THE ASYLUM

John Harwood was born in Hobart and educated
in Tasmania and at Cambridge University. He is
the author of the novels *The Ghost Writer* and
The Séance, and a recipient of the International
Horror Guild's First Novel Award for Outstanding
Achievement in Horror and Dark Fantasy.

ALSO BY JOHN HARWOOD

The Ghost Writer
The Séance

JOHN HARWOOD

The Asylum

VINTAGE BOOKS

London

Published by Vintage 2014

2 4 6 8 10 9 7 5 3 1

Copyright © John Harwood 2013

John Harwood has asserted his right under the Copyright, Designs
and Patents Act 1988 to be identified as the author of this work

First published in Great Britain in 2013 by
Jonathan Cape

Vintage
Random House, 20 Vauxhall Bridge Road,
London SW1V 2SA

www.vintage-books.co.uk

Addresses for companies within The Random House Group Limited
can be found at: www.randomhouse.co.uk/offices.htm

The Random House Group Limited Reg. No. 954009

A CIP catalogue record for this book
is available from the British Library

ISBN 9780099578840

The Random House Group Limited supports the Forest Stewardship
Council® (FSC®), the leading international forest-certification
organisation. Our books carrying the FSC label are printed on FSC®-
certified paper. FSC is the only forest-certification scheme supported
by the leading environmental organisations, including Greenpeace.
Our paper procurement policy can be found at:
www.randomhouse.co.uk/environment

Printed and bound in Great Britain by Clays Ltd, St Ives Plc

FOR ROBIN

Part One

Part One

Georgina Ferrars' Narrative

I woke, as it seemed, from a nightmare of being stretched on the rack, only to sink into another dream in which I was lying in a strange bed, afraid to open my eyes for fear of what I might see. The smell and the texture of the blanket against my cheek felt wrong, and I was clad, I became aware, in a coarse flannel nightgown that was certainly not my own. I knew that I must still be dreaming, for I had gone to sleep as usual in my bedroom at home. Every joint in my body ached as if I had been stricken with fever; yet I had felt perfectly well the night before.

I lay still for a little, waiting for the dream to dissolve, until my eyes opened of their own accord. The ceiling above me was a dull white; the bare walls, a dismal shade of green. Grey light filtered through a metal grille; the glass behind it was clouded and streaked with moisture.

I sat up, wincing at the pain, to find myself in what appeared to be a prison cell. The door to my left was solid oak, with a narrow aperture at eye level, closed by a wooden shutter. The air was damp and chill, and smelt of cold ashes and chloride of lime. A small fireplace was, like the window, entirely covered by a stout metal grille. There was no furniture beyond a bedside table, a single upright chair, a washstand, and a small closet; there were no ornaments, no looking glass; not so much as a candlestick.

It was impossible; I could not be here. But neither could I deny that I was wide awake. And I was not, I realised, at all feverish; my forehead was cool, my skin was dry, and my breath came freely. So why did my body protest at the slightest movement? Had I fallen somehow? or been attacked?—or worse? Trembling, I threw off the bedclothes and examined myself, but I could find no trace of injury, except for some bruises on my upper arms, as if someone had gripped them tightly.

Was it some sort of hallucination? If I lie down, I thought, and pull the covers over my head and try to go to sleep again, perhaps I will find myself back in my own bed. But my feet, seemingly of their own volition, were already on the floor. I moved unsteadily to the door and tried the handle, but it would not budge.

Should I call out? And who would come if I did? I turned toward the window, wondering if this was what sleepwalkers experienced. Half a dozen paces brought me to the grille. The world beyond was obscured by grey, swirling mist, with faint, unidentifiable forms— walls? houses? trees?—hovering at the edge of visibility.

I returned to the door and tried the handle again. This time the panel shot open, and two eyes appeared in the slot.

"Where am I?" I cried.

"The infirmary, miss," replied a young woman's voice. "Please, miss, I'm to say you're to get back into bed, and the doctor will be here directly."

The panel slid shut, and I heard the muffled sound of footsteps receding. Shivering, I did as she had asked, relieved at least to discover that I was in a hospital. But what had happened to me, and why had they locked me in? I waited apprehensively until another, heavier tread approached. A lock rasped, the door swung inward, and a man stepped into the room. From his dress—a tweed suit and waistcoat, somewhat rumpled, a white collar which had sprung loose at one side, a tie of dark blue silk, carelessly knotted—and a certain humorous glint in his eye, you might have taken him for an artist, but there was an air of authority about him, of a man accustomed to being obeyed. He looked somewhere between forty and fifty, not especially tall, but broad-shouldered and trim. His eyes were pale blue, accentuating the blackness of the pupils, deep-set and piercing beneath heavy brows, with dark pouches beneath; his nose strong and aquiline and straight as a blade, the nostrils flared above chiselled lips. A long, lean face, clean-shaven except for a fringe of side-whiskers, tapering down to a creased, prominent chin. He stood silent, surveying me appraisingly.

"Where am I?" I said again. "Who are you? Why am I here?"

A gleam of satisfaction showed in his eyes.

"Do you mean you don't know? — I see you do not. This is most inter — that is to say, most distressing for you. Forgive me: my name is Maynard Straker, and I am the superintendent and chief medical officer here at Tregannon House — on Bodmin Moor, in Cornwall," he added, seeing that my bewilderment had not lessened. "Have no fear, Miss Ashton, I am entirely at your ser — "

He stopped short at the expression on my face.

"Sir, my name is not Ashton! I am Miss Ferrars, Georgina Ferrars; I live in London, with my uncle; there has been a terrible mistake."

"I see," he said calmly. "Well, never fear. Let me order you some toast and tea, and we shall talk it all through in comfort."

"But sir, I should not be here! Please, I wish to go home at once!"

"All in good time, Miss — Ferrars, if you prefer. The first thing you must understand is that you have been very ill. I know" — he held up his hand to silence me — "I know you do not remember: that is a consequence of your illness. Now please; first you must allow me to examine you, and then I shall explain what has happened to you."

Such was the force of his personality that I waited in silence whilst he murmured instructions to someone outside the door. He took my pulse, listened to my heartbeat, tested my reflexes, and seemed quite satisfied with the result. Then he settled himself on the wooden chair so that he was facing me directly.

"You arrived here yesterday morning; without notice, which is most unusual. You gave your name as Lucy Ashton and said that you wished to consult me on an urgent and confidential matter. As I was away on business, the maid referred you to my assistant, Mr Mordaunt. You were, he says, in an agitated state, though striving to conceal your distress. He explained that I would not be back until the evening, and that you would therefore have to stay here overnight, and register as a voluntary patient in order to see me, and to this you very reluctantly agreed. You would not admit to any disturbance of mind; only to extreme fatigue, and, after giving him a few cursory details, asked if you might complete the admission forms later.

"Mr Mordaunt found you a room in the voluntary wing and left you there, assuming you would rest. But several times that afternoon he saw you walking about the grounds in what he described — my assistant is something of a poet — as a trance of desolation.

"I returned at about nine o'clock, and, upon hearing Mr Mordaunt's account of you, called briefly at your room to arrange an appointment for this morning; I had too many calls upon my time to speak to you last night. You were plainly in a state of extreme nervous exhaustion, but again you refused to concede anything beyond fatigue. I naturally ordered you a sedative, which you promised to take, though I fear you did not. Voluntary patients are, I should say, under no compulsion to accept any particular treatment here. So long as they pose no danger to themselves or others, they are free to do as they wish: it is part of our philosophy.

"Early this morning you were found unconscious on the path behind this building; you must have slipped out without anyone noticing. It was evident to me that you had suffered a seizure, which, though rare, is not unheard of in cases such as yours, where extreme mental agitation induces something like an epileptic fit, or, in those actually prone to epilepsy, a grand mal episode. It is nature's way of discharging excessive mental energy. Upon waking, the patient commonly remembers nothing of the preceding days, or even weeks, and is at a loss to account for the extreme soreness of joints and muscles, which is due to the violence of the spasms. Such episodes are, of course, more common in women, whose faculties are more delicate, and more readily overstrained, than those of men—"

"Sir," I broke in, as the full horror of realisation dawned, "am I in a madhouse?"

"It is not a term I favour; say rather you are in the care of a private establishment for the cure of diseases of the mind. An enlightened institution, Miss — Ferrars, run on the most humane principles, dedicated to the advancement of knowledge and the comfort of our patients.

"Now, you assured me at our first interview that you had never suffered from epilepsy, or any form of mental disturbance—but I take it you cannot recall that interview?"

"No, sir."

"And you have no idea of how, or why, you presented yourself to us as Lucy Ashton?"

"None whatever, sir."

"What is the last thing—the very last thing—you can recall?"

I had clung, throughout his recital, to the belief that this was all a ghastly mistake, and that I should be escorted home to London as soon as I could persuade him that I was Georgina Ferrars and not Lucy Ashton. But his question provoked a sort of landslip in my mind. My memory, as it had seemed, of going to bed at home the night before, wavered and collapsed, leaving only a dreadful, buzzing confusion. I must, I thought desperately, *must* be able to remember. If not last night, then the day before? Memories—if they *were* memories— spilled from my grasp like playing cards, even as I tried to order them. I saw my life dissolving before my eyes. The room swayed like the deck of a ship; for a moment I felt sure I should faint.

Dr Straker regarded me calmly.

"Do not be alarmed; the confusion will pass. But you see now why I hesitate to address you as Miss Ferrars. It is possible—I have seen such cases—that you are in fact Lucy Ashton; that Miss Ferrars— Georgina, did you say?—that Georgina Ferrars is your friend or relation, or even just a figment of your disordered imagination. The mind, after an insult such as this, can play the most extraordinary tricks upon us."

"But sir, I *am* Georgina Ferrars! You must believe me! I live in Gresham's Yard, in Bloomsbury, with my uncle, Josiah Radford, the bookseller. You must wire to tell him I am here—"

Dr Straker held up his hand to stop the rush of words.

"Steady, steady, Miss . . . Ferrars, let us say. Of course we shall wire. But before we do so, you should at least consider the evidence of your own possessions . . . Ah, here is tea."

A young maidservant in a neat grey uniform entered with a tray.

"You will be pleased to see, Bella, that our patient is recovering," said Dr Straker.

"Yes indeed, sir," she said. "Very glad to see you looking better, Miss Ashton. Will there be anything else, sir?"

"Yes; run down to Miss Ashton's room, and bring all of her things up here. Ask one of the porters if you need assistance. We can manage the tea."

"Yes sir; right away, sir."

"You see?" said Dr Straker wryly as she hurried out. "Miss Ashton is, at least, not just a figment of *my* imagination. Milk? Sugar?"

If Dr Straker had betrayed the slightest anxiety on my behalf, I think I should have given way to hysteria. But his nonchalance had a strangely calming, or rather numbing, effect upon me. I had come here calling myself Lucy Ashton: so much seemed undeniable, though utterly incomprehensible. I felt certain I knew no one of that name, and yet it seemed vaguely familiar. He has promised to wire, I told myself. I shall be going home soon, and must cling to that thought. I sipped my tea mechanically, grateful for the warmth of the cup in my cold hands.

My mother's birthday! It had been a warm autumn day.

"Sir, I have remembered something," I said. "The twenty-third of September, my mother's birthday—she died ten years ago, but I vowed I would always do something that we should have enjoyed together. It was a Saturday, and I walked up to Regent's Park, and ate an ice, and felt very ill afterward."

"I see . . . and after that?"

I strove to pick up the thread, but beyond that one glimpse, I could not be sure. I could go backward with some confidence, over the events of the summer, and the spring, and indeed all the way back to my childhood—or so it seemed—but when I tried to advance, I could summon only blurred images of myself in my uncle's house; the power of ordering them seemed to have deserted me.

"I—I cannot be sure," I said at last.

"Most interesting. Let us say, then, that your last clear recollection is—or appears to be—of the twenty-third of September. Would you care to hazard a guess at today's date?"

I knew then what had been troubling me about the chill, the damp, even the quality of the light.

"I cannot guess the time, sir, let alone the date."

"It is two o'clock in the afternoon of Thursday, the second of

November. In the year of our Lord 1882," he added, raising one eyebrow.

"November!" I exclaimed. "Where have I . . . How could I have . . . Sir, you must wire my uncle at once; he will be desperately worried."

"Not necessarily. If a Georgina Ferrars had been missing for the past week, let alone the past month, we should have been informed. Asylums, like the hospitals and the police, are kept up to date with news of missing persons; and there is no one of that name—indeed, no one resembling you—on any of our lists. You may have told your uncle that you were going away; though not, presumably, to a lunatic asylum under a false name. So before we trouble him, let us try to set the record straight."

He drew a piece of paper from his coat pocket.

"This is all the information you gave my assistant when he admitted you yesterday morning. 'Name: Lucy Ashton. Address: Royal Hotel, Plymouth. Date of birth: the fourteenth of February 1861. Place of birth: London. Parents: deceased. Next of kin: none living. No history of serious physical or mental illness. No person to be advised in case of illness or decease. "Patient says she is quite alone in the world,"' Mr Mordaunt has noted. Interesting, is it not?"

"Sir, I have never even *been* to Plymouth!"

"I think we can safely say that you have. Amnesia is the most difficult of all conditions for a patient to grasp, Miss Ashton, because there is literally nothing to hold on to. You do not recognise any of those details, then?"

"None, sir. I cannot imagine why—"

"I can think of at least two explanations," he said, producing a notebook and pencil. "But before we come to that . . . Your full name?"

"Georgina May Ferrars, sir."

"And your date and place of birth?"

"March third, 1861, at Nettleford, in Devon."

"That is *near* Plymouth, is it not?"

"I believe so, sir; I have no memory of it. We—my mother and I—moved to a cottage on the cliffs near Niton, on the Isle of Wight, to live with my aunt Vida—my great-aunt, I mean—when I was only an infant."

He listened to this halting explanation with an air of polite amusement, as if to say, And why should we believe you this time?

"I see . . . And your father?"

"His name was Godfrey Ferrars, sir; I never knew him. He died before I was two years old."

"I am sorry to hear it. What was his profession, do you know?"

"He was a doctor, sir—" I almost said, "like yourself," but checked myself. "A medical officer, in London."

"What part of London?"

"Clerkenwell, sir. But he became very ill and had to move to the country; he was convalescing in Nettleford when I was born."

"And did not recover, I take it?"

"He did recover, sir, but then he insisted on taking another situation, in Southwark—"

"Again as a medical officer?"

"Yes, sir. My mother took me to Niton—we were to follow as soon as he had settled in—but he came down with typhoid fever and was dead before news of his illness reached us."

"Do you know the date?"

"No, sir; only that it was summer."

"Well, let us say the summer of 1862." He scribbled in his note-book. "And your mother's maiden name?"

"Emily Radford."

"She died, I think you said, ten years ago?"

"Yes, sir. She had some weakness of the heart—an aneurism, we were told. It was not discovered until after her death."

"A melancholy history. Are you her only child?"

"Yes, sir."

Dr Straker regarded me curiously.

"Do you know, I wonder, whether the weakness was hereditary? Your own heart seems sound enough, on a brief examination, but have you ever suffered from palpitations, shortness of breath, dizziness, fainting fits . . . ?"

"No, sir, I was a very healthy child. She and my aunt were always anxious that I should take plenty of rest and exercise, and not become over-excited, but they never mentioned my heart."

"That, at least, is reassuring," he said, making another note. "And after that?"

"I remained with my great-aunt, Vida Radford, on my mother's side, until we lost—until she died last year. After that I went to London to live with Uncle Josiah—Aunt Vida's brother, so he is my great-uncle, too—"

Again I heard myself faltering.

"And has your uncle any children of his own?"

"No, sir. Like my aunt, he never married."

"I see. And—if you will forgive me—what are your financial circumstances? Have you money of your own, or expectations of your uncle?"

Something in his tone made me even more fearful.

"I have a small income, sir, about a hundred pounds a year, from my aunt. And my uncle is certainly not rich; he says his estate is worth only a few hundred pounds."

"I see. And now we come to your mental health. As Miss Ashton"—he glanced again at the paper on his knee—"you told my assistant that you had no history of mental disturbance. But given that you came here under an *alias*, and have since suffered a seizure, almost certainly brought on by prolonged and violent mental agitation, perhaps there is something you would like to add to Miss Ashton's account?"

Again the room seemed to revolve around me. There were, I thought, with my heart beginning to pound, several things I ought to add; but if I confessed to them, I might never be allowed to leave. The seconds ticked by under his ironic gaze.

"I—I do not think there is anything out of the ordinary."

"Very well," he said, after an uncomfortable pause. "And now I must look in on some of my other patients. In the meantime, you must stay in bed and keep warm; Bella will see to the fire when she returns with your luggage."

"But sir, you will send that wire to my uncle?"

"By all means. The nearest telegraph office is at Liskeard, a good forty minutes' ride from here, so we cannot expect a reply until this evening at the earliest. Mr Josiah Radford, of Gresham's Yard, Bloomsbury, is it not?" he added, glancing at his notebook.

You *must* be able to remember, I told myself as the echo of his footsteps died away. It is like a door that sticks; you have forgotten the trick of it; that is all. Or a name that will not come to you, and then you find it upon your lips a few minutes later. But no matter how hard I strained, I could not even discern a gap where memory should have been. Was it possible that the real Lucy Ashton—where *had* I heard that name before?—looked just like me? Could we have been confused with each other? But that did nothing to explain what *I* was doing in a private asylum in Cornwall, a part of the world I had never visited . . . and so my thoughts went spiralling on, until Bella reappeared, struggling under the weight of a stout leather valise, a hatbox, and a dark blue travelling-cloak, none of which I recognised.

"I am afraid those are not my things."

The girl regarded me with, I thought, a certain compassion.

"Beg pardon, miss, but you was wearing that cloak when you come here yesterday. And look," she added, setting down the case and opening it. "Here's your wrap, miss, the one you asked me to look out when you was cold later on."

She held up a blue woollen shawl—the pattern was certainly one I might have chosen myself—and draped it around my shoulders. I watched numbly as she opened the closet and began to unpack the case—which had "L.A." stamped in faded gold lettering below the handle. Everything she took out of it looked like clothes I might have chosen myself, but none of them were mine. It struck me that my own wardrobe, in its entirety, would fit into a case not much larger than this.

"Wait!" I cried. "I am not staying here; I must return to London as soon as—" My voice trailed away; the fog of confusion seemed suddenly to lift. Why on earth was I waiting for the answer to Dr Straker's wire? He had said I was a voluntary patient, and regardless of how and why they had mistaken me for Lucy Ashton—regardless, indeed, of what had happened to my memory—the sooner I was back in London, the better.

"In fact," I said firmly, "I wish to leave immediately. Would you please help me to dress, and—"

"I'm sorry, miss, but I can't, not without the doctor's say-so." She had a soft country accent which would, in other circumstances, have been pleasing to my ear.

"Then I shall dress myself. Please go at once and find Dr Straker, and ask him to order me"—I was about to say, "a cab"—"a conveyance, to take me to the nearest railway station. You do understand," I added, hearing my voice beginning to tremble, "that I am a voluntary patient here."

"I'll go and see, miss. But please, miss, doctor's orders was for you to stay in bed."

She hurried out, closing the door behind her. I slipped out of bed, suddenly afraid that she might have locked me in. But the door opened readily, onto a dark-panelled corridor, in which Bella's receding figure was the only sign of life.

I closed the door again and turned to the closet. Lucy Ashton's taste in clothing was almost identical to my own; like me, she favoured the aesthetic style; her blue woollen travelling-dress was the twin of one that I possessed in grey, and when I held it up against myself, it was plain, even without a mirror, that it would fit me perfectly. Even the laundry marks were exactly the same as mine: small cotton tags stitched into the lining, with "L.A." sewn into them in neat blue lettering. If I had been asked to outfit myself for a journey, I could not have chosen better.

Again I found myself clutching at the idea that Lucy Ashton must be my double, only to remember that this did nothing to explain why *I* was here. Once more I strove to penetrate the void shrouding my mind, until something brought me back to the immediate present, and the awareness that Lucy Ashton's case contained no purse or pocketbook; no jewellery, no rings, and no money.

And two other things were missing—though of course they were missing, since these were not my things: the dragonfly brooch my mother had bequeathed to me, which I would never have left behind; and my writing case, a present from Aunt Vida, containing the journal I had kept since my sixteenth birthday. It was a quarto-sized case made of soft blue leather, with two gold clasps, and a key, which I always kept on a fine silver chain around my neck, but which was certainly not there now.

The loss of that key somehow brought home the extremity of my plight. My strength deserted me, and I sank down upon the edge of the bed, just as Dr Straker reappeared in the doorway, followed by Bella with a pail of coals.

"Miss—Ferrars," he said sternly, "you must get back into bed and stay there. As your physician, I command it. There can be no question of your leaving; you are far too ill."

"But sir—"

"No more, I pray you. The wire has been dispatched as you requested; as soon as we have an answer, I shall let you know," he said, and strode from the room.

"Bella," I said as she arranged the blankets over me, "I can't find my purse, or my brooch—in a small red plush box; it is quite valuable; or my writing case—a blue leather one. Have you see them anywhere?"

"No, miss, I 'aven't. This is all there was, miss, when I packed up your room just now."

"But I *must* have had money," I said desperately. "How else could I have got here?"

"You gave me a sixpence, miss, when you was still wearing your cloak. P'raps it's there."

She tried the pockets but found only a pair of gloves.

"You don't think *I* took it, miss?" she said, with a look of alarm.

"No, Bella. But *someone* must have, and my brooch and writing case; I would never travel without them."

"I don't know, miss, I'm sure. We're all honest girls here. Might you have put them away somewhere yourself, miss, and—and forgotten? Now please, miss, I must get on."

To this there was plainly no answer. I gave up all hope of escaping that day, and lay with my mind spinning, and a sick feeling of dread gnawing at the pit of my stomach, while daylight slowly faded from the room, until I woke with the glare of a lantern in my eyes, to find Dr Straker standing beside my bed.

"I am afraid, Miss Ashton, that you must prepare yourself for a shock. As well as conveying your message to Josiah Radford, I took the liberty of asking him whether he had ever heard of a Lucy Ashton. This is his reply."

NO KNOWLEDGE LUCY ASHTON STOP GEORGINA FERRARS HERE
STOP YOUR PATIENT MUST BE IMPOSTER STOP JOSIAH RADFORD.

I was sedated, that night, with chloral, and emerged from a pit of oblivion with my body still aching and a foul taste in my mouth. Whether it was the after-effect of the drug, or the accumulated shocks of the previous day, all I could think was that Dr Straker must have wired the wrong Josiah Radford; further than that, my mind refused to go. Bella brought me breakfast, which I was unable to eat, along with a mirror in which I saw a drawn, sunken face, white as a ghost's except for dark pouches like bruises beneath eyes that were scarcely recognisable as my own. Dr Straker, she told me, as she brushed the worst of the knots out of my hair, would be here directly; his orders were for me to stay in bed; and no, I was not to dress on any account. And so I was condemned to wait in my nightgown and wrap until he appeared at my bedside, looking, if anything, even more cheerful than he had the day before.

"Well, Miss Ashton, as I think we must call you until we discover who you really are, I must say that your case is unique in my experience."

"Sir, I beg of you . . . I cannot explain what has happened, but I swear to you, on my dear mother's grave, I *am* Georgina Ferrars!"

"I know. I know that is what you believe, with every fibre of your being. But consider the facts. There is a Georgina Ferrars presently at the address you gave me—no, hear me out. You came here under the name Lucy Ashton, and I think we may say with certainty that Lucy Ashton is not your real name, either. You are, I take it, familiar with Scott's Waverley novels?"

I knew, suddenly, where I had heard the name before.

"Lucy Ashton is the heroine of *The Bride of Lammermoor*. She is forced by her mother to break her engagement to the man she loves, Edgar Ravenswood, and marry another whom she loathes. She stabs her husband on their wedding night, and dies, insane, of a seizure. So it occurs to me to ask whether this has any personal significance for you."

I stared at him, appalled.

"I have never been engaged, sir, let alone . . . !"

"Nevertheless, you will agree that it is a disturbing choice of alias for a troubled young woman presenting herself for treatment at a private asylum. It suggests that there is something in her past—perhaps her immediate past—from which she is fleeing."

"There is nothing, sir, nothing!"

"Nothing that you can remember, I agree."

"But sir, I have told you my history; you wrote it down yesterday.

The person who sent that telegram is lying; I do not know why. If you do not believe me—"

"I have already been in touch with the medical boards of Clerkenwell and Southwark: a Dr Godfrey Ferrars held positions there in 1859 and 1862 respectively. He died at Southwark of typhoid fever on the thirtieth of August 1862, survived by his wife, Emily, and their infant daughter, Georgina."

"Then how can you not believe me?" I cried.

"Because—though I am sure you could give me the most fluent recital of the facts of Georgina Ferrars' life—it does not follow that you *are* Georgina Ferrars. You may, for example, have met the real Georgina Ferrars, or someone who knows her very well, and—for reasons we cannot yet fathom—become obsessed with her. I have seen such cases before; it is called hysterical possession, where the patient assumes the identity of another and comes to believe in all sincerity that she *is* that person. As well as the evidence of the telegram, we have the fact that you presented yourself here as Miss Ashton, suffered a seizure, lost all memory of the past six weeks, and only then declared yourself to be Georgina Ferrars—"

"Sir," I broke in, gathering my courage, "you *must* hear me! That cable is a fraud. I do not know who sent it, or why, but if you send someone to Gresham's Yard, you will find only my uncle; he will come straight away and fetch me. I have a little money saved," I added, praying that it was still true, "and I will pay any expenses—"

"That will not be necessary. As it happens, I have to go up to London by this afternoon's train. I shall call at Gresham's Yard tomorrow, and speak to Josiah Radford—and, I fear, to Georgina Ferrars, and try to persuade her to come down and identify you—since you clearly know a good deal about her.

"And if," he added, before I could speak, "if it *should* turn out that you have a mortal enemy, who has been lurking around Gresham's Yard, waiting to intercept a telegram he could not possibly have known would come, I promise to bring Mr Josiah Radford back with me on the very next train, and eat my hat—a thing I have never promised to do before—as penance. In the meantime, we shall keep you comfortable, at our expense, of course."

"But sir, I wish to leave at once!"

"I am afraid I cannot allow it. You are not well enough to travel, and, if my instinct is right, and you were to appear at Gresham's Yard in your present frame of mind, you would probably be arrested and confined at Bethlem Hospital, which, though much improved, is not a place I should recommend to anyone in my care. And now I must see to my other patients; I shall leave you in the care of my colleague Dr Mayhew until I return—which may not be until Monday."

"Monday! But sir . . ."

He rose, silencing me with a gesture, and strode to the door, where he paused.

"Oh, and I shall ask my assistant, Mr Mordaunt, to look in on you. I think you will find him—sympathetic."

For the rest of that day I saw no one but Bella and Dr Mayhew, a stout, grey-bearded physician who took my pulse, peered at my tongue, felt my forehead, grunted a few times and went away without speaking. Bella helped me to bathe, and brought me meals, most of which I was unable to eat. *You must keep up your strength for the journey home*, I kept telling myself, but the clenched knot in the pit of my stomach left little room for food. Once, after she had taken away my tray, I slipped out of bed and made my way unsteadily to the window. The mist had cleared, and through the grille I looked down upon an enclosed garden, perhaps thirty yards across, surrounded by high brick walls. Gravel paths ran between beds of dark green foliage; there was no one in sight, and no sign of any way in or out. Above the walls I could see only the tops of trees, silhouetted against a leaden sky.

There was no clock within my hearing; nothing to mark the passing of the hours except the slow fading of the light and the occasional spatter of rain against the glass; nothing to do but struggle in vain to comprehend what had befallen me, until I fell at last into a doze and woke in lamplight to find Bella arranging my supper tray. She had brought me another draught of chloral, which I swallowed reluctantly for the oblivion it promised. But instead of sleeping through the night, I woke in a kind of delirium in which I was aware of myself lying in bed, unable to move, spinning through fearful dreams until daylight and the horror of coming fully awake and finding myself still at Tregannon Asylum.

Before this, the idea that I might not even be—myself, was the only way I could conceive of it—would have seemed merely absurd. But here, anything seemed possible; not only possible, but nightmarishly plausible. How could I be sure that I was not insane? I did not *feel* mad, but how was I to know what madness felt like? Dr Straker evidently believed it; and I had only to think of that telegram to feel terror rising to engulf me. Why had I called myself Lucy Ashton—as I must have done, unless everyone here was lying to me? Was there a strain of madness in our family, which had come out in me?

You must not think of it, I told myself, and a great sob burst from my throat. When the fit of weeping had passed, I lay down and closed my eyes and strove to imagine myself back in my own small bed in our house on the cliffs at Niton, with Mama and Aunt Vida murmuring nearby, their voices blending with the ebb and wash of the sea far below.

My great-aunt Vida had found the cottage many years before I was born, and had fallen in love with it at first sight. It stood about fifty yards up from the cliff, with the ground rising steeply behind. Away to the east ran the great sweep of the cliffs, the edge so sharp in places that it might have been cut with a knife, plunging down to two horizontal lines of fluted rock like great jagged teeth, the lower jaw projecting beyond the upper, and then down again to the falls of rock heaped along the shore far below. Whole farms lay buried in some of these mounds, but my aunt insisted that we were too far from the edge to be in any danger.

Our sitting room was upstairs at the front, with windows on two sides looking to the east and south, over the vast expanse of the sea. My mother had a chaise longue by the side windows, and here she would spend hours each day reading, knitting or embroidering, or simply gazing out to sea. Every morning after breakfast, the sitting room would become my schoolroom, and much of my education came from reading aloud—I could not remember a time when I could not read—or being read to, and asking questions whenever I did not understand. We read a great deal of poetry, and Lamb's *Tales from Shakespeare*, and Macaulay's *History*; anything from our small library that my mother considered suitable, and I do not remember her ever condescending to me, or saying that anything was too hard for a child to understand.

My aunt slept in the other front room; my bedroom was across the passage from hers, and my mother had the room next to mine. From my window I could see the long westward sweep of the coast. The dining room, which we seldom used, was downstairs, along with a breakfast room where we took most of our meals, and the kitchen and servants' quarters where Mrs Briggs, the housekeeper, and Amy, the maid, lived.

Aunt Vida seemed, when I was small, to tower above my mother, though I came to realise that there was only an inch or two between them. But my mother was pale and slender, whereas Aunt Vida was as stout and solid as a tree-trunk, her face weathered by long exposure to wind and sun. She was a great walker, and I would often see her striding out in the morning, swinging her blackthorn stick. In summer, especially, she might not return until after my bedtime; I would hear her voice raised in greeting as I was drifting on the edge of sleep, or wake to the murmur of conversation from the sitting room. She spoke, as a rule, in a gruff, staccato fashion, as though dictating her thoughts at the telegraph office. "I should have been born a man," she once said to me, years after my mother had died, and indeed she behaved, for the most part, as if she had been. Once, having seen her snipping at her hair—a thick, white, wiry mane, very like that of Mr Allardyce the vicar—with the kitchen scissors, I decided to try it myself, with predictable consequences. "I am old enough, and ugly enough, to do as I please," she had said sternly, "but you, child, are not." She despised bustles and crinolines; her wardrobe consisted of two summer and two winter walking-dresses, all in the same shade of brown ("doesn't show the mud"), and two pairs of stout boots; in wet weather she would array herself in oilskins and a sou'wester. Years later, when I was fully grown, she insisted upon giving me a set of my own, which I thought deeply unbecoming and would wear only as a last resort. They smelt faintly but persistently of tobacco, and I suspected her of buying them from a sailor.

My own taste in dress was formed by my mother, who, like my aunt, refused to wear a bustle, or endure any form of tight lacing. She, however, had embraced the artistic fashion when I was still very small:

plain, loose-fitting gowns in muted shades and soft fabrics, which she cut out and sewed herself. With me, she was abundantly affectionate; even during my lessons, we would nestle together on the sofa, whereas Aunt Vida, though I never doubted her love for me, could manage no more than a clumsy pat on my shoulder, as you might pat a horse you were not entirely sure of. But sometimes, if I caught my mother unawares, I would find her staring absently into space with a haunted, fearful expression—was it dread, or physical pain? I could not tell, because the instant she caught sight of me, she would shake herself, beckon me into her arms, and assure me that it was nothing, nothing at all. If she was in pain, or visited by some premonition of approaching death, she concealed it resolutely; if I suggested a walk, and she did not feel up to it, she would simply smile and say that she thought she had better rest. And so, with my aunt out roaming the countryside, I was left a good deal to myself in the afternoons.

The only remarkable thing about my bedroom, from a child's point of view, was a full-length mirror in a tarnished gilt frame, fixed to the wall beside my bed. When I was about six years old, I invented a game—at least it began as a game—in which my reflection was my sister, Rosina. The name simply floated into my head one day, and I liked the music of it. I would stare at my reflection in the glass until I drifted into a strange, half-mesmerised state in which Rosina's gestures and expressions seemed independent of my own. Rosina, of course, looked exactly like me, except that she was left-handed. But in personality she was quite different: bold, headstrong, defiant of authority, and entirely fearless. And oddly, though it did not seem so at the time, she was not my mother's daughter, despite being my sister; she had sprung fully formed from the mirror, a law unto herself.

I had a separate voice for Rosina, higher and fiercer than mine, and sometimes our exchanges would become quite heated, if she was taunting me for refusing to do something forbidden, such as creeping downstairs before dawn to play in the moonlight. As I grew more adventurous, it was always fear of Rosina's scorn, which I could summon as vividly as any feeling of my own, that kept me from turning back. When my mother was resting, I liked to play by myself in the garden, which was enclosed by a rough stone wall—I suppose it was no more than six feet high, but to me it seemed immense—partly hidden from the house by a coppice of ancient fruit trees. I was forbidden to climb it, but at Rosina's urging I went a little higher each time, until I was perched on the very top. Looking along the coast, I could see the edge of the cliff, cut as cleanly as a pat of butter, and hear the wash of the sea far below.

That was as far as I dared go for a week or more, and it was even longer before I made my first tentative descent to the rough, tussocky grass outside. The hillside around was overgrown with gorse, which made it easy to keep out of sight of the house, though I learnt to be very careful of the thorns. Despite my apprehension, I knew at once what the next dare would be: to go right down to the edge of the cliff and look over.

I do not know how far I believed in Rosina as a separate being. Part of me, at least, was aware that I was playing a game with myself; yet the Rosina-voice also seemed to come from outside. *I* did not want to be bad, or cause my mother distress, but Rosina simply did not care; *I* was afraid of the cliff and had promised never to go near it; but Rosina was not afraid of anything. And so, day by day, I ventured closer to the edge.

Though the slope down to the cliff was quite steep, there was a place where the ground curled up like a lip: a small patch of grass, growing right to the edge, flanked by two gorse bushes. The afternoon I chose for my attempt was mild and still, but I was scarcely conscious of the sun's warmth on my back, or the droning of the bees amongst the gorse, as I crawled up the lip on my hands and knees, too intent even to notice the stains accumulating on my pinafore. But the grass was higher than it had seemed from above, and I could no longer tell where the edge was; the gorse bushes on either side obscured everything beyond the small circle of crushed grass. All I could see before me was a tangle of green and brown stalks against the shimmering blue of the sky.

It did not occur to me that I could turn back. With my heart thudding violently, I lay flat on my stomach, stretched my hands as far ahead of me as I could reach, and inched forward, expecting every moment to feel empty space beneath my fingers. The coarse, springy grass confused me. Was the ground sloping up, or down? Was I pushing myself along, or beginning to slide toward the brink? Panic seized me. I dug in my toes into the earth, and pressed myself even flatter. I felt my fingers slipping through the grass, until they encountered a large stone, at which I clutched frantically, pushing myself back with all my strength.

The stone stirred like a live thing. It seemed to lift itself slightly, and shiver, before the grass beneath me vanished in a great slithering rush. Something caught me across the chest, and I was left suspended in midair while a mass of earth and rock hurtled down the cliff-face. It struck the undercliff in a silent explosion of debris, followed by a sound like a muffled peal of thunder. A plume of reddish-brown dust hung in its wake.

I found that my hands were gripping a gnarled tangle of roots, projecting from what was now the cliff-face. Small rivulets of dirt were spilling around me. I was lying side-on to the precipice, too terrified to move or breathe. Far below, jagged spurs of rock protruded from a mound of rubble, like teeth waiting to devour me. My perch was trembling in my grasp.

Whimpering with fear, I turned my head very slowly away from the abyss. The gorse bush whose roots had saved me, was now poised on the very edge of the cliff, the base of its trunk half-exposed. With every slight movement I made, more dirt trickled from around the roots.

I was perhaps two feet below the brink. To survive, I would have to pull myself closer to the trunk, wedge my feet amongst the roots, and actually stand up, balanced against the crumbling bank, before I could scrabble over. It was impossible: my feet and hands would not move. I tried to scream for help, but no sound came out.

Climb, you fool! Rosina's voice seemed to explode inside my head, scornful, imperious. The roots shook; a rush of earth and pebbles spurted from the bank. I remember one glimpse, as if looking down from above, of myself pressed against the cliff with my fingers clawed over the brink. The next instant, as it seemed, I was sprawled on the ground, scraped and bloodied and weeping with shock and relief.

I do not know how long I lay there before realisation struck me. I had broken my solemn promise never, ever, to go anywhere near the edge; I had set off a landslip; and what if more of the cliff should fall? I was covered in dirt from head to foot, and my pinafore was torn and filthy. I sprang to my feet, raced up the hillside, heedless of the need to keep out of sight of the house, and scrambled back over the wall with a horrid rending of cloth. I dared not tell the truth; I would have to say that I had fallen in the garden; or perhaps I should say that I had tried to climb the wall to look over and had fallen off. Then at least I should be confessing to a small part of my sin. Yes; I could say that I had heard a strange noise from the cliff, climbed up to see what it was, and slipped. And I knew that I must go indoors straightaway, and not wait to be called and have to explain why I had stayed in the garden in such a dreadful state.

As it happened, my mother was still asleep, and the first person I met was Amy, who scolded me roundly, scrubbed me down, and gave me a clean pinafore. Mama was alarmed rather than angry when she saw my scrapes and bruises, said she hoped I had learnt my lesson, and made me promise, which I did with heartfelt sincerity, never to climb the wall again. I was still afraid that more of the cliff might collapse — what if our house was swallowed up in the night? — but as no one had heard the noise, they assumed I had imagined it.

I tried not to show how shaken I was, but every time I closed my eyes I would find myself back on the cliff-face, and I was so pale the next morning that Mama thought I might be sickening for something. Though I would much have preferred to do my lessons with her, I was made to rest in bed, with nothing to do but brood upon what I had done. If Rosina had not shouted at me — as it had truly seemed — I should certainly have died; but then if she had not taunted me with my fear of the cliff, I should never have gone near it. After a while I slipped out of bed, confronted my reflection in the mirror, and berated her for putting me in such danger. "I might have died!," I was shouting, when my mother appeared behind Rosina — as it momentarily seemed — in the glass, staring down at me with a look of consternation.

"Georgina! What are you doing?"

"I was only playing at charades, Mama," I said lamely. I was not sure what charades were, but I knew that they involved pretending to be other people.

"But you were shouting at your own reflection, and calling it Rosina; you said you might have died."

"She is only someone I made up, Mama; it was just a story I was telling myself."

"Georgina," she said, kneeling down, taking me gently but firmly by the shoulders, and turning me to face her, "I am not angry, but you must tell me the truth. This—what you were doing with the mirror—is not good for you. And what is this about dying? Is it to do with your falling off the wall yesterday?"

"Yes, Mama," I confessed, and to turn my guilty thoughts away from the cliff, I proceeded to tell her all about Rosina, and how the idea of a sister had come to me from the mirror, and that Rosina was the bold and reckless one who had dared me to climb the wall, aware as I spoke that my mother was regarding me with deepening anxiety, until my voice trailed off altogether.

"But why did you name her Rosina?" she asked. There was a note of fear in her voice that I had never heard before.

"I don't know, Mama," I said helplessly. "It just—came to me."

"I see," she said, and was silent for a little. "Now, Georgina, you must not play this—this game anymore; it is bad for you, as I said. We need not trouble Aunt Vida, but I know that she would say the same. I shall ask Mr Noakes to take away the mirror when he comes on Saturday, but meanwhile you must promise me not to do it again. If you are tempted, come and tell me; I promise I will not be cross. And if you are lonely, we must find you playmates; it will be much better for you to have real friends than—"

She did not finish the sentence. I did not think I had been lonely, but I agreed that I should like some real friends, and said that I felt well enough to come and do my lessons. Despite my promise, I tried once more to summon Rosina before the mirror was removed, but all I saw was myself, pale and uneasy, with a bruise upon my forehead. And though she pressed me no further, I was aware, for some time afterward, of my mother's anxious scrutiny.

Though I kept well away from the edge after that, I soon forgot about Rosina, and even the terror on the cliff-face diminished in memory until it seemed no more than the shadow of a bad dream. But alone in the infirmary at Tregannon House—where I found myself sitting up again, with no recollection of having done so—it was my mother's reaction that came back to haunt me. Why had she been so alarmed? Had she thought Rosina was some sort of ghost? Could I have had a sister who had died? No; she would surely have told me.

Madness in the blood, however, was a very different matter. Of course she would have kept it from me, even if—perhaps especially if—she had feared that my fascination with the mirror was the first sign of its coming out in me.

Apart from Aunt Vida, the only relation I had ever met was her elder brother, my great-uncle Josiah, who used to come to us every two or three years for a week in September. He was younger than my aunt but looked much, much older: completely bald, except for a thin fringe of white hair at the back of his skull, and so stooped over that I used to think he must be a hunchback. He had a white moustache, and a narrow, projecting jaw, which, with his stooped, wiry figure, gave him a distinctly simian air. He wore thick-lensed spectacles and used a magnifying glass for close work. His manner was always courteous, though very reserved; you could sit with him for a whole evening and realise at the end of it that he had scarcely uttered a word. There was—or so I felt as a child—a benign air about his silence; he would sometimes look up over his spectacles and smile faintly at me, but by the time I went to live with him, I cannot have been anything more than a familiar blur.

My mother's father, George Radford, who had worked all his life at the Treasury, was the youngest of the three. Mama had talked quite freely—or so it seemed when I was small—about growing up in Clapham, telling me all about her brothers, Edgar and Jack (Mama had been the youngest by six years), and how handsome they had looked in their dress uniforms when they came to visit, tramping about the house in a great clatter of spurs and sabers, until they decided to go out to New South Wales and make their fortunes, and how Grandmama (whose name was Louisa) had missed them so much that she had gone to live in New South Wales, too. Mama had stayed in Clapham with Grandpapa, who had died soon after she married my father.

Mama herself had died before I came to realise that she only ever talked about her father or her brothers, repeating the same few comic stories about the scrapes they used to get into, whilst revealing almost nothing about herself. But from the caustic snippets Aunt Vida let fall in later years, I pieced together a very different version. Louisa Radford had been a vain, foolish woman who had led her husband a dog's life ("poor George never had much backbone") and doted slavishly on her sons, no matter how badly they behaved, to the exclusion of her daughter. Mama had been George's favorite, and Louisa had resented her for it; my mother once told Aunt Vida that if she could have had one magical wish, it would have been for the power of making herself invisible whenever she chose.

Why Edgar and Jack had gone to Australia, my aunt professed not to know, beyond hinting that they had left the army under some sort of cloud. Louisa insisted upon following them ("no more than they deserved"); but my mother refused to accompany her, and my grandfather George, taking courage from his daughter's example, had refused to go either, and so the family split in two. According to Aunt Vida, Louisa had never written to my mother again.

The only likeness my mother had kept was a miniature of her own grandmother—her father's mother, whom she had never known—it showed a fair, pretty young woman with her hair elaborately curled, but gave no sense of her personality. The miniature lived in Mama's jewel box, along with a wonderful array of rings, pendants, beads, bracelets, necklaces, and earrings—nothing of any value, she said, but to me a treasure-trove. Her one truly precious possession was the brooch her father had given her when she came of age; she discovered after he died that he had paid a hundred pounds for it, far more than he could really afford. It was a dragonfly in silver and gold, less than two inches across, with rubies for eyes and a larger ruby, surrounded by clusters of tiny diamonds, set into each of its four wings. There were even smaller diamonds studded along its slender tail; its delicate legs and feelers were made of pure gold, and when Mama pinned it on her dress, the long gold pin was completely hidden; the dragonfly seemed to have settled upon her breast.

About my father I knew even less. I had never seen a picture of him, either, and I had only the vaguest idea of what he might have looked like: bearded—but so were most men—with brown hair—like most men; tall, but not especially tall; handsome, but not in any particular way. As a child, I had simply accepted whatever Mama had told me, which was mostly about their life in London when they were first married, and especially about his work amongst the poor of Clerkenwell, and what a good and kind and conscientious doctor he had been, but somehow these conversations had left me with very little impression of *him*. Papa's parents had died, she said, before she had met him, and if he had had brothers or sisters, uncles or aunts, she had never mentioned them. For all I knew to the contrary, his entire family might have been locked up in Bedlam.

By the time I was eight or nine, I had come to believe that the subject of Papa—and especially their time at Nettleford, where he had taken so long to recover his health, even after I was born—was painful to her, though she tried very hard not to show it, and so I gradually ceased to question her. Perhaps if Mama and I had been living alone, I might have been more insistent. But our little household seemed to me quite complete, until all thought of my father was swept away by the shock of Mama's sudden death.

I had become so absorbed in these recollections that I was startled to hear Bella's voice in the doorway, telling me that "Mr Mardent" would like to see me, if I felt well enough. I did not connect the name with Dr Straker's parting remark, and agreed uneasily, assuming that another doctor had come to examine me. But the young man who appeared in the doorway a few moments later looked, as Dr Straker had intimated, more like a poet than a physician.

He was about the same height as Dr Straker, but slender, almost emaciated, with thick brown hair, parted in the middle and worn quite long. Light from the window fell across his face, revealing sensitive features and dark, liquid eyes. He wore a suit of dark brown corduroy, with a loose white collar and a striped cravat.

"Miss Ferrars? My name is Frederic Mordaunt; I am Dr Straker's assistant; he asked me to call on you."

The name "Mordaunt" struck a faint resonance, like the toll of a distant bell, immediately lost in the relief of being addressed as "Miss Ferrars." His voice was low and hesitant; we might have been meeting in a drawing room. I invited him to sit down, but he remained hovering awkwardly in the doorway.

"Really I should not," he stammered. "I am not a doctor, and it would not be seemly for me to . . . There is a sitting room just along the hall; the fire is lit, and I thought perhaps, if you felt strong enough, we could . . ."

Twenty minutes later, I was walking down the dim corridor, a little shakily but without Bella's assistance. She had done her best to make me presentable, and though I still felt very bedraggled, Lucy Ashton's blue woollen travelling-dress fitted me perfectly. Mr Mordaunt was waiting by the window in a room not much larger than my own, but furnished with a settee, and cracked leather armchairs on either side of the hearth. The walls were papered in dark green vertical stripes, suggesting the bars of a cage, on a background much stained by smoke, with a faded hunting print above the mantel.

"We have already met, Miss Ferrars," he said, once we were seated by the fire. "It was I who admitted you here — as Miss Ashton," he added, colouring a little. "But you do not remember me, do you?"

"No, sir, I am afraid not. May I ask what Dr Straker has told you about me?"

"I know that you have suffered a seizure and lost your memory of the past few weeks. And that you prefer to be addressed as Miss Ferrars — "

"I *am* Miss Ferrars," I broke in. "I presume Dr Straker has shown you the telegram?"

"I am afraid so," he replied. "But Miss Ferrars, I am not here to question your — that is to say, I have no right; I am not a medical man. Dr Straker simply thought that a little conversation might help you recall . . ."

He made an expansive gesture, then clasped his hands self-consciously.

"You must understand, Mr Mordaunt," I said firmly, "that although I cannot explain what has happened to me, that telegram is a mistake or a fraud, and I shall certainly be going home on Monday."

He murmured something which was obviously meant to sound reassuring, but made no further reply.

"May I ask," I continued, "how I appeared to *you* when I arrived here?"

"Well," he said, colouring again, "you seemed agitated, and fearful — as many patients are when they first arrive here — but quite resolved that you must see Dr Straker and no one else, on what you described as 'an urgent and confidential matter.'"

"And did I say anything at all, beyond what you wrote on that paper, about why I had come here?"

"Well, no, Miss Ash—Ferrars, I mean—you did not. You struck me as preoccupied, almost as if—how shall I put it?—as if you were repeating a lesson you had learnt, whilst your mind was elsewhere."

"And after? You told Dr Straker that you saw me walking about the grounds."

"Yes, I did. Even at a distance, you looked utterly desolate. I went out to you once, to ask if there was anything at all I could do to help."

He looked at me appealingly, as if willing me to remember him.

I was about to ask him what I had said in reply, when Bella came in with a laden tray.

"It is almost midday," said Mr Mordaunt, "and I thought you might like—I took the liberty of ordering a light luncheon."

I realised that, for the first time since my awakening, I was hungry. It seemed very strange to be sitting by a fireside, drinking tea and eating bread and butter and potted shrimp with this personable young man, and my hopes suddenly lifted. Why should I not simply say, I am quite recovered now, and need not wait for Dr Straker to return? I remembered that I had no money; but perhaps I could persuade him to lend me enough for the fare to London.

"Tell me, Mr Mordaunt," I said, "what is it that you do for Dr Straker?"

"Mostly, Miss Ferrars, I act as his secretary. There is, as you can imagine, an immense amount of paperwork to be kept up. But he is the kindest, as well as the most brilliant, of men. He has been like a father to me for as long as I can remember."

"You knew him before you came here?"

"No, Miss Ferrars, I was born here."

"Was your father a doctor, then?"

"No, a lunatic."

I stared at him in astonishment.

"Your father was confined here?"

"In his last years, yes. But you see, Miss Ferrars, Tregannon House has only been an asylum for the past twenty years or so. Before that, it was my family home."

"Your *home?*"

"Yes; there have been Mordaunts here since my great-great-grandfather married a Tregannon in 1720 or thereabouts. It was an alliance of two wealthy families, which increased the standing of both. It also brought together two bloodlines marked by a strong hereditary tendency toward melancholy, violent mania, and insanity. My grandfather, George—Mad Mordaunt, they called him; the maddest of the lot—squandered a large part of the family fortune, and of his children, only my uncle Edmund was spared the worst of the affliction. But I should not be speaking thus—"

"No, I should like you to continue," I said. "Is your mother still alive, may I ask?"

"I don't know," he replied. "I can barely remember her. She ran away, you see, with another man, when I was four years old. And who could blame her?"

He spoke without bitterness, and my heart went out to him.

"I am very sorry to hear it," I said. "Do you have any brothers or sisters?"

"No; Uncle Edmund and I are the only surviving Mordaunts—in this unfortunate line, at least. And my uncle's health is failing; I fear he has not long to live."

"Does your uncle live here, too?"

"Yes. He has rooms on the ground floor, which he seldom leaves these days."

"And—how were you brought up?" I asked.

"By Uncle Edmund; he paid for me to be privately tutored here. I owe everything to him, and Dr Straker. They were friends, you see, at Oxford. Dr Straker was already deep in the study of mental disease when they met, and Uncle Edmund had vowed to do whatever he could toward the lifting of the family curse, as he calls it. They dreamt of founding an asylum on humane and enlightened principles, like the Retreat at York—you have heard of it?—"

I had not, but I nodded, not wanting to interrupt him.

"When the estate came to Uncle Edmund, Tregannon Asylum was established, with Dr Straker as its chief medical officer. My uncle had complete faith in him, even though he had scarcely begun to practise. There was just enough capital left to pay for the initial conversion. My uncle used to say—though he is not given to levity—that since it was already a madhouse, we might as well make a business of it. And it has done well, over the years; there has been a great deal of new building, which I suppose is a good thing—though I would far rather see the whole place pulled down for want of patients," he added, with a sudden access of passion.

"And you, Mr Mordaunt? Why do you choose to work here?"

"The family curse, Miss Ferrars: I suffer from bouts of acute melancholia. I could not complete my medical studies, and so Dr Straker took me on as his assistant. Here, at least, my illness is of some use; our patients find me easy to talk to. I sometimes feel, Miss Ferrars, that I am a lay brother in a strange sort of latter-day order: we no longer believe in God, but hope nevertheless for miracles — though Dr Straker would not agree."

"But surely, would you not be better living — " anywhere but here, I almost said "in the world?"

"It is natural to think so, Miss Ferrars, but my duty lies here. Dr Straker has come to depend upon me, and besides — "

He blushed, averting his gaze; I wondered what he had been about to say.

"And you, Miss Ferrars?" he said after a pause. "Would you tell me something of yourself? You grew up on the Isle of Wight, I understand."

Hesitantly at first, I began to speak of the scenes I had recalled that morning, though not of my fascination with Rosina and the mirror. He listened attentively, smiling at my portrait of Aunt Vida. It struck me as I talked that, despite the loss of my mother, my childhood had been far happier than his.

"Was your mother always an invalid?" he asked. "From childhood, I mean?"

The question stirred a troubling memory. I had never thought of her as an invalid; as a child, I had accepted her being delicate, and needing to rest a great deal, as simply part of the order of things. And when I was told, in the first extremity of grief, that her heart had been diseased, I assumed it had always been thus. It was only years after Mama's death that it occurred to me to put exactly this question to my aunt.

We were standing, that afternoon, on the path by St Catherine's Lighthouse, gazing out across the sea. Neither of us had spoken for some time. It was a clear, windless day, early in the spring, and I was wondering whether a faint skein of cloud along the horizon was actually the coast of France, when my aunt said, more to herself than to me, "Emily always liked this spot."

Aunt Vida, when preoccupied, would speak of "Emily" rather than "your mother"; she always talked more freely when we were out of doors. Though we were only about a mile and a half from the cottage, the path was rough, and very steep in places, and I could not imagine Mama negotiating it.

"Was she stronger—her heart, I mean—when she was a girl?" I asked.

My aunt nodded, still in her reverie. "Could walk all day then. No sign of anything wrong."

"So when did she . . . ?"

"At Nettleford, after—" Her expression changed abruptly, as if a blind had fallen across her features.

"After what, Aunt?"

"Don't know. Woolgathering. No good asking me. Never saw the place."

My aunt had scarcely known my father. She had moved to the Isle of Wight when my mother was quite small, and though Mama had spent a good deal of her time there, my father had never visited the cottage. Aunt Vida had met him on a few occasions in London, but she in turn had never been to Nettleford.

"*Why* did you never visit her at Nettleford?" She had always evaded the question, but now that I was as tall as my aunt, I felt entitled to an answer.

"Told you before. Godfrey was too ill; didn't want to be a nuisance. Before that, he was too busy. Asked them here several times, but he could never get away. Always worried about his patients. Would have lived longer if he'd chosen another profession, your mother said."

"Was he—were he and Mama happy together?"

"Of course they were, child. Why do you ask?"

I did not know what had prompted me to ask. I had been possessed, of late, by a strange restlessness, as if I were yearning for a place I had never seen but would recognise at once if only I could find it. I was in my sixteenth year, and on the verge of womanhood, for which my aunt, in her gruff, taciturn way, was doing her best to prepare me. Earlier on our walk, we had seen a cow giving birth to a calf, and not

long after we had passed a field in which a bull-calf was attempting
to mount a heifer—a common-enough sight, with so much farmland
around us. I had once asked Mama about it, and she had told me that
they were playing at leapfrog. I soon learnt to avert my eyes unless I
was quite alone, but by the time I was thirteen, I had deduced what I
supposed to be the essential facts of procreation.

That day, however, as I was studiously ignoring the bull-calf, my
aunt had abruptly said, "Mating. Same with humans. 'Spect you've
guessed. Never cared for the idea myself."

I could not imagine anyone caring for the idea, but as I stood beside her, with the white bulk of the lighthouse towering above us, the
groaning of the cow in its birth throes came back to me, and with it a
dreadful suspicion that I knew why my mother had died so young.

"That was why Mama always changed the subject," I said, my previous question forgotten, "and why you will not speak of it—of Nettleford. It was giving birth to me that strained her heart."

My aunt turned on me, her face white with shock and fury. I recoiled, thinking she meant to strike me, until I saw that she was furi-
ous not with me, but with herself. She seized my shoulders and fixed
me with blazing eyes.

"Never think that, never! Not a jottle of truth in it—none at all.
Always remember—*only* remember—she loved you best. You were
her joy, her happiness: hold to that, and ask no more!"

She drew me close and held me in a rare and crushing embrace
while I wept.

The memory faded at the sound of Frederic Mordaunt's voice.

"I do beg your pardon, Miss Ferrars; I did not mean to distress
you."

"It is not that," I said. "I grieved dreadfully for my mother, but—"
I did not know what else to say. He rose and added more coals to the
fire. We had long since finished our luncheon, but he seemed in no
hurry to leave.

"Were you ever sent to school?" he asked, settling himself again.
"After you lost your mother, I mean."

"No; my aunt used to say that if you could read and do sums, you
could give yourself an education."

"And did you—do you have friends there still, at Niton?"

"I fear not. Most of our neighbours were retired army men; the families all knew one another, and we didn't fit in. We used to converse with the men, if we met them out walking, but we were too unfashionable, and too eccentric—my aunt, I mean—for the women. The farming people would remember me."

"Was it a lonely life?"

"I suppose it was, though I did not feel it at the time; my life in London has been far more solitary. And you, Mr Mordaunt? You must have been very much alone here."

"I was, yes. I had a series of governesses, because none of them would stay very long; they didn't like living in a madhouse. Like you, I found solace in walking, once I was old enough to be let out on my own. I used to roam all over the moor; there are some wonderfully wild places, and huge clusters of standing stones, left by the Druids. The wind has a strange, thrumming note when it blows amongst them; you always feel that something uncanny is about to happen. I used to stand by Dozmary Pool—where Sir Bedivere is supposed to have thrown Excalibur—and hope that the Lady of the Lake would show herself.

"And of course the house—the original part, where I grew up—was built nearly eight hundred years ago. Nobody lives there anymore. I would find it oppressive, even now; to a small boy it was profoundly so."

I shuddered, imagining lunatics shrieking and clashing their chains in the night.

"Oh, it was not the patients," he said, seeming to read my thought. "They were never kept in the old house. The voluntary patients have always lived in the middle wing, where we are now—it was added early in the seventeenth century—and those confined under a certificate are all in the new building, farthest away from the original house. No, it was—well, I suffered very badly from night terrors, and the housekeeper we had then—Mrs Blazeby, her name was—used to play upon my fears, telling me bloodcurdling stories of ghosts until I did not know whether I was more afraid of falling asleep or staying awake. A house as old as that is never entirely still, even in the dead of night, with a myriad of tiny creatures gnawing away at the fabric, not to mention—"

He stopped abruptly, colouring.

"I do beg your pardon, Miss Ferrars—most inconsiderate of me."

"You needn't apologise; I am not afraid of mice, or rats, if that is what you mean. But did you ever—have you ever *seen* a ghost?"

His reply was forestalled by Bella coming to remove the luncheon tray. The sight of her evidently reminded him of something; he started and drew out his watch.

"I am terribly sorry, Miss Ferrars, but I have a duty to attend to; I had quite forgotten. It will take me about half an hour; but if you are not too tired, would you care to remain here by the fire? Then we could continue our conversation; Bella will fetch you anything you need."

I agreed at once, delighted by the prospect. Frederic hastened away, glancing over his shoulder as if to reassure himself that I had not vanished the instant his back was turned. Bella, who seemed to be trying to repress a smile, followed him out.

As I watched them leave, I was overtaken by a sense of absolute unreality. It was exactly like the moment in a dream where you realise that you *are* dreaming, an instant before you wake. So vivid was the sensation that I held my breath, waiting for the room to dissolve, expecting to wake in my bed at Gresham's Yard, or—please God—in my room at the cottage, with my aunt and my mother talking quietly at the far end of the hall.

The smoke-stained walls did not dissolve; the watery light at the window did not fade; the soft creak and trickle of the coals went on. And yet my perception had changed as profoundly as if I had indeed woken to the sound of retreating footsteps. My breath came freely; I no longer felt as if I had swallowed a mass of frozen lead. Warmed by Frederic's evident belief in me, I felt sure that the telegram was, after all, a mistake. I had never been left alone with any young man, let alone one so agreeable. It would be hard, I thought, to imagine two more different upbringings, and yet our conversation had flowed so freely; I could not help feeling that there was an affinity between us and that he was drawn to me as I felt drawn to him. He had been so open, so candid—and it was surely not just professional concern that made his colour change so frequently . . .

I realised with a start that I had almost forgotten I was in a lunatic asylum, waiting not just for Frederic but for Dr Straker to return from London. The thought of Dr Straker struck me like a dash of cold water. Why had he been so willing to believe that I was not Georgina Ferrars, even before the telegram had come?

It was now Saturday afternoon; Dr Straker was due back on Monday. There was really no reason to doubt that he would release me— Frederic, for one thing, evidently admired him above all men—but all the same, just supposing something *had* gone wrong at Gresham's Yard . . .

Frederic was the heir; he must have some authority here. When he came back, I would tell him I wished to leave at once, and ask him to lend me the fare home—which would give me an excuse to write to him. Of course he might refuse me, but I would be no worse off if he did. He might even offer to escort me back to London.

Imagining that prospect, I leant forward and stirred the coals, enjoying the warmth on my face and thinking how absurd my suspicions about madness in my family would seem to Frederic. The nearest I had come to acute melancholia was, I supposed, my grief for my mother, but I could not recall the actual emotion, only a vision of myself weeping, and of my aunt's dry, stricken face as she sat beside me on my bed, awkwardly patting my shoulder; and how could this be a true recollection when I seemed to be looking down upon the two of us from somewhere near the ceiling?

There was also the time I remembered as "the estrangement," for want of any better description. It came on so gradually that I could not say when it had begun; only that I became aware of it in the autumn, a few months after my aunt's passionate outburst on the subject of Nettleford. It was as if an invisible film had come between me and the world; or as if I were looking through the wrong end of a telescope, except that instead of the people around me appearing physically smaller, it was my feeling for them that had grown distant and remote. The lines, "Ye are the salt of the earth: but if the salt have lost his savor, wherewith shall it be salted?" were often in my mind.

I was not unhappy, at least not consciously so, only detached from everything and everyone around me. If anybody had asked me, I would have insisted that I did not love my aunt any less, but my heart was unmoved by the sight of her; I seemed to have lost the power of feeling. I sensed that she was uneasy about me, but I was afraid of hurting her, and there seemed to be some inward prohibition against speaking of it. And so, all that winter, I insisted that nothing was amiss; I was not even aware that my heart was slowly reawakening until the day, early in the following spring, when I realised I was my old self again.

It was then, for my sixteenth birthday, that Aunt Vida had given me the writing case, along with a journal in a slipcover bound in the same blue leather. "Think you should keep a diary. Never got into the habit myself. Often wished I had. Try to write something every day."

I wondered if she was inviting me to speak of the estrangement, but still the strange prohibition kept me silent, and as a sort of recompense I began my journal that very night. I had never corresponded with anyone, apart from dutiful letters to my uncle, and I found the act of setting down my most intimate thoughts both unsettling and compelling. Until then, I had seldom remembered my dreams, but the more assiduously I recorded them, the more frequent and vivid they became. There was one in particular that recurred several times, in which I was moving from room to room, searching for my mother. There was no one else in the house, and the echoes of my footsteps sounded unnaturally loud. The dream always began on the ground floor, but as it went on, I realised, with a growing sense of foreboding, that every surface was covered in a layer of fine white dust. Sometimes the thought, *But Mama is dead!* would flash across my mind, followed an instant later by the realisation that I was dreaming; but in at least one such dream I continued on up the stairs, with the dust growing thicker at every step, until it rose up in a great choking cloud and I woke with a cry of horror.

A coal burst with a sharp crack and a shower of sparks. My writing case and brooch! "We're all honest girls here, miss." I remembered, with another stab of apprehension, Dr Straker saying that I — or Lucy Ashton — had given my address as the Royal Hotel in Plymouth. Could I have left them there? Perhaps, now that I was calmer, I would begin to recall something of those missing weeks. I summoned all of my concentration, but still nothing would come, only a jumble of grey, featureless autumn days in my uncle's shop, and then, with no perceptible interval, my awakening here in the infirmary.

Footsteps sounded in the corridor outside, and Frederic, slightly breathless, reappeared in the doorway.

"Miss Ferrars; I am sorry to have been so long. Bella is bringing us some more refreshment."

To me, the time seemed to have flown, but I discovered to my surprise that I was hungry again.

"I would not have left you," he explained as he sat down, "but there were papers I had to get off to Liskeard in time for the London train."

"Do you mean there are no more trains today?"

"No—why do you ask, Miss Ferrars?"

"Because—how much is the fare to London, can you tell me?"

"Two guineas, for a first-class ticket."

My heart beat faster, and my mouth felt dry, but I made up my mind to ask him.

"Mr Mordaunt, you must have some authority here. You will understand that I am very anxious to see my uncle; I *know* that telegram is a mistake, and I do not wish to wait for Dr Straker. I should like to leave by the first train tomorrow, and if you will only lend me the fare to London, I shall repay you as soon as I am home again."

"Miss Ferrars, you are not a prisoner here, and if you choose to leave, no one will hinder you. But I urge you with all my heart to remain until Dr Straker returns. Remember that you have suffered a seizure; and there is the question of—what happened during the interval, and why you chose to arrive here as Miss Ashton. If you leave us before these mysteries are solved, you may suffer a relapse. I wonder, myself, if some healing instinct drew you to us: Dr Straker is a leading authority on disorders of the personality. I am not saying that you have any such disorder, but *if* you do, you could not be in better hands."

"And can you assure me that if I do wait for Dr Straker, he will let me go whenever I wish?"

"My word upon it, Miss Ferrars. You are a voluntary patient, and need only give twenty-four hours' notice in writing. And, of course, since you are here as our guest, even that would not be necessary."

"But—" I was about to say that Dr Straker had twice refused me permission to leave, when it occurred to me that Frederic might not know this.

"It is only that—Dr Straker seems far too disposed to believe that I am not Georgina Ferrars."

"But you must understand, Miss Ferrars, that he sees many patients who are utterly convinced of things which are—well, quite mistaken. I am not saying that *you* are mistaken, only that he is bound to consider that possibility. I assure you, Miss Ferrars, you have nothing to fear; I would trust him with my life."

He spread his arms wide in a gesture of reassurance. His hands were naturally expressive, the fingers long and flexible, unconsciously dramatizing the flow of his emotions as he talked. Every so often he would become aware of them, and blush, and clasp them tightly in his lap, until gradually he forgot, and his hands would unclasp, and begin to speak again. I wanted to tell him that he need not restrain them on my account, but it would have seemed far too intimate.

"And you have no idea," he said after a pause, "as to why you presented yourself here as Miss Ashton?"

"None at all; I have tried and tried, but nothing will come . . . Have *you* any notion, Mr Mordaunt, of what might have happened to me? How could I have lost all memory of the past six weeks, and yet recall everything before that perfectly—as I assure you I do?"

"Well," he said hesitantly, "it can happen that, after a particularly terrifying experience, one loses all memory of the event—the mind protecting itself, like a scab growing over a wound before the wound itself has healed. But in your case, the seizure itself is the most likely cause, as I am sure Dr Straker has indicated. Indeed, Miss Ferrars, you are fortunate to be alive; two of our patients have died of seizures in the past year—"

He stopped short with a look of consternation.

"I am very sorry, Miss Ferrars; I should not have mentioned that. Dr Straker would be most displeased. You are recovering well; that is the important thing. The real question is what brought you here in the first place.

"Most likely, Dr Straker has already seen your uncle and reassured him; he may even have solved the mystery. Why risk a long, cold, and tiring journey before you are fully recovered? You are safe here, on my word of honour, and I shall be delighted to keep you company whenever I can—if that is agreeable to you—until Dr Straker returns."

I could see the sense in this, and the thought of another day—perhaps two—in his company was tempting, indeed. But a small, persistent voice urged me not to weaken.

"Or," he continued, "if you absolutely insist upon leaving tomorrow, is there someone else—a close friend, a relation?—in this part of the world, to whom you could go?"

"There is no one, apart from my uncle," I said. "I am quite alone in the world." The words echoed in my mind, as if I had heard them very recently.

It occurred to me that I need not leave by the very next train; I could wait until tomorrow afternoon, or even take the first train on Monday morning.

"I should like to think about it," I said at last, "and decide in the morning, if I may."

"Of course, Miss Ferrars; I am entirely at your disposal."

He was interrupted by Bella appearing with a substantial tea of sandwiches, scones, and cake. Again I was struck by the incongruity of taking tea in a madhouse; so much so that I almost laughed aloud. I realised, too, that I had grown even hungrier, and we ate for a few moments in silence, glancing covertly at each other.

"Miss Ferrars," he said suddenly, "since you asked me to lend you the train fare, I presume you have no money with you?"

"None at all; but the valise I arrived with is not mine, and neither are the clothes; though they are exactly what I should have bought if I had to outfit myself for a journey. But why would I have done that, when I had perfectly good clothes already?"

"That is very strange—very strange, indeed. It almost suggests . . . But you must have had money to get here."

"My own thought exactly. Bella says I gave her a sixpence when I arrived, but that she found no purse when she unpacked my—the valise. And I am anxious about two other things I am sure I would never travel without: my writing case, and a dragonfly brooch my mother left me: it is the only keepsake I have of her." I described them both in some detail, hoping that I might have produced the writing case when he admitted me.

"I'm afraid not. Bella, I'm sure, is honest, and we take great pains to ensure that all of our staff are trustworthy, but there is always the possibility . . . The room you occupied is on the floor below this, on the opposite side of the building; I shall start by—"

"Mr Mordaunt, I am not accusing anyone here of theft; I am worried that I have left them somewhere else—the hotel in Plymouth, for example, which I gave as my address, because of—whatever has befallen me."

"Yes, I do see that. Staying alone at an hotel—I know you don't remember, but it suggests that you are accustomed to travelling, are you not?"

"I would not say accustomed, but yes; my aunt and I made several journeys together, after—" I almost said, after the estrangement, but changed it to "after I turned sixteen. She said it was time I saw something of the world; she used to make me buy the tickets at the station, and write ahead for our lodgings, and make the introductions when we arrived. My aunt was determined that I should grow up to be an independent woman, you see."

"And where did you travel—abroad?"

"No, not abroad. We went to Scotland twice, and to Yorkshire, and Kent . . ."

"And Plymouth?"

"No, never—that I can recall, I mean."

And never to Nettleford, I thought. I had tried to persuade Aunt Vida, saying that I should love, more than anything, to see the place where I was born, only to be met with a barrage of objections: she was sure we would never find the house; it had probably been knocked down by now; the countryside there was just like the Isle of Wight, but not nearly as interesting; and so on until I gave up, inhibited by the memory of her distress that day by the lighthouse, and her impassioned cry: "You were her joy, her happiness: hold to that, and ask no more!"

I looked up from the flames and saw that Frederic was studying me intently. He blushed as our eyes met, and we finished our tea in awkward silence. I felt suddenly, overwhelmingly fatigued; he remarked upon it a few moments later and took his leave, promising to return in the morning.

I slept, that night, without the aid of chloral; a long, dreamless sleep from which I woke in grey twilight to the sound of raindrops spattering against the window. I got out of bed, moving much more freely, and pressed my face against the grille. Steady, drenching rain was splashing along the paths below and bouncing off the tops of the walls. The trees beyond were no more than dim, skeletal shapes, wreathed in vapour.

It was raining like this, I thought, when we lost our house. The autumn was almost over, and the weather had been so wet that I had not ventured out of doors for days. The roof had sprung a leak; water was dripping loudly into a bucket on the floor of Mama's old room, and our garden had become a swamp, with rivulets streaming around the house and gouging deep channels in the sodden earth. All week the mercury had hovered beside "Rain"; there had not been much wind, only the relentless downpour. But when we woke on Saturday morning, the glass had fallen toward "Stormy," and a heavy swell was running. As darkness gathered, the roar of the waves grew louder still, and the wind was rising.

Amy and Mrs Briggs were away, staying with relations as they did on the last Saturday of every month. My aunt and I had finished our supper and drawn our chairs close to the sitting-room fire; she was playing patience, as she often did to settle her mind, but I could tell that she was uneasy. I was sitting with my back to the flames, listening to the gusty roar of rain upon the roof, the creaking of the house, the wind shaking the windows and flinging torrents of water against the glass, and beneath it all, the deep, echoing boom of the waves.

Without warning, the house shuddered violently. Ornaments jangled and fell; a cupboard door flew open; the floor lurched and rebounded. A roar like thunder followed, shaking the walls until my teeth rattled; I thought for an instant we had been struck by lightning, but how could that be, when we had seen no flash?

"It is the cliff," said my aunt. "Quick, fetch the lantern."

I seized a candlestick and hurried downstairs, with my aunt close behind me despite her rheumatism. We kept a hurricane lamp on a hook by the kitchen door; I fumbled with the chimney and the box of vestas for an age before the wick caught and the harsh white light flared up.

We hastened along the passage, and threw open the front door to the rush of wind and the deafening roar of the sea, louder and closer than I had ever heard it. I could see our four stone steps, black and glistening, and a little of the gravel path below, but the light was drowned in the confusion of the deluge, like bundles of fine steel rods hurtling past an impenetrable curtain of blackness.

"Shall I go down and see, Aunt?" I shouted, reaching for my waterproof.

"No — too dangerous — must leave now," replied my aunt, struggling into her oilskins as I closed the door against the noise. "We must find the path — make for the vicarage."

"Mama's brooch!" I cried, and was racing back upstairs before she could stop me. I dashed into my room and seized the jewel in its red velvet case. My writing case lay on the bedside table; I seized that too, thrust it into the bosom of my dress, and was back in the hall before my aunt had finished tying on her sou'wester. I threw on my own oilskins and galoshes; we returned to the kitchen door and faced the downpour again. Not long before my mother died, a gate had been let into the back wall: to reach the village, we would have to climb a steep, narrow path up through the gorse for a hundred yards or more, and then follow the road — a welter of mud, after such a deluge — for at least a quarter of a mile before the lights of Niton came into view.

"The rain is too heavy!" I shouted. "If the lamp goes out, we'll be lost!"

"Must chance it — keep together!" She seized the lamp with one hand, clutched my arm with the other, and plunged into the storm.

I must have walked this path a thousand times; even on a moonless night, my feet would carry me from the kitchen door to the gate with scarcely a thought on my part. But the light showed only a teeming chaos of darkness and rain. We were sheltered, at first, from the full force of the wind, but the lamp still flared wildly, and the hot glass hissed and sputtered as we lurched in what I could only pray was the right direction. Branches clawed my face; black, clinging mud wrenched at my galoshes. I could not tell whether the quivering I felt was simply my own body shaking with fear, or the ground itself trembling; with every thunderous crash from the sea at my back, I expected the earth to vanish from beneath my feet.

After an age of splashing and stumbling, I blundered against stone, and felt my aunt tugging me to the right until we reached the gate and began to climb. Black, streaming gorse caught at our oilskins, leaving scarcely room for us to walk abreast, and the wind grew fiercer as we dragged our way upward, tugging at my sou'wester and sending jets of icy water down my neck.

I was trying to count my steps, and had got to something like fifty, when my aunt gasped and fell heavily, dragging me down with her. The lamp flew from her hand and went out in a flare and a clatter of breaking glass, and we were plunged into absolute darkness.

"What is it?" I shouted, drawing her close and trying to sit up.

"Ankle—can't walk."

"I'll help you."

I tried to stand upright, but immediately lost my balance and fell into gorse. Prickles stung my cheek. Fighting down panic, I slid one foot across the mud until it struck something soft; I heard another groan and dragged myself back to my aunt's side.

Slowly and painfully, I managed to get us both sitting up, with our arms around each other and our backs against the gorse. Our gloves and oilskins shielded us from the prickles, but my galoshes were full of water, and I could feel my aunt shivering. I drew her closer still and tried to arrange our oilskins to protect us as best I could. With our heads side by side, we could at least hear each other without having to shout. The gorse gave us some shelter, but the wind still swirled about us, and the rain beat down relentlessly.

"You must go on," said my aunt hoarsely. "Can't be too far from the road. Crawl up the path—use the gorse to guide you."

"I won't leave you, Aunt. I'd only get lost."

"Keep the sound of the sea behind you. When you reach the road, keep the wind on your left till you see the lights."

"No; you'll freeze if I leave you."

"We'll both die if you stay. Might be another collapse any minute. You get help—only chance."

I tried to picture the rest of the climb. Though the gorse bushes grew close, there were gaps quite large enough to deceive me; once off the path, I would get hopelessly entangled, or crawl blindly until I slipped and rolled to my death.

"I can't. I'll never find the way."

"S'pose not," she said after a pause. "But if the sky clears, go at once."

Even halfway up the path—as surely we must be?—the roar of the sea was terrifying. The time could not be much past nine o'clock;

nearly ten hours until the dawn, unless the clouds parted. The moon had been full a week ago, before the rain began, but even starlight would be enough to guide us. We were both shivering now, and I could not feel my feet. I wrapped my arms still more tightly around my aunt and waited for the end, trying not to imagine the ground opening beneath us, the bone-crushing fall, being buried under tons of rock and yet still conscious—and recalled, with terrible clarity, a torrent of earth and rock plummeting down the cliff, and my being suspended in midair by a tangle of roots, with red dirt spilling over me.

"Rosina! Help me!" I heard myself cry.

My aunt gave a violent start and twisted in my arms.

"What? What did you say?"

"It was—only a sort of prayer."

She muttered something I did not catch, and subsided. I remembered my mother finding me at the mirror, and the fear in her voice when she asked me about Rosina. If we lived, I thought, I would make Aunt Vida tell me—whatever there was to tell, about Rosina, and Nettleford, and my father . . .

But still the rain beat down, and the wind whipped about us in the darkness, carrying away what little warmth remained in my body. The shivering increased until I had to clench my teeth against it. It would be the worst of ironies, I thought, if we were found frozen to death with the house still standing. I had read somewhere that shivering was the body's way of keeping itself warm, and I began hugging my aunt rhythmically, hoping to squeeze some warmth into her. Mud squelched beneath us; I kept feeling that we were toppling to one side or the other, with only the pressure of the gorse against my back to tell me it was an illusion. Pinpoints of coloured light drifted before my eyes; for a wild moment I thought they were stars, until I realised that my eyes were tightly shut; the pinpoints were still there when I opened them. I clung to my aunt, and shook, and prayed for rescue.

Her head lolled against my cheek, lurched away, and lolled again. The rain had lessened; even the roar of the waves had receded. I realised that I was no longer shivering. My arms and legs were numb, but that did not seem to matter, as I did not feel cold anymore, only pleasantly drowsy, as if I were sinking into a warm bath . . .

I was lying in soft grass, beside a hedgerow crowded with blossom, the colours richer and more dazzling than anything I had seen: reds and crimsons and violets and pinks and whites so breathtaking I could feel them softly vibrating. Sunlight warmed my cheek; the air quivered with the chirruping of birds and the deep, resonant hum of bees, growing louder and louder until my body shook to the sound. Then the sun vanished with a colossal roar, and I was plunged back into freezing darkness, with the long, booming echoes of another landslide reverberating in the darkness below.

"'S the end," my aunt mumbled. "Mus' leave me."

"Aunt, you must wake up," I said. "We'll die if we go to sleep again."

I began squeezing her once more, with arms I could not feel, assuring her that we had slept most of the night away—and wishing I believed it myself—but she only stirred, and muttered something unintelligible. The rain, at least, had stopped, but the wind still swirled around us, and the sea, now that I was fully awake, sounded even louder and closer than before.

How much more of the cliff had gone? Had it taken the house this time? As I strained my eyes toward the crashing of the waves, it seemed to me that the darkness was no longer impenetrable. Looking up, I caught a glimpse of stars, blurred by a flying skein of cloud. Faint outlines of bracken coalesced around me. To see if the house was still there, I would have to stand, but my legs refused to obey me; for all the feeling in them, they might have been amputated.

What should I do? If the starlight held, and I could make my legs move, and climb the path, I could reach Niton in twenty minutes, and my aunt would be rescued within the hour. If I stayed, she would survive the cold longer—but not until morning, which I felt certain was still many hours away, even if a third landslide did not claim us.

As gently as I could, I withdrew my arm from around her, took one of my lifeless legs in both numb hands, and began to work at it, pushing and pulling until a spasm of cramp seized my calf. I did the same to the other, clutched at the gorse for support, and dragged myself slowly upright.

A pale gleam, low in the sky, appeared from behind a cloud. It was the moon, only just risen—so the time could not be much past midnight—above a seething chaos of foam. Where the silhouette of our house should have been, no more than fifty yards down the slope, there was only an uneven line of darkness, stark against the white of the sea.

Numb with dread as much as cold, I turned to face the climb. Pain shot through an ankle; my foot, I realised, must be trapped in the mud. As I tried to free it, the moon was blotted out, and I was plunged once more into absolute darkness.

No, not absolute. A star—a bright yellow star—shone out above me. And no, not a star but a lantern, swaying as it descended, and voices calling our names.

Though I escaped with only a severe head cold and a lingering chill in my bones, my aunt was stricken with fever. She lay delirious for several days, hovering between life and death, and by the time the fever broke, her lungs had been gravely weakened. We had been taken to the vicarage, where we remained in adjoining rooms, tended by Amy and Mrs Briggs, whom Mr Allardyce had kindly allowed to join us.

If the cottage had been spared, I think my aunt might have regained her health. I had somehow assumed, from her muttered words on the path that night, that she knew it had gone. But the first thing she said to me after the fever had subsided was "When can we go home?" and all I could bear to reply was, "Not yet, Aunt; you must get stronger first."

I walked round to the headland later that morning and stood for a while in pale sunlight, looking down from the top of the path. Our rescuers' trampled footprints were still clearly visible around the place where my aunt and I had waited. Fifty yards farther down, the path ran straight over what was now the edge of the cliff. The rubble was completely hidden from view; of the house and garden, nothing remained but empty air, and the wash and slide of the sea below. Everything we possessed—our clothes, our books, our furniture, my mother's jewel box, the trunk containing her own belongings—everything but my brooch and writing case lay buried under hundreds of tons of earth. I wondered how long I could put off telling my aunt, but someone must have let it slip, for when I returned from an errand a few hours later, she took my hand and said quietly, "It's all right, my dear; I know."

From that day onward, she ceased to struggle. The Aunt Vida of old would have been up and dressed the minute she could stand, waving away objections and declaring that all she needed was a good walk. But now she seemed content to lie propped up on a litter of pillows and watch the last of the autumn leaves drifting to earth. Our windows faced inland, but she showed no interest in what the sea was doing; nor did she ever ask me to describe the scene where the cottage had stood.

Her awkwardness about being touched had gone, too. She no longer withdrew her hand from mine, or held herself rigid when I put my arm around her, but simply accepted my embrace. Even Mr Allardyce, himself now very old and frail, would hold her hand when he sat with her. We kept up the pretence that she was convalescing, but as the days passed, her breathing became more laboured, and when she slept, I could hear a faint, bubbling undertone. Fluid on the lungs, the doctor said; there was nothing to be done but keep her warm and comfortable and hope for the best.

On a wintry afternoon, she seemed to rally. She had slept most of the day, and, on waking, asked for an infusion and had me arrange her pillows so that she was sitting upright. Her hand felt very cold in mine, as it always did now, no matter how assiduously we kept up the fire.

"I think you should go to your uncle," she said.

"But you would hate London, Aunt; you've always said so."

"I meant, when I am gone."

"You are going to get better," I said firmly, "and then we shall find another cottage—not so close to the cliff this time—and live as we always have."

"No, my dear, I'm not getting better. No tears now, child; I've had a good life, and I count myself lucky to have spent these last years with you."

"Please, Aunt, you musn't—"

"Pay attention, child," she said, with a flash of her old self. "Things you need to know. I wrote it all down, but that's at the bottom of the cliff now."

I dabbed at my eyes and tried to compose myself.

"I've provided for the servants, of course. You'll have about a hundred a year. Sorry it's not more, but half our income dies with me because I never married. And there's about two hundred capital, in trust from your mother. The cottage was to be yours, and everything in it—no use now. If you go to Josiah, you'll be able to save a bit. Maybe find an occupation—we've talked of it often enough—more chance for you in London.

"Our solicitor's name is Wetherell—Charles Wetherell, in George Street, Plymouth. When I'm gone, write to him. I've named Josiah as your guardian—has to be someone—told him to let you do as you please.

"Now—marriage. You know what I think, but you're a handsome gel, not like I was. You'll have offers. If you accept someone, write to Mr Wetherell—tell him who you're marrying. Papers to draw up—he'll tell you what's needed."

She slid back amongst the pillows, breathing hard, and closed her eyes. I could not bring myself to disturb her, and three days later she was dead.

I arrived at Gresham's Yard in the midst of a fog that would last another three weeks. I was used to the gentle mists that drifted about our house on the cliffs, and I had vaguely assumed that fog was the same, only denser. But this was altogether different: noxious, laden with soot, a dark, greasy yellow by day, pitch-black by night, clutching at the throat and choking the lungs. My uncle cheerfully informed me that this was nothing compared to the fog of two winters before, which had begun in November and lasted until the following March. And even when it lifted, the streets remained shrouded, either in smoke or driving rain: I woke each morning feeling as if I had inhaled a lungful of coal dust, and I was always catching cold.

My spirits, desolate enough when I arrived, sank lower as the weeks dragged on. My uncle was interested only in bookselling, and since his specialty was obscure theological works, there was little to converse about. To any question about our family, his invariable reply was, "You know, Georgina, it was such a long time ago; I really can't recall," until I gave up asking. What I had taken for benign approval was really benign indifference, an absolute lack of interest in anything beyond the confines of his shop.

As the days lengthened, and I began to venture out of doors, I discovered that everything sounded louder, and smelt worse, than I had ever imagined; my nostrils were constantly assailed by the stench of dung and drains, decaying meat and rotting fish, my ears deafened by the clatter of hooves and the cries of street vendors; yet the sheer extremity of sensation was a relief from the oppression of the house. In my wanderings through Bloomsbury, I was constantly amazed at how quickly the scene could change, from the grand houses in Bedford Square to wretched tenements a mere hundred paces away. The first time I saw a man sprawled dead drunk in the gutter, with passersby taking no more notice of him than of a sack of coals—far less, indeed, for the coals would have been carried off at once—I wondered if it was my duty to help him. But I soon learnt to avoid meeting the eyes of my fellow pedestrians, to walk briskly through the less-salubrious streets, and which streets to avoid altogether.

Gresham's Yard was a small, cobbled square, opening onto Duke Street, close by the Museum. A little sign above the entrance said JOSIAH RADFORD: ANTIQUARIAN BOOKS BOUGHT AND SOLD. There were other shops in the square, including a stationer, a cabinetmaker, a tailor and a haberdasher. You passed through the entrance, which was like a short tunnel of blackened stone, roofed over by the upper floors of the houses, turned left, and there was the entrance to the bookshop, where my uncle sat in the front room at a battered roll-top desk when he was not pottering with the stock.

Despite his shortsightedness, he seemed to know where any book was in the shop, and if the price was not pencilled on the flyleaf, he would always give it without hesitation. The customers were mostly elderly men like my uncle, scholars who worked at the Museum. The whole of the ground floor, a warren of small rooms on several different levels, was crammed with books; shelves extended from floor to ceiling on every available wall. The rooms, some of them windowless, were lit by gaslights in chimneys, and heated by two stoves at the front and back. My uncle was mortally afraid of fire, and would not allow a naked flame anywhere in the house. He was also, I discovered, mortally afraid of spending money on anything other than books. I gave him fifteen shillings a week for my keep, which was certainly more than it cost him, and took over the duties of the boy who had helped him with the parcels in the mornings, but he still blanched at the smallest expense.

Beside the entrance to the bookshop was the area, protected by iron railings, with steps going down to the kitchen and scullery. Beyond that was the house door, opening onto a flight of stairs that ran straight up to the first floor, where my uncle had his quarters overlooking Duke Street. Here also was the dining room, served by a dumbwaiter and another narrower staircase leading down to the servants' quarters. Mrs Eddowes, the housekeeper, was a gaunt, elderly woman with steel-grey hair who kept very aloof, in the manner of one who was doing my uncle a great favour by remaining, though she had been with him a decade or more. She had seven dishes, one for each day of the week, with which my uncle seemed entirely content. There was a washerwoman who came in, and the maid, Cora, of whom I saw very little—the latest in a series of maids, I gathered, though Uncle Josiah did not seem to notice the difference. My uncle did not like servants waiting at table, and had everything sent up in the dumbwaiter. I preferred to clear away myself and to send the dishes down to be washed, which I am sure suited Cora very well.

On the next floor up were a bedroom and bathroom, and above that two more bedrooms on the third floor. I chose the westward-facing one of these for my sitting room, because of the view over the rooftops; when the air was clear enough, you could catch glimpses of the river. It was barely ten feet square, with a small grate; a Persian rug so faded you could scarcely see the pattern; a tattered old chaise longue, which I draped with velvet; a small round table; and two upright chairs. I repapered the walls myself, in a green leafy pattern, which sometimes caught the afternoon light, and placed the sofa beneath the window. There I spent much of that interminable winter, desultorily reading novels and yearning for a friend. But where was I to find one? As the weather improved, I took to visiting the Museum and various galleries, and I would sometimes smile tentatively at other women, but they were almost never unaccompanied; at best they might smile faintly in return, and then move on.

I dreamt of Niton as a lost paradise, and thought many times of returning, but I feared that I would be just as lonely there, mourning the life I had lost. Amy wrote to me in the spring to say that she had married her sweetheart and moved with him to Portsmouth; Mrs Briggs had retired from service and gone to her sister in Felixstowe;

and when I heard that Mr Allardyce had died—even at Niton, the winter had been exceptionally severe—that put the seal upon it.

Depressing as I found my uncle's shop, I decided that I might as well make myself useful instead of moping upstairs. Most of his business was done by post, but he disliked having to close when he went out to sales, or to visit other dealers, and so I offered to mind the shop whenever he did. By the time I realised what a mistake I had made, it was too late: Uncle Josiah was going out every afternoon from two o'clock until five, while I sat moping downstairs instead of up. If there had been no clients at all, I should have rebelled, but the few that called—mostly elderly clergymen—brought in just enough money for my uncle to insist that we could not possibly manage without it.

Standing at the infirmary window, with the rain still falling steadily, I sought to coax my memory beyond those drab autumn days in my uncle's shop. I could recall, vividly enough, feeling that another winter in Gresham's Yard would be more than I could bear, and thinking that as soon as Aunt Vida's estate was settled—it seemed to be taking Mr Wetherell an unconscionably long time—I could draw out the two hundred pounds Mama had left me and travel abroad: in Rome, or Naples, it would at least be warm . . .

Shivering, I returned to bed and tried to make up my mind about leaving, until Bella arrived with a knowing look and the news that, though it was only half past eight, "Mr Mardent" would be pleased if I would join him for breakfast in the sitting room.

He was pacing about the room when I arrived, looking even paler than he had the day before, and there were dark shadows under his eyes. But his face lit up when he saw me, and I felt my breathing quicken in response.

"Miss Ferrars, I am delighted to see you looking so much better."

"Thank you, Mr Mordaunt. I slept extremely well. And you?"

"Not so well, I'm afraid; I am—not one of the world's great sleepers. But no matter."

There was a short silence while we settled ourselves by the fire.

"Tell me, Miss Ferrars, have you decided?—about returning to London, I mean."

"I thought—perhaps by this afternoon's train," I replied, realising, as his face fell, that I was not at all sure it was what I wanted.

"I'm afraid there is no afternoon train on a Sunday. It would have to be this morning at eleven, which would leave you very little time; and in such vile weather . . . Why not wait for Dr Straker?"

Rain spattered against the window; I thought of how bleak and cheerless Gresham's Yard would seem on such a day—and all the fog-bound, wintry days to follow. Of course, I could leave first thing tomorrow, but to depart only hours before Dr Straker returned would seem even more pointed.

"I should be very happy to wait for Dr Straker," I said, "if you would be kind enough to send another wire to my uncle, just to make sure that—that he knows I am here."

"I am sorry, Miss Ferrars, but that is impossible; the telegraph office is closed on Sundays. Of course, we could wire in the morning, but I doubt the reply would be here before Dr Straker."

"Then I think I should . . ." Instinct prompted me to say "take the first train home tomorrow," but Frederic had given me his word, and I was here as their guest, with Bella, seemingly, as my personal maid; they would have every right to be offended. But still the idea of waiting for Dr Straker prompted a cold, clutching sensation in the pit of my stomach.

"I shall stay until tomorrow," I said at last. "As you say, the weather is too wet for travelling."

Frederic's hands, which had been tightly clasped on his knees, relaxed, and his face brightened again. "It rained like this for a week before we lost our house," I added by way of distraction, forgetting I had not mentioned the landslide. He looked suitably startled and begged me to continue. No one—except my mother—had ever listened so attentively, or for so long. Frederic scarcely spoke, beyond murmurs of sympathy or encouragement, and yet his attention never wavered. When I described my ordeal on the path that night, he shivered unconsciously; I found myself speaking more and more openly as I went on, even disclosing what I had meant to conceal, my misery at Gresham's Yard, and my dread of another winter there.

A small silence followed, in which we sat contemplating the remnants of a breakfast I scarcely remembered eating.

"I wonder," said Frederic tentatively, "if that—your unhappiness in London, I mean—might explain your presence here. You say that, in the last days you can recall, you were thinking of wintering abroad.

Let us suppose that you actually did set out on a journey of some length; we don't know when, or where, but you told your uncle not to expect you back until the new year, let us say.

"And then—this is only my hypothesis, you understand—you suffered an accident, or a severe shock, lost your memory—all of it, I mean—and hence your luggage, though you must have retained some money. You outfitted yourself as best you could; perhaps in Plymouth, perhaps before you arrived there. Why you chose to call yourself Lucy Ashton we don't know—a subliminal awareness, perhaps, that your mind had been badly shaken. It was at Plymouth, I suspect, that you consulted a physician, who in turn recommended you to us. The courage and determination you displayed so abundantly that night on the cliff brought you all the way here, but then the strain caught up with you, in the form of a seizure, which restored most, but not all, of your memory. As I think I mentioned yesterday, if the initial shock was—well, exceptionally frightening—that could explain *why* there is still a gap in your memory.

"And, if I'm right, we can even account for the telegram Dr Straker received from your uncle, who, you say, is very much absorbed in his business and—er—not the most observant of men. What he meant to convey was 'Your patient can't be Georgina Ferrars because she is travelling abroad'—assuming he knows nothing of the accident, or its aftermath—but to economise on words, as one does with telegrams, he put 'Georgina Ferrars here,' with the most unfortunate results. Of course, it is only a theory, but it seems at least plausible, does it not?"

"It is more than plausible," I said with a deep sigh of relief. "I am sure you are right. I have been thinking myself that the reason I went to Plymouth is because it is near Nettleford; if, as you say, I had lost all of my memory, instinct might still have drawn me to the place where I was born. Thank you, Fr—Mr Mordaunt; that is such a relief to my mind."

Our eyes met; I was suddenly, acutely, conscious of his hand resting on the arm of his chair, only a foot away from mine. I lowered my gaze, but my awareness of his hand remained. My breathing faltered; blood rushed to my face. His fingers spread across the fabric, seeming to reach toward mine of their own volition.

Footsteps sounded in the corridor. Frederic hastily withdrew his hand, even though it had not moved beyond the arm of his chair. I clasped my own hands in my lap and stared at them, willing my colour to subside and looking, I am sure, as guilty as if Bella had caught us in the most flagrant embrace, while she cleared away the dishes, pointedly averting her eyes. Frederic made some banal remark about the weather, to which I replied in kind, addressing myself to the fireplace. It seemed an age before Bella withdrew and I dared to glance in Frederic's direction, only to catch him glancing at me, looking every bit as flushed and discomfited as I felt. He stirred uncomfortably in his chair, as if preparing to make his excuses and depart.

"Tell me," I said, casting around for a topic, "I realise I know nothing of what an asylum is really like—how you cure your patients, I mean." The words had scarcely left my mouth before I remembered that his father had been confined and died here; but then, he had chosen to work as Dr Straker's assistant.

"The truth is, Miss Ferrars, that for the most part we don't cure our patients; all we can do is provide them with the conditions most favorable to recovery. Dr Straker has come to believe that for the afflictions we commonly see in our voluntary patients—melancholia, nervous exhaustion, inanition, morbid anxiety, and the like—the conventional treatments are largely ineffective. He says that trying to relieve melancholia with mercury, or hydropathy, is like shooting blindfold at a target; if you fire often enough, you are bound to hit it sooner or later, but only by chance. Whereas clean air, kindness, nourishing food, exercise and occupation—and, above all, respite from the cares of everyday life—can only be conducive to healing.

"What we practise here is a form of moral therapy: we encourage every patient to take responsibility for his or her own cure. In my own case, for example, when I feel a bout of melancholia coming on, I know that there is nothing I can do—nothing anyone can do—to forestall it. I can take a glass of wine to ease the oppression, but then I am tempted to take another glass, and another; I can drug myself with opiates, but then I am fit for nothing. My only desire—in so far as I am capable of desiring anything—is to stay in bed and pull the blankets over my head, as I have done all too often, even though I know that it will only make things worse."

We had recovered our composure while he was speaking, and I ventured to ask him whether melancholia was like grief, only worse, or quite different.

"It is different from grief because grief is a living emotion — to grieve, you must have loved — whereas melancholia is at once the worst pain imaginable — worse than any physical pain I have experienced — and the negation of feeling. It is like a leaden blanket of darkness — darkness and fear, because you are possessed by dread: a universal dread that clamps like a limpet onto every passing thought. In the depths of an attack, I wake each morning feeling as if I have committed a capital crime and been sentenced to hang. The overwhelming temptation is to seek oblivion, and at the worst, the thought of the ultimate oblivion is always with you.

"But I also know, even in those depths — and this is where I am fortunate — that the darkness *will* pass, and that if I can drag myself out of bed, and face whatever the day requires of me, the oppression will diminish somewhat. And that, if you like, is the essence of moral therapy. I have Dr Straker to remind me that I will be better if I get up, but only I can do it. He could drag me out of bed — which is what happens in less enlightened asylums — but I would not benefit in the slightest."

"How can you call yourself fortunate," I asked, "when you endure such anguish?"

"Because, for much of the time, I am free of it, whereas for some of our patients, the darkness never lifts. And because my father and grandfather were so much more grievously afflicted; I have been spared, thus far, from mania."

These last words had been accompanied by one of his expansive gestures, but then his expression changed; he looked suddenly stricken, and averted his eyes.

"I am sorry," I said. "I did not mean to stir such painful memories." It struck me as I spoke that he had very little *but* painful memories to draw upon.

"It is not that," he replied, "only . . . But you were asking me about cures. There are some conditions that *can* be cured: phobias, for example. Dr Straker has had remarkable success with a technique he calls dramatic therapy, in which the patient is gradually brought face to face with the thing he fears most. We had a patient who was morbidly afraid of serpents. Dr Straker began by bringing him into a room in which there was a stuffed cobra in a glass case, well away from the door. The man was gently encouraged to approach a little closer each time until he was able to stand right next to the case; then to watch Dr Straker reach in and grasp the snake, and finally to handle it himself.

"For the next stage of the cure, Dr Straker replaced the stuffed cobra with a live one, whose fangs had been drawn, and repeated the sequence—which took a good deal longer—until the man was able to handle a living serpent without any sign of fear, and even to acknowledge that the creature had a certain beauty about it.

"He—Dr Straker—has had equally good results with several other phobias, and so he naturally wondered if the technique might be extended to more serious cases. A couple of years ago we had a patient who was firmly convinced that he had heard the voice of God commanding him to assassinate Mr Gladstone; I remember Dr Straker saying that many perfectly sane men might be tempted to do likewise, without divine instruction. He was actually arrested on his way to the Houses of Parliament with a pistol in his pocket, but because his family were wealthy, he ended up here rather than in Bedlam. Dr Straker wanted to see if he could cure a patient of monomania by allowing him to act out his obsession under controlled conditions—like drawing fluid off the brain, or lancing a boil—and this man, whose name, appropriately enough, was Isaiah Gadd, seemed an ideal subject for the experiment.

"Dr Straker began by getting the attendants to say to one another, within the man's hearing, that Mr Gladstone would shortly be visiting Tregannon House. Gadd was in a locked ward, but he wasn't closely confined; on any subject other than Gladstone he seemed quiet and sensible. He sat and read his Bible, did what he was told without argument, was polite to his fellow patients, and seemed to understand perfectly well why he was confined. And as you might expect, he was greatly agitated by the news of Gladstone's visit.

"As it happened, we had an elderly attendant who looked remarkably like the great man; I am sure he cultivated the likeness. Dr Straker said that if we hadn't found anyone on the staff, he'd have engaged an actor. On the morning of the supposed visit, Gadd was told that we were moving him to another wing, where he would be locked up until Mr Gladstone had left.

"He was taken to a cell on a badly lit corridor in the old wing, got up to look like a Hogarth engraving: a bare stone floor, with an iron door and vertical iron bars, far enough apart to get your arm through, right along the front. Dr Straker and I were in the room opposite, with the door standing open and the light arranged so that we could see Gadd, but he couldn't see us.

"He was left alone for an hour, growing more and more agitated, pacing up and down like a wild animal. Then a couple of attendants came running down the corridor, shouting that Mr Gladstone would be coming this way, and to be sure to bring the guards up first.

"By this stage, Gadd was in a state of uncontrollable excitement, clutching the bars with his face pressed against them. Then a man in a warder's uniform, with a pistol stuffed into his belt, came up and stationed himself right outside Gadd's cage, as it effectively was.

"Gadd's eyes fell on that pistol, and he grew very still; you could see his mind racing. Very slowly, he let his hands fall to his sides and edged along until he was just to the left of the guard, who was standing rigidly to attention, looking straight ahead of him. There was a tramping of feet; two more warders marched past, and then Gladstone appeared. My heart was thumping wildly; in that electric atmosphere, anyone would have sworn he was the Prime Minister.

"It went off like clockwork. Gladstone paused in front of the cell; Gadd reached through the bars, seized the pistol, and shot him through the heart. Even though I knew it was a trick, I cried out in horror when Gladstone clapped a hand to his chest and it came away drenched in what looked like blood. Gladstone sank to the ground and gave a most convincing death-rattle; Gadd dropped the pistol at the warder's feet and cried in a loud voice, 'Lord, now lettest thy servant depart in peace, according to thy word.'

"Dr Straker had hoped that Gadd would be overwhelmed by horror at his bloody deed and shocked back into sanity by the realisation that his delusion had made a murderer of him. Gadd would be left to steep in his own remorse (under covert watch to make sure he didn't attempt suicide) until Dr Straker judged the time was right to tell him that Gladstone had survived the attack. That, with luck, would prompt an equal and opposite reaction of relief—'I am not a murderer after all'—and then, if Gadd showed no sign of a relapse, another visit from 'Gladstone' would be arranged to test him. Last of all, Gadd would be told that the whole thing had been staged for his benefit, and if all went well, he would be discharged as cured.

"But when Dr Straker went into his cell that evening, and taxed him with murdering the Prime Minister and bringing disgrace upon the asylum, Gadd replied that he was very sorry for Mr Gladstone's family, and for all the trouble he had caused, but the Lord had commanded, and he had obeyed, and he would go to the gallows with a clear conscience, knowing that his reward awaited him in heaven. Dr Straker left him to stew in solitude for a few days but found him quite unchanged. When Gadd was told that Gladstone had survived the bullet, he replied calmly, 'It seems my task is not complete; I must await another opportunity.' He's still here, in one of the closed wards; spends a lot of his time painting. His watercolours—they're mostly of flowers—are very fine. I suppose if Gladstone dies before him, he may be released one day."

"Dr Straker must have been very disappointed," I said.

"Well no, not at all; he wrote an account of it for a learned journal. He often says that negative results can be just as useful as positive."

"Has he tried such an experiment again?"

"Not that I know of; he doesn't always tell me what he is working on. He has a private workroom in the old chapel, which he calls the temple of science: no one else is allowed there. His interests are extraordinarily diverse; he has made studies of everything from grafting fruit trees—not only to improve the fruit, but to see how many different varieties will thrive on a single tree—to the mathematics of gambling. At present, he is engaged in electrical research, though I have no idea where it is leading. A couple of years ago he visited Cragside—Lord Armstrong's estate in Northumberland—to see the hydraulic dynamo there, and he immediately commissioned one for us. It is powered by the stream that runs down from Siblyback Water; he says that one day the whole estate will be lit by electric lamps.

"And yet with all this, and a vast establishment to run, he still has time for individual patients—like the man who was terrified of snakes—even the hopeless cases. There was one, only last year . . . but I ought not say more . . ."

"Do his family live here as well?" I asked.

"He has no family, Miss Ferrars; he is a bachelor, like my uncle, and lives only for his work."

At the mention of his uncle, a shadow crossed his face. Outside, the rain was still falling. He rose, added more coals to the fire, and made a show of consulting his watch.

"I am sorry, Miss Ferrars, but I have duties to attend to. Might I join you again for luncheon, in an hour or so?"

"I should like that very much."

"Then I shall return as soon as I can." He smiled, but his eyes were still troubled, and I feared I had driven him away.

He seemed, however, entirely recovered when he returned an hour later. "I have said quite enough about myself," he insisted, "and I want to hear more about you, and your childhood at Niton." My childhood seemed so commonplace and uneventful compared to his, but I sensed that our quiet domestic life was for him a vision of paradise. I told him about the mirror, and my fascination with Rosina, and its aftermath on the cliff, which led somehow to religion, and how Aunt Vida and Mr Allardyce used to argue. My aunt was a declared agnostic, but I felt that they were essentially on the same side. Mr Allardyce used to say that faith couldn't be commanded; so long as you acted *as if* you believed, all would be well. They were both contemptuous of spiritualism: when I expressed curiosity about it, my aunt suggested with a perfectly straight face that we try a method of spelling out messages with a glass and a circle of cut-out letters, and the glass spelled out "Spiritualism is bunkum."

Frederic laughed at this, but his face was shadowed.

"Rationally speaking," he said, "I agree with your aunt, but in this house it is all too easy to believe that the dead live on amongst us. All those centuries of violent emotion, permeating the furniture, the hangings, the timbers, even the stones . . . The old house was always cold and damp, even in summer; the walls are so thick, and the windows so small, and there are strange pockets of icy air—you could be walking along a corridor and feel as if you had been plunged into freezing water . . ."

"Have you ever seen a ghost?"

"Not seen, exactly, but I think I may have heard one."

It had begun last April, he said, on a mild, sunlit afternoon. He had lately emerged from a bout of melancholia and decided to take a stroll in the grounds, with no particular destination in mind. His feet carried him to a long-abandoned stable, overgrown and collapsing, some thirty or forty yards beyond the old house, surrounded now by woodland. He was standing nearby, gazing idly at the ancient, uneven brickwork and enjoying the unaccustomed warmth of sunlight on his skin, when he heard a pickaxe striking upon stone. It sounded like someone chipping at a piece of masonry in an exploratory fashion, and it seemed to come from inside. He looked in through the doorway—the lintel had collapsed, leaving only a narrow, triangular opening—but there was nobody within. Then he heard the noise again—tap-tap, tap-tap—perfectly clear, with a distinct ringing echo to it—only this time it came from the outside, around the corner to the left of where he was standing. Again the sound ceased as he approached. He walked right around the building; the long grass had been trampled in places by something—badgers, perhaps—but there were no bootmarks, and again no one to be seen. He stood and waited for some time, but the sound was not repeated, and he assumed that it had been caused by some rusted piece of metal, a broken hinge or the like, expanding in the sunshine.

A week or so later, he was passing the stables when he heard the sound again, a little louder, coming from around the corner to his right this time. Once again it ceased just before he turned the corner; once again there was nobody to be seen. Then it started up again, from around the back of the ruin. He found himself imagining a man in a convict's uniform and leg irons, tapping away with a pick. His mouth was suddenly dry; he had to force himself to circle the building, and then retreated with his heart beating rapidly.

Over the next few weeks, he was drawn back almost against his will. Sometimes he would stand for minutes at a stretch and hear nothing but the distant lowing of cattle. It seemed to him that whenever he was intent upon listening for the sound—always metal upon stone—it did not come, but as soon as his attention wandered, it would start up again. And though there was no consistent pattern from day to day, he felt that the sound was becoming stronger, the rhythm of the pick faster—though you could not call it a rhythm because it was al-

ways irregular. It frightened and fascinated him in equal measure; he
had come to believe that the place was haunted by the sound of a murderer burying his victim.

Even more disturbing was the suspicion that he had somehow
awakened the sound; that it was aware of him, playing upon his curiosity and leading him on. He imagined himself digging and exposing a shattered skull — but what would follow if he did? He brought
old Trethewey, the head gardener, over to the stables, and kept him
talking by the entrance for some time. But Trethewey knew of no ancient crime, and the sound did not come, and when Frederic said tentatively that he had heard some odd noises of late, Trethewey gave
him a pitying look and all but tapped his forehead, as if to say, "Another mad Mordaunt." The following day he tried again, asking one
of the undergardeners to inspect the brickwork with him; again the
sound did not come, and he felt that this man, too, was regarding him
strangely. But the very next time he approached the stables alone, he
was greeted by a fierce volley of sounds from within — hard, and menacing, and too fast, surely, for human hands wielding a pick — and he
could not summon the courage to enter.

"And what happened after that?" I asked, when he did not immediately continue.

"I knew what I ought to do: confide in Dr Straker and ask him to
investigate. But I feared it might be a symptom of — something worse
than melancholia, and if it turned out that I could hear the noise, but
he could not . . . So I have simply avoided the place ever since, hoping that whatever I disturbed, whether it was in the stables, or in my
head — or, as I sometimes suspect, in both, will stay quiet as long as I
keep away."

"It cannot be good for you," I said, "living here, in the shadow
of so much anguish. Do you not think you might be happier — and
healthier — away from this place?" I remembered asking him this the
day before, but I could not recall his reply.

He hesitated for a long time before he spoke, keeping his eyes fixed
upon the flames.

"I think of it all the time, Miss Ferrars. But as I may have said
yesterday, my uncle and I are the last of our line. Uncle Edmund has
never married, because he believes that the only way to eradicate the

dark strain in the Mordaunt blood is to let it die out. And he expects me to follow his example."

He took a long, uneven breath, as if to say, *There; I have said it.*

"And—does Dr Straker agree with your uncle?"

"Yes, he does. He says that hereditary madness cannot be cured, only bred out—as we do with defects in every other species."

"But is it absolutely certain," I said, "that if you were to marry a woman who was—perfectly well, your children would be afflicted?"

"No, it isn't, and there's the rub. They might—especially if they were girls; it comes out mostly on the male side—they might be quite untouched. But the dark strain would still be there, and it might reappear in the next generation, or the one after that, in all its old virulence."

"But that is like saying that it would be better if *you* had never existed. I have only known you a day, Frederic, and *I* do not think the world would be better without you—"

He took another long, shuddering breath and rose from his chair, still not looking at me. I thought he was about to walk out of the room; instead, he walked over to the window and stood with his back to me and his shoulders shaking. I rose, stiffly after all the hours of sitting, went over, and stood beside him. Racked by harsh, choking sobs, his face wet with tears, he struggled to regain his self-control. I placed my hand on his cold fingers and stroked them gently. No one, I thought, in his entire lonely existence, has ever said that they were glad he had been born. The uncle sounded like a cold fish; to Dr Straker he was a useful part of the machinery of the asylum, and therefore to be encouraged and got out of bed in the mornings so that he could keep up the paperwork. But no one had ever told Frederic that they loved him.

Strangely, I had quite lost my self-consciousness. I was not, I realised, actually shocked at my boldness at calling him Frederic; nor did I repent of it; nor did I fear that he would think me immodest. Nor, strangest of all, did I think that I was falling in love with him. I did not think of myself at all: my heart had opened itself to him, whether I would or no. If I had a brother, I thought, a brother in terrible distress and anguish of mind, this is how I would feel.

Gradually his breathing steadied, and he turned to me with a wan smile.

"Thank you," he said, "thank you. No one has ever—"

"No," I said, still stroking his cold fingers. Our breath misted the glass. "Your uncle is wrong; I know he is, and I think you know it, too, in your heart. Yours is a loving spirit, and it should not die with you. Surely your melancholia would not return if you were away from here."

"And when you are back in London," he said, gazing at me as if memorising every detail of my appearance, "will you want to see me again?" The implication was unmistakable.

"Until I know what has happened to me, I cannot think beyond the present. But I know that I want to be your friend, and to see you again, and yes, I will write to you as soon as I am back in London. And now I think you should go, before Bella returns and—leaps to conclusions."

"But you will wait for Dr Straker, I trust?" he said, mopping his face with his handkerchief, "rather than taking the first train back?"

"Yes," I said, suppressing another small, cold pang of unease. He had given me his word, and he was, after all, the heir: what was there to fear?

"Then I shall certainly join you for breakfast, and perhaps if the weather is fine, we might take a turn in the grounds."

He left reluctantly, walking more or less backward until he bumped into the door-frame. Outside, the rain was still falling steadily, and the light was fading.

I lay awake for a long time that night, and when at last I did sleep, it was only to be wakened an instant later, as it seemed, by light footsteps in the passage outside my door. For a wild moment I wondered if it might be Frederic, also wakeful; then I thought it must be Bella; but would Bella not have come in? I went to the door and peeped out. Oil lamps flickered along the empty corridor; all the doors I could make out were closed. Where, I wondered, did Bella sleep? In one of the rooms nearby? I thought of the ghost in the old stable, and heard Frederic saying, "A house as old as this is never entirely still, even in the dead of night." Chill air stirred around my ankles; I retreated hastily to bed, and lay awake for some time, listening uneasily. But the footsteps did not return.

The next time I woke, it was full daylight. I got out of bed at once, with a feeling of having overslept. Perhaps Frederic was already pacing up and down the sitting room, not wanting Bella to disturb me in case I was still asleep. Rather than wait for her, I got dressed on my own and hastened along the corridor. But the room was empty, and the fire had not been lit; perhaps it was earlier than I thought. I tugged at the bell-rope and went over to the window. The rain had ceased, but the garden below still dripped with moisture, and the paths were saturated.

I stood there for a while, watching the clouds bulge and crumple like grotesque faces floating just above the treetops. Surely Bella had never taken as long as this? I rang again and waited several minutes more, but still she did not come.

Perhaps the bell was not working. I went out into the dim, empty corridor. In the wall to my left, the direction from which Bella and Frederic had always appeared, were two more doors. I tried them as I went along; both were locked. The passage ended at another, heavier door; it, too, was locked.

If you choose to leave, no one will hinder you.

Of course, the door might be locked for my own protection; this was, after all, a lunatic asylum.

I went back along the passage, giving the bell-rope another tug as I passed the sitting room. The wall now on my left was blank except for an opening about halfway along, the entrance to a much shorter passage, ending at another locked door. Apart from a bathroom near the room in which I slept, every door was locked, including the door at the far end, which led, I assumed, to the closed wards in the newest part of the building.

The oil lamp near my room was still burning. Except for the dim shaft of light falling from the open door of the sitting room, the only source of illumination was a pane of opaque glass—a skylight of some kind?—in the ceiling halfway along. I remembered the footsteps in the night.

You are safe here, on my word of honour.

I retraced my steps, trying not to run, to the door at the other end, and rattled and tugged at the handle, then beat upon the oak in a panic, bruising my knuckles until the pain forced me to stop.

As the echoes died away, a floorboard creaked behind me. The hair on the back of my neck bristled.

"Can I 'elp you, miss? You can't go through there, you know."

I spun round. In the light from the sitting-room door, a woman was standing—not Bella, but a heavily built woman twice her age, with forearms like hams and a flat, porcine face, in which small eyes glittered.

"Who are you? Where is Bella?"

"Hodges is the name, miss." A London accent, I thought, with an insinuating edge that seemed to imply, *I know all about you.* She wore a starched uniform like Bella's, but hers was dark blue. As she approached, I caught a whiff of rank breath.

"Where is Bella?" I repeated.

"Bella's got other duties. I'll be looking after you today."

"Then would you kindly fetch Mr Mordaunt? He will be joining me for breakfast."

"Is that so, miss? Would that be young Mr Mordaunt, then?"

"Yes, it would, and you will kindly fetch him without further delay."

"I'm afraid I can't do that, miss."

"And why not?"

"Doctor's orders, miss."

"You are mistaken. I am a voluntary patient here, and if you do not fetch Mr Mordaunt at once"—I could hear my voice beginning to tremble—"he will be most displeased."

"Really, miss?" She sneered, in the tone of one humouring, or rather baiting, a madwoman. "Well, I takes *my* orders from Dr Straker."

"Dr Straker is in London, attending to business of mine—"

"Well, fancy that. We are goin' it this morning, aren't we? Now I could swear Dr Straker give me my orders just ten minutes ago, and them orders was that Miss Ashton was to stay in bed until he—"

"What did you call me?"

"Miss Ashton, miss. That's your name, according to Dr Straker, and he ought to know."

"My name is not Ashton. I am Miss Ferrars; I am a voluntary patient"—my voice was now shaking wildly—"and I wish to leave this place at once. Now fetch Mr Mordaunt!"

"Come along now, miss; no point getting hysterical, now is there?"

"If you do not unlock that door and let me out this instant, I will—

I will have you arrested and charged with false imprisonment!" The last words came out as a shriek.

"Well, I'll tell you what, miss. You can go back to your bed, nice and quiet, and wait there in the warm till Dr Straker comes to see you, or I can 'elp you undress and put you to bed myself. Now which will it be?"

I thought of trying to dodge past her, but she stood squarely in the middle of the passage, with her great hands resting on her hips and her elbows almost touching the walls. If I resisted her, I might find myself in a straitjacket.

"I will go quietly," I said, "if you will promise to tell Mr Mordaunt I wish to see him urgently."

"Now that's more like it, miss. You come along quietly to bed, and I'll tell Dr Straker that you asked particular to see Mr Mordaunt, and we'll see what happens, won't we?"

She moved aside to let me pass and followed me closely back to my room.

"That's right, miss. You get into bed, and I'll be back with your breakfast before you know it."

A massive hand urged me on. As the door closed behind me, I heard a jingle of metal, followed by the scrape and snap of the lock.

Hodges returned half an hour later with breakfast, which I could not eat, and then insisted that I should bathe, locking me in the bathroom while she made up the bed. "Dr Straker will be along presently," was all she would say. As the minutes crawled by, my hope of rescue shrank to nothing. Either Frederic had deceived me all along—hard as it was to believe, remembering those deep, wrenching sobs—or he was so in thrall to Dr Straker that he had not the backbone to defy him. The more I brooded, the more my suspicions increased. Tregannon Asylum, according to Frederic, was a benign, compassionate, enlightened place, but there was nothing benign about Hodges; she was exactly what I had always imagined a madhouse attendant would be. And if Frederic had lied about that, what else had he lied about? How long had Dr Straker been back from London? Had he even *been* to London? I tried to look out through the observation slot in the door, but it would not open.

An eternity later, as it seemed, the lock turned over again, and Dr

Straker appeared in the doorway. He looked so grave that my protests died on my lips; my first thought was that something had happened to Frederic, and I watched him fearfully as he settled himself beside the bed.

"I am sorry to have to tell you, Miss Ashton, that my instinct has been confirmed. I have been to Gresham's Yard, and I met Georgina Ferrars and Josiah Radford, her uncle. The mystery of how you know so much about them is a mystery no longer. The only riddle we have yet to solve is the riddle of your own identity."

He paused, awaiting my reaction, but I could not utter a sound.

"Believe me, Miss Ashton, I understand how distressing this must be, even though I have tried to prepare you. It will be best, I think, if I begin by telling you what transpired. Gresham's Yard is just as you described it, and until the maid said she would fetch Miss Ferrars, I was preparing to eat my hat. But at my first glimpse of Georgina Ferrars, a great deal became clear: the resemblance between you is quite remarkable. Miss Ferrars was profoundly shaken, but not wholly surprised, to learn that I had a patient who not only looked like her and appeared to know everything about her, but was claiming to *be* her. 'It is Lucia!' she exclaimed, 'Lucia Ardent; it can only be Lucia!' The initials, you will agree, can hardly be a coincidence. But I see the name means nothing to you.

"Three weeks ago, around the tenth of October—Miss Ferrars could not recall the precise date—she was alone in the bookshop when a young woman came in. Miss Ferrars felt sure she had seen her somewhere before, but she did not immediately associate the face before her with the one she saw every day in the mirror—did you wish to say something, Miss Ashton?"

Numb with shock, I could only stare at him.

"The young woman introduced herself as Lucia Ardent. They fell into conversation, and an intimacy sprang up. It was Lucia—if you will forgive the familiarity for the sake of concision—who first remarked upon the likeness between them. Within a couple of days, Lucia was living at Gresham's Yard.

"Lucia, or so she claimed, was the daughter of a Frenchman named Jules Ardent, and an Englishwoman, Madeleine Ardent—who, according to Lucia, had refused ever to speak of her past. All she would say was that her childhood had been most unhappy and that she did not wish to recall it, or ever revisit England; she never revealed her maiden name. Jules Ardent died when Lucia was an infant—all this, you understand, rests upon Lucia Ardent's unsupported word—leaving them an income of about two hundred a year. Lucia and her mother lived an itinerant life, moving about the Continent, staying in pensions and hotels until Madeleine Ardent died about a year ago. Lucia Ardent had always wanted to see England, and so, drawn by the mystery of her birth, she came to London, took lodgings in Bloomsbury, and by sheer chance wandered into Josiah Radford's bookshop.

"All this, you understand, is what she told Georgina Ferrars, who had no reason to disbelieve her. As a child, Georgina told me, she had often wished she had a sister, and now it seemed that she had found one. Lucia was, from the beginning, insatiably curious about every aspect of Georgina's past, and it was only later that Georgina realised how little she had learnt in return. As the days went by, Georgina became more and more conscious of the resemblance between them, and they had many long conversations about its possible bearing on the mystery of Lucia's origins. Lucia had brought only a small travelling-case"—Dr Straker glanced meaningfully at the valise Bella had unpacked—"and as they were much the same size, Georgina was happy to share her own clothes with her newfound friend. Josiah Radford, who is exceptionally shortsighted, was soon unable to tell them apart.

"Within a fortnight they were, Miss Ferrars told me, as close as if they really had been sisters. It was already settled, with Josiah Radford's blessing, that Lucia should make her home there, but first—or so she said—she must return briefly to Paris to settle her affairs. Miss Ferrars would very much have liked to accompany her but felt that she could not leave her uncle.

"And so, last Monday—just two days, Miss Ashton, before you arrived here—Lucia Ardent packed her valise and departed in a cab, promising to return within a fortnight. It was only after she had left that doubts began to creep in. Miss Ferrars noticed, first of all, that Lucia had taken every single thing she had arrived with. And then she discovered that her two most cherished possessions were missing: a blue leather writing case given to her by her aunt, and a valuable ruby and diamond brooch in the shape of a dragonfly, which had belonged to her mother."

It is a nightmare, I told myself. *You must wake up now.* But his face refused to dissolve.

"I am sorry," he said. "I wish I could make this easier for you, but we must face facts. You will be wondering—since you are, beyond question, the woman who left Gresham's Yard two days ago—why I do not address you as Miss Ardent. That is because Lucia Ardent is an alias: the account she gave of herself is an obvious fabrication, since it contains not a single verifiable fact. Lucia Ardent is your own invention, and since you came here as Miss Ashton, I propose that we continue to call you by that name, until we discover who you really are."

"I *am* Georgina Ferrars," I said hopelessly, finding my voice at last. With the words came the thought, *He is lying; he must be lying.* "If—if this woman really exists, then *she* has taken *my* place—"

"There is no doubt of her existence, Miss Ashton; I am speaking to her at this moment. Just as there can be no doubt that the young woman I met in London is the real Georgina Ferrars; an imposter might possibly deceive Josiah Radford, who is exceedingly short-sighted, but not the maidservant."

"What was her name—the maid's?" I asked, clutching at straws.

"I have no idea, but I am sure there is nothing wrong with her eyesight."

"It is clear," he continued, when I did not respond, "that when you arrived here as Lucy Ashton, you were well aware that you had trained yourself to impersonate Georgina Ferrars. *Why* you did so remains a mystery. But I would say, without question, that you had become aware that the balance of your mind was disturbed: why else would you have sought out a leading specialist in disorders of the personality, and presented yourself to him under the name of a madwoman?"

I remembered Frederic—not once, but twice—saying exactly that.

"You adopted an alias because you were not yet ready to confess—no doubt for fear of the consequences—but the alias you chose was itself a kind of confession. And then, sadly, your mental turmoil led to a seizure, which seems to have obliterated everything *but* the personality you were so determined to assume."

"No!" I cried. "I swear on my dear mother's grave, it is *my* life I remember!"

"Miss Ashton, Miss Ashton; I am not questioning your sincerity. But the past you think you remember is a dream, woven by your troubled imagination out of the material of Georgina Ferrars' life. You cannot see this, because it is *all* you can see. But rest assured: we will not abandon you; as I said before, you will be cared for here, without charge, no matter how long it takes us to discover your true identity."

I dug my nails into the palms of my hands, fighting down terror.

"If you will only take me to London," I said in a small, strangled voice, "and let me speak to my uncle; and to Cora, the maid; and Mrs Eddowes, the housekeeper; and Mr Onslow, the haberdasher in the square, they will tell you that I am the real Georgina Ferrars, and not this imposter—"

"I am sorry, Miss Ashton, but that is out of the question. I explained to Miss Ferrars that you were not responsible for your actions, and that bringing you face to face with her might help you recover your memory, but she does not wish to see you again. She feels, understandably, betrayed. 'Let her return my writing case and brooch,' she said, 'and apologise for the distress she has caused us, and then perhaps I will consider your request.'"

"She is lying—" I began, but the futility of it was plain. I took a deep breath and summoned the last of my courage.

"Then since you will not help me, sir, I wish to leave this place immediately. I am a voluntary patient—"

"I am sorry, Miss Ashton, but I cannot allow it. I should be derelict in my duty if I allowed a young woman in the grip of a dangerous delusion to wander away unattended. If you were to appear at Gresham's Yard in your present frame of mind, you would probably be arrested for disturbing the peace. You *were* a voluntary patient; I now have no choice but to issue a certificate of insanity."

I saw, too late, that I had made a fatal mistake.

"Sir, I beg your pardon," I stammered, hearing the note of terror all too clearly. "I spoke in haste; perhaps I am not myself. I promise to stay here quietly until—until I am better; there is no need for a certificate . . ."

He regarded me silently for some time, a faint ironic twist at the corner of his mouth.

"Almost convincing, Miss Ashton; but not quite. Unless I am much mistaken, you would make a dash for the gate the moment our backs were turned. No; I'm afraid my duty is plain. You may be a danger to others; you are certainly a danger to yourself. And now if you will excuse me, I must summon Dr Mayhew; I advised him of these developments this morning, but he will need to examine you in person."

"I am not mad!" I cried as he rose to leave. "Ask Fr — Mr Mordaunt; *he* believes me."

"He *did* believe you, Miss Ashton. Mr Mordaunt is — easily led; he has learnt a salutary lesson."

Dr Mayhew's "examination" consisted of his grunting several times, peering at my tongue, and muttering, "Hmph, mmph — highly agitated — danger to herself and others — no doubt about it," after which he took the pen and the document that Dr Straker was holding out to him, added his signature, and departed.

"Well, there we are, Miss Ashton," said Dr Straker. "We shall keep you here in the infirmary for a couple more days, just to be sure, and then transfer you to one of the women's wards. I know it is hard, but try not to think too much. Hodges will bring you a sedative, and in the morning I shall look in to see how you are getting on."

At the sound of the door closing behind him, I buried my face in the pillow and wept as I had never wept before.

I was roused from my misery by a clatter of keys and the heavy tread of Hodges.

"Come along now, Miss Ashton; this won't do. I've brought you a pot of tea and some bread and butter, and a nice sleeping draught."

It was still broad daylight, but I assumed it must be late in the afternoon.

"What is the time?" I asked hopelessly.

"One o'clock. Now you sit up and 'ave your tea, and then you can 'ave a nice sleep."

Rather than have her touch me, I sat up as instructed; she arranged the invalid tray across my knees, and departed.

Even the sight of food turned my stomach; I reached instead for the glass of cloudy liquid standing beside the teacup. Eight hours of blessed oblivion . . . and then? I paused with the glass halfway to my lips. Through the fog of anguish and horror, a single thought loomed: *Once they move you, you will never escape.*

And if I did not eat, I would be too weak to escape. I set down the glass and began chewing the bread in small, nauseating mouthfuls, washing it down with sips of tea, and trying to concentrate what remained of my mind. Why this had happened to me was beyond my comprehension; all that mattered was to escape (though that was surely impossible) within the next two days, find my way to Gresham's Yard (but how? I had no money), and confront the woman (though I did not believe she existed) who had stolen my life away.

The tale of Lucia Ardent was more than bizarre; it was grotesquely improbable. No; Dr Straker had invented the story for his own purposes—purposes I dared not begin to imagine—which made it even more imperative that I should escape.

But he knew about the writing case and brooch.

I could not remember whether I had mentioned the writing case to him, but I felt sure I had not described the brooch in any detail, either to him or to Bella.

But I had described it to Frederic.

Which meant—that I must not allow myself to think about what it meant.

Escape. I could empty the sleeping draught into the chamber pot, and pretend to be asleep—or drowsy—when Hodges returned for the tray. That ought to give me several uninterrupted hours. And I had better do that at once, before she came back and caught me.

Half a minute later I was back in bed, forcing down the last of the bread and listening for footsteps.

Escape. I already knew that the grille protecting the window felt very solid, but if I could find some sort of instrument, perhaps I could loosen it.

Or there was the door. You could pick a lock with a bent hatpin, or so I had read, but I had never tried it, and beyond this lock would be another, and another . . .

When Hodges brought the tray in, she had left the door open and the key in the lock; I was sure of it.

If I hid behind the door, and padded the bed with rolled-up clothes to make it look as if I were asleep, perhaps I could slip past her, slam the door, turn the key and run. But the door opened flat against the side wall; she would feel that I was behind it. And even if she came right up to the bed without seeing me, there would be very little room to squeeze past her. No; she would certainly catch me.

Could I hit her over the head with something and knock her unconscious? I might be able to break a leg off the upright chair, but would that be heavy enough? How hard would I have to hit her? And what if I killed her by mistake?

Heavy footsteps approached. I leant back against the pillows, turned my head toward the door, and half closed my eyes. The lock turned—a hard, effortful grating sound; the door swung against the wall as Hodges entered, and there was the bunch of keys, swinging from the lock.

"Well, that's better, isn't it? You 'ave a nice long sleep now. I'll look in later, and this evening I'll bring you some supper and another drop o' chloral."

I did my best to look drowsy and vacant as she turned away, stepping out into the passage to set down the tray before she closed the door. Dodging past her looked even more impossible than I had imagined. And from the sound of the lock, it would take far more than a hatpin to open it, even if I knew the trick.

Which left the window. As soon as her footsteps had died away, I went over and examined the grille, which seemed to be set into the stonework itself. I could not move it in the slightest, no matter how hard I tugged. Perhaps if I picked up the chair and ran at the grille, I might be able to dislodge it; most likely I would break the chair, and be punished accordingly.

The jug and basin on the washstand were made of enamel, too light to do any damage. I turned to the closet. The empty valise stood to one side, on end, with the hatbox on top of it.

I had glanced into the hatbox on that first afternoon. This time I took out the bonnet—a pale blue one, trimmed in cream—but found not a single hatpin. I was about to replace it when I noticed a pocket in the lining near the bottom of the hatbox. A small, squarish shape was pressing against the silk.

With suddenly trembling fingers I drew from the pocket a familiar red plush box. I pressed the catch, and there was my dragonfly brooch, unharmed.

And there was something else in the pocket—something that clinked softly as I touched it: a small drawstring purse in brown velvet, with five gold sovereigns inside.

I do not know how long I crouched, staring blankly at my brooch and clutching the purse as if it might take wing and fly away, before it occurred to me that my writing case might be here, too. But there was nothing else in the hatbox. I dragged out the valise and felt all around the lining, but again I found nothing except traces of lint.

I let out a great sob of frustration and self-reproach. If only, if *only* I had thought to look sooner, instead of now, when it was too late.

"Let her return my writing case and brooch" . . . If Dr Straker found out, he would take it from me.

I slipped the purse into the pocket of my travelling-dress, put away the valise and hatbox, and got back into bed for warmth, still holding my brooch in its open box. The rubies glowed like drops of blood.

The gold pin, though sharp, was barely two inches long. Hodges would swat it away with one meaty hand and lift me off my feet with the other.

I pictured those small, knowing, covetous eyes leering down at me, and a plan began to form.

The worst that can happen, I thought, is that she turns out to be honest, and hands the brooch straight to Dr Straker.

I sat motionless for a very long time, thinking it out. Then I got up again and put on my travelling-dress, feeling that I would have a better chance with Hodges if I faced her fully dressed. I laid the travelling-cloak and bonnet at the foot of the bed, took two of the five sovereigns out of the purse, and left them loose in the pocket of my cloak. After that there was nothing to do but pace about the room to keep warm, and pray that Hodges would look in on me before darkness fell.

At last I heard a distant thud, and then the approaching footsteps. I moved over to the window and stood with my back to it, facing the door as the observation slide opened. I heard a sharp intake of breath and a rattle of keys; the door crashed against the wall and Hodges strode into the room.

"What's this then? Why aren't you asleep in bed?"

My heart was pounding so violently that I could scarcely speak.

"Because—because I have something to show you."

"And what might that be?" she asked suspiciously, moving closer.

"This." I took the jewel box from my pocket, pressed the catch, and held it out for her to see, angling the box so that the rubies caught the light. Her little eyes flickered between the brooch and my face.

"It is the most precious thing I have in the world," I said. "My mother left it to me; it is worth a hundred pounds."

"And what's that to me?"

"It is yours," I said, "if you will help me escape."

She smiled derisively. The little eyes bored into mine.

"And what's to stop me taking it right now?"

"Nothing," I said breathlessly, willing my voice not to shake. "But then I would tell Dr Straker, and if you were caught, you would be sent to prison."

The eyes flickered over the brooch.

"Or I could give it to Dr Straker," she said, "and 'e might give me a nice reward."

"He might," I said, "but not two hundred pounds."

"You just said it was worth one hundred."

"Yes, if *you* were to sell it. But to me it is worth all the money I have in the world, which is two hundred pounds, in trust with my solicitor. As soon as I am safely home in London, I will buy it back from you for two hundred pounds."

"'Ow do I know it's not paste?"

I had not thought of this, and I racked my brain for an answer, keeping my eyes fixed on hers as if she were a huge, savage dog, bracing itself to spring. Meaty breath wafted over me, prompting a spasm of nausea.

"You don't," I said at last. "But do you think I would have risked bringing it here, of all places, if I could have borne to part with it?"

She was silent again; I could see the eyes calculating.

"And supposing—just supposing, mind—I was to 'elp you escape, I should lose my place."

"Not necessarily," I replied. "You could say that I hid behind the door, dodged around you when you came in with the tray, and locked you in."

She nodded very slightly. There was a hint of complicity in her glance.

"What are your wages here?" I asked.

"Thirty pound and my keep."

"Two hundred pounds is nearly seven years' wages."

"Maybe, but why should I trust you? S'posing you do get back to London, why wouldn't you tell the police I stole your brooch?"

"Because I have given you my word, and . . . because the police might bring me back here, before I can prove that—I am who I say I am."

There was another calculating silence.

"And what if you get caught before you get out of 'ere? You'll say I stole it, and then where am I?"

I had not anticipated this, either.

"If I am caught escaping, you will still be locked in here, and—if you will not trust me—you can put the brooch back before they find you."

"Then I get nothing, 'cept a bad mark on my character."

I thought desperately, but no answer occurred to me. I felt in my pocket with my other hand and held out the two sovereigns.

"Here," I said as the gold caught the light, "they are yours to keep if you will only help me, whether I am caught or not."

The glittering coins seemed to fascinate her even more than the rubies. Her little eyes fastened on them, then on the brooch, then on me, back and forth, back and forth, for a small eternity before she reached out and took first the coins, and then the jewel box.

"All right," she said. "I'll do it."

The floor swayed beneath my feet; I realised I had stopped breathing, and took a long breath, just in time to save myself from fainting.

"When?" I gasped.

"First thing in the morning. I'll tell you what to do when I bring your supper."

"But Dr Straker is coming to see me in the morning—"

"Not till after breakfast. You'll 'ave two hours' start of 'im."

"But he will wire to London; the police will be waiting for me."

"I can't 'elp that, can I? An' I'm not spending the night locked in 'ere."

"Then . . . if you want your two hundred pounds, you will have to find me another cloak to put over mine; otherwise I will certainly be caught. Anything—it does not matter how old."

"Then I'd be 'ad for stealin' a cloak as well. Now do you want to chance it, or not?"

"Yes," I said, "I will chance it."

At dawn the next morning, I was sitting on the side of the bed, shivering in my cloak and bonnet. During the worst and longest night of my life, I had vomited up everything I had eaten the day before, and I could see nothing ahead of me but an eternity of such nights. When the lock rasped and snapped, I did not even believe it would be Hodges until the door opened.

"You look like death warmed up," she remarked, setting down the tray, "and not much of the warmth about it, neither."

"No," I said, "but if I should manage to escape, how shall I let you know?"

"Write to Margaret Hodges at the Railway Arms in Liskeard, to be left till called for. They'll see I get it."

"Thank you. Now tell me again what to do."

"Left out the door, turn right halfway along. Unlock that door— the big key in the middle there—and leave the keys in it; you won't need them after that. Go to the end of the passage, turn right, and keep going till you come to a landing. Go down four flights and you're on the ground floor. There'll be a long corridor on your left, a shorter one straight ahead. Go straight ahead—it's the voluntary patients, so walk like you belong—and the door's at the end on your right. It won't be locked; the time's gone seven. Turn right, follow the gravel path, and keep going in the same direction till you come to the gate. Anyone stops you—well, you'll 'ave to think for yourself. Through the gate and Liskeard's four mile to your right, but you might get a lift with a carter if you're lucky."

We had been through this the evening before, but it seemed impossible; I would never remember. I arranged my bonnet to hide as much of my face as possible.

"Thank you," I said again.

"Good luck, then. Least I got me tea."

She sat down on the bed, which creaked dangerously, took the lid off the teapot, and began to stir the leaves. When I glanced back as I drew the door shut, she did not even look up. I took out the keys and set off down the empty corridor with my footsteps echoing around me.

The next door opened inward, revealing another dark, panelled corridor, with a dim oblong of light at the far end. Hodges had said to leave the keys here, but if someone tried the door and found it unlocked, the pursuit would begin at once. I locked the door behind me, flinching at the noise, and set off with the keys still clutched in my hand, hidden beneath my cloak.

Now my footsteps sounded as loud as gunshots, no matter how carefully I walked. There were doors on both sides of me; I dared not look at them but fixed my eyes on the floorboards ahead of me. I had got perhaps two-thirds of the way along when a female figure appeared, silhouetted against the light, and began to walk briskly toward me. I kept walking, trying to keep my pace steady and my gaze low while holding myself as upright as I could.

"Morning?" said a puzzled, questioning voice as we passed each other.

"Good morning," I murmured without raising my head.

Her footsteps slowed and stopped. I fought the impulse to run as the end of the passage approached. Five paces to go — was it left, or right? Left, left — no, right. Still no sound from behind me. I turned right, into a wider corridor, and saw another woman, in a white uniform, approaching, and beyond her, a staircase. Again I strove to keep my pace steady and my gaze low, like someone lost in thought.

There was no greeting this time, but again the footsteps faltered and stopped behind me. My heart was pounding so violently that I could not tell whether they resumed or not. I reached the head of the stairs — the treads, to my relief, were carpeted — and began to descend, sliding one hand down the banister for support with the keys still clasped in the other.

I glanced over my shoulder when I reached the half-landing. No one was following, but as I came to the floor below, I heard several sets of footsteps approaching from my right. I quickened my pace and went on down.

One more half-landing, and I could see a passage, flagged in stone this time, leading straight ahead. I stumbled down the last flight, hearing voices descending from above. There was the longer passage Hodges had mentioned, leading away to my left. And a man, a tall man in dark clothes, a dozen paces ahead of me, pausing with his hand on a doorknob, and staring in my direction.

If I took the passage on my left and waited a moment, he might go on into the room; then I could double back. But then the people on the stairs would cut me off. There was no help for it: I kept walking toward the man, feigning oblivion.

It's the voluntary patients, so walk like you belong.

Ten paces, five, and still he did not move; I had come within three feet of him when he faced me directly and spoke.

"May I be of assistance?" A sombre, questioning voice, challenging my presence and compelling me to glance up at him. He was older than I had thought at first glimpse, tall and stooped and gaunt, with a long, haggard face, sunken eyes, and scanty grey hair swept back from his forehead. There was something vaguely familiar about him.

"Thank you, no," I murmured, and slipped past him without breaking my stride. I heard something, a cough or an exclamation, I could not tell, and felt his gaze fixed on the back of my neck. But now the end of the passage was in sight. I could see the door, and the glow of stained glass in the fanlight above it. My legs were shaking; the flagstones swayed beneath my feet; distant voices echoed behind me, but still no one cried, "Stop her!" The handle turned in my grasp, the heavy door swung inward, and a moment later I was through, breathing damp, icy air and squinting against the light of day.

A gravel path ran along the side of the house in both directions, bordering a lawn about twenty yards wide, and beyond that, coppices of trees, their autumn colours fading above mounds of dead leaves. Through the branches to my left I caught a glimpse of ivy-covered brickwork. I set off along the path to my right, almost running now, listening for the view halloo and the crunch of pursuing footsteps, but still it did not come. Grey stone gave way to new brick; still the door behind me was in clear view, and still no one emerged. I passed beneath the branches of a copper beech, around the corner and onto a broad gravel forecourt, and there, fifty yards ahead of me, was the gatehouse, with two massive oaken gates standing open, and a wagon drawn by a pair of horses rumbling toward me.

I slowed my pace a little, feeling the great bulk of the asylum at my back and the pressure of a hundred eyes peering down at me. Now, I thought, now someone is bound to catch me. I still had the keys clutched in my left hand, but there was nowhere to drop them. The driver of the wagon, a stout, rubicund man, tipped his hat to me as he passed; I waved timidly in reply.

Twenty yards; ten; still no one in sight. From the gatehouse on my right, I caught the smell of bacon frying, and I felt a mingled pang of hunger and nausea. The wall loomed above me; I passed beneath the arch and onto a rough, stoney road. There was no other dwelling in sight, only bleak, rolling moorland, rising until it vanished into the mist. A fine rain was falling, gathering in tiny beads on the fabric of my cloak.

Liskeard's four mile to your right. I did not see how I could possibly walk four miles. I was shaking with fear and fatigue, but I set off anyway, throwing the keys into a muddy pool. For hundreds of yards, it seemed, the road ran straight alongside the wall; every time I looked back, I could still see the gate. On the Isle of Wight, I could have covered four miles in an hour; at this plodding pace, assuming I did not collapse, it would take me nearer two. Hodges would be found long before I could reach Liskeard, and then Dr Straker would wire—but of course he could not wire from the asylum; he would send people on horseback, perhaps even dogs, to recapture me.

At last the road began to veer away from the wall, and then to slope downward, until the top of the wall had sunk below the skyline. How far had I come? Half a mile, surely. I was beginning to believe that I might actually escape, when I heard the sound of hooves and wheels coming up over the hill behind me. There was nowhere to hide; nothing but low, tussocky grass and boggy ground; a rabbit could scarcely have concealed itself.

I glanced back fearfully, just as a pair of horses, hitched to a wagon, appeared on the skyline and began to descend toward me. It was the wagon I had seen on the forecourt; I recognised the red-faced driver. Yet he seemed in no particular hurry, and as he drew closer, I could hear him whistling.

"Mornin' miss," he said cheerfully as he came up beside me. "Come from the asylum, haven't you? Not much of a day for walkin'." He had a pleasant country accent, not unlike Bella's. Curls of grey hair protruded from beneath a greasy billycock hat; his nose was even redder than the rest of his face.

"No," I replied, thinking frantically, "I was expecting to be met, but the gentleman has been delayed, and I must get to Liskeard station."

"Well, you're in luck, miss; I'm goin' that way myself. Jump up now; there's a step by your foot there."

He leant down, grasped my wrist, and lifted me onto the bench beside him. A flick of the reins and we were off, only at a walk, but at least double my previous pace. I was wondering how to account for myself when it struck me that there must be a constant flow of voluntary patients to and from the asylum; it might be best to stay close to the truth.

"Do you live in Liskeard?" I asked my rescuer.

"Bless you no, miss. George Baker is my name, and I live in Dobwalls, over that way," he said, gesturing to his right.

"And . . . do you have children?"

"Yes, miss, three boys—fine, strapping lads they are—and two girls, both in service now, and a credit to their mother." And with that he was safely launched, needing only occasional prompting. The air seemed even icier now that I was no longer walking. I huddled into my cloak and tried to subdue my shivering.

We had driven for perhaps twenty minutes when I heard the sound of galloping hooves coming up very fast behind us. George looked over his shoulder; I dared not lift my head but shrank lower on the seat. Seconds later, a big bay horse shot past us, with the rider, heavily cloaked and muffled, bent low over the horse's neck; he did not even glance in our direction.

"*He's* in a hurry," was all my companion said before returning to the story of young Bart and the escaped piglets while I weighed my own chances of escape. Was the horseman on his way to the telegraph office? Or to the police, to have me arrested at the station? Would I be better to try and secure a lift to some other town, and catch a train from there? Perhaps I could change my cloak if there was a ladies' outfitter in the town. But that would mean delay . . . and most likely the horseman had nothing to do with the asylum, or he would have stopped to make sure of me.

I was still wondering what to do when we crested a rise and a sizeable town came into view, less than a mile away.

"Not far now," said George. "Come up, there!" He flicked the reins, and the horses broke into a trot.

A few minutes later we were rattling through the streets of Liskeard, with George pointing out various landmarks while I watched covertly for policemen. There were none to be seen, but several people greeted George as we passed, and looked curiously at me. I felt sick with apprehension, but it was a strangely fatalistic kind of fear: I would escape, or I would not, and there was nothing more I could do about it.

When at last we drew up beside a small, whitewashed booking office, still with no policeman in sight, I remembered I had only the three golden guineas.

"Thank you so much for your kindness," I said. "I should like to give you something for your trouble, and if you will just wait until I have bought my ticket—"

"Bless you, miss; there's no need for that. It's a pleasure to have someone to talk to. You have a pleasant journey, now, and I'll be on my way."

I thanked him again and clambered stiffly down. My knees wobbled as I set foot on the pavement, which seemed to sway with the same motion as the wagon.

"Sure you're all right, miss?"

"Yes, thank you, just a little tired."

It struck me, as I waved goodbye to George and made my way unsteadily into the booking office, that he had not asked me a single question about myself.

The clock above the counter said twelve minutes to nine. There were two people ahead of me, and a moment later I felt someone at my back. It took all of my resolution not to glance over my shoulder. My hands were shaking so badly that I feared they would give me away. If the horseman *was* a coincidence, I told myself, and if the people I passed on my way had not raised the alarm—and surely I would never have passed the gate if they had—then it was quite possible that Hodges was still locked in the infirmary; she might not be found for another hour. I clasped my hands and breathed as deeply as I could.

The clock had moved on to eight minutes to nine before I came up to the counter.

"When is the next train to London?"

"Well, miss," said the elderly official, "there's the stopping train at six minutes past nine, or the express at eleven, but the express'll get you there sooner. Or you can change at Plymouth, and take the London express from there."

"When does the stopping train reach London?"

"At ten past five, miss."

I was about to buy a first-class ticket when I remembered asking Frederic about the first-class fare; if they searched the train, that was where they would look for me. Just as they would expect me to catch the express.

"I should like a second-class ticket for the stopping train to London."

"Thank you, miss. One pound three and six, if you please."

He directed me to the second-class ladies' waiting room, where I meant to stay until the last possible moment. The platform was in a deep cutting, reached by a ramp that passed directly beneath the cloakroom window. There were no policemen visible, and no one I recognised from the asylum, but if they *were* waiting for me, they would be standing out of sight, in the shadow of the embankment. A wave of dizziness rolled over me. I felt my knees giving way, and grasped the sill for support, just as a whistle shrilled in the distance.

"Are you all right, my dear?" said a kindly voice.

A stout, grey-haired woman was peering anxiously at me.

"I am feeling faint, but I must catch my train; I think I hear it now."

"Come along with me, then."

Drawing my arm through hers, she picked up a large basket and led me down the ramp and onto the platform just as the train pulled in. Through the sheltering clouds of steam, we must have looked like mother and daughter; I could not, I thought hazily, have hoped for a better disguise.

Three minutes later I was seated beside her on a hard wooden bench, watching the platform slide away behind us.

· · ·

Seen through the grimy windows of a cab, London by night looked truly infernal. Gaslight flared over wet cobbles; blackened figures moved amidst the glow and smoke of braziers, sending grotesque shadows capering across the walls behind them. I had passed beyond exhaustion into a strange, febrile, hallucinatory state in which the prospect of food, bath, and bed receded endlessly before me. I had never been so cold for so long, not even on the night of the land-slide, and yet every few minutes I would sink into a waking dream in which I was simultaneously basking in the warmth of a blazing fire, and jolting through the streets of Marylebone, until the lolling of my head jerked me awake again. I did not know where exactly in Marylebone I was, but in a few more minutes I would be home and safe.

Mrs Tetworth, the second of my rescuers, had kept me company as far as Plymouth, and even fed me with pastries from her basket. After that, it had been an endless procession of stations and fitful dreams, and the grinding discomfort of the uncushioned seat. My fear of cap-ture had diminished as the hours crawled by; I had thought of get-ting out at Acton and taking a cab from there, but instead I had man-aged to attach myself to a middle-aged couple, who saw me through the barrier at Paddington — again without a policeman in sight — and into a hansom.

And now we were turning in to Tottenham Court Road, where the press of vehicles grew even heavier, and the gaslight fell upon crowds of pedestrians hurrying through the thin rain — to me an utterly in-congruous spectacle, for it felt like three o'clock in the morning — and then in to Great Russell Street, past the looming bulk of the Brit-ish Museum, and at last in to Duke Street, halting by the black mouth of Gresham's Yard.

I clambered down stiffly, paid the cabman, and waited for a mo-ment in the shadows opposite. Lights were burning behind the cur-tains on the first and second floors of my uncle's house; the time, I thought, must be approaching seven o'clock, his dinner hour. Today was Monday — no, Tuesday — so it would be curried mutton, the dish I liked least of Mrs Eddowes' seven, but my mouth watered at the thought of it. Two men in greatcoats went by, glancing curiously at me; I could not remain here long. A woman, muffled against the cold, came briskly up the other side of the street and turned into Gresham's Yard, and I followed her upon instinct.

The yard was lit by a single gas lamp on the wall opposite the entrance. The woman disappeared into a narrow passage beneath the lamp: a blind alley, leading to a house whose occupants I did not know. There were lighted windows all around, but I could see no one else in the yard. Ten feet away to my left, the area below the entrance to my uncle's house was in deep shadow.

I stumbled the last few paces, climbed the steps, and hammered on the door. As I waited, I thought something stirred in the darkness of the area below. But then came the welcome sound of hurrying footsteps and the familiar rattle of the bolt. The door swung back. Light dazzled my eyes; my mouth was already opening in greeting when I saw that the person standing there was not my uncle, or Cora, or any other maidservant.

She was myself.

For one stupefied moment, I thought that someone must have left a dressmaker's mirror in the hall. But this was not the haggard and travel-stained reflection I ought to have seen. This was myself as I had been before those missing weeks, before the asylum, with my hair pinned up as I had pinned it a thousand times in my own mirror, wearing my favourite pale blue gown. Glittering upon her breast I saw, as a hand fell upon my shoulder and a sound like rushing water filled my ears, my dragonfly brooch, its ruby eyes glowing like tiny drops of blood.

I woke in the infirmary at Tregannon Asylum, after an interminable nightmare in which I was either freezing cold or unbearably hot, only to realise that the nightmare was, in truth, beginning again, even to the appearance of Dr Straker in the same rumpled tweeds and dark blue tie.

"Good afternoon, Miss Ashton. I am glad to see you looking a little better; we have been quite worried about you."

I did not attempt to reply.

"You do remember, do you not, your escape—very resourceful it was, too—and your visit to Miss Ferrars?"

I nodded slightly; there seemed no point in denying it.

"I am glad to hear it. I knew, as soon as I found Hodges locked in here, that you must have bribed her. I gave her the choice of confessing at once, or risking a long prison sentence: she gave up the brooch, and I dismissed her on the spot. Of course, you were well on your way by then, but we came up by the express—I had only to imagine what I would have done in your place to anticipate your every movement— which gave me just enough time to return Miss Ferrars' brooch and persuade her to cooperate. She is still, I am afraid, very angry about the theft of her writing case, but she agreed to open the door to you when I told her it might be essential to your recovery."

He paused, studying my face.

"Do you remember anything more, of those weeks before you arrived here?"

I shook my head faintly.

"And before that? Are your memories—as they appear to you— any different? Any less distinct? No? I feared as much. But at least you have seen with your own eyes, Miss Ashton, that you are not, and cannot be, Georgina Ferrars. Our task now is to persuade your mind to accept that. Sooner or later, the past you think you recall will begin to fade, and then to disintegrate, and your actual memories will return. By then I hope to have retraced the steps that led you to Gresham's Yard in the first place. Once we know where you came from, we will be able to reunite you with the past—and the people—you have lost. So do not despair, Miss Ashton; we shall not fail you."

He motioned me to be silent, and left without a backward glance.

The fever returned that night, and for days, perhaps weeks—I lost all track of time—I burned, or shivered, or lay in a drugged stupor, through which an endless procession of faces came and went. Some no doubt were real; others, like Aunt Vida's—or Hodges'—could only be hallucinations, but all seemed equally phantasmal. I would wake from dreams so terrible that it was a relief to find myself back in the infirmary, until I remembered why I was there, and then the waking nightmare would begin again. And yet a small part of my mind— my last and only refuge—went on insisting that it was *all* a dream: that if I could only endure for long enough, I was bound to wake in my bed at Gresham's Yard, and find that no such place as Tregannon Asylum had ever existed.

I clung to this thread until the day that Dr Straker pronounced me well enough to be moved to the women's ward. Two sturdy female attendants half led, half carried me along a series of gloomy, windowless passages, panelled with worm-eaten oak and smelling of damp fabric, ancient timber, and stale tobacco smoke. All was quiet, except for the steady tramp of the attendant's feet.

We stopped at last in front of a massive wooden door, which they proceeded to unlock, and passed through onto a bare wooden landing, with another female attendant seated at the entrance to a long, empty corridor. On my right was a staircase, with a narrow window running the full height of the wall; the sky beyond was already darkening. A tall, emaciated woman, dressed in mourning, was slowly ascending the stairs. I thought at first glimpse that she must be very old, but as she dragged herself a step higher, I saw that she was still quite youthful. As the lock snapped home behind me, I realised that she was one of the inmates.

We continued on past a series of closed doors, each with the inmate's name, made up of gold-painted letters on dark wooden squares, arranged in a slot above the observation panel: MISS PARTRIDGE, MRS WARE, MISS LEWES, MRS HAWKSLEY, MISS TRAHERNE, and last of all, MISS ASHTON. When I saw those words, the last of my courage failed me, and if the attendants had not taken me by the arms, I should have fallen to my knees. They propelled me, not unkindly, through the door and into a room very like the one I had occupied in the infirmary. I sank down upon the bed, dimly aware that my belongings—or rather Lucy Ashton's belongings—had arrived before me.

An indefinite time later, I felt a hand upon my shoulder. A large, grey-haired woman in a dark blue dress loomed over me. Her face, the colour and texture of risen dough, was jowled like a man's. Eyes of the same steely shade as her hair regarded me sternly.

"Now then, Miss Ashton, you must pull yourself together. Dinner is at six thirty, and you will want to make yourself presentable."

She spoke like a grand lady admonishing a recalcitrant child. I sat up, dabbing at my swollen eyes, and stared at her in disbelief.

"I am Mrs Pearce, matron of Women's Ward B. We must begin as we mean to go on."

"Then . . . I am not to be confined to this room?"

"Certainly not, Miss Ashton. As I am sure Dr Straker has explained to you, Tregannon House is run on the system of moral therapy: you will find no manacles on my ward. Here, Miss Ashton, you will be given every encouragement to participate in your own cure. In your case, you are suffering from a delusion regarding your identity. But you will learn, with our assistance, to overcome it. So long as you obey the doctors, keep yourself occupied, and join in the society of your fellow patients, your cure can only be a matter of time."

"And if I do not?" The words slipped out before I could stop them.

"Then your cure will take longer; that is all. There are some unfortunate souls in our care, who must be closely confined for their own safety, but I am sure you do not wish to be one of them. Especially not when Dr Straker has taken a personal interest in your case; so much so that you are here, he informs me, as our guest.

"And now I must leave you. When you hear the gong for dinner, make your way along the corridor and down the staircase: the attendant will direct you. In the meantime, I shall send someone to help you dress."

I wanted to shout, I have been robbed of everything, even my name, but I saw in that calm, implacable face the utter futility of protest.

On Women's Ward B, there was no shrieking, no rattling of chains, no caged lunatics gnashing their teeth and rolling in their own filth, and no brutality: none, at least, that I saw. The attendants were mostly kind, and at worst indifferent; Hodges, or so I came to believe, must have been summoned from some darker realm. Yet it was, in every sense, a place of torment. I could not pass along our corridor without hearing the sound of muffled weeping from behind at least one door, and sometimes a dull, regular thud, thud, thud, as of a woman banging her head endlessly against a wall.

My window, again secured by vertical metal bars, overlooked a flagged courtyard, flanked on two sides by outbuildings. I could watch carts and carriages come and go, until the spectacle became too painful. Besides a metal bedstead, it was furnished with a soft chair, a small desk, an upright chair, a washstand, chest and closet. Heating was by way of a device I had never seen before, made of coiled metal tubing and fed with hot water from a boiler somewhere in the depths of the building. It took away the worst of the chill, but I was always cold. At night the gurgling of the water accompanied my anguished thoughts. We were not allowed matches, or any sort of naked flame: the light, as in the infirmary, came from oil lamps enclosed in stout metal grilles. You could extinguish your light by turning a little brass wheel, but only an attendant could light it again. All lights were extinguished at ten, and were not lit again until seven thirty the next morning.

Dr Straker came to see me once or twice a week, always to ask if I had remembered anything more, and to assure me that it could only be a matter of time before he discovered my true identity. Whether I wept or raged or pleaded, or remained sullenly mute, his manner was always calm, courteous, unruffled; even the seemingly careless fashion in which he knotted his tie scarcely varied. I knew dimly that my only hope of escape would lie in accepting whatever character he chose to confer upon me—but what would I be escaping *to*?

The idea that I had seen Georgina Ferrars at Gresham's Yard was at once inescapable—Dr Straker had met and talked to her—and utterly beyond my comprehension. No matter how I racked my brains, there seemed to be only two possibilities. Either I was mad, as Dr Straker believed, or the woman in London, whoever she might be, had stolen my name, my uncle, my brooch—and presumably, by now, the two hundred pounds my mother had left me. Perhaps she intended to push Uncle Josiah down the stairs, and flee with the proceeds as soon as his will was proven. It seemed an extraordinary risk to run for the sake of a few hundred pounds, but as an act of vengeance, for some crime I had never heard of, it might have been diabolically appropriate.

And according to Dr Straker, she had been at Gresham's Yard for three of those missing weeks. Was *that* why I could not remember anything? Again and again I tried to pick up the thread, to move forward, step by step, from those last monotonous days in my uncle's shop, but it was like stepping into a fog-bank, expecting every time to meet my double, only for the fog to lift an instant later in the infirmary at Tregannon Asylum.

If Dr Straker was right, it could only be a matter of time before my mind — or what I believed to be my mind — began to disintegrate. Imagining that, I would be seized by a trembling that I could not control, sometimes for hours on end. I had read, often enough, of the tortures of the damned, and had tried to imagine them continuing forever, just as I had tried and failed to imagine the joys of heaven. In the darkness of those interminable nights, it was all too easy to believe that I had died without knowing it; died, and been condemned to a hell in which even my present torment would seem like a paradise compared to what awaited me. Yet much of the day was occupied by the routine of the asylum, which I absorbed, little by little, through a fog of misery and dread.

Between seven thirty and six, the door to the landing stood open, and we could descend to the ground floor, on which were a library, a women's sitting room, a men's sitting room, a dining room and a chapel. The men's ward must have been a mirror image of ours; the men descended by a corresponding staircase at the other end of the wing. Patients were not allowed in one another's rooms; if you wished to converse with anyone, you had to do so downstairs. Just beyond the foot of the women's staircase was an outer door leading to an enclosed garden, the one I had seen from the infirmary window, where we were exhorted to walk whenever the weather allowed.

As the days grew even shorter and colder, many of the inmates preferred to remain indoors, and had to be chivvied by the attendants into taking a turn in the garden — if so desolate a place deserved the name — whereas I found some relief in movement, and would put on my cloak and tramp round and round for an hour or more unless it was pouring with rain. Sometimes I would look up at the row of barred windows on the second floor; mine, I thought, had been the third from the right, and four windows farther along — though I tried not to think of it — was the sitting room where I had foolishly put my trust in Frederic Mordaunt. The ground-floor windows were barred as well, but those on the first floor were not, and I would often see faces looking down from them; I wondered if this was where the doctors, or the attendants, had their quarters.

The brick walls that made up the other three sides looked even higher from below. Though they were kept clear of ivy, the mortar had crumbled a little, and it seemed to me that a strong and athletic person, not encumbered by skirts or petticoats, might be able to scramble up where the walls met at a right angle. But the alarm would be raised long before they could reach the top; and even if they got over, they would be instantly pursued. There was a massive wooden door at the far corner of the outer wall, but it was so overgrown that it had obviously not been opened for years. Apart from a scattering of white flowers, the only plants that seemed to be thriving were all of the darkest and most dismal shades of green.

Idleness was strongly discouraged. Those who were agitated were exhorted to knit or embroider: there was basket-weaving or raffia work for those who could not be trusted with a needle. When I could not walk in the garden, I read, or pretended to read, so as to avoid being pressed to play cards or backgammon. In summer, or so I was told, patients who had made good progress were allowed, under strict supervision, to walk around other parts of the estate. All of this, according to Mrs Pearce, was part of the system of moral therapy. To me it resembled a form of religious persuasion in which, though all the talk was of salvation, the prospect of hell was far more immediate, in realms far more confined, housing dozens or hundreds more inmates whom I never saw.

We were required, too, to take all our meals in the dining room downstairs unless the doctors considered us too ill to attend. Male and female patients dined together. There were several tables of various sizes; Mrs Pearce and at least one of the doctors (who all seemed to be bachelors, living on the premises) would preside at luncheon or dinner. At one of the tables, the faces changed from day to day; later I learnt that these were patients from the more restricted wards, brought in to show them the freedom to which they might aspire if they progressed. Conversation was encouraged, but meals were sombre affairs at best. If it had not been for the company, you might have imagined yourself in some genteel boarding-house.

Dr Straker assigned me to a place at the middle table, between a Mr Wingrave, who talked continuously, and a Miss Traherne, who never spoke. Miss Traherne, a tall, emaciated woman with a corpse-white face and lank, mousey hair, would sit, radiating misery, staring at the uneaten contents of her plate until one of the attendants reminded her to take a mouthful. Even the seating formed part of the system of moral therapy: Mr Wingrave was an example of a man possessed by a delusion he refused to relinquish, and therefore condemned to live out his days at Tregannon Asylum; Miss Traherne was a terrible warning of the fate awaiting those who succumbed to despair.

In Mr Wingrave, I thought at first that I had found an ally, for he looked and sounded entirely sane, and seemed to know exactly what was wrong with our fellow diners. But then he confided to me that society was controlled by a race of invisible beings called the Overseers; he knew this because he alone could hear their voices. He appeared to be resigned to his fate; the Overseers, he said, had compelled Dr Straker to certify him, so as to ensure that no one outside Tregannon Asylum would ever discover their existence. You could tell when an Overseer had taken command of someone's mind because of the look in their eyes, a distinctive glassy stare that he had learnt to recognise. After everything that had befallen me, it sounded all too plausible, except that Dr Straker was surely the god of our underworld; the attendants, his familiar spirits.

Others at the middle table included a Miss Partridge, small, elderly, very gracious in manner, and possessed by the unshakable conviction that she was the Queen's younger sister. She had been confined by her own children, to spare them embarrassment, I could only suppose, since she seemed entirely harmless. There was Mrs Hawksley, wild-eyed, very tense and jerky in her movements, glaring at anyone who approached her. There was Miss Smythe, a small birdlike lady in middle age, who shook her head unceasingly, even when she was eating; sometimes slowly, sometimes in a seeming frenzy of denial. There was the Reverend Mr Carfax, distinguished-looking, immaculately turned out, who would arrange his cutlery with mathematical precision and then sit brushing invisible specks of dust from the sleeve of his coat; and Mr Stanton, gaunt, grey-headed, with haunted eyes and a permanent expression of dread. There was Miss Lewes, a stout woman in the grip of religious mania, listening to inaudible voices and arguing sotto voce with them; and others whose names I never learnt, like the immensely tall and thin man who moved like some strange wading bird, pausing before each step with his foot poised above the ground, his face set in a look of utter desolation.

Some weeks after my arrival in the women's ward, I was standing by the library window, which, like that of my room above, looked out upon the stable yard. It had rained earlier that morning, and water was still dripping from the eaves of the stable building opposite. A wagon drawn by a pair of horses rumbled into view, and I saw that the driver was George Baker. He pulled up on the gravel nearby, and was warmly greeted by two stable hands who came out to help him unload. If only, I thought, I had gone anywhere but Gresham's Yard that night; I could have got out at Plymouth and begged shelter from the woman who had helped me at the station. Tears sprang to my eyes; I bit my lip and pressed my face against the bars to prevent anyone from noticing.

"Miss Ashton." Frederic Mordaunt's voice, low and hesitant, spoke almost at my ear. I had time to register, as I turned to face him, that he looked flushed, and ill, and wretchedly unhappy.

Then I heard myself say, with cold, bitter contempt, "You broke your word. You betrayed my trust. You should be ashamed to call yourself a gentleman."

Every vestige of colour drained from his face. I heard a gasp from somewhere in the room. His lips parted, but my feet had carried me past him before he could utter a sound. Watching from the doorway, with his habitual air of ironic detachment, was Dr Straker. A moment later, he slipped away, and by the time I emerged into the corridor, trembling from the reaction, he was nowhere to be seen.

As the winter closed in, I felt myself sinking further and further into a dull, listless apathy. At times I still raged against my confinement, but I could no longer sustain the pitch of emotion that had helped me to endure those first terrible weeks. I had often rejected sedatives; now I was taking every draught that was offered and dozing even during the few short hours of daylight. Christmas came and went in a ghastly pretence of celebration, and after that the weather was too cold and wet—or so I listlessly told myself—to walk in the garden. Separated from anyone who cared for me, from anyone who could even recognise me, I came to realise that my life, which had seemed so unshakably real, consisted *only* of memories, which, according to Dr Straker, did not even belong to me. There were times when I actually strove to remember something of Lucy Ashton's past, but nothing would come. Even more fearful than the prospect that I might wake up one morning as Lucy Ashton, a stranger in my own body, was the feeling that I was becoming no one at all: not even a stranger, but a ghost in a body that no longer belonged to anyone.

On a still, clear afternoon, late in March, I set foot in the garden for the first time in months, wrapped in my cloak and moving much more slowly than before. Within the shadow of the building, the air was chill and damp, but sunlight was falling upon a bench in the far corner, and after a couple of turns around the path I sat down to rest. The warmth of the sun on my face seemed to release something within me, and I began to weep, not hysterically, as I had so often, but quietly, naturally, the salt tears welling up and overflowing through my fingers, until I became aware of someone hovering nearby. I looked up and saw that it was Frederic Mordaunt, looking even thinner and more wretched than when I had seen him last, and regarding me with evident distress.

"Please allow me to speak," he said. "I do not seek — or deserve — your forgiveness, but I have something to say to you."

He stood before me like a prisoner awaiting sentence, twisting his hat in his hands.

"If you insist on speaking, sir, I cannot prevent you."

He flinched at "sir," but stood his ground.

"I ask only that you hear me out."

If he had called me Miss Ashton, I would have turned my back on him.

"Very well, sir; I will listen. You may as well sit down," I added, moving to one end of the bench and indicating the other. I did not want him standing over me.

"Thank you. When Dr Straker returned that Sunday night, after we . . . well, when he told me that he had met Georgina Ferrars in London, I did not at first believe him. But when I learnt that the maidservant, as well as Josiah Ferrars, had been present, and still more when I heard the story of Lucia Ardent, and how she had left Gresham's Yard two days before you arrived here, I had no choice *but* to believe him. And yet my heart rebelled; it simply did not square with—with everything I knew of you. I could not see how you could be—so deluded, and yet seem so entirely sane.

"He replied—I'm sure he has said this to you—that the reason you are so certain you are Georgina Ferrars is because the personality you have assumed is *all* that you experience, so that you are utterly sincere in your belief. But I was still deeply troubled; I even put it to him that the woman he had met in London was Lucia Ardent, and that she had somehow tricked you into coming here."

"And what did he say to that?"

"He looked at me pityingly and said that it was the first thing that had occurred to him. And that he had spoken privately to the maid, who had assured him that Miss Ferrars had been at Gresham's Yard throughout the time that—that you and I were conversing here. And—that I had allowed my emotions to get the better of my judgement."

He was speaking with his eyes fixed on the gravel at his feet, his hands clasped so tightly that the knuckles had turned white.

"I told him," he continued, "that I had assured *you*, on my word of honour, that you could leave whenever you chose, and that I was bound to see you the following morning, as I had promised.

"At that, he grew angry. He said I had allowed myself to succumb to a foolish infatuation for a woman who was dangerously ill, and imperilled your sanity by encouraging your delusion that you were Georgina Ferrars; and that your eventual recovery, perhaps even your life, depended upon my *not* seeing you.

"It ended with his ordering me to keep away from you. I felt I had to obey; your health was at stake, and—I doubted my own motives."

"And why are you telling me this now, after all these months?" I asked bitterly. "Has your conscience been troubling you?"

"I tried to speak to you before, in the library, but you did not want to . . . and Dr Straker rebuked me for distressing you; and after that I was ill, though that is of no consequence. The thing is—the reason I am here . . ."

I had not wanted to show him any emotion beyond contempt, but his hangdog air provoked me beyond endurance.

"And why should you imagine, sir, that your feelings are of the slightest interest to me? You deceived me; you betrayed me; it is because of your treachery that I am a prisoner here, and will probably die here; and you think I should care for your excuses? You say you are heir to this place; if you are not lying about that as well, it is your duty as a gentleman to order Dr Straker to release me at once, as you promised he would."

His reaction was not what I expected. He took a deep breath, lifted his head, and met my gaze for the first time.

"Believe me, Miss Ashton—you disown the name, but I must call you something—if I did not know, beyond a shadow of a doubt, that you are not Georgina Ferrars, you would have been released long before this. But I would rather see you here than in the county asylum, or in prison, and they are the only alternatives. If we released you now, you would go straight to Gresham's Yard—would you not?—and Miss Ferrars would have you arrested."

"And suppose your master is—" I wanted to say *lying*, but my nerve failed me. "Suppose he is mistaken, and *she* is the imposter?"

"I fear that is impossible. Dr Straker would never have certified you if he had the slightest shadow of a doubt: he would be risking his reputation, even his livelihood. And if I were to order him, as you put it, to lift the certificate, he would ignore me. He is the superintendent, and his word, in every sense, is law."

"If his word is law, sir," I said, clinging to my anger, "and he has forbidden you to speak to me, are you not afraid of another rebuke?"

"Well, no," he said uncomfortably, "he seems to have changed his mind. He said to me the other day that since you seem disinclined to trust him, it might help you to see that I agree that you cannot be Miss Ferrars. I said I would only attempt to speak to you if I could be the bearer of good tidings as well as . . . Well, at any rate, he agreed."

"Do you mean—to release me after all?"

"No, I'm afraid not—not yet, that is. But when Dr Straker discovers your true identity, it may turn out that you have no money of your own, and—I wanted to assure you that when you *are* released, you will be provided for."

"By whom?" I asked.

"Well . . . by me," he murmured, addressing the gravel at his feet.

"And why, sir, would you wish to provide for a lunatic who does not even know her own name?"

"Because I gave you my word, and because . . . I care about what becomes of you, regardless of your name," he added, in a voice so low that the words were barely audible.

Again I saw myself standing beside him at the sitting-room window above, looking down upon the bench where we now sat, and saying, "Yours is a loving spirit; it should not die with you." Was it possible that he was in love with me, a haggard and desperate madwoman, as he must see me—as perhaps I was? The thought was swept aside by another wave of indignation.

"Your word, sir, is worthless; I am here because you broke it, and I would sooner starve than accept a farthing of your money."

"I feared as much," he said, rising to his feet. "I meant what I said: I do not hope for your forgiveness. I will trouble you no more, but I will not see you starve, however much you despise me."

He made me a miserable sketch of a bow, and walked away without looking back.

I remained on the bench, shaking with emotion and realising, as my anger subsided, how foolishly I had behaved. Extraordinary as it seemed, he evidently felt something for me, and I ought to have kept my temper and played upon that feeling, instead of driving him away. I rose, shivering, and was walking toward the building when I became aware of a face peering down at me from the end window on the first floor: a large, flat, porcine face that contorted in alarm as our eyes met, and turned quickly away.

If it had not been for her reaction, I would have assumed it was simply a woman who looked remarkably like Hodges. But the flash of recognition had been unmistakable.

I remained staring up at the window until it struck me that there might be an advantage in pretending that I had *not* recognised her. I lowered my gaze, shook my head as if in disbelief, and set off at a slow, mechanical pace, keeping my eyes fixed on the path, continuing on up the stairs in the same abstracted fashion, and along the corridor to my room, where I closed the observation slide and sank down upon the bed, struggling to comprehend what I had seen.

If she really had taken a bribe, and helped a patient to escape, Hodges could not possibly have been reinstated. I remembered the attendants I had passed on my way out, all turning to look at me, but none of them raising the alarm; the asylum gate standing conveniently open, with the gatekeeper nowhere to be seen; George Baker appearing so fortuitously on the road; and Dr Straker waiting for me in Gresham's Yard.

They had *meant* me to escape, or rather, to believe I was escaping. I had been led, every step of the way. Everyone—Hodges, the attendants, George Baker, perhaps even the motherly woman with the basket in Liskeard station, and, unwittingly, I myself—had played the parts assigned to them. In a play designed to convince me that I had met the real Georgina Ferrars in Gresham's Yard. Just as Gadd, the monomaniac, had been brought face to face with the man he believed to be Gladstone.

I remembered Frederic saying that if they hadn't found an attendant to impersonate Gladstone, Dr Straker would have engaged an actor.

The woman in Gresham's Yard had been an actress. She could have spent hours studying me through the observation slot in the infirmary.

A faint sound from the passage had me glancing fearfully at the slide. Had it moved a fraction? I dared not go close enough to check. Instead, I walked over to the window, where at least no one could see my face, and stood looking down into the darkening yard where the stable hands had greeted George Baker with such familiarity.

Had George Baker brought me here in the first place? I had woken from the seizure on a Thursday, so I must have arrived on a Wednesday . . .

But that was no more likely to be true than the story of Lucia Ardent.

I had been told so often, and by so many people, that I had arrived here as Lucy Ashton, voluntary patient from Plymouth, that I had come to picture it scene by scene: being admitted by Frederic; wandering restlessly about the grounds in the afternoon; being found, unconscious, early the following morning.

Dr Straker had said that Lucy Ashton was "a disturbing choice of alias for a troubled young woman presenting herself for treatment at a private asylum." Perhaps it was meant to be disturbing; perhaps he had chosen it himself.

Just as he had chosen to tell me that I had suffered a seizure. I might have been lying in a drugged stupor for weeks, not days, before I woke in the infirmary.

The more I thought about it, the more certain I felt that it was all Dr Straker's invention.

In which case Frederic had deceived me—about *everything*. That shy, earnest, sensitive demeanor; those heartfelt tears; perhaps it had all been an act. Perhaps he already had a wife, or a mistress, or both. He had even told me the story of Isaiah Gadd, confident that I was far too naïve to see the application to myself. Remembering how easily he had won my heart, I blushed with shame and mortification.

And if Bella, who had seemed so childlike and innocent—if she, too, had been deceiving me on Dr Straker's orders, then I could trust nothing beyond the evidence of my own eyes. And perhaps not even that.

I found that I was gripping the windowsill as tightly as I had clutched at the gorse on the cliff-face, staring into the abyss.

Everything they had done had been aimed at driving me out of my mind, in the most literal sense, by confronting me with irrefutable proof that I was not myself.

But *why?* Dr Straker, at least, was risking disgrace and imprisonment. Supposing I had gone to Liskeard police station, instead of straight to Gresham's Yard, and the police had believed me? Supposing my uncle had appeared at the wrong moment? Dr Straker knew that I had very little money, and no expectations. Why choose a perfectly sane young woman when he had a whole asylum full of lunatics at his disposal? There was nothing at all unusual or interesting about me.

Only that, except for a half-blind uncle, no one would care, or even know, if I vanished from the world.

I remembered Frederic saying—again, supremely confident that I would miss the implication—that one of Dr Straker's interests was grafting fruit trees.

They had chosen me for an experiment.

Which was why I had received no treatment. Dr Straker was waiting patiently for my mind to disintegrate, while he combed the records of missing persons for another young, friendless woman who had vanished from the world—a woman whose lost soul he intended to resurrect in my body.

And after that? He could not afford to release me—assuming he intended to let me go at all—until he was absolutely certain that every last trace of Georgina Ferrars had been expunged from my consciousness. For a man of his powers, it would be easy to arrange apparent proof that the real Georgina Ferrars was already dead: a mangled corpse fished out of the Thames, dressed in my clothes and wearing my brooch.

The experiment might end with my being hanged for murdering myself.

Each morning after breakfast, Mrs Pearce would read out the names of patients whom the doctors wished to see, and tell them to return to their rooms and wait. I had not seen Dr Straker for several days, but when my name was called the following morning, I felt as if the blood had drained from my body. It was all I could do to climb the stairs without fainting.

The wait, I knew, might be anything from five minutes to an hour or more. Telling myself that I must not show fear only made my trembling worse; I knew, too, that I would not be able to look at him without horror and loathing. Even if Hodges had not confessed, he would sense that something was wrong; and then he would press and press until he found out.

I could pretend to be ill, but when he found that I had no fever, he would know that I was pretending, and that would make me fear him even more. No; I would have to admit that I was afraid—as I had been, often enough, before—but somehow conceal that I was now mortally afraid of *him*. I sat down on the upright chair, with my back to the window, trying to decide what I should say.

When I heard his footsteps approaching, I buried my face in my hands and began to sob, which was easy enough to do in earnest, and when the door opened, I did not even look up.

"Good morning, Miss Ashton. I am sorry to see you distressed."

I drew a long, sobbing breath and slowly raised my head. His tone, as ever, was calm and courteous, but the gleam in his eyes, which I had once taken for amusement, now seemed as cold as ice.

"It should not surprise you, sir," I said. "I am a prisoner here; I will die here; there is no hope for me."

"Come now, Miss Ashton; any day now, we are bound to discover your identity."

"You have been saying that for months, sir—an eternity of torment—and nothing has changed."

"Believe me, Miss Ashton; I understand how hard it must be. Allow me to take your pulse."

I could not repress a shudder as his fingers touched my wrist.

"I beg your pardon; it is a cold morning, and my hand is doubtless cold as well."

His solicitude was like that of a slaughterman, scratching a lamb's head affectionately as he prepares to cut its throat. He was going to tear my soul out of my body, but in as humane and enlightened a fashion as the demands of his experiment allowed, sincerely regretting any distress I might suffer in the process. I wished I could stop my hand from trembling.

"Hmm . . . a little fast, but then you are agitated this morning. Tell me, is there any reason—any specific reason, I mean—for your agitation? Have you remembered anything of those weeks before you arrived here?"

"No, sir, I have not." The fear in my voice was all too genuine.

"A pity. I had a note from Miss Ferrars only the other day, asking whether we had found her writing case. She is still threatening to press charges against you. Of course, you are perfectly safe so long as you are with us, but if you could only remember where you hid it, that would be one less obstacle in the way of your release."

"I do not understand you, sir," I said dully, dabbing at my eyes to conceal my face.

"Well, Miss Ashton, it would be unfortunate if we discharged you as cured, only to see you arrested at the gate."

"How can I ever be discharged, sir, when I have no home, no money, and no name?"

"But you *will* have a name . . . Are you saying that you no longer believe you are Georgina Ferrars?"

My sob of terror was quite involuntary; I clutched my handkerchief and prayed he would take it for distress.

"I do not know what I believe, sir. My reason says I cannot be, but my memory says . . . that if I am not Georgina Ferrars, I am no one."

"Interesting," he said. "And encouraging, though I know you cannot see it. Try to have faith, Miss Ashton; it will not be long now."

The words echoed like a warning bell as the door closed behind him.

It rained all of that day, but the following afternoon I was back in the garden, walking slowly around the perimeter until weariness overtook me, and I sat down on the bench to rest in the pale sunlight.

What had Dr Straker said about my writing case? "If you could remember where you hid it . . ." It was surely not in his interest that I should recall anything of that time; yet he kept on pressing me to remember what I had done with it. What if it was *not* in his possession? Might there be something in it that he wanted—or feared?

Of course: the journal I had presumably kept throughout those missing weeks. I had told Frederic all about Aunt Vida's gift, and how she had encouraged me to keep a record of every day's events, no matter how trivial.

If I had brought my brooch here—assuming I had not been kidnapped—I would have brought my writing case as well.

But the key had not been round my neck when I woke in the infirmary.

A dark figure emerged from the shadows at the far end of the garden and began to walk toward me. I saw with a jolt of alarm that it was Frederic Mordaunt, looking as woebegone as ever. Which was all the more reason to fear him, especially as Dr Straker was doubtless watching from one of the windows above.

"Miss Ashton, I know I promised not to trouble you again, but I have come to tell you that I have persuaded Dr Straker to move you back to the voluntary wing."

I stared at him for several seconds, mute with astonishment. It could only be a trap, but what sort of a trap?

"You had better sit down," I said, indicating the place on my right, so that I would be facing away from the windows.

"Thank you. I'm afraid there are conditions. He refuses to lift the certificate; and you must take all your meals in the closed ward, as at present. But you will have your old room back—the room you were in before the seizure, I mean—and be free, during the day, to walk anywhere in the grounds, so long as you do not try to escape again, which I beg you not to attempt, for your own sake. You will be closely watched; he insists upon it; and if you so much as pass the gate, he will wash his hands of you, and have you transferred to the county asylum as incurably insane."

I had no need to feign bewilderment. Why would they move me to a room I had probably never occupied, and give me the freedom of the grounds? Did they *want* me to try to escape again?

"Why has Dr Straker agreed to this?" I said at last.

"Because I insisted upon it. I took to heart what you said to me—about my being the heir, and my duty as a gentleman. I have never crossed him before—I have never had occasion to—but after I saw you the other day . . . Well, I reminded him of his own guiding principle, which is never to cause a patient unnecessary pain. I put it to him that after several months' confinement, we had inflicted nothing but torment upon you, and were no closer to solving the mystery of your identity. And that the best chance of restoring your memory was to enlist Miss Ferrars' cooperation by any means necessary, and bring you face to face—so that you could speak to each other, I mean. He said that she would never agree to this unless we could recover her writing case; I said that her best chance of recovering it was to meet you, in as tranquil a setting as we could provide, and that if that failed, I would compensate her for the loss.

"He replied that on the contrary, seeing Miss Ferrars again would cause you such agitation that you might well suffer another seizure—a fatal one this time. He is a physician; I am not: I could not argue with that. But I insisted we do *something* for you. It ended with his agreeing, most reluctantly, to move you back to the voluntary wing, on the conditions I have described. He says that if any harm comes to you because of this, it will be upon my head."

He spoke with what I would have sworn was heartfelt emotion.

"But why did he not mention this himself, when he saw me yesterday?"

"I did not speak to him until this morning, and then—he agreed that I might tell you."

"If you had kept your promise, sir, I would not be here now. But I thank you for what you have done. When may I expect to be moved?"

"As soon as you wish. In fact, if you are willing to accompany me, I can escort you there now."

I rose, a little unsteadily. He offered me his arm, and blushed when I did not take it. Could he really make himself blush on cue? Was he Dr Straker's accomplice or his dupe? In either case, I could not afford to trust him.

"If you will lead the way, sir, I will follow," I said.

He bowed with every appearance of mortification and set off toward the house. I could not help glancing up at the windows; there was a pale blur behind one of them which might have been a face.

He led me back to the entrance, and across the hall to a door through which I had seen Mrs Pearce come and go. An attendant unlocked it as he approached, and we passed along a dim, echoing corridor, emerging beside a staircase I recognised: this was where, during my escape, I had seen the tall, grey-haired man who had reminded me of someone—of Frederic, in fact. Edmund Mordaunt had been watching me.

"Miss Ashton?"

He was indicating the stairs; I wondered, as I followed him upward, whether I had misunderstood him, and they were moving me back to the infirmary. But from the first-floor landing he led me along another passage, very like that in the women's ward, except that there were no names on the doors, until we came to one with MISS ASHTON spelt out in the familiar gilt letters.

"I will leave you here," he said reluctantly, with a look—or so, again, I would have sworn—of hopeless yearning. "If you simply retrace your steps at mealtimes, the attendant will let you through."

He opened the door for me, bowed, and departed, and there was Bella, calmly putting away the last of my things.

"Very pleased to see you again, Miss Ashton, I'm sure. Will there be anything else?"

Her smooth, childish face now seemed a mask of deceit.

"No, thank you, Bella."

She bobbed her head and withdrew, leaving me to my new surroundings.

The room, papered in a blue floral print, which, though faded, was distinctly more cheerful, was furnished in much the same fashion as the one in the infirmary, with a small oak chest beside the wardrobe and a writing table by the window. The paved courtyard below was enclosed by the other three sides of the building, with row after row of windows overlooking mine; I was glad to see that there were curtains. Four metal bars were set into the stonework, but outside the glass, making it seem less like a prison cell. The door had no observation slot; there was even a flimsy bolt for privacy, but no key in the lock.

I had not removed my cloak, and since there was still plenty of daylight left, I decided to test my newly acquired freedom at once to see if I really would be allowed out into the grounds. Two fashionably dressed women—visitors? voluntary patients? spies?—were conversing at the foot of the staircase; they glanced at me curiously but did not speak. My heart beat faster as I approached the door, but no one leapt from the shadows to seize me, and a moment later I was standing on the gravel path.

To my left was dense woodland, extending westward to the boundary wall, which looked at least a hundred yards off. A pale sun was sinking toward the treetops. Ahead and to my right, men were working in a patchwork of fields. Cattle grazed beneath the wall, which ran in a great curve round to the north and east, in the direction of the entrance. But for the great bulk of the asylum at my back, I might have been standing in the fields near Brighstone Forest, where my aunt and I had sometimes walked.

I turned right, as I had done before, and followed the path toward the gate. Freedom seemed tantalizingly close; my heart was thumping and my mouth was very dry as I passed beneath the branches of the copper beech, now coming into bud, and onto the forecourt.

The gates were closed. Further proof, if any was needed, that my escape had been contrived. I should have realised that no lunatic asylum would ever leave its main entrance open and unguarded.

You will be closely watched. Imagining Dr Straker's cool, sardonic gaze fixed upon me from above, I fought down a wave of panic and kept on walking around to the right, across the entrance to the stable yard, and round behind the stable buildings, out of sight of the house.

On this side of the estate, the ground sloped up toward the outer wall, which looked even farther away. To the east were open fields and meadows; to the south, more woodland. I came around the back of the stables into a large kitchen garden, bounded on my right by a very high brick wall. An hour earlier, I had been sitting on the other side of it. Two kitchenmaids were pulling up carrots from a bed nearby; they glanced at me curiously, but without any sign of alarm.

I went on through the opening at the far end. Red brick gave way to the grey stone of the middle wing; ahead of me loomed a squat, rectangular tower, built of much older stone, so dark and pitted it was almost black. The windows on the upper levels were no more than vertical slots; the ones on the ground level had been bricked up altogether, along with the doorway.

As I came closer, I saw that the tower was part of a long, rambling building made of the same blackened stone, plainly the original house. It stood about twenty paces from the main building; the two were connected by a flagged path, roofed in stone like a cloister. No smoke rose from any of the chimneys; the flagstones were strewn with rotting leaves, and weeds had grown up through the surrounding gravel.

The walls of the two buildings, the grey and the black, seemed to lean toward each other, forming a lopsided chasm. If I walked to the far end, and turned right, I should be back where I started. High above me, the uppermost windows caught the rays of the sinking sun, but the ground where I stood was already in shadow. *You were found unconscious on the path* . . . Was this where I had suffered the seizure? What had I been doing here, in the middle of the night? And what had caused it? Something I had seen? Or heard?

My feet began to move of their own accord, faster and faster until I was running over the gravel, around the last corner to the door from which I had set out, along the hall—which seemed to have grown much darker in my absence—and up the stairs, pursued by my frantically echoing footsteps all the way to my room, where I closed and bolted the door behind me and leant against it, shaking from head to foot.

Whether Frederic was simply in thrall to his master, or in league with him, Dr Straker would never have agreed to move me unless it served his purpose. *Was* he tempting me to escape again? I could think of no other reason. If so, he would surely expect me to make for Gresham's Yard.

Where something even more terrifying might be waiting for me. Or, at the very least, my arrest as an escaped lunatic claiming to be Miss Ferrars.

Without money, I could go no farther than Liskeard. So if he meant to lure me back to Gresham's Yard, there ought to be another purse conveniently hidden somewhere in this room. And then, when the trap had been baited, I would find the gates open again.

So my one hope of escape was to find the money—if there was any to find—and flee, not to Gresham's Yard, but . . . to Mr Wetherell, the solicitor in Plymouth. I did not think—no, I felt sure—I had not mentioned him either to Frederic or Dr Straker. I had never met him myself, but that might be just as well; my signature, at least, would match.

The last rays of the sun were fading from the roof opposite, but there was still enough daylight left. Might they be watching me at this very moment? I glanced around the walls and ceiling, looking for spy-holes. Impossible to tell; I remembered my aunt showing me that you could see a whole coastline through a hole no bigger than the point of a pencil. If they *were* watching, they would be expecting—indeed hoping—that I would search the room.

The hatbox and valise were placed exactly as they had been in the infirmary. I went through them both very carefully, and felt all around the linings, without success. There was no money concealed amongst my clothes, or underneath the mattress, or in the oak chest: the bottom drawer opened an inch and stuck fast, but when I removed the other two I saw that it was empty, and there was nothing attached to the inside of the cabinet except dust and grimy remnants of cob-web. I examined every piece of furniture in the room, even removing the drawer from the writing desk to look into the cavity, without finding a single farthing.

Defeated, I knelt down beside the oak chest, intending to replace the drawers, but instead began to fiddle with the one that had stuck, rocking it diagonally back and forth until it began to emerge in tiny increments. I braced one hand against the cabinet for leverage. As I did so, I had a sudden vision of a serpent coiled in the darkness beneath, waiting to strike.

I shuddered violently, and the drawer shot out, colliding painfully with my shin. Something gleamed faintly in the dusty recess: not a serpent, but a gold clasp—the two gold clasps of my writing case. Kneeling closer, I saw that it was covered in a fine layer of dust, floating up around me as I lifted it out with unbelieving hands. The impression left in the dust was plainly visible.

Part Two

Part Two

Rosina Wentworth to Emily Ferrars

Portland Place,
Marylebone
10 August 1859

Dearest Emily,

You will scarcely believe what has happened. Clarissa has eloped!
With a young man called George Harrington, the one I told you
about. She was flirting quite shamelessly with him at the Beauchamps',
but I never dreamt that anything would come of it—I thought she
had resigned herself to marrying that horrid dried-up Mr Ingram—
but I must try to tell you everything in order.

On Monday, my father took the early train to Manchester. He was
to be away two days, and that same afternoon Clarissa left—as I believed—to spend a week with the Fletchers in Brighton. She took an
immense quantity of luggage, even for her, but I was looking forward
to having the house to myself, and thought no more of it until my father returned on Friday evening. I was playing the piano in the drawing room when I heard him berating one of the maids; as usual, he did
not even look in but went straight to his study.

A few moments later I heard him tramping along the hall; I assumed that he was going out again, but he burst into the room, seized
me by the arm, and lifted me right off my feet, waving a letter in my
face and shouting, "Where is your sister?" All I could reply was, "In

Brighton, with the Fletchers," which only enraged him more, until I understood that the letter was from Clarissa, telling him that she had run away. He ordered me up to my room to await his summons. By the time Lily brought me my supper, the news was all around the servants' hall, but she knew no more than I did.

When he called me into his study the next morning, he was his usual cold, implacable self. "Your sister's name is never to be spoken in this house again," he said. "Henceforth it will be as if she never existed. And be warned: I will not be embarrassed a second time." He told me that he had dismissed Miss Woodcroft—did you ever meet her?—without a reference. "I will have no more paid chaperones," he said. "I have written to your aunt; she will be coming to live here, and you will be in her charge until I find a suitable husband for you. In the meantime, you are not to leave the house: if I hear that you have disobeyed me, you will be confined to your room."

He did not even raise his voice, but I have never been so afraid of him. I had always assumed—perhaps I mean hoped—that beneath that cold exterior must be *some* feeling for me, but I saw in his eyes that there is none. I am a piece of property, a negotiable security, as he would say, and that is all. It is what poor Mama must have realised, and I am sure it is what she died of. She was a failure as an investment, because she gave him daughters when he wanted sons. And now that Clarissa has run away, he is all the more determined that I, at least, will yield a profit.

He went out soon afterward, and I retreated to the drawing room, too shaken even to open the piano. I still knew nothing of where Clarissa had gone, or why, but a little later I heard the doorbell, and Mrs Harkness came barging in, with Betsy trailing helplessly behind her. She took great pleasure in telling me that Clarissa had fled to Rome with George Harrington—"*quite* the rake, my dear, and *so* untrustworthy, and *fancy* you not knowing, *all* of London is agog"—until I could bear it no more, and showed her out myself. When I went upstairs, I found the entire contents of Clarissa's room—clothes, ornaments, bedding, curtains, furniture, even the carpets—heaped in a great jumble on the landing, and the footmen stripping the paper off the walls—"master's orders, miss"—because she had chosen it, I suppose. Everything was carried off in a cart, to be burnt, for all I know.

I hope that Godfrey is not overworking himself again. I should so love to see you, but I am forbidden all visitors until my aunt arrives. I shall write again as soon as I can.

All my love to you, and to dear Godfrey,

Your loving cousin,

Rosina

Portland Place

19 August 1859

Dearest Emily,

It is even worse than I thought: I am to be a prisoner, and I may not receive visitors or leave the house unless I am manacled, in all but name, to Aunt Harriet—of whom I shall write when I can. She will open all letters addressed to me, and I am not allowed to send anything she has not seen. I shall write you dutiful letters to ward off suspicion—do not believe a word of them, but tell me all your news.

It is Lily's afternoon off, and she is going to smuggle this to the post. I shall write in earnest when I can.

Your loving cousin,

Rosina

Portland Place

7 October 1859

Dearest Emily,

I have not dared to write candidly before this, for fear that Lily would be searched on her way to the post, and then I should be altogether cut off from you. But writing to you with Aunt Harriet peering—sometimes literally—over my shoulder has become intolerable.

All joy withers in her presence; not that there was ever much of it in this house, which seems more than ever like a mausoleum. You would not know to look at her that she is my father's sister, but they are alike in that regard at least. She is gaunt and boney, and wears her hair, which is the colour of cold ashes—indeed, she *smells* of cold ashes—drawn back so tightly that it makes her look even more like a death's head. And she dresses only in black: the dullest, drabbest, most funereal shade that money can buy. She has spent her life as companion to Grandmother Wentworth in Norfolk—a fate that would make

me feel sorry for anyone else—and reminds me frequently of the sac-
rifice her mother is making in "sparing" her.

I tried, at first, to placate her, but she would have none of it. I have
come to realise that she hates me, simply for being young, and—if
I could only escape her—capable of delight. I fear that I am growing to hate *her*, though the worst I have done thus far is to practise
Beethoven very loudly, knowing that she dislikes it, but she cannot
say so beyond complaining that it gives her a headache, because to ask
anything of me would mean that I might ask something in return.

You will not be surprised to hear that, apart from church, I have
not left the house for weeks. My aunt announced when she first arrived that she would accept invitations from those she considered re-
spectable. But wherever we went, she hovered at my side like a gaoler.
And, of course, everybody wanted to know about Clarissa, and no
matter how tactful the allusion, my aunt would fix the enquirer with a
basilisk stare and change the subject, usually to some question of religious doctrine, and so the conversation consisted mostly of silences.
I was pitied by those of our acquaintance who were truly fond of me,
and gloated over by those who were not, until it became easier—
though that is hardly the word—to refuse.

Apart from your letters, Lily is my only comfort. I divined from
the first that my aunt would disapprove of our intimacy, and so I am
always very stern with Lily—who acts the timid and downtrodden
maid to perfection—in her presence. I used to think Miss Woodcroft a martinet, but now I realise how much freedom she allowed
us: a freedom that was, I suppose, poor Clarissa's undoing. If she had
flatly refused to marry Mr Ingram, my father might have allowed
her to wait for another candidate. But she consented, thinking, I suppose—she would never confide in me—that, once married, she could
live her own life. And then as the day drew closer, she found that she
could not bear it, and there was George Harrington, who was at least
young and handsome, however much of a rake he may have been.

I have asked myself many times: if she and I had been close, would
she still have run away? So often I felt that I had offended her, without knowing why, and if I ventured to ask what I had done, she would
deny that anything was wrong, in the tone that says you have committed a further offence by asking. You once said that you thought she

envied me, but I cannot remember *why* you thought so. She was older, she was prettier, she was poor mama's favourite; she was the centre of attention whenever we had company—but I must not write of her in the past tense. I can only pray that she is safe and happy.

Lily is waiting, so I shall seal this now. If only you could write freely in reply, I would not feel so—but what a fool I am! It has only just occurred to me that you could write to me c/o the post office in Mortimer Street for Lily to collect—if you do not mind the deception, that is. I shall guard your letters with my life.

Your loving cousin,

Rosina

Portland Place

3 November 1859

Dearest Emily,

I have terrible news—as you may have guessed, if you saw *The Times* this morning—Clarissa is dead. It happened a week ago yesterday, when she and George Harrington were driving in the hills above Rome—their horse bolted, and they were flung over a precipice, and crushed beneath the wreck of the carriage. The article—it is only a brief paragraph—calls them Mr and Mrs Harrington, but there can be no doubt. My father sent for me after breakfast and said, without preliminary, "Your sister is dead, as she deserved. There will be no mourning, and no further mention of her. You may go." His look said, as clearly as if he had spoken, "Disobey me, and the same may happen to you."

I do not remember leaving his study, or climbing the stairs; the next thing I knew, I was back in my room, possessed by a dreadful suspicion that he had caused her death. It was only when Lily brought me the paper that the worst of my fears were allayed. Even then I wondered how long he had known, and whether he had told me only because he realised I was bound to find out.

Poor Clarissa! I have not even been able to weep for her. All I can feel is black, smothering despair.

I shall write when I am calmer.

Your loving cousin,

Rosina

Portland Place
Tuesday, 17 April 1860

Dearest Emily,

It was such a joy to receive your letter, and to know that dear God-frey is recovering his strength at last. Nettleford sounds enchant-ing—I am sure that you could not have found a better place. I should dearly love to visit you, but my father would never allow me to travel without Aunt Harriet, and I would not inflict her upon you for the world.

I know that I have said very little of myself, all these long months, but I did not want to burden you with my woes whilst you were so anxious about Godfrey. The piano, as always, has been my principal refuge: I play for hours at a stretch and have learnt most of my favor-ite pieces by heart, so that I seldom need a score. And Lily's read-ing is much improved, though we have had to conceal the fact that I am teaching her, both from my aunt and from the other servants. But time hangs very heavily. The only exercise I have is pacing up and down my room, and yet I have grown thinner; I am often hun-gry, in that sick, costive sort of way, but all appetite dies in my aunt's presence. And the shadow of Clarissa's death is everywhere about the house, all the more darkly because I am forbidden to speak of her. So often I resented her sulks and her ill-temper; how I wish now that I had been more forgiving!

It has only just occurred to me that she and George Harrington might have been married in truth. Aunt Harriet dwells constantly upon the wickedness of those who live in sin, and plainly delights in the idea that Clarissa has gone to eternal torment. She finds a hundred ways of alluding to it, without ever mentioning Clarissa by name. But I will not believe in the God she worships. She has made him in her own image: cruel, petty, vengeful, taking pleasure in the punishments he inflicts. Even if such a being existed, it would be wrong to worship him. I still say my prayers, but I have no sense of any answering pres-ence. Perhaps I never did.

I confess, indeed, that I have sometimes envied Clarissa, and thought: better a few weeks' perfect happiness (as I pray she found), a brief moment of terror, and then blessed oblivion, than dragging out my days in this gilded cage. Mary Traill used to say how much she en-vied *me*, living in such a grand house; yet I have come to understand that I have nothing. My father owns even the clothes on my back, and if he chose, he could throw me into the street to starve.

Since Clarissa's death, he has altogether ceased to entertain; he dines out most evenings, breakfasts early, and is usually gone by the time I come down. He no longer keeps a carriage, and has dismissed his butler and all but two of the footmen. Naylor, his new valet—a most unpleasant young man with a perpetual sneer—is now effectively in charge of the household. He (Naylor) is stooped and boney, with disproportionately long arms, and moves in a kind of lunging, spiderish fashion; Lily says that the maids all hate him but dare not show it.

But I have not yet said what is uppermost in my mind. The truth is—even to write it makes me feel as if I am looking over a precipice—I mean to run away. In six months' time I shall be of age, but that may be too late. I know, all too well, the sort of man my father will choose for me, and if I wait until he presents me with my fate, and then refuse him, I shall be still more closely guarded. He may even try to starve me into submission—I have read of such things. My only hope of escape, so far as I can see, is to find a situation—as a governess, or a piano teacher, or—anything that will enable me to earn my own living. But *how* am I to do this, without my father or my aunt finding out? If there is anything you can suggest, I shall be eternally grateful.

I shall seal this now, before my courage fails me, and Lily will take it to the post later on. She has a sweetheart nearby—he is a footman in Cavendish Square—and contrives to snatch a few moments with him on these excursions.

All my love to you, and to dear Godfrey,
Your loving cousin,
Rosina

Portland Place
25 April 1860

Dearest Emily,

I have shed so many tears of joy over your letter that the ink has run all over "there will always be a home for you at Nettleford." It is so generous of you to offer to come up to London and be my chaperone for the journey, and there is just a chance that my father will agree to let me go without Aunt Harriet. It seems that Grandmother Wentworth's health is failing; my aunt's way of putting it is that she has been forced to neglect her duty to her mother in order to fulfill her duty to me. The truth of the matter is that Grandmother will not have me in the house, in case I might rattle a teacup, or cause a floorboard to creak, or—worse still—speak above a whisper.

So yes, if you are quite sure, do please write to my aunt. I do understand that I must return as soon as I am summoned; I did not realise that my father could have me brought back by force. And you are right to remind me that as a governess or a companion, I would be at the mercy of strangers, especially if it became known that my father had disowned me. I promise to be quiet and to do nothing rash.

Your loving cousin,
Rosina

Portland Place
30 April 1860

Dearest Emily,

Alas, my hopes have been dashed. Aunt Harriet says that she could not dream of burdening you with such a heavy responsibility (meaning, I fear, that she does not trust you to keep me under lock and key at all times), and that in any case it would not be seemly for me to visit you whilst my grandmother is ill. So I must try to resign myself to another six months' imprisonment—it seems an eternity. How I shall endure it I do not know.

I will have, at least, something of a reprieve when my aunt goes down to Aylsham in a fortnight. My father is engaged in some new venture, and is here even more seldom than usual.

I shall try to sleep now, and hope to dream of you and Nettleford and freedom.

Your loving cousin,
Rosina

Portland Place
Monday, 7 May 1860

Dearest Emily,

Aunt Harriet has been called away to nurse Grandmother Wentworth, who has taken a turn for the worse; it seems she is dying at last. I sincerely hope that she will be as slow about it as she possibly can, for all her professed eagerness to meet her Maker. I could have danced a jig in the hall as the carriage drove off, but restrained myself.

Of course, my aunt made a great fuss over who is to chaperone me and said she must speak to my father; but by a stroke of good fortune, he was away in Manchester when the news about Grandmother arrived, and he did not return until after she had gone. So it was left to me to tell him what had happened. He said nothing of chaperones, so it seems that I am to be left to my own devices while Aunt Harriet is away. Perhaps all these interminable months of being quiet and dutiful have helped to allay his suspicions: he goes back to Manchester this afternoon and will not return until Friday.

At any rate, I shall have the house to myself for the next three days and can play the piano as loudly as I like!

Your loving cousin,

Rosina

Portland Place

Thursday, 10 May 1860

Dearest Emily,

These last three days have been the most extraordinary of my life. I have met—but I must restrain myself, and tell you everything from the beginning.

My elation at Aunt Harriet's departure did not last. I woke early the following day and stood gazing out of my window, feeling as much a prisoner as ever. It was a perfect spring morning, crisp and bright, and the thought of being shut away all summer was suddenly intolerable.

Then it occurred to me that my aunt had not actually forbidden me to leave the house in her absence. Naylor was in Manchester with my father; the maids all loathe Aunt Harriet, and they would surely not betray me. I do not trust the footmen, but when Naylor is not here to chivvy them about, William and Alfred spend most of their time playing at cards in the boxroom. And so as soon as I was dressed, I went downstairs, meaning to slip out for an hour before breakfast; Lily was to bolt the door behind me and watch for my return from the drawing-room window. But as I was about to leave, I saw several cards on the tray—my aunt must have been too distracted to notice them—including an invitation to take tea in Mrs Traill's garden that very afternoon, with "Do come—I should so like to see you—Mary" pencilled on the back.

I had not seen Mary T since Clarissa eloped; we were never intimate friends, but as I stood holding that card, all the loneliness and misery of these long months seemed to press in upon me, and I felt a great upwelling of anger against Aunt Harriet and my father. Why should I, who had done absolutely nothing wrong, be punished for poor Clarissa's sins?—as if her death had not been punishment enough? Was it not monstrous of my father to seek vengeance upon his own daughter, even beyond the grave? Why should I owe such a man anything in the way of duty or respect, when I was bound to him only by fear? I resolved in that moment to accept Mary's invitation. In the unlikely event of my aunt's finding out, I would play the innocent: "But Aunt Harriet, I assumed you had left it up to me to reply; I thought it only polite to attend." Besides, what more could they do to me?

And so instead of going out myself, I scribbled a note to say that I should be delighted to come so long as nobody asked me about Clarissa, and I sent Lily off to Bedford Place to deliver it. She had not been gone five minutes before misgivings came crowding in. There was, indeed, a great deal more they could do to me. My father could take away my piano, which, like everything else I regard as "mine," is not really mine at all. He could keep me locked in my room until I came of age—perhaps even beyond that. He could dismiss Lily, and engage some coarse, brutal woman to be my gaoler. Or send me to Grandmother Wentworth's house in Aylsham—which he would inherit—and have me kept prisoner *there*.

I asked myself what *you* would advise, and I heard you saying, as clearly as if you were in the room: "Be patient; do not provoke your father's wrath; resign yourself to another six months' confinement; come to us at Nettleford when you are of age, and apply for a situation when you are safely here." I made half a dozen attempts at another note, pleading a headache and asking Mary not to call as I was forbidden visitors, but a hard, stubborn knot of resistance prevented me from giving my whole heart to the task. I saw months—years—of

captivity stretching before me like an endless desert; and how would
I ever summon the courage to defy my father, if I dared not even pass
the front door in his absence?

I was still vacillating when it came time to dress, which threw me
into another dilemma: would the Traills expect to see me in mourning, which my father had forbidden me to wear? In the end, I chose
a very dark grey, and set off in a state of deep foreboding. I can only
think now that some good angel—some prescient instinct, at least—
was urging me onward—but I must not run ahead of myself.

Just to be out of doors again was quite overwhelming. My aunt always insists upon a closed carriage, and so I had not set foot in the
street since last summer. The hubbub of voices sounded extraordinarily loud, the colours dazzlingly bright, the smells so strong that at
first I feared I might faint. I had meant to arrive early, so as to have a
little time alone with Mary, but three o'clock was striking when we
turned into the square, and as we approached the house, my nerve
failed me altogether. I told Lily to go on and say that I had been taken
ill, but she would not have it. "You've been cooped up too long, miss,
and you ought to see your friends while you've the chance; you know
it'll do you good."

I had assumed that there would be no more than a dozen guests, but
when I was shown through onto the terrace, I thought half of London
must be there: the lawn was a sea of elaborate gowns, bobbing with
hats of every imaginable colour, and not a single face I recognised. If
Mary had not come up to greet me, I should have turned tail and fled;
she wanted to introduce me at once, but I pleaded to be left alone until
I had collected myself. I accepted a cup of tea and moved away as soon
as her back was turned, picking my way around the edge of the crowd
until I came to a massive oak, standing close by the wall, and slipped
into the shadow of the trunk.

There I must have remained for ten or fifteen minutes, sipping
my tea and gazing at the spectacle, until I became aware of a man—
a young man—hovering on the path a few paces away from me. I
thought at first glimpse that he might be a Spaniard, because his hair
was jet-black, thick and glossy, and his complexion had a faint ol-
ive glow to it. He was not especially tall, but perfectly proportioned,
plainly dressed in a dark suit with a soft white shirt and stock, and a

mourning band on his arm. As our eyes met, he smiled warmly, and seemed about to speak, but then his expression changed to one of embarrassment, followed by another, more tentative smile.

"I do beg your pardon," he said, approaching. "I mistook you for someone else. Felix Mordaunt, at your service."

He was, indeed, extraordinarily handsome. I could not help smiling in return as we introduced ourselves.

"I take it that you prefer to observe, rather than to be observed, Miss Wentworth."

"Well, yes; I have not been out of doors for many months, and was not expecting such a grand occasion. It is all rather daunting."

"I quite agree," he replied — though he seemed entirely at ease — "especially as I don't know a soul here."

"But surely you must know the Traills?"

"Well, no, I have only just met them. Our families are distantly related by marriage, you see, and I thought — or, to be truthful, my brother thought — that I should pay my respects whilst I was in London, and this invitation was the result."

"You do not live in London, then?"

"No, Miss Wentworth. We have an estate in Cornwall; my father has lately died, and I am in town to see about his will."

I realised, as I murmured my condolences, that I did not want to speak of Clarissa, and contrived, without telling any positive untruths, to imply that I was an only child recovering from a winter's illness. It turned out that he really had been ill — he did not say with what — and had spent the winter abroad. I told him that I played the piano, and discovered that he, too, loves music, and plays the cello — very beautifully, I am sure, despite his protestations to the contrary. Listening to him talk is like hearing a song perfectly rendered in a nearby room, when you cannot make out the words, but the effect is more sublime than any mere words could convey. And, though I tried not to meet his glance too often, I could not help drinking in every detail of his appearance.

All too soon I saw Mary and her mother coming up the path, and all I could think was to ask how long he would be in London.

"I shall be here at least another week. And you, Miss Wentworth, will you be . . . In fact, do you think I might call upon you?"

My heart was pounding violently, and I had only a moment to think.

"I am afraid my father would not allow that," I said, "but . . . if it keeps fine, my maid and I will take a turn in Regent's Park—around the Botanic Gardens—tomorrow morning at about eleven."

He had no time to reply, for the Traills were upon us.

"Rosina, we have been looking *everywhere* for you," said Mrs T archly. "I see you have already made a conquest of Mr Mordaunt. But you must come and tell me how you *are;* such a sad time it has been for you." I caught his questioning glance as Mrs T led me away, sick with mortification as I realised what I had done. I had made an assignation with a young man, within moments of meeting him, in a way that he could only construe as wantonly forward, especially when Mary told him about Clarissa, as she was bound to do. He would assume that I, too, was willing to be carried off by a man I scarcely knew, regardless of the consequences.

"You must excuse me," I said, feeling the heat rush to my face. "I am feeling quite unwell and must go home at once."

"Nonsense; you are simply over-excited. A cooling drink is what you need. Tell me, how is your dear aunt Harriet?" Mrs Traill had never, before this, been actively malicious toward me, and I wondered, as I stammered out my replies, if she saw Mr Mordaunt as a possible candidate for Mary. And when at last I managed to extricate myself, I was bailed up by one acquaintance after another, all of them pointedly not mentioning Clarissa. My face remained scarifyingly hot; beads of perspiration kept trickling out of my hair, and I felt certain that the entire company were talking about me behind my back. And yet I stayed, I confess, in the vain hope that Mr Mordaunt would come up to me, and that I would somehow—but how? — be able to set things right.

When I could bear it no longer, I went in search of Lily, who had been helping with the refreshments, and left without even attempting to thank Mrs T. We had passed out of sight of the house, and I was assuring a disbelieving Lily that I was perfectly all right, only fatigued, when I heard footsteps hurrying up behind us. To my astonishment, it was Mr Mordaunt, rather out of breath and looking, I thought, a little apprehensive.

"Miss Wentworth, forgive me, but I did not want to lose the opportunity of speaking to you again, in case—"

The implication hung in the air between us. I wondered how many people had seen him run after me.

"I slipped out on the pretext of smoking a cigar," he added, as if answering my thought.

"If you really wish to smoke, Mr Mordaunt, I do not mind. This is my maid, Lily."

"Delighted to make your acquaintance, Miss Lily," he said, bowing. She made him a most demure curtsey, but I could tell that she was smiling to herself. "I don't in fact smoke, but it seemed—may I walk with you for a little?"

I glanced uneasily around but saw no one I recognised.

"Yes, sir, you may; but if I should ask you to leave us, please do so at once."

"I quite understand." He went to offer me his arm but checked himself gracefully, and we set off toward Tottenham Court Road, with Lily following a discreet two paces behind.

"The fact is, Miss Wentworth, I was very sorry to be snatched away from you like that. It seemed to me, from the few glimpses I caught, that you did not enjoy the rest of the afternoon any more than I did, but I was given no opportunity to speak to you again. Is Miss Traill, may I ask, a close friend of yours?"

"Not close, no; I thought of her as a friend, but now . . . Did she, by any chance, speak of my sister?"

"I'm afraid she did, yes, and in a less than generous spirit. All I can say, Miss Wentworth, is that I was—I am—deeply sorry to hear of your sister's death."

"You will understand, I hope, why I find it hard to speak of poor Clarissa. My father forbids all mention of her."

"I am very sorry to hear it. By a strange coincidence, I was in Rome myself last winter and heard talk of a young English couple tragically lost in an accident—but forgive me, Miss Wentworth; I should not have mentioned it."

"You needn't apologise," I said. "It is only that—I was not even allowed to weep for her." My tears overflowed, and he stood awkwardly by while Lily fussed over me; she seemed to understand that he was not to blame. When I had collected myself, he offered me his arm, and this time I took it.

"This—Clarissa's disgrace, as everyone else regards it—is why I have not been out of doors for so long," I said.

"I cannot think of it as disgrace. I can scarcely imagine what it must be like for a spirited young woman to be so closely guarded. In your sister's place, I should certainly have run away."

I looked at him in surprise and gratitude; I had never heard such sentiments from a man before, and it emboldened me to speak openly of the long months of confinement, and of my yearning to escape to you at Nettleford, find myself a situation, and be free of my father's tyranny forever. He listened closely, never seeking to bring the talk back to himself; I was conscious all the while, even through my glove and several layers of fabric, of the movement of my hand against his arm. All too soon—again—we were turning into Langham Street.

"You must leave me here," I said, "and return to make your farewells, if only for my sake. They must think you have smoked a whole case full of cigars."

"I shall indeed. But you will still come to Regent's Park in the morning?"

"I cannot promise. But if I can, I will; I cannot say exactly when."

"Then I shall happily wait all day—and the day after, if necessary—in the hope of seeing you there."

With another captivating smile, and a bow to us both, he turned and strode off the way we had come.

"Mr Mordaunt is a charming gentleman, is he not, Lily?" I said as we walked up Portland Place.

"Yes, miss, very charming indeed. But you must be careful, miss. Men—even gentlemen—will take advantage if—well, if you encourage them. And if your father were to hear of it . . ."

I could scarcely deny encouraging Mr Mordaunt. "I know, I know; I promise to be careful. But I must see him again."

She looked at me fearfully.

"But then you'll crave to see him even more, miss. And what if your father comes back sooner than expected? Naylor's always on the lookout; you'll be caught for certain."

"All I want, Lily, is a quiet hour or two's conversation with Mr

Mordaunt tomorrow; if we wish to communicate after that, we shall write to each other, in the same way as I write to my cousin. But you are quite right; I had better not be seen. Is there a way of getting in and out of the house *without* being seen?"

"Not for you, miss, no."

"But for you, Lily? I promise, on my heart, to keep it a secret."

"Well, miss, I'm friends with one of the maids next door; she has the attic room along from mine, and sometimes we open our windows and talk. The roof's not so steep, and there's a bit of a ledge, so I *could* creep across and get in her window—not that I've done it, mind—"

"But then you would have to go down through the house."

"Yes, miss, but the family's away; there's just the maids and the housekeeper on board wages. Only *you* couldn't do it, miss; your gown would be all over smuts, and they'd be bound to talk—and how would you get in again?"

"Yes, I see. Well, supposing, tomorrow, you were to let me out when the coast is clear, and then say I am in bed with a headache? And then when I come back, I can say I felt better, and slipped out for a short walk—or you could watch for me from my window and run down and open the front door. I shall make it up to you, I promise."

"And what if you don't come back, miss? What would I do then?"

"Lily, I am not going to run away with Mr Mordaunt after two days' acquaintance."

But even as I spoke, I remembered the warmth of his arm beneath my gloved hand; I imagined meeting his eyes—which are a deep, luminous, autumnal brown—and not having to look away. Was this how Clarissa had felt?

"What I meant, miss, was if you didn't come back, I shouldn't know what had become of you, so I should have to tell someone."

"Lily, you surely don't think Mr Mordaunt capable of abducting me? From Regent's Park?"

"No, miss, but he might persuade you to go somewhere private. You don't know what any man's capable of, till you're alone with him. I don't mean my Arthur, miss; he's always good to me, but . . ."

I looked at her questioningly, but she said no more.

My elation at seeing Felix Mordaunt again was succeeded by a restlessness, the like of which I had never experienced. I could not settle to anything, even the piano, and went up and down stairs a dozen times, feeling I could not stand another day of captivity, let alone six months of it. I went to bed early, hoping to sleep the time away, but I was pacing my room again five minutes later, caught in a whirligig of contrary emotions. What if he was an accomplished seducer, who amused himself by preying upon foolish young women like me? I imagined him boasting of his latest conquest, or even making sport of me when he returned to Mrs Traill's party; I relived every detail of my humiliation there, and my face burnt more fiercely than ever. My father was bound to find out, and I should be locked away forever, as I deserved.

But then, in the depths of mortification, the image of Felix—it sounds terribly forward, but you will understand, in a little, why I speak of him thus—would come back to me in all his beauty and sunny openness, and my distrust would blow away like so much shredded paper, and all I could think was that I *must* see him again, no matter what the cost.

And so I passed one of the longest nights of my life, tossing between dread and longing. My mattress seemed to consist entirely of lumps; I would grow suffocatingly hot, and throw off the clothes, and then find myself shivering with cold. I was compelled several times to go and stand at my window in case Felix should be gazing up at me from the street, knowing that the idea was quite mad, but unable to restrain myself. And when at last I did go to sleep, I woke with a dreadful start to find the sun streaming in and Lily knocking at my door, and leapt out of bed in a blind panic, thinking I had slept away the whole morning.

And then, of course, I could not decide which gown to wear—but I shall not dwell upon the agonies of indecision I inflicted upon poor Lily as well as myself. Enough to say that I did manage to escape without being seen, and to arrive, breathless and late, at the Botanic Gardens, and that Felix was waiting, and that one look at his face was enough to dispel all of my fears.

All of yesterday, and most of today, we spent walking and talking, or sitting and talking, in the park. We found a bench in a secluded spot, away from the main walks, and subsisted upon tea and chestnuts from the coffee stall; the weather kept fine and warm, and in all that time I saw nobody I knew. I was vaguely aware that I *ought* to be afraid—mortally afraid—of discovery, but in Felix's company I became quite fearless. It was like the moment after you have taken a glass of champagne, miraculously prolonged, when you feel the bubbles fizzing along your veins, but your head is still perfectly clear.

You will perhaps have guessed—I pray that you will not be shocked—that Felix has asked me to marry him, and I have accepted. There! I have said it. I know you will be anxious, but consider: Felix and I have spent twelve uninterrupted hours alone together, and how many couples, before they become engaged, can say as much? You will say that I cannot be sure of him; I can only reply that when you see us together, you will understand. There is an affinity between us—he felt it, too, from the moment we met—as if we have always known each other. He has the sunniest, most open countenance I have ever seen in a man. You can follow the play of his emotions from moment to moment—I am sure he would be incapable of deceit (or of pretending to like someone he did not). And he *listens*, which most men are incapable of doing with a woman for more than a sentence—but I am letting my pen run away with me again.

The obstacle is, of course, my father. Felix will have about six hundred a year after the estate has been sold up and divided, as he means to do, with his brothers. He comes of old Cornish stock—his family have held the estate for many generations—but there is a difficulty there, which I shall come to in a moment. And you know how my father affects to despise the gentry, especially those, like Felix, who have no particular occupation: he will want me to marry some rapacious man of business, like that vile Mr Ingram. Felix insists that he has money enough and does not care about a dowry, only about my being disinherited. He wants to do the honourable thing and call upon my father, but I have persuaded him—or so I trust—that only disaster would come of it. Merely admitting that I went to Mrs T's unchaperoned and met a gentleman there would be enough to have me locked away.

Felix's lack of occupation, I should say, is not from indolence, but because he is sure that his destiny does not lie with any of the established professions. As you will see when you meet him, he would be utterly unsuited to the army, or the law, and—though I am sure he would preach a very eloquent sermon—he says he could not, in conscience, take holy orders, as there is much in established doctrine that he finds doubtful or even abhorrent. He loves music, as I think I told you—it will be such a joy to play together—and he has written a great many poems. When he first discovered Byron, he was so powerfully affected that he thought *Childe Harold* must have been written especially for him (though nowadays he prefers *Don Juan*, which I have never been allowed to possess—we are going to read it together). For years afterward, his greatest ambition was to *be* Lord Byron: he acquired a black cloak, and used to stride about the moors in it, doing his best to look like a tragic hero wrapped in a cloud of gloom.

And, though his disposition is naturally cheerful, he has had much to be gloomy about. There is—again I beg you not to be anxious; five minutes in Felix's company will set your mind at rest—there is a disposition toward melancholia, and sometimes even madness, in his family, especially upon the male side. His mother died when he was ten years old, worn out, Felix believes, by the strain of living with his father, who could not bear to be crossed in the smallest particular. His father's temper was uncertain at the best of times, and when the fit was on him, he could be very violent: he disinherited his eldest son, Edmund, for trying to have him certified insane, and then the second son, Horace, for marrying without his consent, which is why Felix is determined to share with them. He says that if his father had not been carried off by a seizure, he would have been disinherited in turn, and the whole estate would have gone to some distant relation in Scotland. Poor Horace is presently confined to an asylum after a complete nervous collapse—all the more distressing because he has an infant son.

Even Felix, who is the kindest and gentlest of men, has been sadly afflicted by melancholia. It came upon him without warning, in the autumn of his second year at Oxford. He went to bed one night a healthy young man and woke in the grip of the most appalling horror; he felt, he said, as if he had committed a capital crime. At times his mind would race beyond control, whirling from one dreadful prospect to the next, all fraught with the most hideous anxiety; then his thoughts would slow until to think at all was like trying to wade through quicksand, and he would sink into a lethargy so profound that even to leave his bed seemed an intolerable effort. And over all was cast a leaden blackness of spirit, a thing worse than the worst pain he had ever experienced, because it consumed his entire being, suffocating all joy and hope as if he were being smothered by ashes.

After a month in this terrible state, he abandoned his studies and went home to Cornwall. It was, he said, the worst thing he could have done, because Tregannon House is a dismal place even in summer: dark and damp, with great thick walls and tiny windows. In those bleak surroundings, he sank even deeper into the pit, constantly tempted by the thought of suicide, until some instinct of self-preservation prompted him to flee the house and take passage to Naples, where within a few weeks he was his old self again. He returned to Oxford in the spring, believing himself cured, but the following autumn he felt it coming on again.

This time he did not wait for the darkness to engulf him but sailed at once for Italy, where again his spirits were restored. He has wintered abroad ever since. The English climate, he says, brings out the dark strain in the Mordaunt blood, which is why he is determined to sell the estate. Edmund, sadly, does not agree: he has some absurd idea of turning Tregannon House into a private asylum, but Felix hopes that the rift will heal once things are settled and Edmund has money in his pocket. And he is certain that with me at his side, he will never sink into melancholia again.

Felix, as you can see, has been absolutely candid; he wished me to hear the worst about his family from him, rather than from some malicious tattle-bearer, and, knowing that you are my dearest friend in all the world, asked if I would relate it to you. He very much hopes that you will allow him to call at Nettleford when he returns to Cornwall in a week or two, especially since you and Godfrey will be the sole keepers of our secret. Felix does not want to say anything to his brother until the estate is settled.

We intend to marry as soon as I am of age, and since we cannot hope for my father's blessing, it would be a joy to Felix—and of course to me—if you would give him yours. I should love, more than anything, to be married from your house, with you and Godfrey as witnesses.

Six months does not seem so very long to wait, now. I shall have Felix's letters to look forward to, and he will come up to London as often as the business of the estate allows; I am sure I shall be able to slip out and see him sometimes. I shall even try to be kinder to Aunt Harriet!

And now I must make an end of this long letter. We mean to live abroad — somewhere warm and light, where I pray that you will come to visit us — and travel a great deal. It is sad to think that in all of England, the only people I shall sorely miss are you and Godfrey — and Lily. I would love to keep her with me, but I know she would pine for her Arthur, and for London — she is a London girl through and through, whereas I cannot wait to leave here.

Your loving cousin,
Rosina

Portland Place
Saturday, 12 May 1860

Dearest Emily,

The worst has happened. All yesterday I waited for my father to return; no one knew when to expect him, and I dared not leave the house. I had thought that two whole days with Felix would be enough for me to live on, but from the moment I woke this morning, I was consumed by doubts, which grew worse as the hours I might have spent with him crawled by. What if he had changed his mind? What if his way of amusing himself in London was to extract pledges of marriage from foolish girls? I thought I had banished such fears forever, but they came swarming back to torment me. Five minutes — a single minute — or a line of his writing would have set my mind at rest: I stood for ages at my window, praying that he would appear in the street below, even though I knew that he would be engaged on business all day.

My father did not return until late in the afternoon. I was waiting in the drawing room, and at the first glimpse of his face, my heart turned to lead.

"Mr Bradstone — the gentleman I spoke of — will dine here this evening; you will join us at seven and make yourself agreeable to him."

I had forgotten all about Mr Bradstone. My horror must have shown, for his face darkened, and he asked very sharply if I had not heard him.

"I beg your pardon, sir," I said, "but I feel my headache return-

ing"—I am sure I looked stricken enough for it to sound plausible—
"and I hope you will excuse me."

"Headache or no, you will present yourself at seven, if you know
what is good for you," he replied, and left me without another word.

I dragged myself upstairs, feeling as if I had stumbled into a nightmare, and dressed as severely as I could, with no jewellery except a
small silver cross; I had Lily pull my hair back so tightly it hurt. But
nothing could have prepared me for the man my father has chosen.

Mr Giles Bradstone is perhaps forty years old, tall and powerfully built, with a long, boney face and a leprous complexion. His
nostrils flare slightly when he breathes, and his eyes are very prominent: the coldest, palest blue I have ever seen—they fix you with a
look of amused contempt. He is a widower, and I can give you no better idea of the man than to say that when he told me—with, I would
swear, a flicker of a smile—that his first wife (he actually *said* "my
first wife") died in an accident, I felt certain he had murdered her.
His voice is cool and contemptuous, like his stare, and of course he is
a man of business; he deals in property, like my father, and holds the
same views. I kept my eyes lowered, as far as possible, but all too often
he addressed me directly—just for the pleasure, I am sure, of forcing me to look at him. My father gave one of his disquisitions upon
the idleness of the poor, and how much more work could be got out of
them if they were not so leniently treated by the law; he had no sooner
finished than Mr Bradstone said,

"But I fear Miss Wentworth does not agree with her father."

"I have no opinion, sir," I replied, "beyond what scripture tells us,
that it is our duty to care for those less fortunate than ourselves."

My father shot me an angry look; Mr Bradstone smiled and raised
an eyebrow, as if to say, I know that you dislike me, but do not imagine
that you can escape. Later he remarked—in reference to some business venture, but with his gaze fixed upon me—"I never allow myself
to be beaten. At anything."

When dinner was over, my father insisted I play for them, which
he would never ordinarily do; he actively dislikes music. I chose the
most mournful piece I could think of, but still I could feel Mr Bradstone watching me. And when at last I dared to excuse myself, he said,
"It has been a pleasure to meet you, Miss Wentworth, and I look for-

ward to renewing our acquaintance." His tone was just within the bounds of civility, but his eyes laid insolent claim to me, and I left with the dreadful suspicion that my loathing had aroused his interest.

As you will imagine, I scarcely slept. I was dreadfully afraid that Mr Bradstone might be staying here, and I watched from my window until I saw him drive away in a cab. And then I kept hoping that Felix, too, might be sleepless (he is lodging in Sackville Street, near Piccadilly) and would walk past the house as he had said he might. But there was only the flare of the lamps, and the empty street, and the hourly tramp of the constable's boots, until I sank into nightmare visions of Mr Bradstone's face looming out of the dark, over and over until I woke at dawn and realised the nightmare was still before me.

After breakfast came the summons I had been dreading. My father was sitting at his desk when I entered the study, and motioned me to stand before him, like a child about to be punished.

"Mr Bradstone seems favorably impressed with you, despite your sullenness. He wishes to see you again, and when he does, you will make yourself agreeable to him."

I realised, just in time, that my only chance of escape was to placate him.

"If you wish it, sir, I will do my best."

He gave me a long, disbelieving stare.

"You knew yesterday that it was my wish," he said at last. "Why did you not obey me then?"

"I do not like him, sir; I am sorry if that disappoints you."

"It does—and you will not disappoint me again. Mr Bradstone and I are negotiating an alliance of interests; he is in want of a wife, and a marriage between our houses will cement our association. If he should make you an offer, you will accept. Your duty is to obey me, and you will learn to like him, because I wish it."

"And when does Mr Bradstone return?" I asked.

"On Wednesday; he will stay a fortnight. In the meantime, you are not to leave the house—as I am told you have been doing in my absence—"

"It was only to walk, sir," I said, praying that my face would not betray me—and wondering who had betrayed me.

"No doubt Mr Bradstone will be happy to escort you. Until then, as I say, you are to remain indoors: I have given orders to ensure that you do. Disobey me in this, and you will be confined to your room. That is all."

As I crossed the hall, I saw Alfred stationed like a sentry by the front door. He studiously avoided my eye.

I do not know how I managed to keep my composure in my father's presence; by the time I reached my room, I was trembling violently. My first impulse was to escape at once through Lily's window. But if Felix was not at his lodgings—or worse, if I was caught trying to escape with my father still in the house—I realised I had better write to him first, and send Lily to find him and bring back his reply. He and I had talked of what we might do if this should happen, and he told me that under Scots law we could marry as soon as we had lived there for three weeks. It was, I confess, more his wish than mine that we should wait until I came of age. "As soon as you are safe beneath your cousin's roof," he said, "I can do the honourable thing and ask your father for his blessing. The worst he can do is throw me down the stairs; if nothing else, it may lessen his wrath. But if your life at home becomes intolerable, we shall elope at once."

Then I began to think about what I could take. I remembered Clarissa's room stripped bare, her belongings piled on that filthy cart, my father saying, "Be warned; I will not be embarrassed a second time." I imagined him chopping my beloved piano into pieces with an axe and flinging all of my music into the fire, and my resolve wavered. But if I stayed, and refused Mr Bradstone, he might do all of that, and more; and once imprisoned in my room, how would I ever escape? Clarissa had been of age when she ran away—it had never occurred to me, until then, that the law had been on her side, not my father's—but that had not blunted his fury in the slightest. And what if I *had* been seen with Felix? I might have to flee at a moment's notice.

Sick with fear at the enormity of what I was doing, I chose a small valise and set about collecting things: my mother's necklace and brooch; your letters; a ring Clarissa had given me in a fit of generosity; a few miniatures; a small dressing case; a nightgown; a shawl— already the valise was almost full. I would have to travel in the clothes I stood up in—not the morning dress I was wearing, but something in which I could run, if need be, without tripping over layers of petticoats. The only thing I could find was a plain white dress I had worn when I was sixteen: the worst possible colour for climbing over a roof, but it could not be helped. Packing seemed to heighten, rather than relieve, my terror; when Lily tapped at the door, I almost jumped out of my skin.

Lily turned very pale when she saw the valise, and burst into tears when I told her I meant to elope.

"He'll hunt you down, miss; you know he will."

"We need only hide for three weeks; once we are married, he cannot touch us."

"But what if Mr Mordaunt doesn't marry you, miss? He might ruin you and leave you, and then — it doesn't bear thinking of."

"My heart tells me to trust him, Lily. He is the best and kindest man I have ever met, and I cannot stay here. I would rather fling myself from that window than have Mr Bradstone so much as touch me."

"Then refuse him, miss. Even if your father keeps you on bread and water, it's better than being ruined. And if Mr Mordaunt really loves you, he'll wait till you're of age."

"He has already promised to wait for me, Lily. But I dare not stay, and I shall never be surer of Felix than I am now."

"Then go to your cousin, miss. It's a long way from London; you'll be safe with her."

I confess I was sorely tempted, and not for the first time. Nettleford beckons like an earthly paradise; but I cannot come to you. My father's rage at Clarissa will be as nothing compared to his fury at me, and I could not bring that upon you and Godfrey. Nettleford is one of the first places he will think of; our hearts would be in our mouths every time there was a knock at the door. At least in Scotland we have only to evade pursuit for three weeks until we are safe — and then we *shall* come to you, and all your fears for me will be set at rest.

Later: I have heard from Felix, and we have made our plans. I shall slip out of the house very early on Monday morning, through Lily's window if necessary; I shall know by then if the door is to be watched at night. Felix will be waiting for me in a cab; we shall drive straight to King's Cross and take the first train north. Lily and I have shed a good many tears over each other, but I will not take her away from her sweetheart. We went through the advertisements together and found a situation for a lady's maid in Tavistock Square; I have given her the most splendid character, and she will call upon them when she takes this to the post. Lily will write to me at Nettleford—I hope you do not mind—if she is in want of anything.

I wish I could leave sooner, but my father will be at home all day tomorrow; on Mondays he is usually gone by nine, and he will not expect to see me at breakfast. I shall lock my door behind me and leave a note on it saying that I have taken chloral after a bad night and am not to be disturbed. Lily will wait until the middle of the afternoon, and then tell the housekeeper she is worried about me. With luck, that will give us half a day's start; I do not think they will break down the door without sending for my father, and when they do, he will find a letter saying I have run away to Paris.

I am dreadfully sorry to leave you in such anxiety, but if I am caught—I try not to think of it—I shall have no way of writing to you. Felix swears that if I *am* captured, he will not rest until he finds a way of rescuing me.

Pray for me; I shall let you know the moment I am safe.

Your loving cousin,

Rosina

Georgina Ferrars' Journal

Gresham's Yard
27 September 1882

For weeks now I have been too low-spirited to begin a new journal. There is absolutely nothing to record, but I feel I must make the attempt, before all volition slips away from me. I spent this morning as usual making up parcels for my uncle, and the afternoon minding the shop—without a single customer—whilst he attended a sale. How the hours drag! The days are rapidly shortening, and the shop seems more dismal than ever.

I never imagined that books could be so oppressive. I loved our little library at Niton, the comforting smell of the boards, the warm colours of the spines with their faded gold lettering; but here they poison the air with mould and damp. For all my uncle's attempts at airing the place, there are livid splotches like toadstools amongst the pages; the spores rise up and clutch at my throat. And in all this time, I have not found a single volume I would care to read.

I have tried to be content with my lot, and I know that I should be grateful to my uncle for taking me in, but to him I am simply a useful pair of hands, cheaper and more painstaking than the boy who used to do the parcels for him. If I were to say, "Uncle, I am dying of loneliness and boredom," he would not know what to reply; I doubt that he would even comprehend.

No—another winter of wrapping books for elderly clergymen I shall never see is more than I can bear. But what else can I do? I cannot afford to live independently unless I find an occupation. I keep telling myself that I should learn typewriting; even spending my days copying other people's words onto a machine would be better than this. But I have done nothing about it, just as I have not written to Mr Wetherell to ask about Aunt Vida's will, which must surely have been proven by now—it is nearly a year since she died.

Later: I have just woken from a trance in which I was staring at my reflection in the window and trying to will it to move and speak to me, as I used to do with the mirror at Niton. If only I had a sister! If I could summon Rosina now, what would she say? She would scorn me for moping, and tell me to be bold, and take my courage in both hands, and *do* something, anything, to lift myself out of the slough of despond—but what?

Well, what about the two hundred pounds Mama left me? Everyone says it is wrong to spend your capital, but at least I could see something of the world—Rosina would surely want me to, and I hope Mama as well—and perhaps find a friend at last. I *shall* write to Mr Wetherell—in fact I shall do so now, before my resolve weakens.

Gresham's Yard
Monday, 2 October 1882
An extraordinary thing has happened. This morning I received a letter from a Mr Lovell in Plymouth, explaining that Mr Wetherell has been in poor health for some months (hence the delay in settling my aunt's affairs), telling me that I have £212 11s 8d to my name—and enclosing a sealed packet labelled "Papers deposited by Mrs Emily Ferrars for safekeeping, 22 November 1867; retained upon instruction of Miss Vida Radford, 7 June 1871, *in re* Ferrars bequest." Inside was a bundle of letters, tied with a faded blue ribbon, addressed to my mother at West Hill Cottage, Nettleford.

I have read Rosina Wentworth's letters over and over, as my mother must have done before me: some of the folds have worn completely through. *This* is why I called my imaginary sister Rosina—I must have overheard Mama and Aunt Vida talking about her before I was old enough to understand what they were saying. But why did they never mention her in front of me? Did Rosina escape with Felix Mordaunt, or did her father catch her and lock her away—or even murder her, as I fear he murdered her sister? And if Mama wanted me to have the letters when I grew up, wouldn't she have left a note explaining why?

Perhaps she meant to, but her heart gave out too soon—she sent the packet to Mr Wetherell only weeks before she died. Did she send it to him because she knew she was dying? Anything she left with Aunt Vida would have been lost with the house.

Uncle Josiah, of course, says he has never heard of Rosina Wentworth or Felix Mordaunt, "but it was all a long time ago, my dear, and I may well have forgotten . . . unless you mean Dr Mordaunt of Aylesbury—the Jacobean divine, you know—I have an incomplete set of him in the back room . . ." He did not even ask to see the letters.

This afternoon I walked round to Portland Place and wandered up and down, looking at the grand houses and wondering where she might have lived. There is one in particular, with a dark, unfriendly look to it that strikes a chord, but I have no way of telling.

Eleven o'clock has struck, and the house is completely silent. I feel as if I have been sleepwalking through my days, and Rosina's letters have awakened me. I *must* find out what became of her. But how?

Tuesday, 3 October

This morning I wrote to ask Mr Lovell if he could tell me anything of Rosina Wentworth or Felix Mordaunt. I had scarcely returned from the post when a most peculiar letter arrived from him. He says: "If you have not already opened the packet I enclosed with yesterday's comm^n, I most urgently request you to return it to me unopened at your earliest convenience. Even if you have examined the contents, I should be most grateful for their return." It seems that Rosina's letters should have been kept with another sealed packet that Mama had subsequently sent for safekeeping, and that "according to your late mother's instruction, this packet is to be made available to you if and only if a certain condition is fulfilled"—but he does not say what condition.

Mr Lovell—Henry Lovell is his name—sounds quite young, despite all the circumlocutions. He sends his "most abject apologies," which does not sound like a grizzled old lawyer. Reading between the lines, I should say that Mr Wetherell came into the office unexpectedly, discovered what Mr Lovell had done, and berated him soundly. But what can it mean? I wrote back at once, saying that I should like to keep the letters unless the law positively forbids it, and asking him to explain exactly what I need to do to see the rest of the papers. I have copied all of Rosina's letters into the back of this journal, just in case.

Thursday, 5 October

Mr Lovell's reply is even stranger. "I regret that your late mother's instructions explicitly prohibit us from disclosing the terms upon which the packet in question may be forwarded to you. We are likewise prohibited from answering any enquiry relating to the contents of the package, and I am therefore unable to respond to the questions in your previous letter of the 2nd *inst.*" He says that since I have read the letters, I may keep them if I wish, and sincerely regrets that he is unable to enter into any further correspondence upon the subject.

It makes no sense—unless the condition is that I may not see the papers until I am twenty-five, say, in which case why not tell me so? Did Mama not want me to have them until (or unless) I was married?—because of something improper, or shocking? But what sort of thing, and why would she want me to know it at all? And how will Mr Lovell know, if I am not supposed to write to him, whether I have fulfilled the condition or not?

Rosina's fate is at the heart of the mystery: of that, at least, I feel sure. Mama plainly loved her; I know I would have loved her, too, if only we could have met . . . but supposing she is not dead?

Well, since the lawyers will not help me, I must find some other way. But how? Looking through my uncle's directories in the shop this afternoon, I found dozens of Wentworths in London alone, but not a single Mordaunt. What if I were to advertise in the personal column of *The Times*? Mama and Rosina were cousins, so I am Rosina's cousin once removed; and Rosina must have been born in 1839 . . . I could say, "Relative anxious to trace Rosina Wentworth (b. 1839), last known address Portland Place (1859–60); please communicate with Miss G. Ferrars at Mr Radford's bookshop, Gresham's Yard, Bloomsbury." I need not tell Uncle Josiah unless he happens to notice the advertisement.

But what if Rosina's father is still alive? Might I be putting her—

or for that matter myself—in danger? Surely not: he would be an old man now, and the worst he could do would be to come into the shop and make a scene (though that would be quite bad enough). And if Rosina has managed to evade him all this time . . . it is my best chance of finding her. I shall walk down to Fleet Street in the morning and place my advertisement.

Monday, 9 October

No replies. I suppose it was foolish to hope for any. I found a tattered London directory for 1862 in the back room this afternoon, and looked up the residents of Portland Place. But no Wentworth is listed there. And no Mordaunts in *The Upper Ten Thousand*. What am I to do?

Wednesday, 11 October

My prayers have been answered! I was alone in the shop yesterday afternoon—my uncle had been gone only about a quarter of an hour—when a young woman appeared in the doorway. She was beautifully dressed, in a gown of peacock blue, trimmed in cream, and a bonnet to match, the colours wonderfully rich and vibrant in the gloom. I was seated behind the desk, and must have gazed at her for several seconds before she caught sight of me. She looked strangely familiar—about my own height and figure, her hair a similar shade of brown—and yet I knew I had never seen her before. Our eyes met with—or so I felt—a flash of recognition on her side, fading to a tentative smile.

"Pray excuse me," she said. "I hope I am not intruding, but are you Miss Ferrars?" Her voice was low and vibrant, with a slight foreign intonation.

"Yes, I am Miss Ferrars. Won't you come in?"

I rose to greet her, my pulse accelerating. Something in the shape and set of her eyes—a luminous hazel—heightened the sense of familiarity. Her gloved hand trembled faintly in mine, a subtle, quivering vibration, like a current passing between us.

"My name is Lucia Ardent"—she pronounced "Ardent" in what I took to be the French fashion—"and I am here because of your advertisement . . . except that I have come in the hope that you can help *me*. You see, I know the name Rosina Wentworth—I heard it when I was a little child—but I do not know who she was; or why my heart insisted, when I saw that name in the newspaper, that I must not lose the chance."

"That is so strange—won't you sit down? I am sorry it is so gloomy in here, but I must stay until my uncle returns—because it is exactly my own case. But before I say more, will you tell me, Miss Ardent, how you came to hear of Rosina Wentworth, and why you think she may be important to you?"

"Of course. You should know, Miss Ferrars, that I am an only child. I have lived all my life on the Continent; this is my first visit to England. My father, Jules Ardent, was French, and much older than my mother—he died before I can remember—but my mother grew up in England. I lost her only a year ago."

"I am very sorry to hear it."

"Strange to tell," she continued, "I know absolutely nothing of my family on either side. My mother always refused to speak of her past; you would have thought her life had begun on the same day as mine. All she would ever say was that her life in England had been so unhappy that she would never return, and that she wished only to forget. No matter how I coaxed and pleaded, she would not be drawn. She was cultivated, and read a great deal—mostly English books; Mama and I always spoke English when we were alone. I think her family must have had money—perhaps a great deal of it—but we had only a small income from my father. Here it would be worth no more than two hundred a year, but you can live much more cheaply on the Continent. We had no settled home, and we were always moving from place to place—I have lived in Rome, Florence, Paris, Madrid—"

"How wonderful!"

"You would not say so if you had spent your life in pensions and furnished rooms, always packing and unpacking, saying farewell to people just as you begin to like them. When you have seen as many great monuments as I have, you begin to think that one is very like another. If I had had a sister, we would have been company for each other—but you were asking me about Rosina Wentworth.

"All I can tell you is that when I was about seven years old—I am not even sure where we were staying, but I think it might have been Rouen—my mother had a visitor. We were living in a house; I remember that—there was a garden, which was always a great treat for me, with a lake at the foot of it. I was playing at hide-and-seek, pretending that an ogre was hunting me, and had crawled under a tree whose branches came right to the ground, when I heard voices. I peeped out and saw Mama and a tall, grey-faced man, very thin and stooped, approaching. As they came nearer, I realised they were speaking in English. I heard him say, 'I have kept your secret,' and then—it might have been 'but she cannot stay there,' or 'but you cannot stay there.' I could not catch Mama's reply, but as they passed my hiding place, he said something about 'Rosina Wentworth.' I heard only the name, and a sharp exclamation from my mother, before their voices faded.

"By the time I came indoors, the visitor had gone, and Mama was standing at the window, staring absently at the trees; she spun round as I approached, and then tried to pretend I had not startled her. When I asked who the man with the grey face had been, she replied, 'What man? You must have dreamt him.' Even after I told her where I had been hiding, she tried to persuade me that I must have fallen asleep, until I said, 'Mama, who is Rosina Wentworth?' She turned white to the lips, and cried, 'What else did you hear?' She said it so fiercely that I was frightened. I repeated the words I had overheard and assured her that I had not meant to spy on her—Mama was always very stern about not listening at doors—and after a little she began to comfort me, and tried once more to persuade me that it must have been a dream. And the very next day we left that house.

"I never asked about Rosina Wentworth again, but the name is engraved upon my memory, and when I saw your advertisement, I knew I must come to you."

"That is quite extraordinary," I said, and launched at once upon the tale of the mirror, and my imaginary sister, Rosina. I had meant to go straight on to the letters, but Lucia—as she had already invited me to call her—was so fascinated by my childhood, and asked so many questions, that I ended by relating my entire history. I tried several times to turn the conversation back to her—my life seemed so commonplace and uneventful compared to hers—but she would not have it. "You cannot imagine," she kept saying, "what a delight it is to find someone who has lived exactly the life I always yearned for, settled and tranquil, and bound by ties of deep affection." Often as I talked I was aware of her gaze, drinking in every detail of my appearance; a little disconcerting at first, but very flattering. No one had paid me such attention since Mama died. When I came to the loss of the cottage, and my ordeal with Aunt Vida on the cliff-top, she turned ashen pale and slumped forward in her chair: I sprang forward and threw my arms around her, thinking she was going to faint.

I was shaken to realise how long it had been since I had embraced anyone, and how much I had missed that intimacy. I remained kneeling before Lucia's chair, with her head resting upon my shoulder and her cheek against mine until she disengaged herself—reluctantly, I felt—and sat up again. We both began to apologise at once; she for being so affected and I for distressing her, each reassuring the other until she confessed that she had eaten nothing all day except a square of toast and a cup of tea at breakfast.

"But where are you living?" I asked.

"In a temperance hotel in Marylebone. I have only a hundred a year, apart from a little capital, but I am determined to stay in England. My clothes are an extravagance, I know, but I must be well turned out; as I have no friends, no family, and no one to recommend me. I think I must go on the stage, but I wanted to see something of London first."

"I should very much like to be your friend," I said. "And I shall certainly not let you starve; you must come upstairs with me and have something to eat, and then I will show you Rosina Wentworth's letters."

She looked up at me, startled.

"But how can you have her letters, when you lost everything with your house?"

"My mother left them—and some other papers I am not allowed to see—with our solicitor; I shall tell you all about it in a moment."

I closed the shop without a second thought and drew her to her feet, relieved to see the colour stealing back into her face.

After she had eaten—she wanted only tea and bread and butter, and did not seem very hungry, in spite of her fast—we went on up to my own small sitting room, where I told her about my mother's perplexing bequest, and sat beside her on the sofa whilst she read through the letters with rapt attention. Pale sunlight slanted through the dusty pane, heightening the rich colours of her gown and sending tiny sparks through her hair, which she wore pinned up in a fashion very like my own. After she had finished, she was silent for some time, turning the letters in her hands as if she could not quite believe she was holding them.

"It is strange," she said at last, "but I feel as if I know her already. Mama loved the piano, too, and she would play, very beautifully, whenever there was an instrument . . ."

We looked at each other, and I saw my own presentiment mirrored in her face.

"Lucia—may I ask how old you are?"

"Twenty-one."

"And when is your birthday?"

"The—the fourteenth of February."

"Just a month before mine—and a little more than nine months after Rosina's last letter. And your mother loved the piano, and would never talk about her past."

The papers rattled in her grasp; she set them aside and turned to me slowly, like someone waking from a dream.

"It explains everything," she said. "Why we could never stay . . . why Mama never told anyone where we were going next . . . why I was drawn to you, here, today. It is fate, as you said . . . That is what the grey-faced man meant, that day in the garden: *he* had kept her secret, but someone had found out that Rosina Wentworth was in Rouen . . . and so we fled the very next day."

Her hands trembled in her lap; a hectic spot of colour appeared on her cheek.

"Of course it means that I am a . . . that Mama was not married when she . . ."

"We don't know that," I said, placing my hand on hers, which were icy cold. "Perhaps Felix Mordaunt did marry her, and then—something happened to him."

"No, I am certain he seduced and abandoned her, just as the maid Lily feared he would. Mama always warned me: 'When you are in love,' she would say, 'you must never trust your heart, only your head. A man will say anything, promise anything—and mean it quite sincerely—to seduce you, but once you have given yourself, the chase is over: he will cast you aside without a backward glance.' I knew she spoke from bitter experience, though she would never admit it."

"Even if you are right," I said, "your father—Jules Ardent, I mean—took pity upon her. You are his child according to law," I added, wishing I felt more confident than I sounded.

"Perhaps there never was a Jules Ardent. Would an elderly Frenchman really have married a penniless English girl, disowned by her father, who was bearing another man's child? I think Mama invented him for the sake of respectability."

"What did your mother call herself?" I asked. "I mean, her Christian name?"

"She called herself Madeleine."

"And—when was her birthday?"

"The twenty-seventh of July—she never told me her age. When I was small, I often thought how young and beautiful she looked. But then the lines crept over her face, and year by year she grew thinner . . . Of course, it was fear that aged her . . ."

"And—what did she die of?"

"Her heart gave out—just like your own mother's. We were climbing the stairs in a pension—last December, it was, in Paris—she gave a little cough, and then a sigh, and her knees gave way. I caught her, thinking it was a faint, but she died in my arms."

"I am so sorry," I said, chafing her cold hands. "How strange, that our mothers should both . . . not so strange, perhaps, if they were cousins . . . though of course we cannot be sure."

I had a momentary pang of doubt: was this no more than an extraordinary coincidence? If Rosina had become Madeleine Ardent, surely she would have gone on writing to my mother? But perhaps she had; perhaps those were the letters Mr Wetherell was keeping from me.

"I am already sure," said Lucia, regarding me with luminous eyes. Perched on the sofa beside me, she looked like some exotic bird of paradise come to earth. "It is blood that tells. You and I, we look alike, we think alike; already I feel I have always known you."

"And I also," I said, embracing her. "If only those letters had come to me while Rosina—your mother—was still alive; I should so love to have met her—and to have known you sooner."

"I wish you had, too. But even if Mama had seen your advertisement, she would not have replied."

"No, I suppose not—for fear of her father," I said. Lucia shook her head in seeming bewilderment; she was studying Rosina's letters again. A horrid realisation struck me.

"If he is still alive, he may have seen my advertisement, too. You may be in danger because of me."

She looked up from the page and smiled, a little wanly.

"If you had not advertised, Georgina, we should never have met. As for Thomas Wentworth, he would be an old man by now, and surely—"

"Lucia . . . why did you call him *Thomas* Wentworth?"

She started, and glanced at me fearfully. "I must have read it here."

"I am sure she never mentions his Christian name."

We went through the letters again, line by line, without finding it.

"Lucia," I said, "you see what this means. You must have overheard your mother—or someone—speaking of him. Just as Rosina's name came to me." Our shoulders were touching; I could feel a faint, continuous vibration thrilling through her body.

"Of course you must be right. The grey-faced man, perhaps . . ."

"Did you ever see him again?"

"No, never."

"He, at least, was your friend. Did Rosina—your mother—not leave you *any* letters or papers?"

"Nothing. She received very few letters—few, at least, that I saw—and those she burned as soon as she had read them. All she had were her clothes, her *articles de toilette*—I have forgotten the English word—a few necessities—everything she owned would fit into one small trunk, and she brought me up to do the same. 'Possessions are a snare and a burden,' she used to say. 'They only weigh us down. The fewer things we have to carry, the freer we are.'"

"And your income? You said you have a hundred a year; do you know where from?"

"Until today, I assumed it came from the estate of Jules Ardent. I suppose I could write to the advocates—the lawyers in Paris. But they are French lawyers; if you forgot your own name, they would find reasons for not telling it to you."

"English lawyers are no better," I said. "Somehow I must discover what it is I must do to see the rest of the papers my mother left me. These letters—did I explain?—only came to me by mistake. I wonder—might she—my mother, I mean—have been protecting Rosina? By not letting me see the letters until her father was safely dead? Which would mean—"

"That he *is* still alive," said Lucia, and shivered. "And that monster was—is—my grandfather! It is horrible to think of."

"*Why* didn't Rosina go to Nettleford?" I exclaimed. "After Felix Mordaunt abandoned her, I mean. Mama could have kept her hidden until you were born. And after my father died, we could all have lived with Aunt Vida at Niton; you and I could have grown up together . . . Such a waste of happiness!"

"Yes," said Lucia, looking through the letters again, "but do you really not see why?"

"She says, 'I could not bring my father's wrath upon you,' or something like that, but I *know* Mama would have taken her in, without a second thought, and so would my aunt. You would have been far safer—and far happier—with us, than wandering the Continent alone, where nobody even knew who you were."

"But the shame, Georgina, the shame! All of London must have known that she ran off with Felix Mordaunt. And then to bear a child out of wedlock . . . What a burden I must have been to her!"

"You must never think that, never!" I said, taking her in my arms. I tried to imagine what I would feel in Lucia's place: anger at Felix Mordaunt, certainly; sorrow for my mother; but not shame, either on her behalf or mine. Was I somehow deficient in moral sense? Aunt Vida, certainly, had never cared about the world's opinion. I heard, in what I had just said to Lucia, the echo of my aunt's cry: "You were her joy, her happiness: hold to that, and ask no more!" I stroked Lucia's hair and made soothing noises, half wishing I had never shown her the letters (but how could I have withheld them from her?), yet delighting, for all my unease, in the warmth of our embrace.

When she was calm again, I began to talk about that day by the lighthouse, when I had come to suspect that giving birth to me had strained my mother's heart, and what a comfort my aunt's words had been to me ever since.

"You and your mother loved each other dearly, did you not?" I said.

"Oh yes . . . I never doubted her love for me."

"Then think how much lonelier she would have been without you.

The doors of society closed against her the day she ran off with Felix Mordaunt. But her real friends—like my mother—would not have cared . . ."

"I wish I could believe that," said Lucia.

"I am sure that when we see the rest of the letters, all your doubts will be set at rest. And Lucia—?"

"Yes?"

"This will be our secret; no one else need ever know. We shan't even tell my uncle. Not that it would matter if we did; he cares for nothing but his shop and would forget it all five minutes later. To the world you will be simply my friend Miss Ardent."

As I spoke those words, I was seized by a dizzying sense of unreality, as if I was looking down upon the two of us from somewhere near the ceiling. Surely this *must* be a dream? So powerful was the sensation that I dug my nails into the flesh of my wrist.

"You are so kind," I heard Lucia saying. "And yes, I cannot quite believe it, either."

I looked up and saw that she was smiling.

"I am sorry," I said. "I did not mean . . . It is only that . . . I have been so lonely here and have longed and prayed for a friend. And for you this must be a hundred times stranger—your whole life changing before your eyes."

"Yes, it is—and yet I think I always expected something like this. Mama is still my mother, after all; it does not mean she loved me any less than I believed. More, indeed; much more . . . when I think of what she faced each day."

I knew already that I could not bear to lose her. Uncle Josiah would be utterly nonplussed, but if I paid for her keep . . .

"Lucia," I said, "instead of staying in that hotel, why don't you come and live here with me? You could have the bedroom below this: we shall have to air it and find you some furniture, but that is easily done."

Her lips brushed my cheek; the warmth of her breath lingered against my skin.

"I should love to, but I could not impose myself, and besides, your uncle . . ."

"Uncle Josiah will need persuading, but I shall see to that. And if you don't mind helping in the shop sometimes, it will be all the easier to persuade him. Why don't you stay to supper—it is Tuesday, so curried mutton, I'm afraid—and meet him? And then we can come up here again and talk for as long as we like."

She made a polite show of reluctance, but her delight, and her relief, were plain as I rang for Charlotte and told her to warn Mrs Eddowes that there would be three for supper.

"One thing I am sure of," I said when we were alone again, "is that our mothers kept on writing to each other. They loved each other; you can see from the letters that Rosina trusted Emily implicitly. We *must* persuade Mr Lovell to let us see the rest of the papers. Suppose . . . would you be willing, Lucia, to trust him with your secret, if we tell him in the strictest confidence? He is my solicitor, after all; I am sure he would not betray you."

"I suppose not," she said doubtfully, "but in truth, Georgina, I would much rather tell no one else, for the time being at least. There is so much to comprehend—to take in. Could you not simply say that something has happened which makes it vital for you to see those papers? Or if he will not do that, insist that he reveal what you must do to satisfy this mysterious condition?"

"Yes, of course I will. I wonder . . . Mama would have known about you; perhaps that was her condition—that you and I should have met?"

"Perhaps," said Lucia, her face still shadowed, "but I should still like to keep my secret for now."

"Of course; we shall not tell a soul. Oh, if only we could have met sooner! I still don't understand why you couldn't have come to Niton. Once your mother had established herself as a widow—perhaps she really did marry a Jules Ardent; who else would have paid her an income?—she would have been perfectly safe with us. Even Thomas Wentworth wouldn't have dared to hire murderers and send them to Niton. We knew all the farming people; they would have kept an eye out for us. And my aunt was quite fearless; she kept an old blunderbuss in the scullery, in case of burglars, and I am sure she would have used it. 'Any ruffian shows his face around here, I'll have him locked up before you can say Jack Robinson.' That's what Aunt Vida would have said. So how could Rosina have felt safer abroad, especially after what happened to poor Clarissa?"

Lucia shook her head in bewilderment. "I can only think that she was more afraid of meeting people from her past—like that awful Mrs Traill and her daughter—than of her father."

"But if everybody knew her as Mme Ardent—why should she have cared what the Traills thought? Compared to the risk of being murdered in some lawless place? *You* believed your father was Jules Ardent, until today. It makes no sense."

I felt another horrid pang of doubt: how could I be certain that all this was *not* simply a bizarre coincidence?

"I am not sure I ever did believe in him," said Lucia, "not wholly. Mama was always so vague; I could never picture him."

"It was the same with my father," I said. The thought was somehow reassuring, but my doubts persisted, until I remembered where she was staying.

"Lucia," I said, "where exactly in Marylebone is your hotel?"

"In Great Portland Street."

"Which is next but one to Portland Place."

Her eyes widened.

"Even when I saw the letters, I did not realise—it just seemed natural that I should have chosen that place. I *must* have been drawn there."

"Just as you knew—without realising that you knew—Thomas Wentworth's name."

"And what else is lurking in the dark corners of my mind, waiting for me to stumble over? I don't like it. Still"—she set her chin, and made a banishing gesture—"no matter what we find, we have each other now."

My uncle was quite bewildered by the prospect of anyone—let alone a young woman I had scarcely met—dining with us, but Lucia was so charming, and asked so many questions about the bookshop, that I feared we would never escape. Uncle Josiah, to my relief, showed no more interest in her history than he had ever shown in mine. I had always striven to please him, but now I found myself resolved that in the matter of Lucia's staying, I would not give way, no matter how many objections he raised; indeed I promised her, as soon as we were alone again, that I would secure my uncle's permission the following morning.

It was after eight o'clock before we left the table; I expected her to say that she must return to her hotel, but Charlotte had lit the fire in my sitting room, and Lucia showed no inclination to leave. The firelight glowed upon her cheek and in her hair, sparking red and copper and burnt gold when she turned her head. The French intonation seemed to have faded from her voice, or perhaps I had simply grown accustomed to it. I longed to hear more about her life with Rosina, which I could not picture with any distinctness, but I did not like to press her, imagining how I would feel if my own history had just unravelled before my eyes. For her part, she wanted to know everything, no matter how trivial or mundane, about my childhood in Niton; when I showed her my dragonfly brooch, she gazed at it like a holy relic, turning it slowly in her fingers so that its jewelled eyes burned crimson in the firelight.

We gave no thought to the time until the distant sound of the hall clock striking ten brought her hand to her mouth.

"Georgina—I had quite forgotten. The hotel locks its doors at ten; what am I to do?"

"You must stay here," I said. "We can make up the sofa as a bed—or, if you do not mind, you are welcome to share mine."

She accepted gratefully; I fetched her a nightgown and left her to change in front of the fire while I undressed in my bedroom, by the light of the two candles above my dressing table. As soon as I had put on my own nightgown, I opened the door again to let her know that she might enter, and began brushing my hair in front of the mirror.

"Let me do that," said a soft voice in my ear, as the twin of my reflection appeared above my own. I turned with a start, relieved to see that Lucia was actually there; in the wavering depths of the mirror, the likeness was positively uncanny.

"I am so sorry; I must have tapped too softly. I didn't mean to startle you." She took the brush from my hand and continued while I gazed, half hypnotised, at her reflected self, who smiled when our eyes met, exactly as if my imaginary sister had come to life.

When she had finished, we changed places, but the change in the mirror was scarcely perceptible, which made the sensation all the more dreamlike. I had not done this since my mother died, and I had forgotten the intimacy of it: the soft tug and crackle of the brush, the warm scent rising from her hair. After a little, her eyelids drooped, and then closed, but small responsive movements of her head, and the smile that played about her lips, told me that she was not asleep.

At last I set the brush aside. Lucia rose to her feet and embraced me, murmuring, "I did not realise how lonely I have been." She went over to the bed and settled herself in it like a child, her faced turned toward the light. I left one candle burning and slipped in beside her so that we were face to face, each with an arm around the other. Her eyes closed again; within five minutes she was fast asleep, but I kept myself awake for a long time, feeling the soft rise and fall of her breast against mine, her breath stirring my hair. This, I thought, is what people must mean by wedded bliss. But would it be the same with a man? I remembered the bull-calf in the field, and my aunt saying, "Same with humans—never cared for the idea myself." Most novels ended in wedded bliss, but novelists never mentioned the bull-calf. I had always imagined something rough and clumsy and painful; now, bathed in the warmth of Lucia's body, I knew that this was everything I had hungered for, safe within the circle of my arms.

I would happily have stayed awake all night, but sleep at last overcame me, until I woke in darkness to feel Lucia, now lying with her back to me, struggling in the grip of a nightmare. Her voice rose to a shriek; for a moment she fought to push my arm away, then turned, shivering, into my embrace. "Hush, Lucia, hush," I murmured. "You are safe now." I stroked her hair and drew her close, and felt the answering pressure of her lips before her breathing slowed and settled again. Again I strove to keep awake, breathing the scent of her hair and picturing our life together, in a cottage by the sea . . . Uncle Josiah had managed perfectly well before I came here and could surely do so again . . . perhaps at Nettleford?—we must visit, at least, and see the house where I was born . . . or on the Isle of Wight, though not so close to the cliff this time . . .

I woke to grey twilight and the smell of guttered candlewax, alone with the fear that Lucia had been nothing but a dream. Springing out of bed, with my heart pounding wildly, I ran to my sitting room. There was no trace of Lucia; except for my nightgown, neatly folded on the end of the sofa. And I had not even asked her the name of her hotel . . . I sank down upon the sofa, pressing the gown to my face.

Out of it fluttered a slip of paper, on which was written in faint pencil, in a hand not unlike my own: "A thousand thanks—I did not want to wake you. I shall come to the shop this afternoon. L."

Persuading Uncle Josiah proved even harder than I anticipated. I cornered him at breakfast, as I had promised, even though I was more than half afraid that Lucia would change her mind about staying—assuming she had not vanished like a fairy. But, I told myself, if she does still want to stay and I have not spoken to him, she may think that I do not really want her to. And so I steeled myself to interrupt—he was intent on a catalogue that had just arrived in the post—by asking if he had liked Miss Ardent.

"Yes, my dear," he said without looking up, "a charming young lady."

"I am delighted you think so, Uncle, because she is coming to stay with us."

He set down his magnifying glass and peered at me in absolute bewilderment.

"I don't understand."

"Miss Ardent is coming to stay with us," I repeated. "In the spare bedroom, upstairs."

"But, Georgina, you cannot be serious. It is out of the question; we cannot have people staying here."

"Why not, Uncle?"

"Why not? The expense, the inconvenience, the . . ." He threw up his hands in a helpless gesture. I had thought, watching him at dinner with Lucia the night before, how much frailer he had grown in the year I had lived with him. His skull was now entirely bare; even his drooping white moustache seemed thinner. My heart smote me, but I would not be put off.

"There will be no expense, Uncle; Lucia will contribute fifteen shillings a week, just as I do, which is more than enough to pay for her keep."

The last part, at least, was true; I had resolved to pay him myself, without telling her. It would leave me less than ten shillings a week, but I did not care.

"And there will be no inconvenience, either; Lucia will help in the shop, when she can, and we will take our meals upstairs in my sitting room, so that you can read at table in peace, without being disturbed by our chatter."

"Well—I shall think about it," he said, folding his catalogue.

"No, Uncle, we must decide now. She is staying in a hotel, and she needs a home."

"Mrs Eddowes will not like it—she will complain."

"I will deal with Mrs Eddowes," I said, realising to my surprise that I meant it.

"But, but—we know nothing about Miss Ardent."

"I know already that she is my dearest friend," I said firmly. "She and I have a great deal in common."

"No, no, no; I really cannot allow it. The inconvenience has already begun; I was very surprised, Georgina, to find the shop closed when I returned from yesterday's sale. If you are going to be gadding about with Miss Ardent when you should be minding the shop . . . and now I must get on."

"Uncle," I said breathlessly, "if you will not allow Lucia to stay, then I must leave your house. I shall always be grateful to you for taking me in, but I have been very unhappy, and desperately lonely here, and without Lucia's company, I can bear it no longer."

He sank back into his chair, with one hand pressed against his heart.

"But, Georgina, what has possessed you? I had no idea you were unhappy. If you wished to take an afternoon off, you had only to say so. How will I manage without you? The orders . . . the parcels! How will I ever get out to a sale?"

He looked and sounded so feeble that I feared he might collapse on the spot. If he does, I thought, I will be wholly to blame: I encouraged him to dismiss the boy, and I insisted upon helping in the shop; of course he has grown to depend upon me. But the thought of Lucia spurred me onward.

"You managed perfectly well before, Uncle. We can easily find you someone else to do the parcels and mind the shop."

"But he would want to be paid! I cannot afford the expense!"

"In that case, Uncle, you have only to agree that Lucia may live with us."

"Oh very well, very well, if you insist. But it is really most . . . most inconvenient."

"You will not be inconvenienced in the slightest, Uncle. Everything will be exactly the same."

"I do not see how, but I suppose I must put up with it."

He rose unsteadily to his feet and shuffled out of the room, leaving me shaken by my own boldness and wondering if I had grown callous and hard-hearted.

Thursday, 12 October

It is after midnight. Lucia is (or so I imagine) asleep in her room, which is already quite transformed; it is such a delight to have her here, and I know that she shares my feeling. Such a contrast to yesterday: Uncle was wounded and huffish all morning; then, as the afternoon dragged on and still Lucia did not return, I paced about the empty shop like a caged animal, imagining all sorts of catastrophes.

When at last she appeared in the doorway, I confess I shed tears of joy, and then felt very ashamed of myself: she had woken very early and did not want to disturb me. She had been walking and thinking all day, she said, reliving her life as if it were someone else's. Charlotte and I had aired her room and made up the bed, but she chose to spend one more night in the hotel, "to prove to myself that I am not afraid to be alone," she said, "now that I know I don't have to be." I spent the evening composing a letter to Mr Lovell, and tossed and turned most of the night . . . but she is here now, and safe, and that is all that matters.

Wednesday, 18 October

It is only a week since Lucia appeared in the shop, and already I cannot imagine life without her. The likeness astonishes me more every day. Uncle cannot tell us apart, and nor, I think, can Mrs Eddowes; not that she would care. Lucia wears my clothes, having so few of her own apart from the gorgeous peacock gown; she is having two new dresses made in the same pattern as my own. When I teased her about it, she smiled and said, "Yes, I am a chameleon; I take on the colour of my surroundings." We often wonder whether our mothers resembled each other as closely as we do, but without so much as a miniature between us, we can only speculate. Lucia is always constrained when she talks of "Mama"—the mother she remembers—whereas she will speculate freely about "Rosina," as if they were quite separate beings. She finds my childhood inexhaustibly fascinating, and steers the conversation back to me at every opportunity. Mr Lovell has not yet replied, so we have nothing more to go upon.

Uncle is still being huffish and put upon with me (or with Lucia, when he confuses us—she takes it in very good part). I should never have promised him that everything would stay the same. He sighs ostentatiously at the smallest change to his routine, and reminds me at least twice a day that he is far too old to manage without me. I had selfishly imagined that Lucia and I would look after the shop together, but she prefers to walk alone in the afternoons. She is very tactful about it, but I can tell that she craves solitude in which to reflect. "It is like remembering two different lives at once," she said yesterday, "and wondering which of them is mine," but she will not be drawn beyond generalities.

I worry about her wandering the city alone, with very little idea of where her feet are carrying her; she insists that she is not afraid of Thomas Wentworth—or anybody—but is she simply putting on a brave show for my sake? I cannot tell. I suspect she broods, as I would surely do in her place, over the dark strain in the Mordaunt blood, and whether it runs in her veins, but of course I dare not speak of that in case I am mistaken. Sometimes, when her face is shadowed, a chill comes over me, and I fear she would have been happier if we had never met.

I understand completely why she needs this time alone; yet I long to be of more comfort to her: I would happily spend every waking— and sleeping—minute beside her. Every smile, every caress, every kiss, is precious to me: friends and cousins in novels are always kissing and embracing, but every evening—the time I most look forward to—when we embrace and say good night, I long to say, Come to bed with me, and let me hold you as I did that first night.

On Sunday I summoned the courage to say, "Lucia, I know you suffer from nightmares; why don't you stay with me, and then I can comfort you?" She smiled and caressed me, and seemed to hesitate before she replied, "Thank you, dearest cousin, but I'm sure I shall sleep soundly tonight." I am afraid to ask her again, in case she should think—I am not even sure what. Is it wrong of me to feel as I do? Am I like Narcissus, falling in love with my own reflection?

Thursday, 19 October

Today, for once, Uncle Josiah did not go out; he was expecting one of his oldest clients, and said I might take the afternoon off. Lucia, to my delight, insisted that I accompany her. We walked up to Regent's Park, arm in arm, and wandered around until we came upon a little grotto with a seat inside, just out of sight of the path. This, surely, was where Rosina and Felix Mordaunt had sat and talked. There was even a coffee stall nearby, kept by a wizened old man who said he had been there twenty-seven years, perhaps the very same one; it was like being served by a ghost.

We took our tea back to the grotto and sat down on the bench, which was only just wide enough for two. Our shoulders were touching; I took my cup in my left hand so as not to jostle Lucia, and edged a little closer to her, until it came to me that this was how Rosina must have felt, sitting in this exact spot, with Felix Mordaunt beside her.

"Have you ever been in love, Georgina?" said Lucia, as if she had read my thought.

I started, almost spilling my tea, and blushed.

"Not before—I mean, no, no, I haven't."

"But do you think about marriage—do you long to be married, to have children?"

"I don't think I do, no. I—I don't think I have a very high opinion of men. Our little household at Niton seemed very complete, even after Mama died. I knew when I was older that there was *something* I yearned for, and I vaguely assumed it must be marriage, but I have never met—never even seen a man I could imagine marrying. As for children, I know that I am supposed to long for them, but I don't think I actually do; I can't even imagine what it would feel like. I feel—I feel entirely content, sitting here with you."

I felt myself blushing even more.

"And you, Lucia?"

"Oh, I have fancied myself in love with various young men, but like you, I could never imagine marrying any of them. And I am accustomed to freedom, to making my own way in the world; I will not surrender that lightly. I wish I could live many lives, and be many different people; I should like to know what it feels like to be rich, to go to wonderful balls and banquets, and wear extravagant clothes, and be admired by everybody; but only for the experience: to walk on stage, so to speak, with the cream of society, play my part to perfection, and slip away again. Perhaps we shall do such things together, one day; it is what fascinates me about being an actress. But the theatre is so artificial, so mannered; I should love to be an actress in real life. The secret of acting, I feel sure, is to become the person you mean to play; not simply *pretend* to be them, but to cast off your usual self as completely as you shed one costume and put on another."

"It sounds fascinating, but I have no talent for acting."

"I am sure you have. Your uncle is always saying he could not manage without you; let us prove him wrong by changing places for a day. I will be you, and do the parcels and mind the shop; you shall wear my peacock blue, and I shall make up your face a little—in the most delicate fashion—and I will wager that even Charlotte will not realise what we have done."

"Yes, let us try it," I said, feeling my heartbeat quicken at the prospect. "What will you wager?"

"What would you most like to win?"

I longed to say, "Your heart," but could only blush, and try to hide my face in my cup.

"Perhaps you have won it already," she said, touching my wrist with the tip of her gloved finger. "We shall change places tomorrow. And if we succeed, we shall not tell anyone, just yet; it will be another of our secrets."

Saturday, 21 October

Lucia was right; Charlotte addressed me as "Miss Ardent" from the moment we came downstairs. Aunt Vida used to say that only vain, foolish women use powder and paint, but when Lucia allowed me to look in the glass, I confess I was very much taken with the result: she had made my eyes darker and more luminous, my eyebrows finer; my cheekbones more prominent, but so subtly that I could scarcely tell how it was done. And the peacock blue gown suited me to perfection. She had only watched me do the parcels once, but she carried it off flawlessly, sweetly turning aside my uncle's peevishness. She even insisted that I should go out for the afternoon while she kept the shop; I would far rather have stayed, but she said firmly, "No, Lucia; it is very kind of you to offer, but you must have some time to yourself."

We continued to play each other even when we were alone; I found it extraordinarily exciting, and (in a brief lapse of concentration) told her so. "You see?" she replied. "It is just as I promised; that is the delight of acting. Of course, you and I are so alike that it is easy for us to change places. And now, Lucia . . ." I never contradict her when she says we are alike, because it pleases me, but—despite the extraordinary resemblance—I am not at all sure that we *are* alike. And yet I could not say how we differ. Lucia is still a mystery to me—I feel that she is opaque where I am transparent, and it is the mystery that fascinates me.

When it came time for bed, we rose and embraced as usual, standing by the sitting-room fire—only not as usual, for she held me closer than ever before, and murmured, with her lips almost brushing my ear, "Lucia, why don't you sleep with me tonight? Then I can comfort you if you have nightmares."

I was about to say, "Oh, Lucia, I should love to," when I remembered that I was supposed to answer for her, not myself. My heart sank; the words died on my lips. Was she hoping I would say yes? Or subtly rebuking me for being too forward? I drew back, her hands still warm upon my shoulders. A faint, teasing smile flickered about her mouth; she regarded me as a teacher might regard a prize pupil faltering over a recitation.

"Thank you, dearest cousin, but I'm sure I shall sleep soundly tonight." Her smile broadened; I had won the prize, but lost what I most desired.

"Good night, dearest cousin," she said, drawing me close again, and adding, in a low, throaty whisper, "We shall make an actress of you yet." Her lips brushed mine as she turned toward the door. But instead of crossing to the stairs, she turned right, and disappeared in the direction of my own room. A moment later I heard my door open and close.

I was halfway down the stairs when I remembered my writing case. The key was around my neck—the chain is entirely hidden when I am dressed, so Lucia had not asked for it—but had I locked my journal away in the case, and put the case back in the drawer as usual, or was it lying on my writing table? Should I go up and make sure? But if I knocked, Lucia would think . . . She would think, at the very least, that I had something to hide. *You always lock your journal away*, I told myself. *The reason you cannot remember is that you do it automatically.* But I could not actually picture myself turning the key, and I hovered on the stairs for a long time before I went miserably on down to her room, where I lay awake most of the night, alternately tormenting myself by imagining what I had forfeited—perhaps she had *wanted* me to say yes, and was now lying awake in my bed, thinking that *I* did not want *her*—and enduring agonies of humiliation at the thought of her reading my journal. In the end I overslept, to find my bedroom empty, my writing case safely locked away, and Lucia already downstairs, back in her own character and behaving as if we had never so much as thought of impersonating each other.

Monday, 23 October

Mr Lovell has replied at last, apologising for the delay: it seems that Mr Wetherell has suffered another stroke, and retired from the practice, leaving Mr Lovell in sole charge of his clients. Lucia and I were at breakfast when the letter arrived; she watched eagerly as I opened it, but her face fell as I began to read aloud:

I deeply regret that your late mother's instructions expressly prohibit me from forwarding the packet as you request. You say that your circumstances have changed in a way that makes it vital that you see the remaining papers; I wonder whether you could be more explicit about the nature of that change? I should add that the remainder of the bequest consists of a single sealed packet. Beyond the impression that it contains papers or documents, I know nothing of its contents. I think I may indicate, without exceeding my instructions, that in the event of your death—or certain other events, which I am forbidden to disclose—the packet is to be destroyed unopened. If you wish to instruct me on any other matter, I shall, of course, be honoured to act for you . . .

"I suppose it was foolish of me to hope," she said, with a look of desolation that pierced my heart.

"You musn't despair, Lucia. You *shall* see what is in that packet, if I have to engage a burglar to steal it from Mr Lovell's office. But we shan't need a burglar; he is weakening, you can see. Inviting me to be more explicit: that is surely a hint. Lucia, we must tell him that we have met; I am certain that is what my mother intended."

"Perhaps you are right," she said, "but I would feel happier if we had met him—so that I could feel sure of his discretion."

"Then let us go down to Plymouth and see him," I said.

"But your uncle—he will be most put out."

"Uncle Josiah will have to manage without us soon enough."

"But not like this; you must break it to him gently, for your own sake. And what does Mr Lovell mean by 'certain other events'? Your mother might have ordered him to destroy the packet if anyone else enquired about it . . . and there is another way. What is the point of your having a solicitor in Plymouth? Why don't we find one here in London and ask Mr Lovell to send the packet to him? A new man would be so much easier to persuade."

I had not thought of this. Her suggestion made obvious sense; yet all my instincts were against it.

"But changing solicitors might be another of those 'events,'" I said, trying to justify my reluctance. "Mr Lovell wants to help us, I am sure of it. If I write to him and say—in the strictest confidence—that you and I have met, and that you are the daughter of Rosina Wentworth, who married Jules Ardent—what harm can come of that?"

"I—I don't know what it is I fear," she said uneasily. "If only I could meet him, then I would know whether to trust him with my secret . . ."

"But Lucia, we needn't tell him. He doesn't know what's in the packet; as far as he is concerned, you are the legitimate daughter of Jules Ardent, who married Rosina Wentworth in France. Mama wouldn't have told him any more than that."

"But what if we are wrong, and this is *not* the condition she laid down?"

"Then I will go down to Plymouth and tell Mr Lovell that I shan't leave his office until he hands over the packet."

"You are right," she said, taking a deep breath and lifting her chin. "I know I am being foolish—it is only that . . . Suppose I were to go to Plymouth in your place? Mr Lovell has never met you, after all."

"But Lucia, he might want you to sign something—"

"I am sure I could imitate your signature, if I practised a little."

"No, dearest, no, I won't have it. If Mr Lovell so much as suspected, he might destroy the papers; you could even be sent to prison.

No, *I* will go down to see him—I need only be away one night—and, if you are sure you don't mind, you can pretend to be me again, and then Uncle Josiah will have nothing to complain of. You are right: I must give him time to get used to the idea and find someone to help in the shop, but I mean to tell him as soon as I return from Plymouth. And I promise you, Lucia, if I have the slightest reservation about Mr Lovell, he will never know of your existence."

"But then how will you persuade him to hand over the packet?"

"You mustn't fret, Lucia. Mr Lovell wants to help us; I feel it in my bones. I promise I shan't return empty-handed."

Her face was still troubled, but I had confidence enough for two, and my letter to Mr Lovell was in the post an hour later.

Wednesday, 25 October

Mr Lovell has replied by return; a good omen. My appointment is for two o'clock on Monday. He even advises about trains, and recommends Dawlish's Private Hotel, which is only fifty yards from his office. I had hoped to return that night, but the London express leaves Plymouth at four forty-two, and I cannot be sure of catching it; it may take more than one visit to persuade him.

Lucia was very subdued all day; I tried several times to persuade her to come with me, but she assured me that she was happy to stay with Uncle Josiah. "It is nothing; just low spirits; it will pass," she kept saying, until at last, as we were about to retire, I took her in my arms and implored her to tell me what was wrong.

"It is nothing, only . . . I have no right to ask, but I should have loved to be there when you opened the packet."

"You have every right," I said, reproaching myself for being so obtuse. "Come with me, and we shall open it together."

"No, one of us must stay with your uncle."

"Then I shan't open the packet until we are together again."

Her face lit up at this, and she kissed me very warmly.

"Thank you, Georgina. Shall we tell your uncle in the morning that I will be going away for a little while? In fact, why don't you travel under my name?—not with the lawyer, of course, but at the hotel? You shall wear my things, and take my travelling-case; then the illusion will be complete, and even Charlotte will not suspect."

Dawlish's Private Hotel,
George Street,
Plymouth
Monday, 30 October

There is so much to record, but I must begin with my interview with Mr Lovell, while it is fresh in my mind. His rooms are in a high, narrow building of dark brown stone; an elderly clerk led me up several flights of stairs to a landing, where I was warmly greeted by Mr Lovell himself. My intuition was right: he is tall and gangly and fresh-faced, and looks no more than twenty-five, though I think he must be at least thirty. His office was lined on three sides with bookshelves, filled with an extraordinary array of objects: stones, shells, birds' eggs, paperweights by the dozen, fishhooks, brass instruments, lumps of coloured glass, ornaments of every size and shape—as well as the books, which are crammed in higgledy-piggledy. His desk was heaped with bundles of papers, interspersed with yet more books, many of them lying open and face-down. An armchair stood in a patch of sunlight by the window.

"I am afraid we are all at sixes and sevens, Miss Ferrars," he said, ushering me to the armchair. Henry Lovell, I could not help noticing, is really quite handsome. He has thick fair hair, rather dishevelled, and a long, clean-shaven face, slightly reddened around the jaw as if the razor irritates his skin. His suit—a coarse brown tweed, patched with leather at the elbows—looked like something a farmer might wear. He dragged an upright chair across the carpet and settled, or rather draped, himself upon it, and for the next few minutes we talked about my journey, and about Mr Wetherell's illness: despite his remark about sixes and sevens, it soon became clear that Mr Lovell had been doing most of the work of the practice for several years now—my mother's estate was one of the few that Mr Wetherell had kept to himself—and that his room is in permanent chaos.

By the end of our small-talk, I had resolved to trust him with everything except the secret of Lucia's birth, which I had promised not to reveal unless there was no other way of securing the papers. He listened closely, and without interjecting, to the account I had rehearsed on the journey down, in which Rosina had fled from a cruel and violent father, married Jules Ardent in France—I made no mention of

Felix Mordaunt—and refused ever afterward to speak of her child-hood.

"So you see, Mr Lovell," I concluded, "why I am sure that my mother would want me to have that packet, now that my cousin and I have met."

He had listened intently, without once interrupting, and remained silent for a little, regarding me with troubled eyes.

"I am very sorry, Miss Ferrars," he said at last, "but your mother's instructions were quite explicit, and the condition she specified has nothing to do with your cousin, Miss Ardent. I don't for a moment doubt that your mother would have *wanted* you to have the packet in the circumstances you describe, but the law, alas, compels me to abide by the letter, rather than the spirit, of her wishes in the matter."

"Then surely, Mr Lovell, you can at least tell me what the condition *is*."

"I am afraid not. Your mother was, as I say, absolutely explicit. Unless your circumstances should change in a very particular way, I may not give you the packet, or reveal to you anything whatsoever about the bequest. If I had not made the unpardonable error of sending you those letters, you would never have known of its existence."

"Unless my circumstances should change in a very particular way," I repeated thoughtfully.

"Yes; that is correct."

"But how would you know, Mr Lovell, if that change were to occur? Wouldn't my mother have wanted to be sure that you *did* know?"

"Well, yes," he said uneasily. "But really, Miss Ferrars, I should not be discussing this at all—"

"I appreciate that, Mr Lovell, but I am your client, too."

"Yes, and it puts me in something of a quandary." He gave me a wry smile, in which I detected a hint of encouragement. *Unless your circumstances should change* . . . Of course! How could I have been so obtuse? I had a sudden vivid recollection of Aunt Vida on her death-bed, saying, "You're a handsome gel, not like me—you'll have offers . . . Write to Mr Wetherell—tell him who you're marrying. Papers to draw up . . ."

"I have guessed the condition, Mr Lovell. I am to have the packet if I marry—or become engaged to marry."

Now he looked deeply uncomfortable.

"Well, yes, but—"

"But?"

"I take it, Miss Ferrars," he said, glancing at my left hand, "that you are not engaged—or contemplating an engagement?"

"Certainly not," I said.

"Then I fear it is absolutely impossible for me to hand over the packet."

"But if I *were* to become engaged . . ." To an obliging young man, I thought, willing to play the part . . . or why not simply invent one?

"Then you should write and tell me, yes. But that in itself would be exceedingly unlikely—astonishingly unlikely—to fulfill the condition. And now, Miss Ferrars, I really cannot say any more . . ."

Astonishing unlikely . . . "Tell him *who* you're marrying," Aunt Vida had said . . .

"I am to have the packet if I become engaged to someone in particular," I said flatly. "Mr Lovell, you have been so helpful; will you not take the last step and tell me who it is?"

"That, Miss Ferrars, I absolutely cannot do. I have trespassed thus far because I am to blame for your receiving those letters in the first place. But carelessness is one thing; knowingly breaching a client's trust is quite another. I should deserve to be struck off if I did any such thing."

A small silence followed. Our eyes met, and I smiled encouragingly.

"But, Mr Lovell, you would not be breaching my mother's trust. It is absolutely essential, for my own peace of mind and Lu—Miss Ardent's—that I should see what is in that packet, and if my mother were here now, she would tell you so herself."

"Are you quite certain of that, Miss Ferrars?"

"Of course I am, Mr Lovell. Don't you think I know what my own mother would have wanted?"

"I meant, are you sure that seeing those papers *would* bring you peace of mind?" he said.

"You said in your letter, Mr Lovell, that you didn't know what the packet contained."

"Nor do I. But—no, I am sorry; it is quite impossible. Now really,

Miss Ferrars, there is nothing more I can tell you. Would you care for some tea?"

"Yes, I should, thank you."

"Then pray excuse me one moment." He rose with evident relief and left the room.

All I need do, I thought, is ask the right question. A man Mama did not want me to marry—or did not want me to grow up and marry without reading the rest of the papers—which *must* have to do with Rosina and Lucia, Thomas Wentworth, and Felix Mordaunt . . . Could Thomas Wentworth have remarried and had a son? Then why all the secrecy? Why had Mama, or Aunt Vida, not simply warned me against him? And why on earth would Mama have feared that, of all the eligible men in the kingdom, I would choose this particular one? She had sealed the packet at least ten years ago: he might easily have married someone else by now. Or died.

And there was something else . . . something Mr Lovell had said in his last letter, which I had brought with me. "In the event of your death—or certain other events, which I am forbidden to disclose—the packet is to be destroyed unopened." "Certain other events" . . . Surely the man's death. So he must still be alive!

But Mr Lovell had written "events." I had just realised what it must mean when he returned to his chair.

"Tea won't be long," he said, glancing uneasily at the paper on my knee.

"I am sorry to plague you," I said, "but I have divined so much that you may as well tell me the rest. You are to give me the packet only if I become engaged to marry a certain man"—his expression changed at this, in a way I could not interpret. "If he dies—or if I marry anyone *but* this man—you are to destroy it unopened. I am right so far, am I not?"

He groaned and ran his hands through his hair.

"This is my own fault, Miss Ferrars; I have dug myself a pit, and fallen into it; but I cannot answer you."

"Then I am sorry for you, Mr Lovell, for I have vowed not to leave Plymouth without that packet."

"You are a very determined young woman, Miss Ferrars," he said with a rueful smile.

"You may think it unbecoming—"

"I did not say that, Miss Ferrars, nor did I mean it. On the contrary," he said warmly, "you have every right to press me. But the fact remains: I am bound by my oath of office not to surrender that packet unless your mother's terms are met."

"But surely, Mr Lovell, if her intention was to save me from marrying this man, she would want you to tell me his name—now that you have revealed so much?"

"You would make a formidable barrister," he said, ruffling his hair again. "But all I can do—speaking from the heart, and not simply as a lawyer—is advise you to trust in your mother's judgement. At least some good has come of my carelessness; it has brought you and your cousin together, and I can see that you are deeply attached to her. Indeed—am I right in feeling that you are here for her sake rather than your own?"

"For both our sakes," I said, avoiding his eye as I felt my colour rising.

"All the same, Miss Ferrars, given what you have told me, I don't see how your cousin's happiness can possibly depend upon the contents of that packet. I do earnestly advise you to trust in your mother and leave things as they are—ah, thank you, Mr Pritchard," he said, springing from his chair as the elderly clerk appeared with a tray.

I was glad of the interval, for I could not decide what to do next. Instinct warned me that revealing Lucia's secret would not be enough to sway him; I would have to divine the forbidden suitor's name or coax Mr Lovell into revealing it . . . and then I saw how it might be done.

"Tell me, Mr Lovell," I said when he was seated again, "have you always lived in Plymouth?" The look of relief on his face was almost comical, and for the next few minutes I encouraged him to talk about himself. He had indeed grown up in Plymouth, and until quite recently had lived at home with his parents—his father had also been a solicitor—and his two youngest sisters; there were two married sisters and a brother, all living within twenty miles of the town. His parents had lately retired to the village of Noss Mayo, leaving Mr Lovell in bachelor quarters near the Hoe. He spoke of them all with great affection, and sounded entirely content with his lot.

"But, Miss Ferrars," he said suddenly, "I am forgetting my duty; you did not come all this way to listen to my ramblings."

"It is a pleasure to hear about your family. But yes, there is something else: a separate matter."

"You have only to name it," he said eagerly.

"There are two men about whom I should like some information; I should like to know if either of them is still alive, and if so, where they are living. But I don't want either of them to know of my enquiry."

His face, which had cleared at the words "a separate matter," fell again.

"And their names?"

"The first," I said, studying him closely, "is Thomas Wentworth—Rosina Wentworth's father."

"That," he said uneasily, "I may be able to help you with. What else can you tell me about him?"

"Only that he was wealthy—a businessman or financier of some sort—and lived in Portland Place, at least from 1859 until 1860. And he had an elder daughter, Clarissa, who eloped in the summer of 1859; she and her lover, a man called George Harrington, were—they died together in an accident in Rome, in October of that year; there was something about it in *The Times*."

"I see." He fetched a piece of paper from his desk and scribbled a few lines on it, looking troubled, but not unduly alarmed. "And the other?"

"Felix Mordaunt, of Tregannon House, in Cornwall."

This time the shock was palpable; he bent over his paper, writing studiously, but the rash along his jaw was suddenly livid.

I had guessed the riddle, but it made no sense. Felix Mordaunt might have been a notorious libertine, but how could Mama possibly have imagined that of all the men in the kingdom, I would meet and marry *him*? And again, even if she had, why not simply warn me herself?

"May I ask why?" he said, without raising his eyes from the page.

I was about to say, *Because he is the man my mother named*, but realised I did not actually know that for certain.

"Oh—a family connection," I replied as coolly as I could manage.

"My aunt mentioned the name once or twice; is it familiar to you, Mr Lovell?"

His head flew up, his face reddening with anger.

"If you *knew*, Miss Ferrars, then why? — " His mouth snapped shut as realisation dawned.

"I assure you, Mr Lovell, that when I arrived here this afternoon, I had not the faintest suspicion. If you had not led me to the answer, I should never have guessed. But now that you *have* told me — "

Once again he groaned and ran his hands through his hair, rumpling it so wildly that I feared it would come out in tufts.

"Will you tell me," he said at last, "how you arrived at that name?"

"I cannot do that, Mr Lovell, without betraying a confidence. But I know exactly why my mother did not want me to marry this man" — again that indecipherable flicker of reaction — "and I can assure you that my happiness, and that of my cousin, depends upon your handing over that packet, as my mother would instruct you to do, if only she were here. And I promise you — I will swear on the Bible, if you wish — that no one except Lucia and I will ever know you gave it to me."

He leant back in his chair, swirling the dregs in the bottom of his teacup.

"I confess, Miss Ferrars, that I simply don't know what to do. Sometimes I think I am not cut out for the law . . . But the fact remains: the terms of your mother's bequest have not been met, and again I urge you to trust in her judgement. You say that your happiness depends upon it, but you don't know what that packet contains, any more than I do, and you may be mistaken."

"I am sorry, Mr Lovell, but my mind is made up."

"I feared as much. Will you allow me twenty-four hours to think it over?"

"Might I be able to see you in the morning? I should like to be home tomorrow night."

"I am afraid that every minute of the morning is spoken for," he said. "But I shall be free by half past two at the latest."

He rose and offered his hand, which was reassuringly warm and dry, to help me up, and for a moment we stood smiling at each other, our hands still clasped.

"You have been very kind," I said as he accompanied me to the landing, "and exceedingly forbearing; far more than I deserve."

"On the contrary, Miss Ferrars, I have nothing but admiration for you. Until tomorrow, then, at half past two."

I had gone halfway down the stairs before I realised that I was quite unsteady on my feet, and trembling with emotion.

It is only nine o'clock, but the hotel is completely silent; not surprisingly, as there is only one other guest. My room is quite large, and perfectly comfortable; Mrs Gifford, the proprietor—she has the most extraordinarily elaborate coiffure of snow-white hair—is most obliging. From my window I can see a line of gaslamps stretching away in both directions along the empty street.

After I had written down everything I could recall of the interview, I put on my cloak (or rather, Lucia's cloak) and set out again, meaning to walk down to the Hoe and look at the sea. But the light was fading, and the evening chill had settled, so I went only as far as the telegraph office on Royal Parade—it felt very strange, addressing a telegram to myself—to let Lucia know that I hoped to be home tomorrow night. Mrs Gifford, who was hovering in the foyer when I returned, invited me to take tea by the sitting-room fire; I was about to decline when it occurred to me that she might know something of the Mordaunt family.

The sitting room is as dismal as most of its kind; I remember half a dozen like it from my travels with my aunt: crammed with chairs and sofas in faded Regency plush, along with their attendant footstools and side tables. There are the usual heavy maroon curtains shrouding a bow-fronted window; the wallpaper, also faded and Regency, is on the verge of peeling. But the fire was crackling cheerfully, and to forestall any more questions about myself (I *must* learn to answer to "Miss Ardent" without the slightest hesitation) I asked her at once about the Mordaunts of Tregannon House.

"Mordaunt, Mordaunt . . . No, I can't say that I do," she replied, taking the chair beside me. "But Tregannon—now, that rings a bell. There's an asylum at Liskeard of that name."

So Edmund Mordaunt must have prevailed, I thought.

"I think that might be it," I said. "Can you tell me where Liskeard is?"

"About twenty miles to the west, Miss Ardent, just this side of Bodmin Moor."

"I think the Mordaunt family may own Tregannon Asylum," I said, realising as I spoke that someone had entered the room.

"Ah, Mrs Fairfax," said my hostess, bouncing to her feet. "Would you care to join us for tea? Miss Ardent; Mrs Fairfax."

I had passed her on the stairs that afternoon, on my way to Mr Lovell's office. She had the figure of a young woman, and her hair, a few shades darker than my own, showed no trace of grey. But her face was gaunt, with deep lines scored downward from the corners of her mouth, and bruised pouches like crumpled snakeskin beneath her eyes, which were very dark and lustrous.

As we exchanged greetings, a maid came in and murmured something to Mrs Gifford.

"I am afraid I must leave you," she said, "but do make yourselves comfortable; Martha will bring an extra cup."

I did not want to make conversation with Mrs Fairfax, but there was no escaping short of rudeness, and so I resumed my seat.

"A very comfortable hotel, is it not, Miss Ardent?"

"Yes, very."

"And a fine view of the town; I am in number seven, on the floor above you, I think. Will you be staying long in Plymouth?"

"No — that is to say, I am not sure. And you, Mrs Fairfax?"

"I think I shall stay a few more days . . . Forgive me, Miss Ardent," she said in a lower tone. "I hope you will not think me impertinent, but I could not help overhearing: you were speaking of Tregannon Asylum." Her voice had a throaty, musical quality which seemed vaguely familiar; she must, I thought, have been talking to Mrs Gifford just before I met her on the stairs.

"Yes, that is correct."

"Forgive me; I don't mean to pry. It is only that — I have just been visiting a dear friend there."

I gave her what I hoped was an encouraging look, wondering if I should offer my condolences.

"Oh, it is not a painful duty," she said, smiling. "My friend is a voluntary patient; she can come and go as she pleases. She is prone to nervous exhaustion, and says that a month at Tregannon Asylum is as good as a visit to Baden-Baden."

"So it is not a lunatic asylum, then?"

"Oh yes, there are lunatics confined there—quite separately from the voluntary patients—but they are treated very kindly. Dr Straker, the man in charge, prides himself upon running the most humane and enlightened asylum in the country."

"I believe it is owned by the Mordaunt family," I ventured.

"Yes, Miss Ardent; do you know them?"

"No," I said, rather too hastily. "I—er—I have a friend who is distantly related. And you, Mrs Fairfax, are you acquainted with the family?"

"Not personally, no. But my friend has met Mr Edmund Mordaunt, the present owner—though that was some years ago now; I believe his health is failing, and he seldom leaves his quarters."

"Does he live at the asylum, then?"

"Oh yes; the estate has been in the family for centuries—but perhaps you know that," she added, regarding me curiously. *Trust me; confide in me,* her gaze seemed to say. The pupils of her eyes glowed like polished jet; I could see the pinpoint reflections of the flames burning in their depths.

"My friend has told me a little," I said, as casually as I could manage. "She mentioned a Felix Mordaunt, I think; have you heard of him?"

"No, I don't think I have—unless you mean Frederic Mordaunt, Edmund Mordaunt's nephew, a charming young man: my friend is always singing his praises. He acts as Dr Straker's personal assistant and will presumably inherit the entire estate."

"Edmund Mordaunt has no children of his own, then?"

"No, he never married."

"And Frederic Mordaunt?"

"He, too, is a bachelor, Miss Ardent—and a very eligible one, I am sure," she added, glancing at my left hand.

"I am sure he is," I said mechanically, remembering Mr Lovell, and how his expression had changed at the words "my mother did not want me to marry this man" . . . this man, *this* man . . . and suddenly I saw that Mrs Fairfax had handed me the key to Mr Lovell's strongbox.

"Miss Ardent?"

I realised that I was staring vacantly into the fire.

"I do beg your pardon," I said. "I am a little preoccupied . . . a family matter."

"You mustn't apologise," she said, in a tone that invited confidences. I could not think how to respond to this, and an awkward silence fell, until Mrs Gifford returned with the maid and the tea tray.

It was a bad mistake to call myself Miss Ardent, as I realised from the moment I set foot in the hotel. I could not borrow Lucia's actual history, as it would have made her too anxious: I am supposed to have lost my parents before I could remember, and to have lived with my great-aunt, in various parts of the country, ever since. But Lucia's faith in me is misplaced; I have contradicted myself several times already, and I fear that Mrs Fairfax, at least, suspects me of dissembling. There was another awkward moment in the sitting room, when Mrs Gifford suggested that since Mrs Fairfax and I were the only guests, we might like to share a table at dinner. Travelling as myself, I would have seized the opportunity to press her about the Mordaunts. As it was, I hesitated, and was spared embarrassment only because she happened to be dining with friends. I met her coming upstairs, presumably to change, as I was going down to dinner.

A half-moon is rising above the rooftops opposite; I have scarcely seen a moon since I left Niton, let alone one so clear. Tomorrow I mean to visit Nettleford. There is a ferry across the harbour to Turnchapel, and then a walk of about three miles along the coast; if I leave straight after breakfast, I shall be back well before half past two. I hope Lucia will not mind—mind my not waiting until we can see Nettleford together, that is. It is the perfect way to fill what would otherwise be several long and anxious hours; and of course she would want me to go, just as I would want her to go in my place.

If only she were here with me, my happiness would be complete. But I shall be home tomorrow night, with the packet—I am certain I have guessed the riddle—and we shall open it together. And then we shall leave Gresham's Yard, and never have to be apart again. She said to me last night, as we lay in bed: "You must not be anxious for me, dearest: no matter what we discover, it will be a relief to *know*."

Strange that a quarrel—well, only a spat, really, and only on her side, but horribly distressing all the same—should bring such joy.

It was shortly before bedtime; we were in her room, packing her valise, and were about to close it when I thought of my writing case and brooch, and said I would run upstairs to fetch them.

"But that will spoil the illusion," she said sharply. "If Charlotte notices, she may realise what we've done."

"I am sorry, Lucia," I said, "but I would never travel anywhere without them. They are all I have left from the wreck of our house"—as you know perfectly well, I almost added—"and Charlotte won't know, because I always keep them in the drawer of my writing desk."

She looked, for a moment, quite mutinous; her eyes flashed, and she opened her mouth to protest, then turned on her heel and left the room. I heard her running upstairs, and then my own bedroom door slamming. My heart seemed to shrivel in an instant; I dared not run after her, and sank down on her bed, engulfed in misery.

An eternity later—as it seemed—I felt her arm steal around my shoulders. Looking up blearily, I saw that she had brought my writing case and brooch.

"Forgive me, Georgina," she murmured, drawing me closer. "I am such a stickler for perfection, when it comes to acting a part, that I forgot myself. Of course you must take them."

I allowed myself to be kissed but could not surrender to her embrace. She took me by the shoulders and turned me gently to face her. My happiness, I thought, is utterly in your keeping; but is the same true for you?

"I am so sorry, dearest," she said. "It was not just . . . I know it is foolish, but I am anxious about your going; I could not bear it if anything happened to you."

"Then come with me," I said. "It is not too late."

"No, that would only make it harder for you—when you come to tell your uncle that we are going to live together, I mean—and I won't have that. And I am being foolish; I know it. Only . . . may I sleep with you tonight?"

"Of course you may," I said, all misery forgotten. "But what about Charlotte?"

"I do not care about Charlotte; I want to stay with you, here, tonight, in my bed."

As I was brushing her hair and gazing at her reflection in the mirror, it struck me that something about her appearance had changed since our first night together; something that for a moment eluded me. Her dressing table was the same size and shape as mine; the candles were in much the same places; we were wearing the same nightgowns; yet . . . And then it came to me: the first time, I had been overwhelmed by the resemblance; now, I was conscious only of the differences between us: the shape and set of her eyes, the exact curve of her cheekbones, the play of her expressions; and I was overjoyed at the realisation. I am not like Narcissus, I thought. We *are* different; and that is what draws us together. Our eyes met in the glass, and she made a small kissing gesture with her lips, as if she had divined my thought.

"Lucia," I said, "where would you most like us to live?"

"Where would you, dearest?"

"Somewhere by the sea; but I will be happiest wherever you are happiest."

"And I feel the same. I used to think—I remember saying to you, when we first found each other—that all I craved was to be settled in one place, to put down roots, and never have to move again. But what I really craved was *this*"—she took my hand and pressed it to her breast—"and wherever we are together, that will be our settled place."

Her breast swelled beneath my hand; my heart was suddenly pounding. She rose to her feet and into my arms; our bodies melded together; our lips met and parted, and I was filled with a sweetness beyond imagining. My hands moved of their own accord over her body, discovering, dwelling, delighting; her arms tightened around me; I felt the soft pressure of her tongue against mine; but then she drew back, keeping her hands on my waist and regarding me with huge, troubled eyes. We were both trembling violently.

"I am so sorry," she gasped. "You must not think . . . that I do not want to; I do, but . . ."

"But . . .?"

"I was cruel to you, cruel and hateful: I have Mordaunt blood in my veins."

"Lucia, Lucia, my darling, I don't care whose blood runs in your veins. All that matters is that I love and adore you, and as long as you love me, too—"

"What if I should stop loving you?"

"Then I should die," I said, more seriously than I intended. "But I would never regret loving *you*. And it wasn't the Mordaunt blood; it was only because you are anxious about that packet. Remember what you said: we can face anything, so long as we are together."

"You are so good to me," she said. "Once I *know* . . . I still want to stay with you tonight, only . . ."

"Of course," I said, kissing her gently. "Can we leave the candle burning for a little, so that I can look at you?"

"Yes, my dearest; I should like that too."

I would have been perfectly content to stay side by side, but she took me in her arms and drew me close again, so that we were lying face to face.

"*This* is our settled place," she murmured, "and when you are home again . . ." Her eyelids drooped; a small smile played about her lips, and a few minutes later she was fast asleep. But I lay awake until the candle guttered, softly caressing my beloved, remembering that first night when I had thought no greater joy was possible, dreaming of paradise to come.

Dawlish's Private Hotel
Tuesday, 31 October 1882

I shall be resolute and start at the beginning—perhaps it will help me to decide what I must do.

I slept badly last night—the moon was shining full on my face, but I did not want to draw the curtains—and woke with a headache and no appetite for breakfast. I felt distinctly queasy aboard the ferry, but my spirits lifted on the road to Nettleford, which took me along the coast, through open pasture like the country beyond Chale, only lower and gentler. I had always imagined Nettleford as a smaller version of Niton, with paved streets, and a post office, and an inn like the White Lion, but it proved to be a mere scattering of cottages around a disused church. Several of the cottages were plainly untenanted; smoke was rising from the chimney of another, but as I approached the gate, a dog began barking hysterically. The front door opened a little; a harsh voice commanded the dog to be silent, and a sour-faced, grey-haired woman peered out, regarding me suspiciously.

"And what might you want?"

"I am looking for the house where Dr Ferrars lived—about twenty years ago, but perhaps you might—"

"No one of that name here," she said, and closed the door firmly. I saw a curtain twitch as I retreated.

I went on as far as the church without seeing any other sign of life, and stopped by the lych-gate, contemplating the wilderness within. The graves were overgrown, the headstones flaking and pitted with lichen. As I stood gazing at this dismal scene, my eye was drawn by a name that looked like "Ferrars."

I lifted the latch and pushed at the wooden gate. The hinges groaned; shards of rotting wood fell about my feet; it opened just far enough for me to squeeze through into the churchyard.

The name, I saw as I came closer, was not Ferrars but Fenner—Martha Fenner. "Departed This Life" . . . The rest had crumbled away. Many of the inscriptions were quite illegible, but beneath the opposite wall, about twenty paces away, was a much newer stone, the original pink of the marble still gleaming faintly through the lichen. Trampling down weeds, I made my way over to it.

IN LOVING MEMORY OF
Rosina May Wentworth

b. 23 November 1839
d. 6 March 1861

Dearly Beloved Cousin
Of Emily Ferrars

REST IN PEACE

Useless to dwell upon the hours of fearful speculation that followed. I arrived at Mr Lovell's office half an hour early, certain of only one thing: I could not return to London until I had secured that packet and found out what was in it. I paced about the waiting room, anxiously observed by his clerk, whose name I could not recall, until I heard footsteps bounding up the stairs.

Henry Lovell's face brightened when he caught sight of me, but his smile changed to a look of concern as he showed me into his room.

"Miss Ferrars, is something wrong? You are as white as—as if you had seen a ghost."

All too true, I thought.

"Yes, I have had a shock—something which makes it all the more imperative that I find out what is in that packet."

"I see. But first you must take some refreshment: a glass of wine, perhaps? Tea? Some cake?"

"Thank you, I want nothing; only my mother's bequest."

"Then—can you not tell me what has happened?"

"No, Mr Lovell, I cannot."

Still he seemed to hesitate.

"Mr Lovell," I said, launching upon the speech I had rehearsed many times, "I am afraid I was not entirely frank with you yesterday afternoon."

"I suspected as much. Please be assured, Miss Ferrars, that nothing you say here will ever pass beyond these four walls."

He leant forward encouragingly.

"You asked me if I was engaged to be married, and I said I was not. The truth is, I am secretly engaged to Mr Frederic Mordaunt, of Tregannon House—Tregannon Asylum, as it now is—at Liskeard, in Cornwall."

He recoiled as if I had struck him.

"Miss Ferrars, you cannot be—I am afraid I don't believe you."

"Sir, that is most discourteous!" I replied, with all the indignation I could muster.

"I am very sorry for it, but truly, Miss Ferrars, there is no need for this—this charade. I had already decided to give you the packet."

If he truly meant it, why had he had not said so at the beginning? Was he trying to trap me? I could not take the risk.

"My engagement, sir, is no charade. I did not tell you yesterday because I needed time to reflect. Even Frederic's uncle, Mr Edmund Mordaunt, does not yet know of our engagement. And so, Mr Lovell, my mother's condition is fulfilled. Will you now hand over the packet?"

He rose slowly from his chair, his face a welter of conflicting emotions: doubt, confusion, concern; even, I thought, disappointment.

"Yes, Miss Ferrars, I will. I only wish I knew . . ." I thought he was going to add, "whether to believe you," but he said no more. From the top of an unstable heap of papers on his desk, he picked up a large grey envelope and handed it to me.

It struck me, as I declined another offer of refreshment, that I need not have lied to him.

"If there is anything more I can do, Miss Ferrars," he said as we parted, "anything at all, I hope you will not hesitate to call upon me. Here is my card. I have written my parents' address on the back, and if you should ever find yourself at Noss Mayo, you will always find a welcome there.

"Oh, and there is one thing more. You asked me to find out if Thomas Wentworth was still alive: he died bankrupt, in November of 1879, by his own hand."

So intent was I upon the envelope in my hand that the words scarcely registered. When I reached the landing below, I looked back and saw him still standing at the top, regarding me with troubled eyes.

Rosina Wentworth to Emily Ferrars

Kirkbride Cottage,
Belhaven,
East Lothian
Friday, 18 May 1860

Dearest Emily,

I am so sorry to have left you in suspense, and can only hope that you received the notes I scribbled from King's Cross and Dunbar. I am safe, and well, and happier than I ever imagined possible. And now I must gather my wits, and try to tell you everything as it happened.

Last Sunday was the longest of my life. I had intended to feign illness, and keep to my room to avoid my father, but there was no need of feigning; I was sick with dread and could eat nothing all day. I had, at least, the consolation of knowing that Lily had made a great impression upon the people in Tavistock Square, a widowed physician and his daughters, who live very quietly, and do not seem to move in any of the circles Clarissa and I used to frequent; they said she might start with them as soon as she liked. But such was my disordered state of mind that, when Lily offered to take my clothes to Felix's lodging, I tormented myself all the while she was gone with visions of Felix running away with her instead of me — all the more unpardonable as I would never have escaped without her help.

Lily and I said our farewells that night. At five o'clock on Monday morning, I dressed, put on my cloak, and crept downstairs. Alfred had not taken up his post until eight the previous day, but the front door is always locked overnight, and Naylor keeps the key, so I had decided to leave by way of the area below. I stole across the first-floor landing—my father's room is just along the corridor—and went on down into the gloom of the hall. The blood pounding in my ears sounded appallingly loud; I thought I saw movement in the shadows behind a pillar, but nothing emerged. Moving as quickly as I dared, I entered the foyer and passed through the narrow door that opens onto the servants' staircase; I had to leave it ajar to see my way down.

The only light came from a frosted pane of glass above the area door; the rest of the passage was in darkness. I had slipped the upper bolt, and then the lower, and was turning the handle when a voice at my back said, "You can't do that, miss; master's orders."

Naylor was standing a few feet away. The light fell upon his pale, smirking face, red lips parted in triumph. I wrenched open the door and darted up the steps; his hand seized my shoulder and came away with my cloak, in which he became entangled, gaining me precious seconds in which to open the area gate and slam it behind me. I heard Naylor shouting at the top of his voice; I saw Felix beginning to run toward me from a hansom twenty yards away; I heard the clash of the area gate and the thud of Naylor's boots close behind me.

"Run to the cab!" cried Felix as he passed, but I could only turn and watch. He planted himself squarely in Naylor's path; Naylor, who was at least a head taller, tried to dodge around him, but Felix stuck out a foot and tripped him. He was up again in a moment, flailing savagely; one blow struck Felix across the mouth and sent him staggering back. Naylor seized him by the collar and made to fling him to the ground, but Felix twisted from his grip with a rending of cloth, and it was Naylor who fell heavily; I heard the crack of his head striking the cobbles. A paper fluttered from Felix's torn coat pocket as he turned toward me, and this time I did not hesitate. We ran side by side for the cab, and Felix lifted me bodily in.

"Victoria Station, the boat train, fast as you can!" shouted Felix as he jumped up beside me and the cab jolted forward. Looking back through the window, I saw Naylor picking himself up off the pavement, and another man emerging from the house.

"Let us hope he heard that," said Felix, dabbing at his mouth with a handkerchief. Two minutes later we were rattling along Weymouth Street, with no sign of pursuit.

We had intended to breakfast at King's Cross and take the ten o'clock express to Edinburgh, but Felix thought it would be too dangerous to wait, with the hunt already up. If my father dismissed my note about running away to Paris as a blind, the Scottish express might be the next thing he thought of. Worse still, the paper Felix had lost was a letter from his solicitor. And so we took the first available train to Leicester, travelling as Mr and Mrs Childe, and made our way north from there in a series of steps, arriving very late in the afternoon at Dunbar.

From the moment we set out, it seemed absolutely right and natural to be sitting hand in hand with Felix; I never once felt—and have not since—that I was travelling with a man I barely knew. Felix kept a wary eye on the platform whenever we stopped, but my anxiety diminished as London receded behind us, until I felt only a sublime assurance that all would be well. I slept much of the way from York to Newcastle: a sleep of utter contentment in which I dreamt I was lying in Felix's arms, and woke to find it true.

Dunbar, as you may know, is right beside the sea, very popular in the summer, but in May almost deserted; the coast is very wild and beautiful. The man who brought us from the station happened to know of this cottage, which sounded perfect: about a mile farther up the coast, a little way from Belhaven village, looking toward the sea. I wanted to drive out and see it at once, but Felix said we should think about it first, and so we took rooms in a lodging house near the castle.

And now for my confession. I have hesitated a great deal over whether to tell you, but I resolved this morning that I would. If our situations were reversed, I would want you to speak freely and trust in my love, knowing that I would never judge you harshly; and so I should place the same trust in you.

Felix had said on the train that he thought I ought to stay in a separate lodging until our three weeks were up, but I refused to be parted from him. "We may be snatched away from each other at any moment," I replied, "so every moment together is precious."

"But we must keep apart until we are married; you are under my protection, and I would never want you to regret—to feel that I took advantage of you."

We said no more at the time, but in the evening, after we had dined—we were the only guests in the house, and took our supper in front of our sitting-room fire—he returned to the subject. His arm was around my shoulders, as it had been much of the day; my fingers were twined through his hair; every so often he would kiss my temple, or my cheek, and whenever our lips met, my breathing would quicken and I would twine myself closer still, and then Felix would sigh, and quiver, and gently draw back.

"You know," he said, "if we take that cottage, it will be even harder to keep apart, living alone under the same roof."

"I do not want to keep apart from you," I said. "My reputation is lost forever, so far as people like the Traills are concerned, and I do not care a jot. The proprietor thinks we are married; we are pledged to each other; I am wearing your ring; and if my father should trace us; well, I do not want to die without knowing . . ."

"But my darling, even at the very worst—suppose I were to be arrested for abducting you, and assaulting Naylor, and you were carried off to your father's house by force—it would be terrible, but we would only have to wait until you were of age; he wouldn't dare harm you."

"My father is capable of anything; he thinks the law applies only to lesser mortals. I have never quite shaken off the fear that he murdered Clarissa. Not with his own hands, of course, but by hiring footpads to force their carriage over that cliff. I shall never forget the look on his face when he told me she was dead."

"But the authorities said it was an accident. You remember I heard talk of it myself in Rome: a young couple tragically lost when their horse bolted."

"I shall try to believe it. I can only pray that she died happy—as happy as I am now," I added, moving closer again. "So let us take that cottage tomorrow—we will be safer away from the town—and have no more talk of keeping apart."

"Rosina—you do understand what that means?"

"Not—not exactly, but I think I can imagine. I have trusted you with my life; why should I not trust you with—in every way?"

His arms tightened around me, but then he drew a long breath and disengaged himself, his expression suddenly sombre.

"Rosina, there is something I must say to you. I meant to tell you when we next met in London, but there was no time . . ."

"Anything, so long as you are not married already."

"No, not that, but . . . I have not always lived celibate. If only I had known we were to meet, I should never have looked at another woman, but alas . . . I have made no promises, and broken no vows, but I have been—intimate before this; I wish with all my heart I had not. So you must think on whether you still wish to marry me. No matter what you decide, I shall protect you with my life so long as there is blood in my body—"

"All I desire of you," I said, "is to be certain that you love me with your whole heart, and that there is no other attachment—nothing in your past that could ever come between us."

"I swear it by all I hold sacred. If there is anything—anything at all—you wish to ask of me, you have only to ask it—only—"

"Only?"

"Only that—if you really can forgive me—might it not be better to begin life together anew, without looking back?"

He rose, made up the fire, and left the room, murmuring something about the landlady and breakfast. I realised, staring into the red glow of the coals, that he had told me nothing I had not already divined. But if I knew everything about every woman he had ever embraced, would I feel any more secure in his love? Or would that knowledge prey upon me, no matter how firmly I tried to push it away, until I grew jealous of every kiss, every caress . . . ?

A coal burst in a shower of sparks, vanishing upon the instant. "You are right," I said as his shadow fell across the couch. "Let us begin anew."

Felix had warned me that the act might be painful; I had always vaguely assumed (I suppose because of all the talk of sin and shame) that it would have to be done in complete darkness, but we left the candles burning, and came to it so tenderly, and so gradually, that the pain was no more than momentary. We made love until dawn (now I truly understand why it is called making love), so rapturously, and with such exquisite caresses, that I feared we might wake the landlady with our cries. Marriage—between people who truly love and adore each other, I mean—must be like a secret society (I can write this, since you and Godfrey belong to it): how could anyone be ashamed of such delight, such ecstasy of body and soul, the heart overflowing with love?

We woke in each other's arms, and drove out to Belhaven in a daze of happiness. I had never seen countryside so beautiful, or colours so rich and radiant; everything—the songs of birds, the scents of blossom, the tang of the sea—seemed so *alive*, like the first day of spring after a long drab winter, but infinitely more so.

And the cottage itself is ideal—only a hundred yards from the shore, and hidden from its neighbours by a coppice of trees. A woman from the village comes in the mornings; the rest of the time we have the house to ourselves and can do exactly as we please. Felix knows how to make tea and fry a beefsteak: we supped last night in bed, upon bread and cheese and potted meat and cake, and were utterly content.

I must finish here; we are about to walk into the village to catch the afternoon post. I dare not read this letter over, and can only remind myself that if I were in your place, I would want to know everything. We are to be married—I have only just thought to mention it, such is my conviction that we are married already—on Monday, the fourth of June, in Dunbar, if we are not discovered. I should have loved to have you and Godfrey for our witnesses, but it is such a long way, and perhaps you may feel—I must not entertain such thoughts, or I shall lose my nerve, and tear this up instead of posting it. May we come to you at Nettleford, as soon after the fourth as will suit? I long to embrace you, and will write again very soon. Have no fear for me, dearest cousin; I am blessed beyond measure.

All my love to you, and to dear Godfrey,

Your loving cousin,

Rosina

> Kirkbride Cottage,
> Belhaven
> Wednesday, 23 May 1860

Dearest Emily,

I burst into such tears of joy when I read your letter that Felix thought something terrible must have happened! Your loving words mean more than I can say until I embrace you on the ninth. And to know that Lily is safe in Tavistock Square—truly, my cup runneth over.

We have been here nine days now, without the slightest alarm. No one else knows where we are, except for Mr Carburton, Felix's solicitor, who is to write care of the post office in Dunbar. Because of the letter he dropped in the struggle with Naylor, Felix decided he must write to Mr Carburton to explain the circumstances of our elopement, and warn him against believing anything my father may say. If my father should call at the office, Mr Carburton is to tell him that we will shortly be married, but nothing more.

Felix has also written to his brother, as he feels is only right, though Edmund is bound to disapprove of our marriage, believing as he does that no Mordaunt should ever marry. Edmund remains bitterly opposed to the sale of Tregannon House, despite Felix's assurance that the proceeds will be equally divided—which is all the more generous of Felix, since he has had to borrow against his own share and is anxiously awaiting the deed of sale. Mr Carburton will forward the letter, as Felix does not want Edmund to know where we are until we are married.

But that is the only cloud on our horizon, and most of the time we scarcely notice it. The weather, for the most part, has kept wonderfully mild and sunny: we walk for miles along the coast, with scarcely another human being in sight. Those last fearful days at Portland Place already seem like a distant nightmare, apart from the odd superstitious moment when I have to pinch myself to make sure I am truly awake, and free, and happy beyond my wildest imagination. Felix has the most extraordinary vitality; he scarcely needs to sleep, and often I wake to see him scribbling verses by candlelight, or gazing at the stars. And then, if he hears me stirring, he turns to me with a look of such delight that my heart overflows. His mind teems with ideas: sometimes his thoughts tumble over one another so fast that I cannot keep up with what he is saying, but I feel I always understand the music, even when I miss some of the words. He dreams of finding, or even founding, a community—apparently there are several like it in New England—built upon love and respect, a brotherhood of the spirit, he calls it, in which women would enjoy the same rights as men, and property would be held in common, for the benefit of all. To me he seems the very embodiment of that spirit, always so ardent and loving, filled with the joy of life.

Until the ninth—Felix sends his warmest and most heartfelt

thanks for your invitation, and joins with me in hoping that all is well with you and Godfrey—

Your loving cousin,
Rosina

Kirkbride Cottage,
Belhaven
Friday, 25 May 1860

Dearest Emily,

Alas, I spoke too soon. I was unwell yesterday morning and so did not accompany Felix when he walked to Dunbar to see if the deed of sale had arrived yet. He returned, looking very grave, with a disturbing letter from Mr Carburton, enclosing another, even more distressing, from Edmund. My father, it seems, went straight to Marylebone police station on the morning of our escape and had warrants sworn against Felix for abduction and assault. He then stormed into Mr Carburton's office, demanding to know where we were. Mr Carburton, of course, knew nothing of what had happened (he did not receive Felix's letter until Friday), but he was sufficiently alarmed to write to Edmund at Tregannon House, telling him of my father's visit. This was Edmund's response:

Dear Felix,

I have long despaired of your profligate ways, but I never imagined you capable of such an outrage as this. To have abducted an heiress (even if she accompanied you willingly, it is still abduction), and assaulted the loyal servant who sought to defend her honour: these are acts so heinous that I can only suppose — I might almost say hope — that you have altogether lost your reason. I have been in communication with Mr Wentworth, whose wrath would scarcely be appeased by seeing you hanged, and pleaded the only thing I could plead: that you ought to be confined as a lunatic rather than as a felon, but he is adamant, and will not rest, he says, until you are locked up in Newgate.

There is, nevertheless, a faint chance of your avoiding the disgrace of a prison sentence. You must ensure that this foolish young woman is returned to her father's house at once — unless, as I greatly fear, you have already debauched her. If Mr Wentworth re-

fuses to take her back, then I suppose we must make provision for her. You yourself, however, must not accompany her to London, but return home at once. Maynard Straker has very kindly offered to come down and examine you as soon as he is summoned; assuming—I cannot see how there can be any doubt of it—that he is prepared to issue a certificate, we can declare you unfit to plead, and arrange for your confinement here.

As for your unconscionable scheme of selling the roof from over our heads: I have written to Mr Carburton, apprising him of the facts of the matter, and advising him not to act upon any further communications from you, or to advance you any further funds, as you are plainly not of sound mind.

I urge you, once again, to arrange for Miss Wentworth's immediate return to her father, and to present yourself here without delay. Fail in this, and I dare not answer for the consequences.

Your aff^{t} brother,

E. A. Mordaunt

Mr Carburton, for his part, advises Felix to "consider very carefully whether you still wish me to draw up a deed of sale, since your brother will certainly contest your fitness to sign this or any other document pertaining to the sale of the estate. This would place me, as a trustee of the Mordaunt estate, in a most invidious position, since I cannot, of course, act for one member of the family against another. I do most earnestly counsel you to come to terms with your brother before you proceed."

"What does he mean, 'come to terms with your brother'?" I asked. The day was overcast, the fire unlit; our little sitting room seemed, for the first time, cold and drab.

"He means—though being a lawyer, he will not say so plainly—that he agrees with Edmund: he thinks I am as mad as my father and should meekly present myself to his friend Straker to be certified and shut away like poor Horace—as soon as I have delivered you to the nearest police station, that is."

"That is monstrous—absurd. No one could possibly believe you mad."

"You forget the family history, dearest. Edmund regards my desire to sell that wretched mausoleum as proof in itself."

"All the same . . . do you think, if we were caught, that you really might be sent to prison?"

"If you were able to swear that you came away willingly, and that Naylor was as much the aggressor as I, probably not. But you would be locked away in your father's house—that is what they are counting on—in no position to swear to anything, leaving them free to blacken my character. So yes, I might very well be convicted and imprisoned, assuming that Edmund did not contrive to have me certified, which would be far worse—but fear not, my darling; in ten days' time we shall be married in law, and that will draw most of their teeth."

"Most?"

"Well, they could still have me arrested and thrown in gaol to await my trial. And then, if your father had you kidnapped—it would be illegal, but he might still risk it—they could contend that I was insane at the time of our marriage, and try to have the marriage annulled. Until you come of age in November, we must be on our guard. But don't look so alarmed, dearest: we shall be gone long before then. I shall call at the shipping agent's this afternoon, and see what sailings are available."

"Shall we not see Emily, then, before we leave?" I asked, striving to conceal my disappointment.

"Your cousin's house is likely to be watched. But," he added, studying my face, "I know how much it means to you; we shall find a way of throwing them off the scent."

"Must you go back today? Is it safe? What if Mr Carburton has told your brother that he is writing to you at Dunbar?"

"I was on my guard from the moment I opened the letter—which I did in the post office, thinking it was the deed—and saw nothing suspicious; I am certain I wasn't followed. There is always that danger, yes: the devil of it is, I must be able to communicate with Carburton about the sale, and so if we move, the same difficulty will arise. And it will be easier to prove our three weeks' residence if we remain here. From now on, I shall go to Dunbar alone; if I have to run for it, that will give me a better chance of escaping. You must try not to worry too much; the only danger is at the post office, and I shall be watching like a hawk."

"But if Mr Carburton has taken your brother's side? . . ."

"That is why I must go back: I have decided to consult a medical man and have him write me a certificate of sanity. Unusual, I know, but if you can be certified insane, why not the reverse? I shall send it straight to Carburton, with instructions to draw up the deed of sale and advance me a further two hundred and fifty pounds. I am the heir, after all, and he is already acting for me; I think, when it comes to it, he will have to do as I ask. And now I must be off; it may take me several hours, but the sooner it is done, the sooner we can set sail."

Watching him stride away across the grass, I realised that, in spite of the threat hanging over us, I no longer wanted to live abroad. We had talked a great deal—or rather Felix had talked, and I had listened, utterly content in his embrace—of faraway cities like Rio de Janeiro: places he had never seen, but could conjure, with the utmost vividness, from fragments he had read and pictures he had glimpsed, as if recalling a vision of heaven. And yet it had never seemed quite real to me; reality was the bed we lay in, the sun on the coverlet in the mornings, the salt air wafting in from the sea, the beating of his heart against mine. I had said to myself, "I can be happy anywhere Felix is happy," and believed it, but now, newly conscious of the damp stains on the wallpaper and the musty odor rising from the carpet, I envisaged a bleak procession of furnished rooms and lodgings, and my spirit rose up in revolt and said, "No, I want us to live here, in our own country, and have a house of our own, a place where our children can grow up amongst friends, and music, and laughter, not as strangers in a strange land." Yet when we had talked in Regent's Park, the prospect had seemed wholly delightful. What had come over me? I reproached myself for inconstancy of feeling and for putting my own comfort above Felix's, but I could not recapture whatever it was I had felt that day.

I emerged from my reverie to find that Felix had vanished from sight. I had locked the front door behind him, but what of the others? The house was surrounded on three sides by trees, which until then had looked peaceful and sheltering, but now seemed alive with shadows. The front windows looked over a low stone wall, beyond which was an expanse of meadow, then a long curving line of pale sand, and the sea stretching toward the horizon. If you went out by the kitchen door at the back, you could pick your way through the trees—the copse was very much overgrown, and choked in places with nettles— past the collapsed remains of another wall, and scramble down onto the Edinburgh road, in clear view of the village. We had never gone that way to Dunbar, having always taken the path along the coast.

I went around the ground floor, making sure that all the windows were latched and the kitchen door bolted. Fear prickled at my spine. I went on upstairs, forcing myself not to look back, and into our bedroom. Not a soul was in sight; only the ragged meadow, and an iron grey sea fading into mist. My head ached dully, and there was a griping in the pit of my stomach, which might have been apprehension, or simply the discomfort I had felt all day. I was shivering, too, but reluctant to light the fire, telling myself it was not really cold enough and trying to suppress the voice that whispered, *The smoke will give you away.*

In the end, I got into bed fully dressed, wrapping the chill bedclothes tightly around me until the shivering diminished, and I began to drift in and out of uneasy dreams, starting awake whenever the hall clock chimed, or a bird's claws scrabbled on the sill. Two o'clock struck, and then the half hour, and then three. And then I must have fallen into a deeper sleep, from which I woke with the impression that someone had been knocking at the door below.

I threw off the bedclothes in a panic, wondering how long Felix had been waiting, and was halfway to the landing before I came fully awake and realised that it might not be Felix at all.

The sound was not repeated. I crept back to the bedroom, knelt down beside the bed so that I could not be seen, and crawled toward the window. My skirts chafed against the carpet—or was that footsteps on the gravel beneath? Very slowly, I raised my head.

A man was standing just inside the front wall, no more than ten yards away, looking up at the house; he seemed to be staring directly at me. A stocky, powerfully built man in a dun-coloured suit like a uniform, with a cap of some sort protruding from his side pocket. His head was completely bald, lumpish and irregular in shape, the skin so transparent that it gleamed like polished bone. Down the left side of his face, a livid scar ran from temple to jaw, narrowly missing the eye.

I dared not move. He stood as though he had a right to be there, his eyes flicking back and forth over the house, but always, it seemed, returning to me, with a chill as palpable as the draught from the casement. At last he turned and walked away, pausing for one more glance at the window before he disappeared behind the trees.

Had he seen me? He had turned to the left, as if to go around the outside of the copse and rejoin the Edinburgh road, but there was no way of telling. He could be lurking amongst the trees, waiting for me to emerge. Any minute now, Felix might be approaching from the other direction, oblivious of danger.

Unless they had captured him already.

The hall clock began to strike, startling me to my feet before I realised what the sound was. If the man was still watching, he had certainly seen me now. Five o'clock. Felix had been gone nearly four hours.

If he *had* seen me, and Felix was already in their hands, they would have broken down the door by now. Which meant . . . The thought was lost in a wave of panic, but I knew well enough what it meant. My only hope of escape was to slip out by the kitchen door, seek another way through the coppice, and pray that I could find Felix before they did.

There was no one in sight. I went over to the closet, pulled on my walking-shoes and cloak with trembling hands, and went downstairs as quickly and quietly as I could.

Was there anything I could use as a weapon? I could think of nothing more formidable than the poker, and one thought of the scar-faced man was enough to dissuade me. I crept into the kitchen and sidled up to the window. Misty grey cloud hung low over the treetops; again there was no one to be seen, but any number of men might have been lurking amongst the trees.

No help for it. I drew back the bolt and lifted the latch. Silence, except for the terrible pounding of my heart. Inch by inch, I eased the door open, willing the hinges not to creak, and looked out through the gap. Nobody sprang at me, but the floor beneath my feet felt very strange. It began to sway, and then to revolve; the door slid through my hand, and darkness engulfed me.

I came to my senses with my cheek pressed against cold stone and a throbbing in my temple. For a moment I had no idea where I was, only that I was lying sprawled across a doorway with something digging into my shins. How long had I been lying here? Shivering, I rose stiffly to my feet and looked around.

The overgrown garden was deserted; nothing stirred in the shadows beyond. Keeping close to the wall, I moved toward the far corner of the house and peeped around. Still there was no one; only the low front wall and a glimpse of meadow. Twenty paces away, across a stretch of ragged grass, loomed the edge of the coppice.

The ground was uneven and littered with dead foliage, so I had to watch where I trod. Five paces; ten; I was almost there, when a voice on my left cried, "I seen her!"

I began to run, tripped over my cloak, and fell. Footsteps pounded toward me; I picked myself up and turned, hopelessly, to face my pursuer—and realised that he was Felix, calling my name.

"Rosina! What on earth . . . ?"

I gabbled out my story, but he seemed strangely unperturbed.

"One man alone, you say? No one you recognised?"

"No, but—"

"Well, then, he couldn't have known who you were. You see—I was thinking about it on the way back—they would have to send someone who could identify you: Naylor, for instance. Even your father wouldn't risk kidnapping the wrong woman. And now we must get you indoors, my darling; you are shivering, and white as a sheet."

"Felix, you don't understand; they will be back any minute—"

"No, dearest, they won't, because they don't know where we are. We haven't been followed on any of our walks; I'm certain of it. You were anxious—all my fault; I shouldn't have alarmed you so—and out of sorts. Your scar-faced man, however menacing he seemed to you, was most likely an innocent wayfarer in need of sustenance. And remember, you were fast asleep; you might very well have dreamt the knocking, and even your sinister visitant himself."

Calmly ignoring my protests, he led me back to the house and put me to bed as tenderly and efficiently as Lily would have done. Only after he had got a good fire going, and mixed me a glass of hot spiced wine, did I think to ask how he had fared in Dunbar.

"All is well, my darling. The physician I consulted was a little nonplussed by my request, but after fifteen minutes' conversation he agreed readily enough. And then, while I was looking for a notary, I remembered my will—the one Carburton persuaded me to sign a few days after my father died, leaving everything to Edmund as the next in line—poor Horace isn't allowed to manage his own affairs. So I found a solicitor instead—a Mr McIntyre, in Castle Street, well away from the post office—and had him draw up a new one, leaving the entire estate to you. It is drawn 'in anticipation of marriage,' as the lawyers say, so it will still be valid after we are married."

"But dearest, you have promised to share with your brothers; it is not fair to them—not even to Edmund, abominably as he has behaved."

"Well, that is the point, in a way. As soon as the will was signed and sealed, I wrote to Edmund, telling him what I had done; but I didn't enclose a copy, and I didn't tell him who had drawn it. So, at least until the estate is sold up and divided, it would be very much against his interest for me to die."

"Felix—are you afraid he might try to have you murdered?"

"No, but it will show him that I am not to be swayed by his threats: that, and the certificate of sanity I sent to Carburton along with my instructions about the sale. One copy of the will is in Mr McIntyre's strongbox; the other is for you to keep. And now you must rest, and promise not to dream of any more scar-faced men; we would not be here now if I thought there was the slightest danger."

Reassured by his certainty (and doubtless by the hot toddy, which he insisted I finish), I agreed that I could easily have dreamt the scar-faced man, and by the time I fell asleep, I almost believed it myself.

It is almost midday on Friday; I have let my pen run away with me again, but I will abide by my principle of doing what I should want you to do (or rather posting what I should want you to post) in my place. I am still in bed, at Felix's insistence, still headachy and uncomfortable, but with only a few scrapes and bruises to show for yesterday's fright. He blames himself for alarming me unnecessarily by rushing home whilst he was still upset over Edmund's letter. For my part, I feel ashamed of getting into such a panic over a harmless stranger, as he surely was. In ten days' time we will be safely married, and then, God willing, I shall embrace you on the ninth.

All my love to you, and to dear Godfrey,

Your loving cousin,

Rosina

Kirkbride Cottage
Friday, 1 June 1860

Dearest Emily,

Once again I had to reassure Felix that the tears I shed over your letter were tears of joy. It is such a delight to know that Godfrey is his old self at last—such a long and anxious time it has been for you—and eager to return to his work. And such a relief that neither you nor your neighbors have seen anything suspicious.

All is quiet here, too. The man with the scarred face has not returned, not even to trouble my dreams. And Felix is in wonderfully high spirits; he told me last night that our love has brought him a happiness beyond anything he could have imagined. "Before I loved you," he said, "even at the best of times, there was always a grey cloud hovering somewhere about my heart. At the worst, it was Stygian darkness; I could scarcely lift my head from the pillow, and longed only for oblivion. But now I am filled with light; I have fed on honeydew and drunk the milk of paradise, and the cloud is banished forever." He says it is why he needs so little sleep; he feels light in every sense, and can easily believe that human beings could soar like birds if only they had sufficient faith, as with the disciple who was able to walk on water until he grew fearful and began to sink.

Yesterday afternoon we walked along the coast to a place called St. Baldred's Cradle, a steep, rocky cleft at the mouth of a river. Felix insisted upon climbing the outer cliff, though he did not so much climb it as run straight up a spur of jagged rock, fifty or sixty feet high, and then leap from crag to crag along the top, waving delightedly whilst I watched with my heart in my mouth. He assured me when he came down that he could not possibly have missed his footing, but I do wish he could learn to be just a *little* fearful, if only for my sake!

As yet he has heard nothing from Carburton, but in Dunbar this morning he had a strong presentiment that he should call at the shipping agent's. There he learnt that a ship called the *Utopia* will be sailing from Liverpool for Rio de Janeiro on the twenty-ninth of June. It seemed to him such a good omen that he reserved a cabin for us; the passage money does not have to be paid until the fifteenth, and he is certain the deed of sale will have reached him by then.

I confess that my heart sank at the news—it seems so terribly soon—but I am determined to subdue my misgivings. Felix is so elated by the prospect that I cannot bear to disappoint him. "We shall never have to endure another winter," he said when he came in, "because in Rio it is warm and light all the year round." Even though he is certain his melancholia will never return, it would be unpardonably selfish of me to try and keep him here, where the winters would remind him of that terrible darkness. All I could bring myself to say was that I should hate to be separated from you forever, to which he cheerfully replied that of course we should come back for visits. And perhaps when we have stayed in Rio for a while, he will be happy to live somewhere closer—Spain, perhaps, or the isles of Greece (he read me those wonderful lines from *Don Juan* the night before last)—so that we can spend whole summers in England—by which, of course, I mean Nettleford, and take a house close by, and see you every day.

All my love to you, and to dear Godfrey,

Your loving cousin,

Rosina

Kirkbride Cottage
Tuesday, 5 June 1860

Dearest Emily,

Well, we are married according to law, though the ceremony itself was a miserable affair, conducted by a dour and (I thought) disapproving clergyman in the presence of two paid witnesses who shuffled their feet whenever there was a momentary silence. I wept at the cheerlessness of it all, and even Felix was quite cast down; though the day was fine, we were in no mood for celebration, and were about to return home when he noticed a livery stable and suggested we hire a dogcart for the afternoon. A brisk drive along the coast restored our spirits, and a mile or so beyond the village of Skateraw we came to a little bay that was quite deserted. We tethered our horse near a grassy hollow, where the same thought came to us both: that we had been married not three hours, but three weeks. We made a bed of our cloaks and lay down, sheltered from the wind; and afterward, holding Felix in my arms while he slept (such a rare delight) with the sun's warmth on my skin, I felt as though we had been taken up to heaven without the need of dying, floating in perfect light.

Only four days until I embrace you at last. We shall take the London express on Friday morning and stay in the Great Northern Hotel that night, so that Felix can see Mr Carburton about the deed of trust. I feel a little apprehensive about staying so close to Great Portland Street, but Felix insists that, despite what he said the other day, there is not the slightest risk of his being charged with abduction. "I was upset by Edmund's letter," he said, "and not thinking clearly; you are my lawful wedded wife, and if anyone accosts us, I shall have him arrested then and there." He will call at Mr Carburton's office on Saturday morning; as soon as that is done, we shall drive straight to Paddington, and should reach Nettleford by six at the latest. And then my happiness will be truly complete.

Your loving cousin,
Rosina

Station Hotel,
Durham
Thursday, 7 June 1860

Dearest Emily,

I have been staring at this page for the past hour, wondering what I shall say to you, and trying to imagine your replies, but all I can hear is my own voice telling me how unutterably foolish I have been. I should have known—but how *could* I have known? Felix—I must try to set it down plainly, from the beginning.

This morning—it seems a century ago—I accompanied Felix to Dunbar. "The law is on our side," he said, "and I refuse to skulk." The day was bright but chilly, and rather than go into the post office with him—he was certain, as he had been every day for the past week or more, that the deed of sale would have arrived—I waited on a bench in the sunshine. I was feeling perfectly content, and not in the least apprehensive, when I happened to glance at an alleyway across the street. Standing just inside the entrance was the man with the scarred face, his gaze fixed upon me. He was wearing his cap this time, with the peak drawn low over his brow, but the scar was unmistakable. As soon as our eyes met, he withdrew into the shadows and disappeared.

I sprang up and hurried into the post office to warn Felix, who was engaged at the counter. For the first time ever, he betrayed irritation. "It is just some local farmer or the like," he said curtly, and returned to his interrogation of the postmistress. The man was nowhere to be seen when we emerged, and we walked home in uncharacteristic silence, Felix brooding (I presumed) over the absence of the deed of trust; I feeling wounded and uneasy, glancing frequently over my shoulder and receiving (so I felt) disapproving looks from Felix.

"You must forgive me, my darling," he said as we came up to the house. "I am out of temper with Carburton, not with you. Shall we walk on a little?"

"No, thank you," I said, "I have a slight headache. But you must keep on; I shall be quite all right."

If he had insisted upon staying, I should have forgiven him completely. But he kissed me perfunctorily, and strode off in the direction of St. Baldred's Cradle, leaving me to make my own way indoors.

Wishing I had a piano, which I had scarcely missed until that moment, I wandered restlessly about the cottage. Felix had always come from the post office in high good humour, saying the deed was sure to arrive tomorrow, but I had never been with him at the moment of disappointment. He should not have been so dismissive, but then I should have been more sympathetic; no doubt he was right about the scar-faced man, who would surely have followed us if he had any sinister intent. And this was our last day at the cottage; we must not leave here on a sour note.

Felix had been gone about a quarter of an hour; I ran downstairs and out to the front gate, meaning to follow him; but what if he had circled inland? The wind had dropped, and the sun's warmth was comforting, so I sat on top of the wall to watch for his return.

Several minutes passed; I grew restless again and was about to go back indoors, when I heard the clatter of wheels and the jingling of a bridle coming up the lane behind the trees to my left. I darted toward the house, but before I could reach it, the vehicle—an open carriage, with the driver perched on a box, and a veiled woman in a dark cloak and bonnet seated within—had turned the corner and pulled up at the gate.

Half-fearful, half-curious, I remained in the doorway. The driver got down to help his passenger—whose bonnet concealed her face—descend. It is someone come to see the house, I thought. The landlord has told her that we are leaving tomorrow.

She spoke softly to the driver, who resumed his seat and took up the reins again. As she turned and began to walk toward me, I saw that she was heavy with child. I saw, too, that there was something familiar about her; something that chilled my blood and settled like ice around my heart.

She was Clarissa.

Not an apparition, not an hallucination, but my sister, smiling in a fashion I remembered all too well.

"So, Rosina, you are Mrs Mordaunt now? Felix will have to choose between us."

I did not feel anything at all; I suppose I was incapable of feeling, even of thought. I invited her into the house—what else could I do?—I think I even offered her tea. She looked as striking as ever, despite her condition. The gown beneath her travelling-cloak was a rich, pale blue satin, abundantly trimmed with lace, whereas I was dressed as plainly as a girl of fourteen: anyone coming into the room would have taken me for the parlourmaid. Her eyes seemed even larger and darker than I remembered—kohl, perhaps, and belladonna, but so cleverly applied I could not be sure—her hair more abundant, the lines of her face if anything finer. She had kept her old trick of regarding you—regarding me, at least—with every appearance of interest, tinged with a derision as subtle as the hint of rouge about her cheekbones. But the old mockery had taken on a new edge—wry, bitter, undeceived—along with a cool resolve I had not seen before. Only her hands betrayed any agitation, twining and untwining beneath the fringes of her sleeves.

I listened as one listens in a nightmare, powerless to move or speak, whilst she explained that the woman who had died with George Harrington had been her maidservant, an English girl she had engaged in Dover. Clarissa had caught them in flagrante, as she put it, a week before the accident (while they were still in Florence); she had left him that same day, taking everything she could lay her hands upon. She supposed the girl had decided to call herself Mrs Harrington when she and George moved on to Rome.

In Siena, travelling as Caroline Dumont, a young widow, Clarissa heard the news of her own death, and decided then and there to leave Clarissa Wentworth in her grave. She did not say whether she suspected my father of having anything to do with the accident, but once she had made the decision, there was no going back on it. And then, at a masked ball in Venice, she met Felix Mordaunt.

Their affair, which lasted about a month, ended when she took up with a Mr Henderson, a wealthy American of forty or so. "Felix was a younger son," she said coolly, "with no obvious prospects: he never mentioned that he was the heir, or I might have stayed with him." I remember, as she said this, glancing at a pair of crossed daggers on the wall behind her, and picturing myself, quite unemotionally, taking one of them down and plunging it into her bosom. Something must have showed in my face, however, for she added, "You would have done the same in my position. I had no choice. I sold what I had to sell, for the best price I could secure; it was that, or starve."

They parted, she said, on good terms; Felix went on to Rome, whilst she remained with her American suitor in Venice, where she very soon discovered that she was expecting Felix's child. She had hoped to pass it off as Mr Henderson's, but his suspicions gathered as the months passed, and once again she found herself alone. Soon after that, she learnt from a new acquaintance that a certain Rosina Wentworth—it was the talk of London—had followed her late sister's example by running away with Felix Mordaunt, the heir to the Mordaunt estate.

With no other prospects in sight, she returned to England and made her way to Tregannon House, thinking she would find us there. Instead, she met Edmund Mordaunt. "He did not like me any more than I liked him, but we had interests in common. His man had only just traced you, and Mr Mordaunt was hesitating over whether to pass the information on to our father. He feared that if Felix were to be carried off to prison, he would do something wild, such as deeding the entire estate to you.

"Edmund Mordaunt was seeking a way of prising you and Felix apart; and, of course, being a very moral and upright man, he felt some obligation toward me, as another of the women his brother had ruined. And so, reluctantly, he gave me your address."

She had been Felix's mistress; she was carrying his child. I knew that I ought to be angry, but anger would not come; as at that moment when you have cut yourself badly and time seems to freeze. You know that the blood will spurt, but all you can see is white, severed flesh; and then the pinpoint drops begin to form.

"What do you want?" I said dully. The question sounded foolish as soon as uttered; not only foolish, but beside the point.

"Money, of course. Or perhaps we could all live happily together in one of those Ottoman countries where a man is allowed more than one wife; it would certainly suit Felix. And now, Rosina, it is your turn for confidences; you must tell me how you met him."

Her expression changed; she shrank back in her chair. I discovered that I was on my feet, with no memory of having risen, frozen by the realisation that it was not Clarissa who had deceived me, but Felix. My hands fell slowly to my sides.

And even Felix had not lied. "I have been intimate before this." If he had added "with your sister," then of course I should never . . . but he had not known; he could not have known she was my sister, any more than Clarissa could have known that I, of all the women on this earth . . . Lily had warned me, as you would surely have done if I had waited for your reply, instead of rushing headlong into Felix's arms. My father could not have forced me to marry Mr Bradstone. I had deceived myself.

If it had not been for this monstrous coincidence . . . but no; not entirely. That first intimate smile, when he first caught sight of me at Mrs Traill's: the memory I had tried so hard to suppress, for fear it would make me jealous. "I do beg your pardon. I mistook you for someone else."

He had been drawn to me because I reminded him of Clarissa.

I was still standing motionless, staring down at her, when I heard the front door open, then the sound of whistling in the hall. Felix appeared in the doorway, smiling his warmest smile and saying, "My darling, I am so . . ."

The smile faded and died.

"Caroline," he stammered at last. "What—what on—"

"She is not Caroline," I said. "She is Clarissa; my sister, and the mother of your child."

His face crumpled; lines appeared where none had ever been, like cracks opening in a wall at the point of collapse; he seemed to shrivel beneath my gaze, until the last remnants of the man I had loved had crumbled into dust.

His mouth opened, but no sound came out; he took a step toward me, stretching out his arms in a gesture of hopeless appeal.

"Do not touch me!" I said in a voice I scarcely recognised. "You have no claim upon me: *she* is your wife. I am going upstairs to fetch my things; I do not wish to speak to either of you, ever again."

Felix made another attempt to speak; for a moment I thought he would try to grasp my arm, but his hand fell away, and I left the room without a backward glance. My hands were steady, my eyes perfectly dry; I went up the stairs like an automaton, gathered the few remaining things I had not packed—including ten guineas in gold that Felix had given me to keep in case of an emergency—put on my travelling-cloak, and closed the lid of the valise.

He was waiting, ashen-faced, near the foot of the stairs when I came down.

"Rosina, I beg of you—"

Again he made as if to touch me, and again his hand fell nervelessly to his side. I was aware of Clarissa hovering at the edge of my vision, but neither of them spoke again, and a moment later I had closed the front door behind me.

I did not weep then, and have not since. Tomorrow I shall take the train to London, and thence to Plymouth. It means I shall be with you a day early; I hope you will not mind. I do not know what I shall do—only that I should like to see you first.

There is no point in posting this. Perhaps I shall burn it—or keep it to remind me of my unutterable folly.

Georgina Ferrars' Journal (continued)

I HAVE BEEN THROUGH everything in the packet, and shaken out the envelope, but there is certainly no letter from Mama. Perhaps there *were* other papers left behind after she died, which were then lost with the house. That must have been what Aunt Vida meant when she was dying: "Things you need to know. I wrote it all down, but that's at the bottom of the cliff now."

Poor Lucia! There is no denying it: Clarissa, not Rosina, was her mother. Mama left me the letters because she did not want me to marry a Mordaunt—because of what happened to poor Rosina—that is all. Rosina died three days after I was born, and *that* is what strained Mama's heart, just as Aunt Vida said—or would have said, if only she had felt able to.

But *how* did Rosina die? Did she take her own life, as I fear? I shall not think of it. I must think of Lucia, and of what I am to do.

I could burn the letters, and tell her that Mr Lovell refused to hand them over. And say nothing about the tombstone.

And the wills? And Rosina's marriage certificate? Could I burn those as well?

It almost looks as if Mama believed we had a claim upon the Mordaunt estate. There is a copy of the will Felix made in Belhaven, "in anticipation of my marriage to my beloved fiancée, Rosina May Wentworth," leaving his entire estate to her. And a copy of Rosina's own will, made at Nettleford on the twelfth of December 1860, leaving everything to "my beloved cousin Emily Ferrars, in accordance with the sealed instructions to be opened by her in the event of my death"—but no trace of any instructions.

If Felix Mordaunt is still alive . . . But no, Edmund Mordaunt inherited the estate. Felix must have changed his will again before he died.

Unless he really did go mad, like his brother Horace, and is locked away at Tregannon Asylum.

Must I tell Lucia? She is bound to suspect—the thing I will not think of—and then I will surely lose her.

But if our happiness is built upon a lie . . . I am hopeless at deception. She will sense that I am keeping something from her, and press me until I confess, and then it will be worse than if I had told her the truth in the first place.

No; if I try to deceive her, the shadow will come between us, and I will lose her anyway.

But what if I am wrong? Suppose Clarissa was *not* her mother? If she sees those letters, Lucia will leap to that conclusion, just as I did. I am clutching at straws, I know, but if there is one chance in a thousand . . .

I must try to discover what became of Clarissa—and Felix—before I go back to London. Of course I could ask Henry Lovell to find out—but no, not after telling him I was engaged to a man I have never even met.

If anyone knows, it will be Edmund Mordaunt. Liskeard is only twenty miles off—it cannot be more than half an hour by train. And if Tregannon Asylum is close to the town, I could go there in the morning and still be home tomorrow night.

But even if he is at home, and agrees to see me, I cannot tell him why I want to know, without giving away Lucia's secret. And I am forgetting those wills. If he has looked up Rosina's will—supposing there was some sort of claim on the property—he is scarcely going to welcome a Miss Ferrars. Or agree to keep our secret. I think I must go as Lucia Ardent; but no, not without asking her.

L.A. Her initials are on the valise. Laura? Lily? Lucy Ashton. The name just popped into my head.

Of course! I will say that I wish to consult Doctor—what was his name?—Straker, as his patient. Then I can tell him as much as I need to, under a pledge of secrecy. He has known the Mordaunt family all this time; if I throw myself upon his mercy, perhaps I can persuade him to be frank with me. Even if he refuses, I shall be no worse off.

I shall take all of my things with me in the morning; that way, as soon as I have seen Dr Straker, I can return to London at once.

Part Three

Part Three

Georgina Ferrars' Narrative

K NEELING IN THE DUST, with my writing case clasped to my breast, I reached instinctively for the chain around my neck—and found, of course, neither chain nor key. Both catches were locked. I grasped the cover and tugged reluctantly, thinking I would have to break the stitching, before it struck me that keeping the case intact might help to secure my release. And so I spent an age prying at the locks with a hairpin I had managed to bend into a hook. My hands shook so badly that I cut myself several times; by the time I had both catches open, the blue leather was stained with blood.

I took out my journal, along with two bundles of letters in a hand I did not recognise, a packet containing what appeared to be legal documents, and a solicitor's card, with an address written on the back— "C. H. Lovell, Yealm View Road, Noss Mayo"—and began to read. I was still crouched on the floor, with the last of the daylight filtering over my shoulder, when I heard a distant gong, and had to cram everything back in its hiding place in a mad rush and set the room to rights before Bella came to find me. I must have eaten—if I ate at all—in a kind of trance, for the next thing I recall is being back in my room, with the door bolted again, and Rosina's last letter in my hand.

Throughout my incarceration in Women's Ward B, I had assumed that if only I could discover what I had done in those missing weeks, the fog would lift from my mind. Yet even after I had read through my journal for a third time, there was no answering chord. I could half convince myself that I remembered walking with Lucia in Regent's Park, or confronting Uncle Josiah and demanding that she be allowed to stay with us. But it was like sifting through my earliest recollections, and trying to distinguish actual memories from things Mama had simply told me I had done. The fog remained as impenetrable as before.

I felt, indeed, as if I had lost a whole existence, rather than a few weeks of my life. Lucia had stolen my name, my money, my heart, and left me here to rot. Everything she had told me—even the name Lucia Ardent—had been a lie, carefully woven to draw me in. And I could not remember so much as a syllable she had uttered, or recover the smallest glimpse of her face, except for that hallucinatory moment on the doorstep in Gresham's Yard, on the evening of my escape.

Had she deceived Dr Straker, too? The shock of finding Rosina's grave, and reading her last letters, and realising (even as I fought to deny it) that Felix Mordaunt had been my father as well as Lucia's, and that Rosina had died within days of giving birth to me—the shock of all that had brought on the seizure, just as Dr Straker had said.

Calling myself Lucy Ashton, and coming here on that deluded, foolhardy quest: I might as well have been acting on Lucia's instructions.

As perhaps I had been. I looked again at my description of Mrs Fairfax; of how she had been singing Dr Straker's praises; how much she seemed to know about Tregannon Asylum. I had, indeed, heard that voice somewhere before. She had reminded me of Lucia. And if I had left those wills with Henry Lovell, as any sensible person would have done, instead of bringing them with me, Lucia could have retrieved them, and, in the person of Georgina Ferrars, laid claim to the Mordaunt estate.

When I heard the clock strike ten, I hid everything away again and put out the light, so that Bella would not come tapping at the door. Stars glittered above the rooftop; I wrapped myself in the coverlet and went over to the window, gazing down into the moonlit courtyard.

I knew that I ought to be consumed with rage and mortification, but I seemed to have lost the power of feeling. I might as well have been reading about someone else; someone for whom I felt a degree of sympathy, but whose fate did not directly concern me. I wondered if I would ever feel anything again. My childhood with Mama and Aunt Vida seemed quite untouched, only now immensely distant, as if seen through the wrong end of a telescope. The numbness seemed vaguely familiar.

But I still had to decide what I should do.

I could hand over the papers—except for the most intimate passages about Lucia (though was that not most of the journal?), which I would tear out—to Dr Straker. That would surely persuade him that I had been telling the truth.

But unless Felix had made a later will, I would be presenting Dr Straker with proof that I was the rightful owner of Tregannon House. Edmund Mordaunt would be disgraced; Frederic would lose his inheritance, and Dr Straker his kingdom. I could say that I did not want the estate, only my freedom, my name, and my own modest income; but why should he believe me? It would be safer by far to burn the papers—"Miss Ferrars" in London could do nothing without them—and lock me away in the darkest corner of the asylum.

I could show the papers to Frederic, but again I would be gambling with my life.

Or I could try to escape again. But with no money, no name, and no one to help me—Lucia would surely have made a conquest of Henry Lovell by now—all roads led back to Women's Ward B. Or worse.

Perhaps there was another way.

I stood at the window for a long time, watching the shadows climb slowly up the opposite wall, thinking how it might be done.

At ten o'clock the next morning, I was seated on a bench near the entrance to the voluntary wing. I had told Bella that if she should happen to see Mr Mordaunt, I would be grateful if she could mention that I wished to speak to him. Now all I could do was wait.

The air was chill, but I could feel the sun's warmth on my back. Through the woodland to my left, I could see a patch of red brickwork: the ruin of the old stable, perhaps, where Frederic had heard the mysterious tapping sounds. Away beneath the wall, men were tilling the fields, just as they had been the evening before. I felt strangely, almost unnervingly calm.

At least I know I am not mad. The thought had come to me upon waking: I might have Mordaunt blood in my veins, but I had endured five months in the family asylum without succumbing. It came to me again, like a current of warm air, as I sat gazing across the fields. I realised, too, that I did not greatly mind about being Rosina's child and not Mama's. No one could have loved me more dearly; if Rosina had lived, I should have had two loving mothers, as well as an aunt. I thought of the game I had played with the mirror, and the look on Mama's face when she heard me shouting "Rosina" at my reflection, and I understood that in her place I should have done exactly the same. Her anxious, haunted expression when she thought no one was watching . . . I could well imagine her being possessed by a superstitious dread that if she made no provision, I would choose, of all the men in the kingdom, to marry a Mordaunt *because* she had not done so.

And indeed she had been right to fear it. Of all places in the kingdom, I had come to Tregannon Asylum, and might, in different circumstances, have fallen in love with Frederic Mordaunt, never imagining that he was my cousin. Only I had not come here by chance, but because of Lucia—Mordaunt blood calling to Mordaunt blood?— and if I had loved her so passionately, could I really have loved Frederic with the same—?

"Miss Ashton?"

I sprang to my feet. Frederic Mordaunt was standing two paces behind the bench.

"I am very sorry; I did not mean to alarm you."

"Yes—I mean, no, I was just—shall we walk a little?" I said.

"By all means," he said, falling into step as I set off, at random, toward the trees. He was bareheaded, and dressed much as I had seen him on that first morning, in brown corduroy and a white stock. The shadows beneath his eyes were darker than ever.

"You—er—mentioned that you wished to speak to me."

"Yes, Mr Mordaunt, I did. I feel—I have come to realise that I owe you an apology. I have been—unjustly harsh, and ungrateful—"

"Miss Ashton, Miss Ashton, it is I who should apologise—"

"But you have done so already, Mr Mordaunt, and I ought to have accepted your apology with more grace. It is not your fault that I am here."

His hands unclenched; he took a deep breath, almost a sob, and turned away to hide his emotion.

"Your generosity, Miss Ashton, means more than I can say; especially when—"

"Especially?" I prompted.

"Well—especially since you still believe you are Miss Ferrars."

"I have been thinking about that," I said. "Now that I am more at liberty, thanks to your kindness, it is easier for me to consider the possibility that—that I may have been ill, as Dr Straker has always maintained. As I say, it is not your fault. I must not keep you from your work, Mr Mordaunt; I only wanted to express my gratitude."

"I see." He sounded surprised, almost startled.

"But," I continued, "I need time to reflect, before I speak to him, and so, if you are willing—"

"Upon my honour, Miss Ashton, I shall not breathe a word to him."

His colour had risen; he was studying me as intently as politeness allowed, with every appearance of adoration. I kept my own gaze demurely fixed upon the prospect before us, wondering how he would respond if I told him we were cousins.

We were now approaching the edge of the wood. The trees were mostly oaks and alders, growing very close together; a narrow path wound its way in amongst them. Frederic began to bear away to his right.

"Shall we walk through the wood?" I asked innocently.

"Perhaps better not," he said. "It is very overgrown, and you might . . . There is a very pleasant walk along the western side."

He sounded natural enough, but it seemed to me that he averted his eyes from the ruin, and we walked for a little in silence, following a rough track that led us across a stretch of open field and around the end of the wood, until we were out of sight of the house.

"I remember you saying," I ventured, "how lonely it was for you, growing up here."

"You remember our conversation?" he exclaimed, with another

heartfelt glance, which I pretended not to see. I had allowed the distance between us to diminish, so that our shoulders were almost touching. "After all you have suffered here—I am—" He seemed about to say "overwhelmed," but checked himself.

"Yes, it was; I had no playmates, as I may have mentioned."

"And no other relations—uncles or aunts, or cousins . . . ?"

"None living. Uncle Edmund had a younger brother, but, like my father, Horace, he took his own life."

I stared at him in shock, caught my foot in a tussock, and grasped his arm to save myself from falling.

"I did not know," I said. "About your father, I mean."

"I did not like to mention it. He had been closely confined, for his own safety, but somehow . . ."

"I am truly sorry to hear it," I said, thinking how dreadfully inadequate that sounded. Through the cloth of his jacket, I could feel his arm quivering—or was it my hand? I steeled myself to continue.

"And—the younger brother?"

"The same, I fear. He—my uncle Felix—was lost overboard, on a voyage to South America, but given the family tendency, there can be very little doubt. I came upon the report of it quite recently, when I was sorting through some papers. The ship—the *Utopia*, she was called—was just three days out from Liverpool. He had dined as usual that evening—the weather was calm, with only a light swell running—and that was the last anyone ever saw of him."

"And—do you remember him at all?"

"No, he died before I was three years old; in the summer of 1860, I believe it was. I know almost nothing about him. The subject is distressing to Uncle Edmund; he prefers not to speak of it."

I found that I was still gripping his arm, and hastily released it. Felix had not stayed with Clarissa; he had boarded the ship on which he had planned to sail with Rosina, and drowned himself, surely out of despair at losing her. He would never have made another will in Edmund's favor; not when Edmund had been the agent of his ruin.

"Miss Ashton?—I fear I have distressed you."

"No, no, it is only—" I took a step forward, and realised I was quite unsteady on my feet. "I should like to sit down for a little."

I made my way over to a fallen tree, anxiously attended by Frederic, and sat down on the trunk. A few paces to my left, a path led back into the wood; I saw Frederic glance over his shoulder, and wondered if it went to the ruined stable.

"You must understand," he said, "that, bleak as it must sound, these sad histories are part of the furniture of my mind. They have lost their power to hurt."

A brief silence followed.

"Miss Ashton," he said hesitantly, "what you said to me, before, has lifted a great weight from my mind. I hope you will not take it amiss if I remind you that, when you leave here, my purse will be at your disposal."

In fact, sir, I imagined myself replying, it is *my* purse, and I have documents to prove it. But only if I could prove that I was Georgina Ferrars.

"You are very kind, Mr Mordaunt," I murmured, hoping I was not overplaying my part. "I should have been more gracious when you first made the offer."

He gave me another of his heartfelt looks, in which a sort of incredulous hope was dawning. No one, I thought, could counterfeit such transparent emotion, those rapid changes of colour . . . I felt a wild impulse to confide in him, to trust in his sense of honour and his evident feeling for me; but then I thought of my journal, of how I had trusted just those signs in Lucia (if only I could *remember* trusting her). I reminded myself, too, of how much he idolised Dr Straker, and resolved to stick to my plan.

"You spoke, Mr Mordaunt, of *when* I am released. Are you confident, then, that Dr Straker will let me go?"

"Yes, Miss Ashton, I am—though I cannot, as you know, force his hand."

"But why is it, may I ask, that he will not release me now? I am not a danger to myself, or anyone else; I accept that I cannot be Georgina Ferrars, and I am prepared to wait patiently for my actual memory to return: what, then, is the obstacle?"

"I am afraid there are several. He fears that if he releases you prematurely—his word, not mine—your actual memory, as you call it, may *never* return. And he still hopes that by combing through records of missing persons—which he spends a good deal of his time doing—he will discover who you really are, and restore you to your friends and family, assuming, of course . . ." He trailed off awkwardly.

"But do *you* think it fair, Mr Mordaunt, that he should keep me here, as a certified lunatic? If I am capable of living in the world, should I not be allowed to?"

"I—speaking for myself, I agree with you. I find it impossible to think of you as a lunatic, or to imagine . . ." He shook his head, as if to clear it. "The difficulty, according to Dr Straker, is that yours is such a rare condition—he knows of only four comparable instances, all reported from France—that he simply can't predict how, or how soon, it will resolve. My own belief, as I said to you only yesterday, is that if you could—I hesitate to say converse with, but speak to Miss Ferrars, in a setting acceptable to you both, the spell might be broken. But Dr Straker, as I told you yesterday, is vehemently opposed to it: he fears the shock might kill you."

"I cannot see why, Mr Mordaunt. I agree with you; I am convinced that it would help me. In fact—of course I have no right to ask," I said, meeting his eyes with all the appeal I could muster, "but would *you* be prepared to call upon Miss Ferrars at Gresham's Yard, and try to persuade her to see me?"

"Nothing would give me greater pleasure, Miss Ashton; but Dr Straker would never agree."

"But supposing he is wrong? Should you not trust your own instinct? If it helps me recover my memory, and leads to my release, will he not forgive you? And have the largeness of heart to acknowledge that you were right and he was wrong? I should be eternally grateful," I added, with another beseeching look.

"Miss Ashton, I only wish . . . The thing is, even if I were to defy him, Miss Ferrars has said that *she* won't agree to it unless we can return her writing case."

"But, as you said yourself, Mr Mordaunt, if it helps me to remember what I did with it . . ."

He was plainly torn; his hands, clasped in his lap, were trembling.

"Something has just come to me," I said, playing my last card. "About that writing case."

"Yes, Miss Ashton?"

"'Aunt Rosina's will': I don't know what it means—the words just came into my head, but my heart insists that Miss Ferrars will understand them."

My heart, in fact, was beating very fast, and my mouth was dry. I had gambled on his not recognising the name.

"I see. Do you think, Miss Ashton, that your memory is already returning? Dr Straker will be most—"

"Please, Fre—Mr Mordaunt; you promised you would not breathe a word of this conversation to him, until I have had time to reflect."

"Of course not, if you wish it," he said, regarding me with a sort of troubled adoration. "I shall do my utmost to persuade him—about Miss Ferrars—as if it were solely my own idea."

My heart sank at "do my utmost."

"But he will never agree; you said so yourself." I had no need to exaggerate my disappointment.

"You are right," he said, after a pause. "It is time I . . . I will not go behind his back, but I shall write to Miss Ferrars—I had better make sure she is at home—regardless of his response. And I shall certainly mention Aunt—Rosina, is it?—Aunt Rosina's will."

"Thank you," I said. "I am very much in your debt. And now, I think, if you do not mind, I should like to return to my room, and rest for a while."

He rose and held out his hand to help me up, and we stood for a moment facing each other, my hand still in his. He took a deep breath, as if about to make a declaration.

"You must know that I—this time I shall not fail you," he said, restraining himself with palpable effort.

I smiled and thanked him again, and let my fingers brush across the palm of his hand as I released it, sternly repressing the thought that perhaps I was no better than Lucia.

I had intimated to Frederic that he might find me any day at about three o'clock, so long as the weather kept fine, reading by the fallen tree. He appeared that same afternoon, looking even paler than before.

"I cannot stay long," he said, "but I wanted to tell you that my letter to Miss Ferrars will be in tomorrow morning's post."

"You have spoken to Dr Straker, then?"

"Yes, and he was most displeased; even more so when he realised that I meant to write to Miss Ferrars, with or without his consent. He again accused me of—well, it does not matter. 'I cannot prevent you from inviting Miss Ferrars to Tregannon House,' he said, 'but if any harm comes to Miss Ashton because of this, it will be upon your head. I have a good mind to move Miss Ashton back to the closed ward, for her own safety, but doubtless you will object to that, too. Very well; in the unlikely event that Miss Ferrars accepts, we will bring them together, under the most careful supervision. I repeat: upon your own head be it.'

"Neither of us alluded to it, but the implication was clear: he agreed only because Uncle Edmund could die at any time, and as the owner, I could make things very difficult for him—I hope I am not distressing you, Miss Ashton."

"No, no, it is—only the thought of being confined again; I could not bear it."

"I would not allow that, I assure you, unless you were to become—so violently agitated that there was no alternative. Indeed, I went further: I pressed him once more to lift the certificate. But there he is adamant. 'If I did that,' he said, 'Miss Ashton would be off to London on the next train. She would go straight to Gresham's Yard and make a scene. Miss Ferrars would summon a constable, and Miss Ashton would be hauled off to Bethlem. I hardly think she would consider that an improvement, do you?'"

"But I accept that I cannot be—" I stopped, realising that I had tied his hands by pledging him to secrecy.

"Yes," said Frederic, "but *he* will not accept that, unless he is certain that your memory has returned."

I had considered that possibility during the night: to tell Dr Straker that I had remembered I was Lucia Ardent, exactly as she had presented herself to me. But he would want to check; he had already dismissed Lucia's story as an obvious fabrication (as it surely was), and if he caught me in a lie, I would lose Frederic's regard, and find myself back in Women's Ward B.

Again I was tempted to present him with the wills and Rosina's letters and say, here is the truth, you must decide. But would he—would any man—meekly hand over a lucrative private asylum to a certified lunatic, wholly within his power? Even if he was infatuated with her? The idea that I was the lawful owner of this vast estate was too much for me to hold in my mind; I could grasp it only in bewildering flashes. Regardless of what the law might say, did I really want to deprive Frederic of his inheritance? The question was unanswerable. I could not think beyond escaping, and recovering my own name and fortune from Lucia.

"—Miss Ashton?"

I realised that Frederic had been speaking.

"I beg your pardon," I said. "There is—so much to take in."

He gave me a searching glance, as if hoping to detect some personal meaning, and looked hastily away. In the fields by the wall, work continued as usual. A light breeze blew from the west, stirring the leaves overhead and carrying fragments of song from the workmen. Patches of sunlight drifted across the hills. I thought of all the anguished souls incarcerated a mere hundred yards away, and shivered.

"I must go," he said. "And perhaps you should not stay too long; you must be getting cold. I shall let you know as soon as there is any news."

I thanked him once more. He did not offer me his hand this time, but he stood for a moment gazing down at me. Then he squared his shoulders and walked away without looking back.

The following morning after breakfast, Mrs Pearce, the matron, stopped me on my way out with the words I least wanted to hear: Dr Straker wished to see me in my room. There I waited, imagining worse and worse consequences as the minutes ticked past. By the time he appeared in the doorway, I had resigned myself to being dragged away in chains, to the deepest, darkest cell in the asylum. But all he did was take my pulse—he seemed not to notice my agitation—and ask his routine questions about whether I had remembered anything more, to which I thought it safest to reply that I had not. I thanked him for moving me to the voluntary wing, and said that I felt better already for being able to walk amongst trees and open fields; he heard me out with his ironic smile and a faint inclination of his head, said he would look in again soon, and departed.

My relief, however, was tempered by—I could not tell exactly what—an atmosphere, an undercurrent, an uneasy feeling that his manner had been a little *too* casual, his habitual detachment too studied. Frederic, after all, had confronted him twice in the last few days. Did he really believe that I had not the faintest inkling of this? Or was he trying to lull me into a false sense of security?

Or was it simply my overwrought imagination running away with me? How could I be certain, for that matter, that Frederic *had* confronted him? Perhaps the only person I had succeeded in deceiving was myself.

Three days passed without my seeing Frederic; I told myself that it might be weeks before Lucia replied—if she ever did—but my spirits sank lower nonetheless. The voluntary patients—there seemed to be about a dozen of them, all much older than I—avoided me whenever possible; I wondered who had told them that I was still certified.

On the fourth morning, I resolved to visit the old stable, to see if it would suit my purpose. A fine, misty rain was falling, which made it more natural that I should hug my cloak around me and draw the hood close around my face as I set off along the path I had taken every afternoon. When I had gone about halfway to the wood, I knelt and pretended to remove a stone from my shoe, glancing behind me as I did so. There was no one following, but every window seemed alive with watchful eyes; the pressure on my spine did not relent until the path had carried me out of sight of the asylum.

Grey, drifting vapour hung low overhead, curling amongst the treetops. Sheep wandered in and out of patches of mist, their cries muffled by the damp. Beneath the wall, indistinct figures hunched over their spades.

You will be closely watched. Beyond the fearful promptings of my imagination, I had seen no sign of it. Could Dr Straker really have stationed watchers all around the estate? How could he know which direction I would take?

I had only to imagine what I would have done in your place, Miss Ashton, to anticipate your every movement.

There was the fallen tree, and the path leading into the wood. Except for the distant labourers, there was still no one in sight as I passed beneath the canopy.

The trees grew even closer on this side. Some had been felled many years ago, and new ones had grown up around the stumps. I could not help leaving a distinct trail as I hurried along the path, flinching every time a twig snapped beneath my foot. Sooner than I expected, I emerged into a clearing in which stood a dark, ivy-covered mass, dripping with moisture. Frederic had described the stable as it had appeared on a sunlit afternoon; in that grey, murky light it was scarcely recognisable as a building. There was the broken lintel, with rubble heaped around a narrow opening.

I held my breath, listening. Though the asylum was no more than fifty yards away, I could hear only the dripping of water and the muted calls of birds. I moved reluctantly closer.

Frederic had said that the tapping sound came only when he was not listening for it. I knelt by the opening and tried to peer into the darkness within. A dank, chthonic smell wafted out at me—followed by a metallic clang.

I scrambled over the rubble and fled, realising too late that I was running in the wrong direction, with the noise still ringing in my head.

Not the sound of a murderer burying his victim, but the tower clock striking the hour.

As the last echoes died away, I caught a glimpse of black stonework amongst the trees ahead of me: the side—no, the back—of the original house. I picked my way through mounds of sodden litter until the path ended by the uneven remnants of a flagged walk. The rain was falling more heavily now, pattering over the leaves and splashing onto the stones.

No one has lived there for years. Many of the windows on the ground floor were choked with ivy; the panes above were black with grime. In places, where sections of the house had been built out from the rest, there was scarcely room to squeeze between the foliage and the crumbling masonry.

If I could find a way in, I thought, this might be just the place; no one, surely, would think of looking for me here. The first door I came to was massive, banded with rusty iron and quite immovable, but around the corner of a buttress, I found an alcove, about six feet square, with a door in the right-hand wall. Glancing up, I saw the tower looming overhead.

The door was narrow, arching to a point at the top, like the entrance to a vestry, with a massive keyhole below the latch, and a rusty iron ring hanging from a pivot in the centre. I lifted the latch and tugged, without much hope, but to my surprise it opened with only a rasp of hinges.

I stepped over the threshold, into a cylindrical stairwell, lit by a single window no more than a foot wide. Stone steps, deeply worn, spiralled upward into the gloom. There were no other doors.

Outside, the pattering of the rain increased to a roar. I have done nothing wrong yet, I told myself. If anyone catches me, I am simply looking for shelter.

After three complete circuits of the staircase, I came to an archway in the wall. The stairs continued upward, but I passed through the opening, into a bare stone chamber with an even narrower door set into the wall beside me.

Either the rain had stopped again, or the walls were so thick as to muffle the sound entirely. I grasped the handle, half hoping it would not turn. But this door, too, was unlocked; it opened halfway, and stopped against an obstruction.

All I could make out, at first, was a jumble of furniture, mostly chairs and tables and benches—no, church pews—stacked so close to the wall that only a narrow passage, leading away to my left, remained. Murky light filtered down from above; the pile was too high for me to see over.

I crept along the passage, wincing every time a board creaked, toward a strip of light—a window?—at the end. The floorboards were thick with dust, which clung to the damp hem of my cloak, leaving an all too visible trail. A few paces from where I had entered were two massive wooden doors, both immovable.

The oblong of light broadened as I approached; what I had taken for a sill was a railing, waist high, with solid oak panelling beneath. I emerged onto a gallery running the width of the building. The light was coming from lancet windows in the walls high above me. Through a circular hole in the floor, an open staircase spiralled downward.

I stole toward the balustrade and peered over, into what had once been a chapel, but was now a storeroom or a workshop of some sort. All of the windows below had been bricked up, as had the entrance; the only visible door opened into a vestry nearby. I remembered Frederic saying, "He calls it the temple of science," and understood why there were no windows. I had blundered into the very heart of Dr Straker's domain.

Ranged around the walls were tables, benches, and cabinets bearing tools, bottles, racks of tubes, notebooks, coils of wire, and pieces of apparatus made up of brass wheels and polished rods and glass cylinders, with cables snaking away from them. A dozen or more oil lamps hung suspended from wires above the benches. Amidst all of this equipment were homelier touches: a teacup, a tantalus with a single glass beside it, a biscuit tin. A closet stood open; I could see clothes hanging from a rail, a tall hat on a peg, a pair of boots beneath. A long trolley, like a narrow bed on wheels, stood by the vestry door; it had two handles projecting from one end, and rails around the side: the sort of thing, it struck me, that might be used to transport an unconscious patient—or a corpse.

I became aware of a low, continuous humming, just above the threshold of perception. A swarm of bees, perhaps, trapped inside the wall? No, the sound was too constant; I could not tell where it was coming from, but there was a strange, underlying vibration to it that set my teeth on edge.

As I began to back away, I heard, from somewhere below, a key turning in a lock. I dared not run, and could only crouch below the balustrade as footsteps, heavy and confident, approached. The footsteps halted at the foot of the stairs, as it seemed; through the opening in the floor I heard a drawer open and close, followed by the sound of riffling paper. Then silence, until at last the footsteps retreated, the door closed, and the echoes faded into silence.

The rain kept up for several days, but every afternoon I put on my damp cloak and tramped about the grounds, approaching the meeting place from a different direction each time. Frederic came to find me on the third day, a Monday, to tell me that he had received a note from Miss Ferrars, saying that he might call upon her at Gresham's Yard if he wished. He would be going up to London on Wednesday. Despite the pricking of my conscience, I would have been glad of his company, but he seemed to feel himself honour bound not to linger. It occurred to me, as he walked away, that a young man as susceptible as Frederic might easily fall in love with Lucia.

Through the interminable days and nights of waiting, I pored over my journal until I knew it by heart, and could almost convince myself that these were genuine memories; except that the gaps between the entries remained as blank as ever. I imagined, in a sort of waking nightmare, returning from a walk to find Dr Straker with my journal in his hand, saying, in his cool, ironic way, "It is a fiction, woven out

of your disordered mind. Those wills exist only in your imagination."
I had loved Lucia, and she had betrayed me, and yet, no matter how
often I reread those passages, I could not feel as I knew I ought to feel,
or think beyond the prospect of escape.

By Thursday the rain had cleared; I arrived at the fallen tree an
hour early, and paced restlessly about until Frederic appeared, looking so disconsolate that I assumed the worst. He could muster only a
wan shadow of his usual smile.

"Good afternoon, Miss Ashton; I am sorry to have kept you waiting. You will be pleased, I hope, to hear that Miss Ferrars is to visit us,
a week from today."

He sounded so funereal that I thought I must have misheard him.

"Has she agreed to see me, then?"

"Yes, Miss Ashton, she has. She seems to have quite forgiven you,
and she hopes that her visit will do you good—though of course she
also hopes that it will lead to the recovery of her writing case. She
would happily have made her visit sooner; only Dr Straker reminded
me, before I left, that he would be away in Bristol on Monday and
Tuesday, and so we settled upon the Thursday."

He spoke as if his mind were not really upon what he was saying,
and he would not meet my eye.

"I am truly grateful to you, Mr Mordaunt, for all the trouble you
have taken on my behalf. But—you do not seem very happy about it."

"Well yes—no—it is only—no, it is nothing, I assure you."

It is just as I feared, I thought. He has fallen in love with Lucia.

"No doubt Miss Ferrars is very charming," I said. "I only wish I
could remember her."

"Well yes, Miss Ashton, she—no—that is—" he stammered,
looking even more uncomfortable.

"I trust that she was not distressed—or displeased—by your
visit."

"No, not at all, Miss Ashton. She was most hospitable—and
charming, as you say—only—"

It struck me that he was using "Miss Ashton" far more frequently
than before, with a peculiar emphasis upon the "Ashton."

"I wish you would tell me, Mr Mordaunt, what is troubling you."

"Only that—" He took a deep breath, and seemed to make up his mind. "Until yesterday, Miss Ashton, I had hoped—against all the evidence—that Dr Straker might have been mistaken; that perhaps the woman he had met in London really was the imposter, as you so vehemently believed. You had given me such a vivid picture of your childhood on the cliffs; your mother, your aunt, the loss of the house, that I simply could not—"

He paused, groping for words. I felt as if I had swallowed a lump of ice.

"But now I have met Miss Ferrars—the physical resemblance between you is indeed remarkable—and heard her describing those very scenes, sometimes in far greater detail, and spoken to her uncle, and the maid, and heard all about you—Miss Ardent, as you called yourself—and your extraordinary powers of recall, and mimicry, and—well, I can hope no longer. She even invited me to accompany her on an errand to the haberdasher in the square; they were reminiscing about the winter before last, when she first came to London."

Clever Lucia, I thought. She has made absolutely sure of him.

"I am sorry, Miss Ashton, but we must face facts. Dr Straker has been saying all along that when your memory does return, your personality, your facial expressions, even your voice, may change beyond recognition. It will be quite painless, he assures me; you may not even realise it has happened. You will wake up one morning as a different person in the same body, with your true history returned to you. But you will not remember me, or anyone here; you will not even know who I am . . ."

He had been gazing directly at me as he spoke, but his voice broke on the last phrase, and he averted his eyes. After a long, paralysed interval, I heard myself speaking, as I had that winter's morning in the library, with cold contempt.

"Never mind, Mr Mordaunt. You will have Miss Ferrars to console you."

His head shot up again.

"You surely cannot think—you *do* think. No, I cannot—I will not have it. Miss Ferrars is quite charming, yes, but I could never—it is *you* that I love, you that I have longed for since the day we met. I would infinitely rather you remained forever as you are. To me, *you* are the real woman, and Miss Ferrars a pale imitation. I will love you no matter how you may change—of that I am sure—but you will never love me. You will look back on this time—if you remember it at all—with horror, and upon me as one of your gaolers. Detest me if you will, but never, never doubt my love for you."

He spoke with such passion, his face flushed, his hands gesturing eloquently, that I was moved in spite of myself; moved, but also exasperated beyond measure. Then why, why, *why*, I thought, can you not believe that Lucia *is* the imitation? I imagined him getting down on his knees, and my replying, I cannot marry you because we are cousins; because I have Mordaunt blood in my veins; because everything you are offering me is lawfully mine (though I do not think I want to claim it); and because I cannot return your passion. But he is not on his knees, I reminded myself, and you cannot afford to feel sorry for him.

"I do not think of you as my gaoler, Mr Mordaunt, and I am truly grateful for what you have done for me. But you must understand that until I am released, I can think of nothing else."

"Miss Ashton, you must not imagine that I cherish any false hopes," he said earnestly, though his face suggested otherwise. "I should never have spoken, only—" An awkward silence followed.

"At what time next Thursday," I asked, "do you expect Miss Ferrars to arrive?"

"She said she would take the early express, and she hopes to be here in time for luncheon. I have arranged for a fly to meet her at the station. She will stay with us that night and return the following day."

"And—will you tell Dr Straker that you have spoken to me?"

"Yes. In fact, he insisted that I should convey the news to you; he still believes that this was entirely my idea. Relations between us are—strained. But I find I do not greatly care. No doubt," he added, staring bleakly at the distant hills, "we shall be back on our accustomed footing before long. I doubt I shall ever have cause to defy him again."

There seemed to be nothing more to say, and after another awkward silence he rose, and, with a last, desolate, searching look, made his farewells and departed.

The following morning brought another summons from Dr Straker, and an even longer wait before he appeared in the doorway of my room. My mouth was very dry, and I could feel my arm shaking as he took my wrist.

"You are agitated, Miss Ashton. Mr Mordaunt has told you, I believe, that Miss Ferrars is to visit us. Is that, do you think, the reason for your agitation?"

"I—I cannot tell, sir."

"You do understand, Miss Ashton, that you are under no obligation to see her? My first duty is to you, as my patient, and I will not have you exposed to unnecessary nervous strain."

"But sir," I pleaded, "I *want* to see Miss Ferrars; I shall be quite calm, I am sure of it. If I seem anxious, it is because—because I hope this meeting will lead to my release."

"Mr Mordaunt is certainly of that opinion," he said drily. "Well, I shall allow it. You may speak to Miss Ferrars—in my presence, of course—but if you seem in the smallest degree distressed, I shall close the proceedings forthwith. And if you should change your mind in the meantime, do not hesitate to send for me—remembering that I shall be leaving for Bristol on Monday afternoon and will not return until Tuesday evening."

He rose, and seemed about to leave, then paused by the door.

"I take it, speaking of remembering, that you still have no recollection of where you hid Miss Ferrars' writing case."

I was suddenly, acutely conscious of the oak chest, a mere three feet from where I was sitting. I felt sure I could smell leather and parchment. My eyes were irresistibly drawn toward the chest, even as I tried to keep them fixed upon the floor at my feet, pretending to reflect. The air was heavy with suspicion.

"I am afraid not, sir."

"A pity. Well, good day to you, Miss Ashton. I shall look in again on Wednesday, if not before."

His cool, sardonic smile seemed to linger as he closed the door behind him; the rhythm of his departing footsteps was exactly as I had heard it from the gallery above his workroom.

At a little before five o'clock on Monday, I was standing at the back of the old house, scanning the woods around me for signs of pursuit. Birds were making a great clamour, and there were constant rustlings and cracklings in the undergrowth around me. I could not get enough air, no matter how rapidly I breathed, and at every movement amongst the trees, my heart would give a great jolt and seem to stop altogether.

All afternoon I had waited beneath the copper beech by the forecourt, pretending to be immersed in a book, alternately wondering if the tower clock had stopped and wishing the quarters would not strike so frequently. The shadows were lengthening, and the evening chill beginning to descend, before the gatekeeper emerged from his lodge and opened the gate. A few minutes later I saw Dr Straker cantering up the drive on a glossy bay horse. He passed through in a flurry of gravel, spurring his horse in the direction of Liskeard. The gatekeeper did not lock up after him but remained by the entrance. As the hoofbeats faded into the distance, I heard a rumble of wheels from the opposite direction.

A small black carriage, enclosed like a London hansom, turned in through the gate and pulled up in the middle of the drive, about twenty yards from where I was sitting. No one got out; the driver remained on his box. I could not tell if there was anybody within.

Nor could I afford to delay any longer. I rose to my feet, made a play of stretching, and set off across the grass, fighting the temptation to hurry or look back until I had passed out of sight of the carriage.

My original plan had been to entice Lucia away from the house, by way of hints dropped during our supervised conversation. She wanted the wills; I wanted my freedom. If she believed I was prepared to strike a bargain with her, she might slip out and meet me somewhere private. I would force her to change clothes with me, and then somehow imprison her for long enough for me to reach Plymouth, show the papers to Henry Lovell, and trust in my powers of persuasion. Lucia, or so I had persuaded myself, would not have risked an interview with him; far safer just to forge my signature on a letter whenever she needed money.

It had seemed a desperate enough scheme when I first thought of it; as the day approached, it looked altogether hopeless, but without a disguise of some sort, I would certainly be apprehended. I had thought of stealing into the servants' quarters and taking a maid's uniform, but every foray had ended at a locked door, until I realised that the key was already in my hand. Dr Straker was not especially tall; dressed in the clothes from his workroom, I would have a far better chance of escape. If necessary, I would fill my pockets with biscuits and walk all the way to Plymouth. I had found a place on the boundary wall, on the far side of the wood, where the trees grew close enough for me to scramble onto the top.

If I found enough money for the train, I would leave at once. I had brought my writing case with me, secured beneath my dress with strips torn from a petticoat; the outline was visible, but my cloak concealed it. Otherwise, I would hide everything I needed and leave immediately after breakfast the following morning. I had excused myself from luncheon often enough that my absence would not be noticed until the evening, by which time I ought to be in Plymouth. And even if the alarm was raised earlier, they would be looking for a woman, not a man.

I reached the alcove in the wall, took one more fearful look round, and eased the door open. Before, the sound had been muffled by the rain; now, every creak of the hinges echoed like a gunshot. As I stepped inside, I thought I heard a twig snap somewhere nearby. But I dared not look back. I hastened up the stairs, through the door at the top, and on to the gallery. The muddy trail I had left ten days ago seemed quite undisturbed.

On legs that shook as though I had been stricken with palsy, I let myself down through the hole in the floor, with the whole flimsy staircase quivering in sympathy. Clothes, money, food, I told myself. The fear will not kill you unless you give in to it.

The space beneath the gallery floor was much darker. Several large pieces of machinery, partially covered by dust sheets, were ranged along the wall: they looked like massive spinning wheels except that the wheels were made of glass. A desk, littered with papers, stood in the corner by the staircase. The wall itself was blank except for a doorway at the far end.

Clothes, money, food. The closet door was shut, but not, to my overwhelming relief, locked. I took down a shirt, a waistcoat, and a frayed tweed suit, such as a countryman might wear for rough walking, wondering why he kept a wardrobe here. The shoulders were too big, and the sleeves too long, as were the trousers, but not outlandishly so, and his heavy tweed overcoat—with a scarf to cover my throat—would help to conceal the disparities. I felt in all the pockets, hoping for coins, but found only lint and fragments of paper.

The hat would have covered my ears if my hair, which I had pinned as high and as tightly as I could manage, had not held it up. I saw at a glance that the boots were far too large, but the cuffs of the trousers would cover my own shoes.

Money and food. The biscuit tin was half full of ginger biscuits, stale but perfectly edible; I crammed them all into the pockets of the overcoat and returned to the desk, where I draped the clothes over Dr Straker's chair, and rifled through every drawer, but I found only papers, many of them filled with elaborate diagrams and mathematical symbols. Every nerve was screaming, *Take the clothes and go;* but without the train fare, I would have to stay another night, or sleep in the open; a woman dressed as a man could not ask anyone for shelter.

I looked frantically around the room, wondering if there was anything I could take to a pawnbroker in Liskeard. But I had never pawned anything in my life, and all I could see were tools and scientific instruments, which were sure to arouse suspicion.

There was, however, a cabinet on the other side of the floor, with a drawer at the top. An invalid chair, with an opening in the seat like a commode, stood nearby; I was sure it had not been there ten days ago. As I approached, I saw that leather straps had been attached to the arms and legs: once secured, the occupant would not be able to move. I imagined, all too vividly, a patient in a fit of mania, teeth bared, face distorted with fury, straining to break loose.

Hanging from one of the handles was a curious piece of headgear, like a coronet made of thick brown leather, with black-coated wires trailing away from it. Inside the circlet were two polished metal discs, about the size of a half-crown and six inches apart.

Take the clothes and run.

I opened the drawer.

Inside were dressings and bandages, several stout leather straps, neatly rolled, some crescent-shaped pieces of gutta-percha, about the size of my hand, an open case of surgical instruments . . . and a fine silver chain, glittering faintly as I drew it out.

The key to my writing case.

Again I became conscious of that low, resonant hum, not so much a sound as a faint vibration coursing through my bones and teeth. I put the chain over my neck and ran, scooping up the clothes and clutching the hat by the brim as I scrambled back up the stairs, squeezed past the furniture and through to the antechamber. Should I change my clothes here, or in the chamber below? I would rather freeze in a ditch than stay another night within these walls.

Throwing the hat and the clothes down the stairwell, I followed unsteadily after. But at the lowest step, my foot caught in my skirts, and I went sprawling across the tangled clothing. My head struck the floor; dazzling pinpoints of light flashed before my eyes, and I lay for a few seconds unable to move, wondering if I had broken anything.

Escape. I dragged myself painfully to my feet and went over to the window to make sure there was no one outside. Only my blurred reflection, staring back at me through the grimy pane.

My reflection recoiled from me, its mouth opening in a soundless cry of surprise or alarm as darkness swallowed it.

I was woken by hands undoing—no, doing up—the buttons of my dress. A young woman was crouching over me. I had seen her last in the doorway at Gresham's Yard, dressed in my favorite pale blue gown. Now she was wearing a grey travelling-dress and cloak exactly like my own. Her face blurred and re-formed; I wondered hazily if she might be a dream. As she rose to her feet, the cloak fell open, revealing my dragonfly brooch pinned to her bosom, its ruby eyes glowing like drops of blood.

Lucia.

And, clasped in her gloved hand, my writing case.

I tried to stand, but a wave of dizziness swept over me. She murmured something that might have been "I am sorry," turned, and was gone.

Using the wall for support, I dragged myself to my feet and over to the doorway. She was already ten yards away, hastening toward the ruined stable; I would never catch her now. And even if I did, who would believe me? I was the lunatic; she was Miss Ferrars, and the writing case was hers, not mine. And soon, very soon, she would be the owner of Tregannon Asylum.

She had almost reached the far corner of the house when Dr Straker, still in his riding clothes, appeared from behind a buttress and seized Lucia by the arm. I saw, as I drew back from the doorway, that he was steering her toward me.

I tried to gather up the clothes, but stooping made my head spin so badly that I feared I would faint again. I left them where they were, scrambled back up the stairs on my hands and knees, and into the stone chamber above. There I halted, crouched by the entrance, trying to control my breathing as voices echoed in the stairwell: Dr Straker's as cool and ironic as ever; Lucia's shrill with fear.

"And what, pray, are my clothes doing here?"

"*She* had them."

"I see. And where is she now?"

"I—she must have run away. Now please, you must let me go—"

"Perhaps she is within; I think we should make sure. You first, Miss Ferrars—or should I say, Miss Ardent?"

I heard a gasp from Lucia, and faint sounds of struggle.

"You may climb on your own, or be dragged, as you prefer. And do not try to escape me. All the other doors are locked."

A sparrow could not have concealed itself in that featureless chamber. I had no choice but to retreat through the inner door, which I dared not close, along the dark passage, and onto the gallery. Daylight was fading fast.

Should I go on down to his workroom? I darted toward the stairs—but where would I hide? I fled along the gallery instead, boards squeaking beneath my feet. There was no passage at the far end: the furniture was heaped against the wall. Too late to go back. I squeezed into the only possible hiding place—beneath a small table, with chairs stacked on either side of it—and huddled there, quivering like a cornered animal. If Dr Straker came even halfway along the gallery, he was bound to see me.

The floor trembled. I heard muffled voices, then the sound of a lock turning over. My last chance of escape had gone. The footsteps drew nearer.

"Down the stairs, if you please." Though he was speaking quietly, Dr Straker's voice rang through the chapel. I could feel the staircase shaking as they descended. Lucia was making incoherent sounds—or sobs—of protest.

To hear without being able to see was more than I could bear. I crawled forward, keeping close against the side wall, and raised my head until my eyes were just above the balustrade.

Dr Straker was standing with his back to me, one hand clamped around Lucia's arm, my writing case in the other. He set the case down on a bench and steered Lucia toward the invalid chair.

"Pray take a seat, Miss Ardent. I am afraid the accommodations are rather limited."

She struggled, but, with a single deft twist, he forced her down into the chair and stooped over her right arm as she flailed at him with her left. Within a few seconds he had her other wrist pinned and strapped; she kicked wildly and tried to bite him, but her legs were secured in turn, and then her upper arms, until she could only writhe helplessly as he stood back and straightened his coat.

"You will feel no pain, I assure you. It is not often that I have the luxury of working with an intelligent, fully sentient subject, let alone one to whom ethical considerations do not apply. I shall make the most of the opportunity."

"Please, I beg of you, let me go! You have the papers; I promise, on my life, we will never speak of it to a living soul."

"Your promise, I fear, is not a currency I can accept. Blackmailing Edmund Mordaunt was one thing; attempting to blackmail *me* was quite another. It amused me to let you believe that you had deceived me as you deceived your unfortunate — cousin, is she not? Miss Ashton, as she is destined to remain. Whereas you will continue in the role of Miss Ferrars — the *late* Miss Ferrars, if I may anticipate a little.

"And now I must go in search of Miss Ashton. We shall renew our acquaintance after dark; I regret I cannot make you more comfortable, or prescribe anything stronger than a mild sedative. A few drops of laudanum, perhaps? No? Then I must leave you. And please do not waste your breath in calling for help; these walls are immensely thick. You could scream all night, and not a soul would hear you."

He picked up the writing case, and seemed to hesitate. I heard him murmur something that sounded like "Best not risk it." Then he turned abruptly and strode toward the stairs. I shrank into the corner beneath the balustrade, not daring to retreat in case the floor creaked. But the staircase did not move. I heard a drawer open, followed by a muttered exclamation. The drawer closed again; a key turned in a lock.

I peeped over the edge again and saw him standing over Lucia. The writing case was no longer in his hand.

"Did you take the key?" he said sternly.

She shook her head wildly.

Caught between the terror of being seen, and the terror of not being able to see him, I dared not move my head. He moved to a panel on the wall and ran his hand across it. All around the room, yellow light sprang from what I had thought were oil lamps, shaded so as to direct their illumination downward, leaving the gallery in near darkness.

He stood in the middle of the floor, surveying his domain, and then began to move around the room, glancing under benches and opening cupboard doors—including that of the closet, which I had, after all, remembered to shut—until he passed directly beneath me. I heard the rasp of sheeting being pulled off the machines below.

My only chance, I thought, is to crawl back to my hiding place as soon as I feel his tread on the stairs, and pray that the sound of his ascent will cover any noise I make. But again the staircase did not move; he reappeared beneath the far end of the gallery and completed his circuit of the room.

Once more he paused beside Lucia, so that his shadow fell across her face. He drew a watch from his waistcoat and considered it, frowning. Then he raised his head, scanning the gallery. I held my breath.

"No," he said at last, "I must not delay."

He crossed to the panel. Lights around the room began to go out, one by one, until only a lamp above the vestry door remained. With a mocking sketch of a bow to Lucia, he drew out a bunch of keys, strode to the vestry door, unlocked it and departed, turning the key behind him. The echoes flitted around the chapel, fading into silence.

My first thought was to remain where I was, wait for his return, and try not to make a sound while he was doing—whatever he meant to do to Lucia. Then, perhaps, I could escape when everything was quiet. But he would surely go straight to my room, and then the hunt would be up. And how long could it be before he decided to make a thorough search of the gallery?

No; my only chance was to recover my writing case, find a way out, and hope that Dr Straker's clothes were still where I had left them. Dressed as a man, I might pass for one of my pursuers.

I rose stiffly to my feet and moved unsteadily along the gallery and down the stairs.

"Georgina! For pity's sake, help me!"

I did not look at her but went straight across to the other door I had seen. It was heavy and close-fitting; when I tried the handle, it did not even move against the frame.

Keys. Or an implement; something heavy enough to break open the gallery door. Or to use as a weapon against Dr Straker. The light was too dim to see into cupboards and drawers. I thought of trying the panel on the wall, but if he was watching from outside and saw the light . . . I moved from bench to bench, ignoring Lucia's pleas.

"Be quiet," I said as I passed behind the chair. "If you speak again, I will bind your mouth shut."

She began to weep instead. I would not look at her.

After a hasty circuit of the room, I had found a hammer, a chisel, a heavy screwdriver, a candle and a packet of vestas. Fury at this woman I had never truly known, except through the pages of my journal, had kept the worst of my fear at bay. I turned to face her at the last.

"Georgina! I did love you, I swear! I would have come back for you!"

"You are incapable of love," I said. "Or truth." I stood looking down at her, trying to recover something of those lost weeks, but nothing would come. Terror had blurred the likeness that had deceived so many. Her eyes were glazed; the kohl had run in dark, glistening streaks.

"At least untie me," she pleaded. "Give me a chance of life."

"What chance did you give me? I would sooner release a serpent."

Her head sagged forward; the chair shook to her trembling.

"What will he do to me?" The words were scarcely audible.

"He may tear your heart out and roast it before your eyes, for all I care." But then I thought, If I leave her thus, I am no better than she is.

"If I escape him, I will save you if I can. For a prison cell."

"Let me loose for a moment, or I shall soil myself."

"You have soiled yourself already," I said, and turned my back on her.

It was so dark in the corner by the desk that I had at last to light the candle. I worked the blade of the chisel into the gap between the drawer and the frame and pounded it with the mallet—the noise was so deafening that I expected Dr Straker to appear at any moment—until the whole front of the drawer broke loose with a rending of timber. My hands were shaking uncontrollably; it took me an age before the writing case was safely buttoned inside my dress. And then I could not manage the lighted candle as well as the tools; I blew out the flame and dragged myself up the stairs, pursued by Lucia's cries.

With the tools clutched to my bosom, I was forced to edge sideways into the darkness between the wall and the heaped furniture. I had gone only a few steps when the hammer slipped from my grasp. Stooping blindly to retrieve it, I lost my balance and fell against the stack, dropping the candle.

An ominous tremor ran through the floor. I was scrambling back toward the gallery when the whole pile collapsed with a roar like thunder. Something struck me between the shoulder blades, and I was flung violently forward, into oblivion.

I knew, as the throbbing in my head became too insistent to ignore, that I had been unconscious for a long time. I was lying on my back, in darkness, with one arm against a stack of chairs and the other jammed against a wall.

I grasped the rung of a chair. The whole pile shifted alarmingly as I levered myself onto my side, wincing at every movement, then rose painfully to my feet and tested my limbs. There was a cold, sticky patch on my temple, which stung like fire when I touched it, but nothing seemed to be broken. If I could find another way out, I might still escape.

As I emerged onto the gallery, I heard, far above me, the tower clock striking the half hour. But it was surely much too dark for half past six; it must be half past seven. They would have been hunting me for an hour at least.

On the western side, the windows still glowed with a dim, purplish light, which seemed to float in the upper part of the chamber. All was deathly quiet, except for the pounding of my heart, and a faint singing in my ears. Or was it the vibration I had felt before?

Below, the lamp still burned by the vestry door. Lucia's white, terrified face peered upward; the marks left by the kohl looked like streaks of blood.

If I were to hide beneath a bench nearby, I might be able to slip out while Dr Straker was occupied—I shuddered in spite of myself—with Lucia. But I could not descend without her seeing me; she would surely betray me if she thought it might save her life.

No; the safest thing would be to remain hidden up here until he had—finished with her. When daylight came, I might be able to move enough of the debris to reach the gallery door.

The invalid chair creaked. Lucia was fighting to free herself, straining until her eyes stood out in their sockets and the chair rocked back and forth on its wheels. She forced her head forward, struggling in vain to reach the straps with her teeth, and at last collapsed into harsh, choking sobs.

No, I thought, no; I cannot bear it. My feet had carried me to the stairs, without the slightest notion of what I meant to do, and my hand was upon the rail, when I heard a lock turn over. The vestry door flew open; Dr Straker appeared, and strode across to the panel without so much as a glance at Lucia. Lights sprang up along the wall behind her. He moved on to a black cabinet nearby, opened the door, and reached inside; I heard a series of rapid clicks, like a ratchet, followed by a flash of blue light.

"Well, Miss Ardent," he said, speaking over her shoulder, "you have caused me trouble enough for one night. Miss Ashton is still at large; we will recapture her soon enough, but I have no more time to spend on you."

Lucia tried to speak, but it came out as a sob.

"You will feel nothing, I promise you; nothing at all," he said, turning back to the cabinet. "It may comfort you to know that your death, at least, will serve some useful purpose. Your body—or, as the world will believe, Miss Ferrars' body—will be found in the wood tomorrow morning. Heart failure—regrettable in one so young, but then her mother had a weak heart. Foolish young women will persist in wandering about strange woods at night, exposing themselves to shocks of all kinds—if you will forgive the expression . . ."

Lucia was making a low, keening sound, like a wounded animal in its death throes. He took the leather coronet in both hands, pressed it down on her head until the outer band was almost covering her eyebrows, and tightened it at the back, with the wires looping down from the chair. Then, from the bench, he picked up a small dark box, with more wires attached to it. He came around the chair and stood looking down at the terrified Lucia, with the wires trailing behind him. Then he raised his right hand in a gesture of finality.

"*No!!*" My voice rang through the tower. Dr Straker spun round, scanning the gallery.

"Miss Ashton, is it not?"

"Yes," I said hopelessly.

"Pray descend, and join us. *You* have nothing to fear, I assure you." I did not reply.

"Now please, Miss Ashton, be sensible. This apparatus is capable of every degree of effect, from a faint tingling sensation in the temples to instant death. I give you my word of honour that you will suffer only the mildest of seizures: you will wake tomorrow and recall nothing of these—unfortunate events. Frederic will have learnt a valuable lesson, and will, I am sure, remain just as devoted to you. Indeed, we may even anticipate your becoming mistress of Tregannon Asylum: a poetic irony I shall savour.

"As for Miss Ardent here, you cannot possibly care what becomes of her. I suggest you avert your eyes."

Lucia appeared to have fainted with terror; she lay slumped in the chair, her head lolling sideways, her eyes closed. Now that all hope had gone, I felt strangely calm.

"If I escape you," I said, "you will be hanged for murder."

"So be it," he said, and brought his hands together.

Lucia's body convulsed so violently that I thought her spine had snapped. Whatever sound she made was lost in my own cry of horror and despair.

"Miss Ashton, Miss Ashton, calm yourself. Think of all the lives that may be saved—your own included—by this machine. We must all die, sooner or later, and some lives are not worth prolonging. So long as she lived, my life's work was in jeopardy. You might even say that she died in the cause of science, that others might live longer and happier lives. The greatest good of the greatest number, Miss Ashton: it is the best we can hope for."

He bent over Lucia and removed the coronet from her lifeless head. From the wreckage at my feet, I managed to free a piece of wood about three feet long. More lights came on; he tilted one of the shades so that the light caught my face.

"Now really, Miss Ashton, this is sheer foolishness. The last thing I wish is to cause you pain. You shall wake tomorrow, I promise you, feeling better than you did the first time; I shall reduce the current to ensure it."

I moved closer to the opening in the floor, grasping the piece of wood with both hands, and placed myself so that I could bring it down on his head without striking the railing. My unnatural calm had deserted me; I was trembling more than ever.

"How did you know—the first time?" I said.

"Ah, well . . . I thought it best not to mention that you *did* come to see me, on the night of your arrival, with a most affecting tale about Felix Mordaunt, and the Wentworth sisters—you seemed excessively anxious about your late cousin's parentage—and their testamentary arrangements. If you had known that Clarissa Wentworth had been blackmailing Edmund Mordaunt for the past twenty years, you might have been more circumspect. I myself knew nothing of this until last spring, when Edmund confessed to me that he had claimed the estate under the terms of a will he knew to be null and void. And, as he soon discovered, Clarissa Wentworth knew it too. She came to him with what appeared to be a copy of Felix Mordaunt's last will and testament, threatening to produce the original if he did not make her a handsome allowance. To this he agreed, on condition that she lived abroad.

"He never dared called her bluff, but I had no such inhibition. I wrote to tell her that there would be no more money, only the certainty of imprisonment for blackmail if she ever dared contact us again. All would have been well if she and her daughter had not crossed your path, but as it was . . .

"Of course, I could not allow you to leave, and so I brought you here. It was a textbook demonstration of the apparatus; all it lacked was a professional audience. My one mistake was to assume that you had left your writing case in your room, but when that wire arrived, purportedly from your uncle, I saw how the game might be played. I have a gambler's instinct, Miss Ashton, and am not averse to risk: I chose to play it long. I pretended to believe that Lucia Ardent was indeed Georgina Ferrars; I knew that sooner or later she would have to come here in search of those papers—where *did* you hide them, by the way?—and so it has transpired. Frederic's falling in love with you did complicate matters rather, but I was able to turn even that to my advantage. He brought Lucia Ardent to me, thinking he was doing your bidding, when in fact he was doing mine: letting her believe that I would be away this afternoon was the surest way of luring her here unannounced.

"All that remains, Miss Ashton, is to relieve you of these unpleasant memories. You will come to no harm, my word upon it. So kindly lay down that chair leg, and descend."

If you faint, you will die. I cast frantically around for something, anything that might delay him, and remembered Frederic saying, "Two have died in the past year."

"Why should I trust you? You have murdered three people already." My mouth was so dry that I could scarcely form the words.

"What do you mean?" he said sharply, pausing in midstride.

"Your two patients who died of seizures. Frederic told me."

"Are you saying that he *knows?*"

"He—he suspects."

Dr Straker stared up at me.

"No," he said at last, "I don't believe you. Frederic is incapable of concealing anything from me."

"But *I* know," I said. "You have just admitted it, and now you mean to murder me."

"Upon my honour, Miss Ashton, you are mistaken! You may call this murder if you will," he said, gesturing toward Lucia's body, "though I prefer to think of it as self-defence; she would happily have murdered *you*. But the others, no; I meant to cure, not kill them. Both men were in the grip of incurable melancholia, and had been so for years. Both had tried repeatedly to end their own lives; one had spent more than half his adult life in a straitjacket. And we have—or had—no effective treatment for such patients. None whatsoever. For all my experience and training—in theirs and so many other cases—I might as well have been the proprietor of a country hotel.

"And then—why should I not tell you, since you will not remember?—I had been experimenting with galvanic stimulation of the brain, and thought I might as well try it upon the younger of the two. With the dynamo recently installed, I had all the power I needed at my disposal, and also the means of controlling it precisely. At the accepted levels, the treatment had no effect whatever, but as I increased the voltage, he began to report some relief. The benefit, however, was fleeting. I raised the level still further — and induced a seizure.

"When my patient regained consciousness, he had lost all memory of the treatment, and of the fortnight preceding it; so far as he could recall, he had never set foot in this room. And for the first time in years, he was free of his affliction; the black cloud had lifted from his mind. The remedy that had eluded so many had been delivered into my hands.

"But I have seen too many false dawns. I watched, and waited, and kept my counsel, and all too soon, the darkness began to encroach again. I decided to risk another treatment, and this time, the seizure proved fatal.

"Judge me if you will, Miss Ashton, but what else could I have done? On the one hand was the certainty that, without my intervention, the man was doomed to a life of torment and would sooner or later make away with himself. On the other was at least the possibility of a cure. I dared not confide in anyone; if the Commissioners had heard of it, we might have lost our licence. But I vowed that my patient's death would not be in vain."

Dr Straker's gaze had not left my face. He was standing no more than five paces from the foot of the stairs, his head thrown back. He seemed to be summoning all of his eloquence; his voice had grown louder as he went on, until it echoed like a preacher's in the darkness overhead. Surely, I thought, the attendants must be searching the grounds for me? Clutching my makeshift weapon, I kept as still as I could, praying that someone would overhear him.

"For the next few months, I devoted every moment I could spare to testing and refining the apparatus. I felt certain there must be a level at which the memory of past suffering would be purged altogether, the mind cleansed of its morbid tendencies, the patient freed to begin life anew — and so I ventured to try it upon the older man. You may recoil, Miss Ashton, but consider: you can establish how much power it takes to stun a rat, and how much more to kill it. But you cannot ask the rat if it recalls the shock, or whether its state of mind is in any way improved. For that, you must have a human subject: how else can the science of mind ever advance?

"This time I proceeded with the utmost caution, raising the voltage so gradually that he recovered from the initial seizure within minutes, but still with no recollection of what had happened. And again, the relief from melancholia was short-lived. I induced two more, at slightly higher voltages, and was on the verge of proving my theory, when—it was a fault in the apparatus, a fault I have since eliminated, but sadly too late for my patient.

"But I had kept my vow; their deaths were *not* in vain, Miss Ashton, for I had learnt exactly how much power I could safely employ, and I had perfected my apparatus, albeit at grievous cost. And so, when it became necessary to—eliminate your memory of certain events—I was able to proceed with confidence. It was, as I said, a textbook demonstration; I only wish the Commissioners could have witnessed the proceedings.

"And now, Miss Ashton, now that I have been absolutely candid, you must be able to see that I mean you no harm. I understand your reluctance, but you must think of the greater good. If I were to release you now, my work would be lost, my reputation ruined, and Tregannon Asylum bankrupted. Frederic would lose his inheritance; and besides all that, I should very likely be hanged for murder. Whereas you need only undergo a brief, painless treatment for all these unpleasant consequences to be averted.

"Now—will you come down, or must I fetch you?"

The floor seemed to be dropping away beneath my feet. I dared not reply, for fear of betraying my weakness.

"No? Then I fear I must disarm you. You have the advantage of position, but I have always fancied myself at singlesticks. I shall try not to hurt you any more than—"

He was interrupted by the jangling of a bell on the wall behind him.

"That will be Frederic; I told him my engagement in Bristol had been cancelled. He knows not to ring unless the matter is urgent, but it will have to wait."

Crossing to a stand by the vestry door, he drew out a heavy blackthorn stick and moved toward the stairs. All the blood seemed to drain from my body.

The bell rang again, more insistently. Muttering irritably, he strode over to it and stabbed with his finger at a bell-push.

"That should silence him."

"But now he knows you are here," I said desperately. I took a deep breath and cried, "Frederic!" thinking he must be close by, but Dr Straker merely laughed.

"That is an electric bell, Miss Ashton. Frederic is in the asylum; if you had a steam whistle, he would not hear you."

"But he knows I have escaped; he will wonder why you are not directing the search."

"He may wonder all he likes. You will be found unconscious in the wood, close by Miss Ferrars' body, as it will seem; he will blame himself for defying me."

In a few strides he had reached the foot of the stairs. The railing shook; I leant forward, raising the length of wood, and flung it like a spear at his upturned face. He tried to fend it off, but it struck him lengthwise across the forehead; his stick clattered to the floor, and he slid back down the stairs, clutching at the railing. I was back at the head of the stairs with another piece in my hand, shaking like a leaf but determined now to survive, before he had recovered his balance.

"You leave me no choice," he said, breathing hard. "I meant every word: I would have spared your life, but you have made that impossible."

He drew a key from his waistcoat pocket, turned toward his desk, and froze.

"I should have known better. Throw down those papers while you still have the chance."

I made no reply. He moved out of sight beneath the gallery, and I heard the scrape of a key. When he reappeared, he had a pistol raised in his right hand.

"You cannot escape me, Miss Ashton. I promise I will not shoot you if you come quietly."

I flung the wreckage at him and recoiled from the opening. The crash reverberated around the tower; but the echoes did not cease. Someone was pounding on the vestry door.

"Damnation," he muttered. There was a brief silence, followed by the sound of rapid footsteps as the hammering resumed. I peeped over the balustrade, just as he turned to look up at me. His face was very pale, and there was a smear of blood across his forehead.

"Be silent, and you may yet live," he said, slipping the pistol into his coat pocket. A moment later he had reached the door, but he did not open it.

"Frederic!" he shouted. "What is the meaning of this?"

I heard a muffled reply but could not make out the words.

"Go back to the house! I will join you shortly!"

The reply evidently did not please him.

"Frederic! I insist that you return to the house!"

Another flurry of hammering.

He turned the key in the lock and braced himself. The door, I remembered, opened outward: he evidently meant to force Frederic back and confront him on the other side. But the door was wrenched from his grip, and Frederic, lantern in hand, burst into the room.

"Dr Straker, you must come *now!* We have searched every . . ."

He set down his lantern, took a few tentative steps toward the invalid chair, and froze, transfixed by the sight of Lucia's body.

"In God's name, sir, what have you done?"

Dr Straker's hand went to his coat pocket. I tried to scream but could not utter a sound.

"She would have ruined us—everything we have worked for."

Frederic turned to face him and caught sight of the pistol in his hand, the barrel downward to the floor.

"You—you murdered her?"

"If you had only obeyed me, you need never have known."

Frederic took a step toward him. Dr Straker half raised the pistol. Then his shoulders sagged, and his hand fell to his side.

"Enough," he said wearily. "Miss Ferrars has defeated me."

He contemplated the weapon for a moment, and with a faint, ironic smile, laid it carefully on the bench beside the lantern.

"Frederic," I said, finding my voice at last. He stared as if mesmerised while I descended, weak from the reaction. Dr Straker, too, stood motionless until I had come up beside Frederic. Then he bowed to me, extended his hand to Frederic (who shook it mechanically), and crossed to the cabinet on the wall, taking up the leather coronet as he passed.

"You should leave now," he said, settling the coronet over his head and turning to the cabinet. With wires trailing from his head and hands, he looked like the high priest of some bizarre sect, dedicated to the worship of electricity. The vibration crept back into my bones, gathering power as I watched. Frederic stood mute. I opened my mouth to protest, but the words died on my lips. Dr Straker raised his right hand and was flung into the air, where he seemed to hang for an instant, his arms outstretched and smoke curling from his temples, before he crashed to the floor.

The vibration did not cease. It rose in pitch and volume until it sounded like a swarm of angry hornets. Flames burst from the cabinet, followed by a vicious blue flash; then silence.

All the lights went out, except for the lantern and the yellow flames licking at the wall. Acrid fumes caught at my throat; I smelt burnt hair and flesh.

"We must run," said Frederic, waking from his trance and urging me toward the door. I stopped beside the chair, looking down at Lucia. Her cloak had fallen open again, revealing my brooch; I had not given it a thought until that moment.

"We cannot leave her," I said.

"We must. She is beyond our help; we will never get her through the tunnel."

I went to unpin my brooch, and found that I could not bear to.

"Please let us try."

"Then we must leave by the other door."

He darted across the room, returning with the lantern and a bunch of keys.

"Let me," I said, and wheeled her toward the far corner, where I held the lantern while Frederic tried one key after another. Burning fragments spilled from the cabinet, sending flames licking along the bench. As the lock turned over, I heard a muffled explosion, followed by a flare of white light. Liquid fire raced across the floor; I caught a glimpse of Dr Straker's body lying in a sea of flame.

"This way!" cried Frederic, slamming the door behind him. The chair lurched and swayed; I had a fleeting impression of rough stone walls, mottled with damp, as we stopped at the last door. Again I held the light while he wrestled with bolts and bars. Lucia's head was hanging over the side of the chair; as I leant forward to straighten it, I saw the flicker of a pulse—faint, but unmistakable—in her throat.

We emerged into a confusion of lights, and voices shouting above the clangour of fire bells. Every window in the tower was pulsing with a fierce orange glow; men with lanterns converged upon us as we wheeled Lucia toward the dark bulk of the asylum. Someone recognised Frederic and called for orders.

"Dr Straker is dead!" he shouted. I could barely hear him above the roar of the fire. "Too late to save . . . Bring water . . . Demolish the cloister and defend the house . . . Run to the wards . . . Get the patients ready . . . Evacuate in case it spreads."

A window burst in a shower of glass, and smoke boiled upward; the noise of the fire redoubled.

"Round to the voluntary wing," said Frederic. "They can take her up to the infirmary from there. If it's safe."

We hastened along the gravel walk between the two buildings and halted within sight of the entrance I had left only a few hours before. The old house had been dark as we passed, but now the upper window nearest the tower began to glow, and then the next, and the next. Frederic was shouting to someone nearby. Two attendants ran up and hurried Lucia away; a hand plucked at my sleeve, and I saw that it was Bella, with Frederic urging me to follow. I had forgotten that I was bloodstained, dishevelled, and filthy; I had forgotten even my exhaustion, but now the weight of it descended as if my bones had turned to lead. Leaning on Frederic's arm, I heard him say something about a bed in the stables, and wondered if he meant me to sleep in the ruin, until we set off along the side of the building, toward the main gate.

Doors were opening all along the wall ahead of us, with people spilling out of them in every form of attire from dress clothes to nightshirts: doctors, lunatics, voluntary patients and attendants, mingled indiscriminately in the glow of the burning tower, swarming into the night.

I woke in a strange bed, with a coarse blanket prickling my neck, feeling as if I had fallen down a staircase. For a few terrible moments I was back in the infirmary, with the nightmare beginning again. Then a

chair creaked and I opened my eyes, to find myself in a whitewashed
attic room, with rain pattering against the window, my brooch and
writing case on a little table by the bed, and Bella sitting beside me.
The asylum, she told me, had been saved, but Mr Edmund had died
from the shock of it all; Mr Frederic was the master now, and very
anxious to see me. "And yes, miss"—it was plain she did not know
what to call me—"the other lady" was alive, though still unconscious;
they had carried her across to the infirmary as soon as it was safe.

At first I could barely walk, but after a perilous descent to the tack
room below, the worst of the stiffness had begun to wear off. I declined, with a shudder, Bella's offer to fetch an invalid chair, and settled for an umbrella instead. Everything looked exactly the same, even
to the distant figures labouring by the boundary wall, but the sour,
acrid reek grew stronger, reminding me of the fogs around Gresham's Yard. I made my way slowly down to the far corner of the asylum and stood gazing at the devastation. All that remained of the old
house was a jagged, roofless shell. Wisps of smoke still curled from
the wreck of the tower; the surrounding trees were blackened and
scorched.

I shivered, recalling my last glimpse of Dr Straker, and thinking
how much ruin and anguish would have been spared if Felix Mordaunt
had never made that will, or, indeed, if he and Rosina had never met
. . . but then I would not be standing here, with my writing case in my
hand, trying to decide what *I* should do about those wills. The rain
had all but ceased; I lowered the umbrella and drifted into a reverie,
from which I was woken by the sound of Frederic's voice.

"Miss Ferrars, I am delighted to see you up and about so soon."

His suit was stained and crumpled, his face grey with exhaustion,
but he smiled nonetheless. There was an air of quiet resolution—or
was it resignation?—about him that I had not seen before.

"Mr Mordaunt; I was sorry to hear of your uncle's death."

"You need not be; he was in constant pain and would not have lived
much longer. And . . . he was not an affectionate man. Or, as I discovered this morning, a prudent one. He had been withdrawing large
sums for many years, with no explanation and nothing to show for the
money. The estate is mortgaged to the hilt; the sale of the asylum will
barely cover its debts.

"So much for my promise to provide for you," he said wryly, "let alone . . . But enough of this. There is so much I don't understand, about you, and Miss Ardent, and why Dr Straker acted as he did . . ."

"It was for these," I said, handing him the wills and the marriage certificate. "And all for nothing."

We talked most of the day by the fire in his private sitting room. I gave him Rosina's letters to read, but said nothing of what I had felt for Lucia, who was lying, still unconscious, in the infirmary, only a few doors away. We were now, as cousins, on intimate terms. I had wondered if the discovery would change his feeling for me, but it plainly had not, and the memory of his impassioned declaration hovered between us.

I offered to burn the wills, thinking he might salvage something from the wreck of his fortune, but he would not have it.

"No, Georgina, the estate is yours by right, moral as well as legal, and if anything can be salvaged, you shall have it. Uncle Edmund was a thief and a hypocrite—when I think of all those lectures on morality!—and I will not profit from his wickedness. Not, I fear, that there is likely to be any profit. An asylum is a business like any other, and when the world hears of Dr Straker's crimes, its reputation will be lost. And to think I worshipped that man . . . the ruler of a madhouse, and he was mad himself."

"Frederic," I said hesitantly, "have you told anyone else about— what you saw last night?"

He shook his head.

"Then I think the secret should be ours alone. Not because of the asylum's reputation; but if word of that machine gets out, someone else will try to build one."

"But then the world will believe he was a great man."

"I think that is the lesser of two evils," I said. "Perhaps he began with the best intentions. But with so much power in his hands . . ."

"And the patients he killed? What of them?"

"We cannot disclose that," I said, "without revealing *how* they died. And then more lives will be sacrificed to someone else's ambition."

We both fell silent, staring into the flames.

"I see what you mean," he said at last, "about keeping silent. Dr Straker acted alone, so there is no question of defrauding the buyer."

"Then I shall sign the property over to you. I insist upon it, Frederic; I have a small income of my own, and I will not see you left with nothing."

"Then I shall insist upon sharing with you—if there is anything to share."

Another silence followed.

"What will you do now?" he asked. His tone was studiously matter-of-fact.

"I shall go first to Plymouth, to see Mr Lovell about the transfer—and find out how much of my money Lucia has stolen. And then I suppose I must call at Gresham's Yard to collect whatever is left of my belongings. So far as Uncle Josiah is concerned, I have been away only a few days, and it would be pointless trying to tell him otherwise; he will be huffish enough about having to pay another boy to help him in the shop."

"And then?"

"Then I shall return to Plymouth. Mr Lovell kindly invited me to stay with his family at Noss Mayo, and if the invitation still stands . . . Don't misunderstand me, Frederic; I know Mr Lovell only through the pages of my journal, but he was kind to me, and I should like to rest for a while in a place where I can walk, and think, and be alone, and say as much or as little about myself as I choose. And you, Frederic? What will you do?"

"I shall look after things here until the asylum has been sold. And then, with luck, the new owners will keep me on."

"But Frederic—"

"I know, I know; I should go out in the world. But this is all I know, and if I have a vocation, it lies here—or somewhere like this. I can at least try to ensure that, in future, no superintendent ever wields such power; if I achieve nothing else, I shall not have lived in vain."

Though he strove to repress it, the note of desolation was unmistakable.

"Frederic," I said gently, "you told me, five days ago, that you loved me, and I fear that your decision to remain here has—something to do with that."

"Yes," he said simply. "I did, and I do. But it is impossible, for every possible reason, and so—"

"No, Frederic; it is impossible only for one reason. I love you as if you were my brother—but not as a woman should love the man she is to marry. If I did, I should not care a straw about money, or Mordaunt blood, or anything else. But I do not want you to cherish false hopes of me, and lose the chance of happiness because of it. You have a loving spirit—I said so at the beginning, and I feel it all the more deeply now—and you ought to marry. You will always have me as your friend, your cousin, but I cannot be your wife."

"If I had been—if I had stood up to Dr Straker at the very beginning . . ."

"Frederic, Frederic, there is nothing you could have done, or not done; you must believe me. Perhaps you feel that you have given your heart to me, and can never love anyone else, but you will—it is why you must go out in the world, as you put it, even if your work is here . . ."

"You sound as though you speak from experience," he said, with a touch of bitterness.

"No, only from intuition. I don't know that I will ever marry, Frederic; after everything I have lived through here, I cannot imagine . . ."

Unsure of what it was I could not imagine, I trailed off, leaving him plainly unconvinced. Frederic, I wanted to say, I loved Lucia as a woman is supposed to love her husband, though I have only the evidence of my journal for it. And yes, she is my half sister, but I did not know that, any more than I knew that she meant to deceive and betray me. And though I may never remember what I felt for her, I believe she showed me something of myself; something that perhaps explains why I cannot return your love as you would wish.

But then I feared he would simply be shocked to no purpose, and so I did not speak, and another awkward silence followed, until a man I had not seen before, a Dr Overton, came in to say that Miss Ardent was awake, and asking if she might speak to Miss Ferrars alone.

"Please tell her I shall be along in a few moments," I said.

"Surely you do not *want* to see her?" said Frederic as soon as Dr Overton had gone. "Should we not send for the police and have her arrested at once?"

"No," I said, "I should like to speak to her before I decide—for my own part, I mean. But how can she possibly remember me, when I recall nothing of her?"

"I think," said Frederic, "that Dr Straker was deluded about that machine, as about so much else. It was sheer chance that he did not kill you. Now really, should you not spare yourself this encounter?"

"No, I want to speak to her."

"Then, if you are quite sure, may I see her first? I have something to say to her myself."

They had put her in the very same room where I had woken on that cold November day a lifetime ago. She was deathly pale, and her face had been scrubbed clean; the resemblance was still plain, but I was far more struck by the differences in the shape of her eyes, the set of her lips, the curve of her cheekbone; so much so that I wondered how anybody, excepting Uncle Josiah, could have mistaken one of us for the other. Standing there in the doorway, I thought of what I had said in my journal about the likeness increasing every day, and I understood just how closely she had studied me.

"Georgina," she said, in a small, chastened voice, "will you sit by me for a little?"

I moved the upright chair—the one Dr Straker had always occupied—closer to the bed, and sat down beside her.

"I can't remember anything of—what happened," she said, "but Mr Mordaunt told me that you risked your own life to save mine, and saved me again when you might have left me to burn. Why did you do that?"

"Because I could not bear to watch you die, without at least trying to save you. Not out of any feeling for you—I have none. You deceived me and betrayed me, and left me here to rot."

A long silence followed.

"I have not had a moment's peace," she said at last, "since I sent that telegram in your uncle's name. It was done on the spur of the moment, and then—I was afraid to go back."

"I would have shared with you," I said, "if there had been anything to share. But Edmund Mordaunt is dead, and the estate is bankrupt; you and your mother had already bled him dry."

She stared at me, horror stricken—or so I would have sworn.

"I knew, I knew, I *knew* you would have shared. But my mother said you would be bound to find me out. And now I shall be sent to prison for years and years—as I deserve."

She burst into heartrending sobs and buried her face in her hands. I knew better than to trust in this show of contrition, and yet I longed to comfort her, and felt cold and heartless for restraining myself.

"Lucia," I said when she was quiet again, "why did you not go on the stage, as you said you wanted to? You are a consummate actress; you could have made your fortune, and been admired for your talent, instead of lying and deceiving your way through life."

"I wish I had," she said, "but it is too late now."

"How much of my money did you steal?" I asked.

"Only your allowance. My mother said I must not risk going to see Mr Lovell until . . ."

She lowered her eyes and let the words trail away.

"That was your mother—Mrs Fairfax—the woman who tried to befriend me in Plymouth."

"Yes," she said faintly.

"And where is your mother now?"

"In London. At the hotel where we—the one in Great Portland Street."

"Where you went every day on those walks of yours. To plan how you might ensnare me."

"And now I must pay for my wickedness. Oh, how you must hate me!"

"No more tears," I said firmly. "I hated you last night, when I said he might tear your heart out for all I cared, but that is gone now, like the fortune you set out to steal. As for sending you to prison: your mother's fate is not for me to decide, and if Mr Mordaunt decides to have her charged with blackmail, she must take the consequences. But for myself, I should rather see you on the stage than in a cell.

"You will write me a full account of every wrong that you and your mother have done me. You will promise, in writing, never to commit another crime. Mr Mordaunt will witness your signature. And you will keep Mr Lovell informed of your whereabouts. Fail me in any particular, and your confession will go to the police."

"I promise," she said in a very low voice. "If I may have pen and paper, I will begin at once." Her face was ashen; she looked utterly spent.

"You should rest now," I said, "and begin in the morning."

"I am truly sorry, Georgina. If only—I wish I had been worthy of your love. I shall try to deserve your trust."

"I wish I could believe you," I said. I rose stiffly to my feet, suddenly aware of my bruised and aching body, and stood looking down at her. She held my gaze with dark, pain-filled eyes, the very picture of remorse, and it seemed for a moment that I could truly remember, could see and feel her trembling in my arms, on our last night together in Gresham's Yard. But then my mind was shrouded again, as if a curtain had fallen between us, and I left the infirmary without looking back.